"An Aztec pr...
murder myst...
even more ...
portrayal of an interesting...
fresh fantasy novel."

– *Kevin J Anderson*

"An amazingly fresh and engaging new voice in fantasy: the shadows of the Aztec underworld drip from these pages."

– *Tobias Buckell*

"A gripping mystery steeped in blood and ancient Aztec magic. I was enthralled."

– *Sean Williams*

"Amid the mud and maize of the Mexica empire, Aliette de Bodard has composed a riveting story of murder, magic, and sibling rivalry."

– *Elizabeth Bear*

"Acatl deserves to become as well known as that other priestly investigator, Cadfael."

– *Strange Horizons*

TIGARD PUBLIC LIBRARY
13500 SW HALL BLVD
WITHDRAWN
A member of Washington County
Cooperative Library Services

# ALIETTE DE BODARD

## Servant of the Underworld

OBSIDIAN AND BLOOD
VOL. I

**ANGRY ROBOT**

ANGRY ROBOT
A member of the Osprey Group

Lace Market House,
54-56 High Pavement,
Nottingham
NG1 1HW, UK

www.angryrobotbooks.com
Jaguar born

Originally published in the UK by Angry Robot 2010
First American paperback printing 2010

Copyright © 2010 by Aliette de Bodard
Cover by Spring London (www.springlondon.com)

Distributed in the United States by Random House, Inc., New York.

All rights reserved.

Angry Robot is a registered trademark and the Angry Robot icon a
trademark of Angry Robot Ltd.

This is a work of fiction. Names, characters, places, and incidents are the
products of the author's imagination or are used fictitiously. Any
resemblance to actual events, locales, organizations or persons, living or
dead, is entirely coincidental.

Sales of this book without a front cover may be unauthorized. If this book is
coverless, it may have been reported to the publisher as "unsold and
destroyed" and neither the author nor the publisher may have received
payment for it.

ISBN 978-0-85766-031-2

Printed in the United States of America

9 8 7 6 5 4 3 2 1

6958

# ONE

## Odd Summonings

In the silence of the shrine, I bowed to the corpse on the altar: a minor member of the Imperial Family, who had died in a boating accident on Lake Texcoco. My priests had bandaged the gaping wound on his forehead and smoothed the wrinkled skin as best as they could; they had dressed him with scraps of many-coloured cotton and threaded a jade bead through his lips – preparing him for the long journey ahead. As High Priest for the Dead, it was now my responsibility to ease his passage into Mictlan, the underworld.

I slashed my earlobes and drew thorns through the wounds, collecting the dripping blood in a bowl, and started a litany for the Dead:

*"The river flows northward*
*The mountains crush, the mountains bind..."*

Grey light suffused the shrine, the pillars and the walls fading away to reveal a much larger place, a cavern where everything found its end. The adobe floor glimmered as if underwater. And shadows trailed, darkening the painted frescoes on the walls – singing a wordless lament, a song that twisted in my guts like a knife-stab. The underworld.

*"Obsidian shards are driven into your hands, into your feet,*
   *Obsidian to tear, to rend*
   *You must endure th–"*

The copper bells sewn on the entrance-curtain tinkled as someone drew it aside, and hurried footsteps echoed under the roof of the shrine. "Acatl-*tzin*!" Ichtaca called.

Startled, I stopped chanting – and instinctively reached up, to quench the flow of blood from my earlobes before the atmosphere of Mictlan could overwhelm the shrine. With the disappearance of the living blood, the spell was broken, and the world sprang into sudden, painful focus.

I turned, then, not hiding my anger. A broken spell would have left a link to Mictlan – a miasma that would only grow thicker as time passed, darkening the shrine, the pyramid it sat upon, and the entire temple complex until the place became unusable. "I hope you have a good reason–"

Ichtaca, the Fire Priest of the temple and my second-in-command, stood on the threshold – his fingers clenched on the conch-shell around his neck. "I apologise for interrupting you, Acatl-tzin, but he was most insistent."

"He?"

The curtain twisted aside, and someone walked into the shrine: Yaotl. My heart sank. Yaotl never came for good news.

"I apologise," Yaotl said, with a curt nod of his head towards the altar, though clearly he meant none of it. Yaotl answered only to his mistress, Ceyaxochitl; and she in turn, as Guardian of the Sacred Precinct and keeper of the invisible boundaries, answered only to Revered Speaker Ayaxacatl, the ruler of the Mexica Empire. "But we need you."

Again? Even though I was High Priest for the Dead, it seemed that Ceyaxochitl still considered me little better than a slave, to be summoned whenever she wanted. "What is it this time?"

Yaotl's scarred face twisted in what might have been a smile. "It's bad."

"Hmm," I said. I should have known better than to ask him about the nature of the emergency. Yaotl enjoyed keeping me in ignorance, probably as a way to compensate for his station as a slave. I snatched up my grey cotton cloak from the stone floor and wrapped it around my shoulders. "I'm coming. Ichtaca, can you take over for me?"

Yaotl waited for me outside the shrine, on the platform of the pyramid temple, his embroidered cloak fluttering in the breeze. We descended the stairs of the pyramid side by side, in silence. Beneath us, moonlight shone on the temple complex, a series of squat adobe buildings stretching around a courtyard. Even at this hour, priests for the Dead were awake, saying vigils, conducting examinations of the recently dead, and propitiating the rulers of the underworld: Mictlantecuhtli and his wife, Mictecacihuatl, Lord and Lady Death.

Further on was the vast expanse of the Sacred Precinct: the mass of temples, shrines and penitential palaces that formed the religious heart of the Mexica Empire. And, still further, the houses and fields and canals of the island-city of Tenochtitlan, thousands of small lights burning away under the stars and moon.

We walked from the bottom of the steps to the gates of my temple, and then onto the plaza of the Sacred Precinct. At this hour of the night, it was blessedly free of the crowds that congregated in the day, of all the souls eager to earn the favours of the gods. Only a few offering priests were still abroad, singing hymns; and a few, younger novice priests, completing their nightly run around the Precinct's Serpent Wall. The air was warm and heavy, a presage of the rains and of the maize harvest to come.

To my surprise, Yaotl did not lead me to the Imperial Palace. I'd expected this mysterious summons to be about noblemen. The last time Ceyaxochitl had asked for me in the middle of the night, it had been for a party of drunk administrators who had managed to summon a beast of the shadows from Mictlan. We'd spent a night tracking down the monster before killing it with obsidian knives.

Yaotl walked purposefully on the empty plaza, past the main temple complexes and the houses of elite warriors. I had thought that we were going to the temple of Toci, Grandmother Earth, but Yaotl bypassed it completely, and led me to a building in its shadow: something neither as tall nor as grand as the pyramid shrines, a subdued, sprawling affair of rooms opening on linked courtyards, adorned with frescoes of gods and goddesses.

The girls' *calmecac*: the House of Tears, a school where the children of the wealthy, as well as those vowed to the priesthood, would receive their education. I had never been there; the clergy of Mictlantecuhtli was exclusively male, and I had trouble enough with our own students. I couldn't imagine, though, what kind of magical offences untrained girls would commit.

"Are you sure?" I asked Yaotl but, characteristically, he walked into the building without answering me.

I suppressed a sigh and followed him, bowing slightly to the priestess in feather regalia who kept vigil at the entrance.

Inside, all was quiet, but it was the heavy calm before the rains. As I crossed courtyard after courtyard, I met the disapproving glances of senior offering priestesses, and the curious gazes of young girls who stood on the threshold of their ground-floor dormitories.

Yaotl led me to a courtyard near the centre of the building. Two rooms with pillared entrances opened on this. He went towards the leftmost one and, pulling aside the curtain, motioned me into a wide room.

It seemed an ordinary place, a room like any other in the city: an entrance curtain set with bells, gently tinkling in the evening breeze, walls adorned with frescoes of gods – and, in the centre, a simple reed sleeping mat framed by two wooden chests. Copal incense burnt in a clay brazier, bathing the room in a soft, fragrant light that stung my eyes. And everything, from the chests to the mat, reeked of magic: a pungent, acrid smell that clung to the walls and to the beaten-earth floor like a miasma.

That wasn't natural. Even in the calmecac, there were strictures on the use of the living blood, restrictions on the casting of spells. Furthermore this looked like the private room of a priestess, not a teaching room for adolescent girls.

"What happened–" I started, turning to Yaotl.

But he was already halfway through the door. "Stay here. I'll tell Mistress Ceyaxochitl you've arrived, Acatl-tzin." In his mouth, even the tzin honorific sounded doubtful.

"Wait!" I said, but all that answered me was the sound of bells from the open door. I stood alone in that room, with no idea of why I was there at all.

Tlaloc's lightning strike Yaotl.

I looked again at the room, wondering what I could guess of the circumstances that had brought me here. It looked like a typical priestess's room: few adornments, the same rough sleeping mat and crude wicker chests found in any peasant's house. Only the frescoes bore witness to the wealth of the calmecac school, their colours vibrant in the soft light, every feature of the gods sharply delineated. The paintings represented Xochipilli, God of Youth and Games, and His Consort, Xochiquetzal, Goddess of Lust and Childbirth. They danced in a wide garden, in the midst of flowers. The Flower Prince held a rattle, His Consort a necklace of poinsettias as red as a sacrifice's blood.

Dark stains marred the faces of both gods. No, not only the faces, every part of Their apparel from Their feathered headdresses to Their clawed hands. Carefully, I scraped off one of the stains and rubbed it between my fingers. Blood.

Dried blood. I stared at the floor again – at what I had taken for dark earth in the dim light of the brazier. The stain was huge – spreading over the whole room, soaking the earth so thoroughly it had changed its colour. I'd attended enough sacrifices and examinations to know the amount of blood in the human body, and I suspected that the stain represented more than half of that. What in the Fifth World had happened here?

I stood in the centre of the room and closed my eyes. Carefully, I extended my priest-senses and probed at the magic, trying to see its nature. Underworld magic, yet… no, not quite. It was human, and it had been summoned in anger, in rage, an emotion that still hung in the room like a pall. But it didn't have the sickly, spread-out feeling of most underworld magic. Not a beast of shadows, then.

*Nahual*. It had to be nahual magic: a protective jaguar spirit summoned in the room. Judging by the amount of blood in the vicinity, it had done much damage. Who, or what, had been wounded here?

I had been remiss in not taking any supplies before leaving my temple – trusting Yaotl to provide what I needed, which was always a mistake with the wily slave. I had no animal sacrifices, nothing to practise the magic of living blood.

No, not quite. I did have one source of living blood: my own body. With only my blood, I might not be able to perform a powerful spell; but there *was* a way to know whether someone had died in this room. Death opened a gate into Mictlan, the underworld, and the memory of that gate would still be in the room. Accessing it wouldn't be a pleasant experience, but Huitzilpochtli, the Southern Hummingbird, blind me if I let Ceyaxochitl manipulate me once more.

I withdrew one of the obsidian blades that I always carried in my belt, and nicked my right earlobe with it. I'd done it so often that I barely flinched at the pain that spread upwards, through my ear. Blood dripped, slowly, steadily, onto the blade – each drop, pulsing on the rhythm of my heartbeat, sending a small shock through the hilt when it connected with the obsidian.

I brought the tip of the knife in contact with my own hand, and carefully drew the shape of a human skull. As I did so, I sang a litany to my patron Mictlantecuhtli, God of the Dead:

*"Like the feathers of a precious bird*
*That precious bird with the emerald tail*
*We all come to an end*
*Like a flower*
*We dry up, we wither…"*

A cold wind blew across the room, lifting the entrance-curtain – the tinkle of the bells was muffled, as if coming from far away, and the walls of the room slowly receded, revealing only darkness – but odd, misshapen shadows slid in and out of my field of vision, waiting for their chance to leap, to tear, to feast on my beating heart.

> *"We reach the land of the fleshless*
> *Where jade turns to dust*
> *Where feathers crumble into ash*
> *Where our flowers, our songs are forever extinguished*
> *Where all the tears rain down…"*

A crack shimmered into existence, in the centre of the chamber: the entrance to a deep cavern, a *cenote*, at the bottom of which dark, brackish water shimmered in cold moonlight. Dry, wizened silhouettes splashed through the lake – the souls of the Dead, growing smaller and smaller the farther they went, like children's discarded toys. They sang as they walked: cold whispers, threads of sound which curled around me, clinging to my naked skin like snakes. I could barely make out the words, but surely, if I stayed longer…

If I bent over the cenote until I could see the bottom of the water…

If I…

*No*. I wasn't that kind of fool.

With the ease of practise, I passed the flat of the knife across the palm of my other hand – focusing on nothing but the movement of the blade until the image of the skull was completely erased.

When I raised my eyes again, the crack had closed. The walls were back, with the vivid, reassuring colours of the frescoes; and the song of the Dead had faded into the whistle of the wind through the trees of the courtyard outside.

I stood, for a while, breathing hard – it never got any easier to deal with the underworld, no matter how used to it you became. Still…

I had seen the bottom of the cenote, and the Dead making their slow way to the throne of Lord Death. I had not, however, made out the words of their song. The gate to Mictlan had been widening, but not yet completely open. That meant someone in this room had been gravely wounded, but they were still alive.

No, that was too hasty. Whoever had been wounded in this room hadn't died within – yet I didn't think they'd have survived for long, unless they'd found a healer.

"Ah, Acatl," Ceyaxochitl said, behind me. "That was fast."

I turned much faster than I'd have liked. With the memory of Mictlan's touch on my skin, any noise from the human world sounded jarringly out of place.

Ceyaxochitl stood limned in the entrance, leaning on her wooden cane. She was wearing a headdress of blue feathers that spread like a fan over her forehead, and a dress embroidered with the fused-lovers insignia of the Duality. Her face was smooth, expressionless, as it always was.

I'd tensed, even though she had barely spoken to me, preparing for another verbal sparring. Ceyaxochitl had a habit of moving people like pawns in a game of *patolli*, deciding what she thought was in their best interests without preoccupying herself much with their opinions, and I seldom enjoyed being the target of her attentions.

"I don't particularly appreciate being summoned like this," I started to say, but she shook her head, obviously amused.

"You were awake, Acatl. I know you."

Yes, she knew me, all too well. After all, we had worked together for roughly nine years, the greater part of my adult life. She had been the one to campaign at the Imperial Court for my nomination as High Priest for the Dead, a position I neither wanted nor felt comfortable with – another of her interferences in my life. We'd made a kind of uneasy peace over the matter in the last few months, but right now she was going too far.

"All right," I said. I brushed off the dried blood on my fingers, and watched her hobble into the room. "Now that I'm here, can we dispense with the formalities? Who was wounded here, Ceyaxochitl?"

She paused for a moment, though she barely showed any surprises. "Hard at work, I see."

"I do what I can."

"Yes." She watched the frescoes with a distracted gaze. "What do *you* think happened here?"

I ran my fingers over the traces of the skull I'd drawn on the back of my hand, feeling Mictlan's touch cling to me like damp cloth. "A nahual spirit. An angry one."

"And?" she asked.

It was late, and someone was in mortal danger, and I was tired, and no longer of an age to play her games of who was master over whom. "Someone was wounded – at Mictlan's gates, but has not yet gone through. What do you want to hear?"

"The nahual magic," Ceyaxochitl said quietly. "I mainly wanted your confirmation on that."

"You have it." I wasn't in the mood to quarrel with her. In any case, she was my superior, both in years and in magical mastery. "Do I get an explanation?"

She sighed; but she still didn't look at me. Something was wrong: this was not her usual, harmless games, but something deeper and darker. "Ceyaxochitl…" I said, slowly.

"This is the room of Eleuia, offering priestess of Xochiquetzal," Ceyaxochitl said. Her gaze was fixed, unwaveringly, on the hollow eyes of the goddess in the frescoes. "Most likely candidate to become Consort of Xochipilli."

The highest rank for a priestess of the Quetzal Flower. "And she was attacked?" What was Ceyaxochitl not telling me?

"Yes."

I stared at the blood on the frescoes – felt the anger roiling in the room. A nahual spirit would have had claws sharp enough to cut bone, and even a trained warrior would have had trouble defending himself against it.

"Did you find her?" I asked. "She needs a healer, at the last – if not a priest of Patecatl." There were healing spells – meagre, expensive things that the priests of the God of Medicine jealously hoarded. But a priestess such as Eleuia would surely have a right to them.

"I've had my warriors search every dormitory. We don't know where Priestess Eleuia is. No one has been able to find her, or to find her trail. She is the only one missing in the whole calmecac, though."

My heart sank. If it had been a beast of shadows... there were ways, and means, to track creatures of the underworld. But a nahual... There were too many of them in Tenochtitlan at any given time: any person born on a Jaguar day could summon their own nahual, though it would take years of dedicated practise to call up something material enough to carry off a human, or even to wound.

"I can attempt to track it," I said, finally, even though I knew it was a futile exercise. Nahual magic was weak to start with, and the coming of sunlight would annihilate it. We had perhaps four hours before dawn, but I doubted that would be enough.

Ceyaxochitl appeared absorbed in contemplation of the brazier: a studied pose, it suddenly occurred to me.

"But I still don't see–" I started, with a growing hollow in my stomach.

She turned, so abruptly I took a step backward. "I arrested your brother tonight, Acatl."

Her words shattered my thoughts, yanking my mind from worries about Eleuia and the nahual to something much closer to me – and much more unpleasant. She had… arrested my brother?

"Which one?" I asked, but I knew the answer, just as I knew why she'd asked about the nahual magic, and why she'd waited for my confirmation before telling me anything. Only one of my brothers had been born on a Jaguar day.

"Neutemoc? You can't arrest him," I said slowly, but Ceyaxochitl shook her head.

"He was in this room, covered in blood. And there was magic all over him."

"You're wrong," I said, because those were the only words that got past my lips. "My brother isn't–"

"Acatl." Her voice was gentle but firm. "When the priestesses arrived, he was searching the room, overturning the wicker chests and even the brazier. And I've never seen so much blood on someone, except perhaps the Revered Speaker after the Great Sacrifices. Your brother's hands were slick with it."

I finally dragged my voice from wherever it had fled. "My brother isn't a killer."

That made no sense, I thought, trying to close the hollow deepening in my stomach. Neutemoc was a successful warrior: a member of the elite Jaguar Knights, a son of peasants elevated into the nobility after his feats in the Tepeaca war. My parents had all but worshipped him, back when they had both been alive. He could do no wrong. He had always been the precious, beloved child – whereas I, of course, was less than nothing, a humble priest who had never had the courage to seek wealth and honour on the battlefield. Of course he was a warrior. Of course he'd know how to kill.

But surely... surely he wouldn't do such a thing?

"I'm sure your brother can explain what he thought he was doing in her room. So far, he hasn't been helpful." Ceyaxochitl's voice was ice again. She disapproved of Neutemoc's arrogance, but I wasn't sure why. Knowing my brother, he'd have said the wrong things to her. The Duality knew it didn't take much to anger her these days.

I tried to think of something to say, but couldn't form any meaningful words.

Ceyaxochitl tapped her cane against the clay of the brazier, with a hollow sound. "You're the High Priest for the Dead, in charge of the Sacred Precinct. A case like this is your province, and mine."

Guardian, and priest: a Guardian to wield the magic of the Duality, and a priest that of the underworld. We'd done it before; many, many times, both here and in the smaller town of Coyoacan. But this was different. I couldn't...

Not Neutemoc. Duality, no. We'd parted ways four years ago, and the last thing I wanted was to see him again. I had left him alone in his grand house with his success, freeing him of the burden of my presence. His acts, in any case, had made it painfully clear that he might not completely share my parents' disapproval of me; but that he would do nothing to change it, that he would not even speak up in my defence when Mother was screaming at me from her death-bed. The hollow in my stomach wouldn't close.

I should walk away. That was the sensible option. Leave him to face the magistrates on his own, as he no doubt wished. But if I did this – if I ran away from him, at this moment – then I would be no better than him. I would prove, once and for all, that Father and Mother had been right: that I was a coward, unworthy of the battlefield.

The Storm Lord's lightning sear him! What had he been thinking of?

"You want us to take the investigation," I said to Ceyaxochitl.

She said nothing for a while. "No," she said. "Not quite. I didn't call you here at night for my own amusement, despite what you might think of me."

"You don't know what I think of you," I protested, which was not quite true. I was wary of whatever she offered, with good reason.

Ceyaxochitl turned, slightly. Her face in the brazier's wavering light was a statue's: majestic, expressionless. "I could have dealt with this on my own. After all, guilt has already been established–"

"It hasn't," I protested – a reflex that surprised me by its vehemence.

"It has," Ceyaxochitl said. She banged her cane on the floor; its deep sound punctuated each of her words. "Listen to the end, young man. As I said: I have no need for you. Strictly speaking, nahual magic isn't your province, and it dissipates in daylight anyway. There has been no encroaching of the boundaries."

"No," I finally admitted. Aside from saying the death-rites, I maintained the boundaries: the fragile balance between the underworld and the world of the Fifth Sun. I dealt with the minor gods of Mictlan: the Wind of Knives, the Owl Archer, the Faded Warrior. "But–"

Ceyaxochitl banged her cane a scant hand-span from my exposed foot. I flinched. "Be silent. I summoned you to do you a favour."

As you did by pushing my name for promotion at the Imperial Court? I thought, but bit my lip before the words could escape me.

Ceyaxochitl saw me, all the same, and smiled grimly. "You might not think it's much of a favour. But the fact is, Acatl, I have no time to investigate this as it should be investigated. Either I end it swiftly by condemning your brother on scant evidence, or I leave it to you."

"No time?" No time for my own brother – after all I'd done for her? No time to find a priestess who might be, if not dead, in mortal danger? "What's so important?"

Ceyaxochitl grimaced. "Revered Speaker Axayacatl-tzin is ill. All the healers are by his bedside day and night. As Guardian, my place is with them."

That the Emperor was ill wasn't news. But, still, I had to ask. "Do you think it's–"

"Magical?" She shook her head. "No. But he's a man, Acatl. He may be Huitzilpochtli's agent on earth, but even a god's powers don't guard you against wounds, or fatigue."

"And so that takes precedence," I said. Again, not a surprise. The Imperial Family always took precedence over us: a bitter, but necessary thought.

"It has to," Ceyaxochitl said. "The fight for his succession has already started among the Council."

The Imperial succession wasn't my concern. Whoever was elected Revered Speaker would still want the dead to be honoured, and the balance to be maintained between the Fifth World, the underworld Mictlan, and the Heavens. Neutemoc was the one I needed to focus on. "So what you're telling me…"

"Is that you can investigate this matter, but, as I said, you'll be on your own. I'll offer resources, but I can't do more than that, or I risk my own position." She didn't sound thrilled by that consideration. But then she had always been independent, like me.

"You know I can't refuse," I said.

Her gaze was sceptical. She knew exactly the state of my relationship with my family, and the grievances between Neutemoc and me. I owed nothing to my brother – nothing at all. I could just walk away...

There was a tight knot in my belly; a constriction in my throat, as if I would vomit. I couldn't let Neutemoc be executed. I couldn't stand by and do nothing.

"Very well," I said. I crouched on my haunches in the middle of the room, trying to forget the nausea in my stomach. "I assume you've sent search parties out into the Sacred Precinct."

"Yes," Ceyaxochitl said. "With jade amulets."

I shook my head. "Jade won't be of use against a nahual." But it couldn't hurt, either. "What can you tell me about Priestess Eleuia?"

Ceyaxochitl's cane tapped against the frescoed walls. "An ambitious woman," she said. "Still beautiful, considering that she was five years older than you."

Thirty-five. For a woman, definitely past her prime. "And?"

"All this is hearsay, of course," Ceyaxochitl said. "Gathered from those few students bold enough to talk to me. But the head of the calmecac, Priestess Zollin, wasn't overjoyed about Eleuia being foretold as the next Consort of the Flower Prince, Xochipilli. Zollin had ambitions of her own."

"Was she born on a Jaguar day?" I asked.

Ceyaxochitl shrugged. "That can be verified. She could have hired someone to do the summoning, though."

I shook my head, still feeling the roiling anger in the room. "Too much rage in here. Whoever did this had personal stakes."

Ceyaxochitl bent to lift the reed mat from the ground with her cane. "I'll defer to your expertise in such matters. What else? You'll want to know about the people present in this section of the calmecac. Surprisingly few, considering how spread-out the place is."

"You can't account for them all," I said.

"You'd be surprised," Ceyaxochitl said, "at how many priestesses are awake at night."

Of course. They would be going through their devotions, just like the priests in the other temples: blowing their shell-conches at regular hours, burning copal to honour their goddesses, and kneeling on the cold stones to pray for the welfare of the Fifth World. "So who was here?"

"In the vicinity of this room," Ceyaxochitl corrected. "A handful of students. Another Jaguar Knight, Mahuizoh. And, of course, Zollin, whose rooms are just next to Eleuia's."

"A Jaguar Knight?" Men in the girls' calmecac weren't rare or forbidden, but they usually left by sunset.

"Visiting his sister," Ceyaxochitl said. "The girl says he didn't leave her side."

"She would."

Ceyaxochitl nodded. "Of course. Blood stands by blood." Probably another jab at me.

Or perhaps I was being too sensitive about the whole matter. The idea of Neutemoc arrested and tried had rubbed me raw, and I wasn't really fit to judge Ceyaxochitl's actions.

"What was Neutemoc's reason for being here?" I asked.

Ceyaxochitl shrugged. "He won't tell us."

I turned, took a good look at the room. "I guess you've already searched it?"

Ceyaxochitl didn't move. "Yaotl did. But if you want to see for yourself…"

I nodded. Yaotl had no magical sight. It was possible he might have missed something, though unlikely.

It was a brief search. Like all priestesses, Eleuia had been living in near-poverty. In the wicker chests I found a few personal belongings, and an unfolding codex on maguey paper, which opened with a rustling sound, to reveal the history of the Fifth World – from the primal fire from which Tonatiuh the Sun God had emerged, to the very end: the Celestial Women and monsters that would consume us before the earth-quakes tore the land apart.

Aside from that… a few tokens, safely hidden under a pile of embroidered cotton skirts: an exquisite chalcedony pendant set in silver, in the shape of a dancer entwined with a warrior; and the same kind of pendant, this time in coral, with the dancer alone. Presumably, a third pendant with another type of inset stone, depicting the warrior alone, would complete the set. It was a fairly safe guess, though, that Eleuia had it around her neck.

I walked out of the room with Ceyaxochitl in tow, wondering how to proceed.

Outside, the night was dark, with only a few stars winking in the sky. Like all the rooms in the calmecac, Eleuia's quarters opened onto a courtyard with a small garden – in this case, a pine-tree. There was faint magic in the courtyard: traces of a nahual, though without living blood I couldn't place it more precisely.

"Satisfied?" Ceyaxochitl asked.

I took a quick look at the layout of the place. Only two sets of rooms opened on this particular courtyard: two wide entrances flanked by painted pillars, their curtains painted with the same dayflower design. The first were Eleuia's, which I had just searched; I guessed that the others had to be those of her rival, Zollin.

I would have to talk with Zollin, to see what she'd really thought of Eleuia, and whether she'd summoned the nahual. I would also have to talk to Neutemoc – and the Southern Hummingbird knew I wasn't looking forward to that.

But the most urgent thing was tracking the nahual. Which meant I needed to cast a spell; and unlike Ceyaxochitl, who was the agent of the Duality and had been entrusted with some of Their powers, I could only rely on my personal magic. Other than magical obsidian, our patron Mictlantecuhtli, God of the Dead, did not give His powers into human hands. Without the gods' help, I could only work magic with living blood.

For this, my own blood would not suffice: I needed much more than I could spare.

"Do the priestesses have supplies here?" I asked.

"For using the living blood?" Ceyaxochitl rose, as regally as an Imperial Consort. "That depends what you want. They're mostly small animals: birds, rabbits…"

I shook my head. For what I had in mind, I needed an animal connected with Mixcoatl, the Cloud Serpent, God of the Hunt. "I'll return to my temple."

# TWO
## *The Jaguar Born*

I walked back to my temple in a preoccupied mood –
trying to keep my thoughts away from Neutemoc and
what awaited him if I failed. My brother had brought
me many problems, but so far most of those had come
only from my own doings: if I had chosen the path my
parents wanted for me, if I had gone to war and dis-
tinguished myself on the battlefield, they would have
found no need to compare us to each other – and in-
variably find me, a priest with few possessions of his
own, a failure too great to be encompassed in words.

I reached the temple, and found my priests still up.
My second-in-command Ichtaca, who was obviously
done with the vigil I'd left him, was leading a group of
novice priests to one of the examination rooms. Overhead loomed the bulk of the pyramid with its shrine;
and several buildings of the temple opened on the
courtyard: rooms where the priests would make offerings; places where the lesser dead (those not of
Imperial blood) would be honoured; closed rooms for
examinations in the case of suspicious deaths; and our
storehouse, a discreet, unadorned door hidden at the
back of the temple complex.

The offering priest who was watching the store-house's entrance – Palli, a burly nobleman's son who looked more suited for the military than for the priest-hood – bowed as I came towards him. "Good evening, Acatl-tzin. You need something?"

I nodded. "Living blood. Do you know what's inside tonight?"

Palli shrugged. "Mostly owls. There's probably some other animals, too."

For what I had in mind, owls would not do – they were connected with the underworld and not with the hunt.

"I'll take a look inside," I said.

Palli frowned. "I can fetch what you need."

"No, there's no need." Huitzilpochtli blind me, I wasn't so respectable yet that I couldn't find my way through a storehouse.

I picked one of the torches outside, and held it against the flame of the torch on the wall until it blazed. Then I entered the storehouse, making my way between the carved pillars. They each bore the image of a minor deity of the underworld: the hulking shape of the Owl Archer, leaning on his feathered bow with the suggestion of coiled strength; the simple, al-most featureless carving of the Faded Warrior, with his obsidian-studded *macuahitl* sword by his side; the glit-tering mass of obsidian shards that made up the Wind of Knives.

I made my way through the storehouse, my torch falling on the piled riches: on the quetzal feathers and ocelot cloaks, on the jade and silver which safeguarded us from the underworld…

I felt as though I had spent an eternity in this place; and still I had seen no animals. The nahual trail in the courtyard would be vanishing further and further; and so would my chances of finding Eleuia alive. Unless…

Near the back were a series of wooden cages. I quickened my pace – but when I shone the torchlight on them, I saw that they held only owls, as predicted.

Tlaloc's lightning strike me, did we have nothing but this? I shone the torch left and right, hoping to see more than hooting birds.

There. Near the back, two wooden cages held weasels. They pressed themselves against the bars when I shone the torchlight on them. They weren't Mixcoatl's favourite animals, but they would do.

I transferred them both to the same cage, and went back to the calmecac.

In the courtyard near Eleuia's room, I knelt in the darkness, and traced a quincunx on the ground with the point of my dagger: the fivefold cross, symbol of the universe and of the wisdom contained therein. I put myself in the centre of the pattern, and started singing, softly, slowly:

> "You who come forth from Chicomoztoc, honoured one,
> You who come with the net of maguey ropes
> The basket of woven reeds
> You who come forth from Tziuactitlan, honoured one..."

I reached inside the cage for the first weasel, and slit its throat in a practised gesture. Blood spurted, covering my hands, spilling over the ground, where it pooled in the grooves of my pattern, pulsing with untapped power.

> "You who seek the deer
> The jaguar, the ocelot
> You who hold them in your hand..."

I plucked the second weasel from where it was

26

cowering at the back of the cage, and drew my blade across its throat. Its blood joined that of the first one: where they melded, the air trembled and blurred, as if in a heat-haze.

*"You who come forth from Chicomoztoc, honoured one,*
*You who come with the arrows,*
*The spear-thrower, the grips of shell*
*You who seek, you who find,*
*Let flow the blessing of Your craft."*

Power blazed across my pattern, wrapping itself around me until I stood completely enfolded. My head spun for a moment. But when the dizziness passed, I could see the tendrils of magic in the courtyard: a trail of sickly green that came from Eleuia's room and exited the courtyard in a wide, loping arc.

I rose carefully and followed it. A minute resistance, like the crossing of a veil, slowed me down as I crossed my quincunx, but it was swiftly gone.

The nahual's trail traversed a handful of other courtyards. For the most part, they were deserted, though a few had girls making offerings of blood on the beaten earth. The trail grew fainter and fainter with every passing step, and that was not normal. Whoever had summoned the nahual had taken the precaution of covering their tracks.

In the last courtyard, the trail made a straight line upwards, the beginning of a leap over the outer wall of the calmecac; but halfway through, it completely faded. It seemed Priestess Eleuia wasn't within those walls any more, which only confirmed the results of Ceyaxochitl's search.

I stared at that wall for a while, but I couldn't find anything more than what I'd already seen.

The Southern Hummingbird curse me.

I hadn't actually expected to find the nahual – but at least to find something, anything that might prove Neutemoc innocent. Here I had nothing, not even a trail. Something about that wall was bothering me, though. But the more I sought to identify the problem, the more it eluded me.

I was about to turn away and leave, when a swish of cloth made me stop.

In the doorway of one of the rooms opening on the courtyard stood a young girl, no more than six or seven, barely of age to be educated in the calmecac. Her face was as pale as a fawn's hide. Her eyes, two pools of darkness in the dim light, turned, unwaveringly, towards me. She wasn't offering blood, or incense: she simply watched me.

"You should be in bed," I said, slowly. I'd never been at ease with young children, having none of my own.

She shook her head.

"Are you supposed to be awake?"

She watched me for a while, and then she said, tentatively, as if afraid I'd berate her, "Can't sleep."

I sighed. "I suppose all the noise we made in the calmecac woke you up?"

Again, she shook her head. "I don't need sleep," she said. "Not a lot."

Comprehension dawned. "Oh." I'd heard of sicknesses like hers, though they were unusual. "You've been awake all night?"

She shrugged. "Most of it. It's not so bad. It's calm, at night."

"Except tonight," I said, ruefully. I pointed at the room behind her. "This is where you sleep?"

"Yes," she said.

"Did you hear anything unusual?" I asked. "I mean, before we came."

She watched me, as unmoving as a deer before it

28

flees. There was something in the liquid pools of her eyes: fear, worry?

"I won't tell anyone you were awake," I said, forcing a smile I knew was unconvincing. "It will be our secret."

"The priestesses don't like it," she said. "They say I'm a disobedient girl."

An intelligent thing to say to a six-year-old with sleeping troubles. "For not sleeping? You can't help it."

She clutched the doorjamb as if for comfort. "Someone screamed," she said. "And a huge thing crossed the courtyard. I heard its breath."

"But you didn't see it?"

"No," she said. "It sounded scary."

I wished she'd been outside, close enough to see it. And then I realised that if she had indeed been outside, she would have died. What had I been thinking of? "It *was* scary," I said. "But we're going to hunt it down."

She didn't look impressed. I had to admit I probably didn't look very impressive. I'd never been as tall or as muscular as Neutemoc – no, I couldn't afford to think of Neutemoc now. I needed to focus on understanding the crime if I wanted to help him.

"Chicactic will protect me," the girl said, proudly.

The name meant "strong", but I couldn't see to whom it would refer, in a house of women and young girls. "Your brother?" I asked.

She shook her head, closed her eyes, and frowned; and the ghostly shape of a jaguar coalesced into existence at her feet.

A nahual. A small, insubstantial one: it batted at me with its paws, as the jaguar's children will do, but its swipes went right through me, leaving only a faint coldness in my legs. For a brief, wild moment, I entertained the idea that this nahual could have carried off Eleuia,

29

but I dismissed it as ridiculous. This animal was young, ghostly. With the Hunt-God's sight still upon me I could see the magic wrapped around the girl, and it wasn't the same one as in Eleuia's room. It was weaker, and not angry, simply tremendously self-focused.

"You're very strong," I said, and my admiration wasn't feigned. It was impressive. Most people born on a Jaguar day would never even get this close to materialising their protective spirit. Only the Duality knew what this child was going to become as she grew older. "I'm sure the priestesses are proud of you."

She made a grimace. She didn't look as though she thought much of the priestesses. "They tell me not to summon him." The jaguar had come back to her, rubbing itself against her legs, purring contentedly. Impressive indeed. "They don't like boastful people."

"They're surprised, that's all," I said. "Most people can't do that."

"No," she said. And then, with more shrewdness I would have guessed for a child of her years, "They're afraid. They think I'll take their place when I'm older."

I'd hoped this calmecac was different from the others: a true place of retreat, and not a battlefield for those who would rise in the hierarchy. But it was everywhere the same. And, judging by the enmities surrounding Eleuia, perhaps worse here, in the shadow of the Imperial Palace. "People are always afraid of what they can't understand. But you know what? If you can do that already, then you'll be very powerful when you're older, and nobody will bother you."

She looked sceptical, as if that wasn't a good thing. In truth, I wasn't sure it was.

Her jaguar spirit was prowling at the foot of the wall, and growling – its small, insubstantial frame dwarfed by the bulk of the calmecac's wall. It could probably smell the spoor of the other nahual.

I finally realised what had been bothering me about that wall. It was too high to leap, even for a nahual. In spite of their supernatural origins, nahuals retained the characteristics of mundane jaguars: teeth, claws, muscles. No jaguar, not even an adult, could have leapt over that wall.

Then how had the nahual left the calmecac? And why did the trail lead here, if it hadn't jumped over that wall?

"Do you know what's behind that wall?" I asked the girl.

She shrugged. "The outside."

"The Sacred Precinct?"

"Yes."

I glanced at the nahual jaguar, and then at the rooms, which appeared quiet. Surely, if the nahual was still in this school, Ceyaxochitl's warriors would have flushed it out? "If you remember anything about that beast – anything about tonight, will you ask the priestesses to send for me?"

She nodded, eagerly. She seemed to care far more for me than for the priestesses. Not that I could blame her. I mostly felt the same about the other clergies: those of the great gods like Tlaloc, God of Rain, and Huitzilpochtli, Protector of the Mexica Empire. Their top ranks were filled with social climbers too cowardly to go to war. As I had been, back when I had left the calmecac and chosen to become a priest.

It wasn't a subject I was ready to dwell on; especially not in the middle of the night, at the hour when the aimlessness of my life weighed like layers of gold on my chest.

I gave the girl my name and bade her a good night. Then I went out of the calmecac, to see what was on the other side of the wall.

As the girl had said, not much. This particular section of adobe wasn't connecting with another temple, or warriors' barracks: it simply faced the deserted expanse of the plaza. A little further away, the ground sloped down, towards the elongated shape of the ball-game court. With the Cloud Serpent's sight still on me, I should have seen the trail, had there been one. But there was nothing. It was as if the nahual had vanished in mid-air.

Feeling faintly ill at ease, I went back into the school, to look for Neutemoc.

Yaotl took me to where Neutemoc was kept: a room at the back of the calmecac. He walked by my side with a faint trace of amusement in his dark eyes, but said nothing. Neither did I – I, too, could play the game of withholding information.

Two of Ceyaxochitl's warriors, with the fused-lovers insignia of the Duality on their cotton-padded armour, stood guard at the door. They let us pass in silence.

It must have been a teaching room for the girls: weaving looms and discarded threads littered the ground. Neutemoc was sitting in its centre, cross-legged on a woven reed mat, hands on his knees, staring distantly at the frescoes on the walls, as if deep in meditation. He wore his Jaguar Knight's regalia: the jaguar's skin tightly covering his body, and his face showing through the animal's open jaws.

I stopped for a moment, suddenly unsure of what I'd say to him. He wasn't quite the brother I remembered from four years ago. His features had hardened in some indefinable way, and slight wrinkles marred the corner of his eyes, lessening the aura of arrogance that had once permeated every part of his body. He smelled, faintly, of the magic in the room, but most of it was gone: washed, no doubt, at the same time as his hands, which were now clean, their skin the colour of cacao beans.

Neutemoc raised his eyes when I came in. "Hello, brother," he said. He didn't sound surprised, or angry, just thoughtful. But his fingers tightened on his knees.

I had been bracing myself for seeing him again, trying to calm the frantic beating of my heart. His face, in the dim light, looked like a younger, softer version of Father's: an unexpected, additional discomfort.

I knelt by his side and looked at him, trying to see evidence of guilt, or remorse – of anything that would indicate he'd summoned the nahual. His face was clear, guileless, as smooth as that of a seasoned patolli gambler. "Dealing in magic?" I asked, as calmly as I could.

He shook his head. "I had nothing to do with that, believe me."

The anger in his voice belied his calm assurances. "I don't," I said, curtly. "Why don't you tell me what you were doing in Priestess Eleuia's rooms, overturning furniture?"

Neutemoc didn't move, but his eyes flicked away from me. "I don't have to explain myself to you."

"Have you no idea of what trouble you're in? What happened tonight, Neutemoc?"

He opened his mouth to say something, changed his mind with a visible effort, and finally said, "It's none of your concern."

None of my concern? Huitzilpochtli curse him, could he be so unaware of what he risked? He'd always been more concerned with the turmoil of the battlefield than with politics, but still… "I think you'll find it has become my concern tonight," I said, with some exasperation, remembering that his silence was one of the reasons we'd quarrelled four years ago. "From the moment magic was used to abduct her."

Neutemoc shifted, looked at the frescoes. "I know I'm in a bad situation, but I didn't do anything wrong. I'll swear it on any god you name."

If only it were that simple. "An oath, even by a Jaguar Knight, won't be enough in a court of law," I said. "Why don't you explain to me what happened?"

Neutemoc just stared at the frescoes. Finally he said, "I came to visit my daughter Ohtli. She entered the calmecac a few months ago, and Huei thought I could see how our daughter was doing. I was halfway to Ohtli's room when I heard a noise coming from a nearby courtyard, and..." He trailed off, closed his eyes. "When I entered the room, something leapt at me and knocked me against the wall. I was thrown unconscious and, when I woke up, your people had arrested me for the Duality knows what offence."

His story was barely coherent. It didn't account for the blood, or the marks on him. "And you overturned the furniture because you weren't sure what had leapt at you?" I asked, fighting to keep my sarcasm in check. "Come on, Neutemoc. I'm sure you can do better than this."

He shook his head. "It's the truth, Acatl."

I didn't believe a word he had said. But he was obviously not going to admit to anything, not unless I forced him into it.

I went to the door, and motioned Yaotl in.

"Anything you want?" he asked me.

"Can you ask the priestesses if there's a girl named Ohtli here, of the Atempan *calpulli* clan? She'd be about–" I thought back to the last time I'd seen Neutemoc's daughters – "seven years old."

Yaotl shrugged. "Easily done," he said. "They keep records of every girl-child in the school."

I glanced at Neutemoc, who was watching me, his eyes widening slightly. It was not a kind threat, the one I was about to make, either for him or for Ohtli, but his life was at stake. "If you find her, can you have her brought here? Tell her I have some questions for her."

"Acatl, no! She's only a child. At least have the decency to keep her out of this."

The insult stung, but I didn't move. "You were the one who introduced her name into the conversation."

Neutemoc's hands clenched. "It was a mistake. Ohtli has nothing to do with this, nothing at all. I didn't get to her room, I swear."

"Then please show a little more co-operation."

"Acatl–" He was pleading now, and it made me ill at ease. I'd never enjoyed reducing people to helplessness.

"It's a pretty story you told me," I said. "But it doesn't fit what I saw in that room, or what the Guardian saw."

Neutemoc looked at me, and at Yaotl, who already had a hand on the entrance-curtain. "Very well," he said, finally. "I'll tell you. But in private."

"Nothing is private," I said. "Your testimony–"

"Acatl." His voice cut as deep as an obsidian blade. "Please."

He was my brother, the threat of death hanging over him, yet I could afford no favouritism. Everyone should be treated according to their status, noblemen and Jaguar Knights more harshly than commoners. "I'll listen to you in private," I said. "But I'll make no guarantee I won't pass it on."

Neutemoc's face was flat, taut with fear. He glanced at Yaotl – tall, scarred, unbending – and finally nodded.

Yaotl slipped out, drawing the entrance-curtain closed in a tinkle of bells. He barked orders, and footsteps echoed in the corridor: the warriors, moving away from the door.

I sat by Neutemoc's side, keeping one hand on the handle of the obsidian daggers I always had in my belt, just as a protection. He hadn't looked violent, but his mood-swings could be unpredictable. "So?" I asked.

He said, slowly, "I... I knew Priestess Eleuia. We fought together in the war against Chalco. She was a novice priestess of Xochiquetzal then, at the bottom of the hierarchy – but she was magnificent." He shook his head. "We slept together."

Priestesses of Xochiquetzal were sacred courtesans, accompanying the warriors on their campaigns. They were also warriors in their own right, fighting the enemy with their long, deadly spears. "You slept with her in Chalco," I said, flatly. "That was sixteen years ago."

I was starting to suspect what Neutemoc had been doing in Eleuia's room. The idea was decidedly unpleasant.

"Yes," Neutemoc said. "I didn't think much of it, at the time. I had my marriage coming, and we drifted apart." He closed his eyes, spoke with care, as if he were composing a poem: each word slowly falling into place with the inevitability of a heartbeat. "I met her again two months ago, when I enrolled Ohtli. I had no idea she'd been posted here. We sat together and reminisced about the past, and all we'd lived through together... She hadn't changed, Acatl. Still the same as she'd been, all those years ago. Still the same smile, the same gestures that would drive a man mad with desire."

The Storm Lord smite him, surely he hadn't dared? "Neutemoc–"

His lips had gone white. "You asked, Acatl. You wanted to know why I was here tonight. I had an assignation. She... she flirted with me, quite ostentatiously."

And he'd gone to her rooms. "You gave in?" I rose, towered over him. "You were stupid enough to give in?"

"You don't understand."

"No," I said. "You're right. I don't understand why you'd endanger all you've got for a pretty smile." Eleuia was no longer a sacred courtesan: to sleep with her was adultery. And for that, they would both be put to death. And then... No more quetzal feathers, no more showers of gold brought to his luxurious home; no more calmecac education for his sons or his daughters, or for our orphaned sister.

I said, haltingly, "For the Duality's sake! You've got a family, you've got a loving wife." Everything – he had everything my parents had wished for their children: the glory of a successful warrior – and not the poverty-ridden life of a measly priest, barely able to support himself, let alone take care of his aged parents...

Neutemoc smiled. "You're ill-informed, brother. Huei and I haven't talked for a while."

I blinked. "What?"

He shrugged. "Private matters," he said.

"Such as your sleeping with a few priestesses?" I asked, rubbing the salt on his wounds. If he had indeed been unfaithful, Huei would have kept silent: if not for his sake, then for the sake of their children.

He finally opened his eyes to stare at me, and his gaze was ice. "I haven't committed adultery. Even tonight, though that was rather unexpected." He laughed, sharply, sarcastically. "I know what you think. What a man I make, huh?"

"Don't push me. Or I might just leave you in peace."

"You've already done too much as it is." Neutemoc's hands clenched again.

"You were the one who brought me into this, all because you were incapable of resisting a woman's charms," I snapped.

Neutemoc was silent for a while, looking at me with an expression I couldn't interpret. "You're right. I shouldn't have said that. I apologise. Can we go back to where we were?"

I had been bracing myself for a further attack; this extinguished my anger as efficiently as water poured on a hearth. Struggling to hide my surprise, I nodded. "So you came to her rooms with the promise of a pleasurable evening. I assume you got in by pretending you were here to see your daughter?"

He shrugged. "It was before sunset. Nothing wrong with my visiting her."

"But you didn't."

"No," Neutemoc said. "I– Eleuia had told me where her rooms were. I went there and found her waiting for me. She poured me a glass of frothy chocolate, with milk and maize gruel – good chocolate, too, very tasty. That's the last thing I remember clearly. Then the room was spinning, and…" His hand clenched again. "There was darkness, Acatl, deeper than the shadows of Mictlan. Something leapt at her. I tried to step in, but everything went dark. When I woke up, I was alone, and covered in her blood."

It still sounded as though he was leaving out parts of the story – probably Eleuia's seduction of him, which I didn't think I was capable of hearing out in any case – but this version sounded far more sincere than the first one he'd given me. Which, of course, didn't mean it was the truth. If he and Eleuia had consummated their act, he could have panicked and decided she was a risk to him while she still lived. I didn't like the thought, but Neutemoc was a canny enough man, or he wouldn't have risen so high in the warrior hierarchy.

"You could at least have had the intelligence to get out as soon as you could," I said. "What about the furniture?"

He stared at me. "Furniture? I... You know, I don't quite remember about that. I think I must have wanted to make sure I hadn't left any trace of my passage."

Not a sensible thing to do. But then, would I be sensible, if I woke up in a deserted room, covered in blood, with no memory of what had happened?

"Very well," I said. "Do you have anything that can prove your story?"

Neutemoc stared at me, shocked. "I'm your brother, Acatl. Isn't my word enough?"

He was really slow tonight. "We already went through that, remember?" I tried to keep my voice as calm as possible. "Your word alone won't sway the magistrates."

"Magistrates." His voice was flat.

"It will come to trial," I said.

I'd expected him to be angry. Instead, he suddenly went as still as a carved statue. His lips moved, but I couldn't hear any word.

"Neutemoc?"

He looked up, right through me. "It's only fair, I suppose," he said. "Deserved."

My stomach plummeted. "Why did you deserve it?"

But he wouldn't talk to me any more, no matter how many times I tried to draw him out of his trance.

Ceyaxochitl was waiting for me in the corridor, talking to Yaotl. He threw me an amused glance as I got closer.

"So?" Ceyaxochitl asked.

I shrugged. "His story holds together."

"But you don't like it," she said, as shrewd as ever.

"No," I said. "There's something he's not telling me." And my brother had tried to sleep with a priestess; had tried to cheat on his wife. I was having trouble accepting it. It did not sound like something that would happen to my charmed-life brother.

"Where does the world go, if you can't trust your own brother?" Yaotl asked, darkly amused.

As far as I knew, Yaotl, a captive foreigner Ceyaxochitl had bought from the Tlatelolco marketplace, had a wife – a slight, pretty woman who seldom spoke to strangers – but no other family. At least, not the kind that lived close enough to get him embroiled in their troubles. Lucky man.

"What about the nahual trail?" Ceyaxochitl asked.

"It vanishes into thin air, halfway up a wall no animal could jump."

"Hum," Ceyaxochitl said. "Odd. We've searched every room, and the nahual isn't here."

"They don't just vanish," I said.

"I know," Ceyaxochitl said. She frowned. "We're no nearer finding Priestess Eleuia than we were one hour ago. I'll instruct the search parties to cast a wider net."

She waited, no doubt for my acquiescence. It was an unsettling thought to be in charge of the investigation. Eleuia had been about to become Consort of Xochipilli. This meant that she would have been connected to the Imperial Court, in one way or another. Given the political stakes, I had better be very careful of where I trod; and politics had never been my strength. "Shouldn't you be back at the palace?" I asked her.

Ceyaxochitl snorted. "I can spare one night to help you start. But only one."

I nodded. She'd been clear enough on that. I couldn't fault her for her frankness, even if sometimes she wounded me without realising she did so.

If the blood in the room and on Neutemoc's hands had indeed belonged to Eleuia, time was against us.

"Send them out," I said. "I'll go and talk to Zollin."

# THREE
## *Dancers*

When I arrived, the courtyard was deserted again, and the entrance-curtain to Eleuia's room hung forlornly in the breeze. But from the other set of rooms – Zollin's – came light, and the slow, steady beat of a drum. Music, at this hour?

I pulled aside the curtain, and took a look inside.

In a wide room much like Eleuia's, two young adolescents went through the motions of a dance. One was tall, her hair cascading down her back, and the seashell anklets she wore chimed with each of her slow gestures. The other wove her way between the tall one's movements, like water flowing through stone. It was not all effortless: beads of sweat ran down the first dancer's face, and the other one kept whispering under her breath, counting the paces.

The drum-beater was older than either of her dancers: her seamed face had seen many a year, and she kept up her rhythm, even though her eyes were focused on the girls. Smoke hung in the room: copal incense, melding with the odour of sweat in an intoxicating mixture.

I released the curtain. The chime of the bells crashed into the music, a jarring sound that made both dancers come to a halt. The drum-beater laid her instrument on the ground, and looked at me, appraising me in a manner eerily reminiscent of Ceyaxochitl. It was very uncomfortable.

"Priestess Zollin?" I asked her. "I am Acatl."

The drummer nodded. She turned, briefly, to the girls, "That was good. But not enough. A dance should be done without thinking, in much the same way that you breathe." She waved a dismissive hand. "We'll practise again tomorrow."

The girls remained standing where they were, staring at me in fascination.

The older woman's full attention was on me. "The High Priest for the Dead, I suppose. Come to question me. I've had the Guardian already, you know, and you've already arrested a culprit. I don't see what good it will do."

She was sharp. Used to getting her own way, to the point of discarding Neutemoc as of no importance to her. Already, I longed to break some of that pride. She was also singularly unworried, if she could dispense music lessons in the middle of the night, with one of her priestesses missing, or killed.

"One of your priestesses has vanished," I said. "Doesn't that–"

She shrugged. "Why should it interfere with the running of this house? I grieve for Eleuia" – that was the worst lie I'd ever heard, for she made no effort to inflect any of those words, or to put sadness on her face – "but she was only one woman. The education we dispense shouldn't halt because of that."

"I see," I said. "So you think she's dead." I closed my eyes, briefly, and felt the magic hanging around the room like a shroud, clinging to the frescoes of flowers and musical instruments: not nahual, not quite, but something dark, something angry. Zollin was clearly powerful.

"There was so much blood," the tallest dancer said suddenly. Her face was creased in an expression that didn't belong: worry or fear, or perhaps the first stirrings of anger.

"Cozamalotl," Zollin snapped. The girl fell silent, but she still watched her teacher. Her younger companion hadn't moved. A faint blush was creeping up her cheeks.

"Eleuia could still be alive," I said.

"Then go look for her," Zollin said. She was truly angry, and I had no idea why. "Do your work, and I'll do mine."

The Duality curse me if I was going to let her dominate me. "My work brings me here," I said, softly. "My work leads me to ask you why you're not more preoccupied by the disappearance of a priestess in your own calmecac."

Zollin watched me. "She never belonged to this calmecac. It was only a step on her path to better things."

"Becoming Consort?" I asked.

"Whatever she could seize," Zollin said.

Cozamalotl spoke up again, moving closer to Zollin as if she could shield her. "Everyone knows Eleuia grasped at power the way warriors grasp at fame."

The younger dancer did not answer. She was shaking her head in agreement or in disagreement, though only slightly. It seemed that Cozamalotl wasn't only Zollin's student, but her partisan. If Eleuia was indeed dead, or incapacitated, Cozamalotl would have her reward, just as Zollin would.

The Southern Hummingbird blind my brother. How in the Fifth World had he managed to embroil himself in such a bitter power struggle?

I probed further. "So you think someone didn't like what Eleuia was doing?"

Zollin snorted. "No one did. It's not seemly for a woman."

Hypocrite. She condemned Eleuia for her ambition, but she still wanted that office of Consort for herself. I liked Zollin less and less as the conversation progressed, though I couldn't afford to be blinded by resentment if I wanted to solve this.

"Women have few paths open in life," I said, finally, thinking of my own sister Mihmatini, who would be coming of age in a few months, and would either join the clergy or look for a husband of her own.

"But we know our place," Zollin said. "Eleuia's behaviour was hardly appropriate. Flaunting herself before men with her hair unbound and her face painted yellow – red cochineal on her teeth, as if she were still a courtesan on the battlefield–"

"When did she come here?" I asked, knowing I had to regain control of the conversation if I wanted to find anything to help Neutemoc.

Zollin looked bewildered for the first time. "Nine, ten years ago? I'm not sure."

"And how long have you been here?"

"A long time," Zollin said.

"Long enough to feel you should have been Consort, instead of Eleuia?" I asked.

She looked at me with new eyes. Yes. I might look harmless, but I could still wound.

When she answered, some of the acidity was gone from her voice. "Some of us," she said, "take what we have. And we do the tasks we were charged with, and do them well for years. Eleuia was young and inexperienced. But she was alluring. And men like that in a woman."

Of course they did – the warriors, and maybe even some of the priests, though they shouldn't have. And the men, as she had no need to remind me, held the power: the clergy of Xochiquetzal was subordinate to that of her husband, Xochipilli.

"She had power," Zollin went on. "A great mastery of magic, and a reputation won on the battlefield. But all that doesn't make a good Consort of Xochipilli."

"Then what does?" I asked.

"Dedication," Zollin said shortly. "Eleuia's heart wasn't in the priesthood. You could see it was only her pathway to something larger."

"I see," I said. She was only repeating herself. But her final assessment of Eleuia sounded more sincere than everything she'd said before. A woman bent on power – and wouldn't Neutemoc, with his status as a Jaguar Knight, have been a good embodiment of that power? My hands clenched. I wouldn't think about Neutemoc, not now. I couldn't afford to. "What were you doing tonight?"

"None of your concern."

Had she and Neutemoc decided to act together to vex me? "I've had my share of foolish excuses for tonight," I said. "Tell me what you were doing."

It was the dancer Cozamalotl who answered. "She was with us," she said. "Teaching us the proper hymns for the festivals."

Given the slight twitch of surprise on Zollin's face, that was clearly a lie.

"I see," I said, again. "Would you swear to that before the magistrates?"

She gazed at me, defiant, but it was Zollin who spoke. "Cozamalotl," she said. "The penalty for perjury is the loss of a hand. Don't waste your future."

Cozamalotl did not look abashed, not in the slightest. Her young companion, though, was bright red by now, and looked as if she wanted to speak but couldn't get the words past her lips. I would have to talk to her later.

"I–" Cozamalotl started.

Zollin cut her. "I was alone. In my rooms. And I can swear that I had nothing to do with that."

"But you hated Eleuia," I said.

"I won't deny that."

"Tell me," I said. "What day were you born?"

She looked surprised. "That's no concern of yours."

"Humour me."

"Why should I?"

"It's only a date," I said. "What are you afraid of?"

"I'm not a fool," Zollin said. "There's only one reason you'd be asking for it. I didn't summon the nahual, Acatl-tzin."

"But you could have."

She watched me, unblinking. At length: "You'll go to the registers anyway. Yes. I was born on the day Twelve Jaguar in the year Ten House."

She'd been quick to react. Too quick, perhaps, as if she'd had prior knowledge? She'd been in the room: it was conceivable she'd have recognised the scent of nahual magic, though highly unlikely. It wasn't a widespread craft among priestesses.

I said nothing. "Will that be all?" she asked, drawing herself to her full height. "I have offerings to make."

"That will be all," I said. "For now." I caught the eye of the younger dancer, who was still standing unmoving, her face creased in worry. She nodded, briefly, her chin raising to point to the courtyard outside.

I exited the room, and waited for the girl there. She did not come immediately: an angry conversation seemed to be going on inside, between Zollin and her two students. But try as I might, I couldn't make out the individual words, not without re-entering the room.

Two things worried me. The first was Zollin's singular unconcern for the summoning of a nahual, and the spilling of blood in her own calmecac school; the second, the sheer incongruity of teaching girls how to dance at this hour of the night.

But then, if she was indeed complicit in Eleuia's disappearance, the first wasn't surprising. As to the second: I'd known men and women who would bury themselves in activities, no matter how ludicrous, in order to escape guilty consciences.

The younger dancer joined me outside, after a while. She was even younger than I thought: not much more than a child, really, her body barely settling into the shapes and contours of adulthood. "Acatl-tzin? I thought–"

"Go on," I said, gently.

"My name is Papan," she said. "I…" She looked at me, struggling for words. "Is Zollin-tzin a suspect in your investigation?"

"I don't know," I said, though she most surely was.

"There was a man found in Eleuia's rooms," Papan said. "With blood on his hands."

I nodded, curtly, trying not to think too much of Neutemoc, of what I'd have to tell his wife, Huei, once I'd gathered enough courage to go to her. "There are unexplained things," I said, finally. I started walking towards the end of the courtyard, crushing pine needles under my sandaled feet. Their sweet, aromatic smell wafted upwards, a relief after the stifling atmosphere of Zollin's room.

Papan followed me. "You're looking in the wrong place."

"Your loyalty brings you credit," I said. "But–"

"No. You don't understand. Zollin-tzin has worked hard for this calmecac. She's always been fair. She would never kill or summon forbidden magic."

"Nahual magic isn't forbidden," I said. "And I only have your word for Zollin's acts."

"But I have only your word that Eleuia was abducted," Papan said, obviously frustrated. "No one has found her. No one even knows if she didn't summon the nahual herself."

I shook my head. "Priestess Eleuia wasn't born on a Jaguar day. She couldn't have summoned the nahual." Curious, I asked, "Why would she do such a thing?"

Papan came to stand by my side, under the red arch leading out of the courtyard. A fresco of conch-shells and butterflies ran along the length of the arch. The insects' wings, painted with dark-red lac, glinted with the same reflections as Papan's eyes. "Eleuia was very beautiful," Papan said. "But always frightened. Cozamalotl and the other students didn't see it, but she always moved as if the ground would open under her feet."

"She had enemies?" I asked.

Papan shrugged. "I didn't know her."

"But you understood her."

"No," Papan said. She blushed. "I just saw. But it wasn't just now. She'd always been like that. For years and years, ever since I entered the calmecac school."

"And you think she wanted to disappear? Why, if she'd always been afraid?"

Papan turned her face away from me. "I– I'm not supposed to tell you. But if it helps..." She twisted her hands together, but didn't speak.

"Go on," I said. "It could save her life."

Papan was silent for a while. "I saw her once, at the bath-house. She was coming out of the pool." Papan blushed again. "I saw the marks on her body."

"What marks? Scars?"

"No," Papan said. "Stretch-marks."

49

"She'd borne a child?" It wasn't forbidden for a priestess of the Quetzal Flower, but it was certainly unusual. Many herbs would expel a child from a woman's body, and there were spells which would summon minor gods from Mictlan to end an infant's life in the womb. Priestesses would know all of these.

"Yes," Papan said. "I asked her; and she laughed and she said it was a long time ago, when she was much younger, in the Chalca Wars. I asked her why she'd done that, and she told me she'd wanted a keepsake of her warrior lover."

My heart went cold. "You're sure it was in the Chalca Wars?"

Papan nodded.

In the Chalca Wars, Eleuia and Neutemoc had slept together. But surely... Nonsense. She was a sacred courtesan. She'd slept with many, many men, even in the Chalca Wars. There were dozens who could have been the father of that child. But it had been someone she'd loved. You couldn't say that about just any warrior.

And there lay the root of the problem: for a warrior, sleeping with a courtesan was an inalienable right, a reward for facing the hardships of the battlefield. A long affair between a warrior and a courtesan, though – that wasn't tolerated. It would lead to exclusion from the Jaguar Brotherhood, no matter how long ago the affair had taken place. If Neutemoc had indeed conceived a child with Eleuia – and if Eleuia had kept it – then it meant they had been more than casual lovers.

It also meant that Neutemoc had an even stronger motive to keep Eleuia silent. A child.

I did not like the thought. I had to consider it, like everything linked to the investigation – but it was an itch at the back of my mind, claws softly teasing apart what I had believed I knew about Neutemoc.

"Why do you think it may be connected?" I asked Papan.

Papan shrugged. "I don't. But she didn't name the warrior."

I had noticed that. "And she didn't tell you anything about him?"

"No," Papan said. "But she looked scared, as if she'd told me something I wasn't meant to know. She made me swear to keep it secret. And I have, haven't I?"

I knew what she wanted. Gently, I said, "Secrets are no use to her if she's dead."

Papan stared at me for a while. I couldn't tell if I'd convinced her. "Don't tell Zollin-tzin I told you," she said, as we walked out of the courtyard. "She thinks Eleuia was only an opportunist."

She didn't use any honorific for Eleuia, I noticed, just her name. "You were close?" I asked.

Papan bit her lip. "Until Zollin-tzin started teaching me," she said, miserably. "It's hard, being torn in two halves."

I hadn't known that. But I could guess, given Zollin's acidity, that it was indeed hard. "You did the right thing," I said.

"I'm not sure." Papan bowed, deeply. "I'll go back to my room now. But thank you for listening to me, Acatl-tzin." And she walked off into the darkness, leaving me to my own worries.

A child. Neutemoc's child? The Storm Lord smite him, couldn't he have been more careful? A warrior was meant to marry in his calpulli clan, to love his wife, to raise her children. And it seemed that Neutemoc – who'd always been held up as an example before me, the shining representation of all I should have done with my life, whom I'd always admired and hated at the same time – it seemed that Neutemoc had not had great success with his marriage.

Ceyaxochitl and Yaotl were waiting for me at the entrance to the calmecac school, by a fresco of quetzals in flight. The birds' long tails spread against the painted background like waterfalls of emerald. Ceyaxochitl's face was flushed, and she was muttering imprecations under her breath. "Arrogant bastard. Who does he think he is?"

"Something the matter?" I asked, stifling a yawn.

Yaotl turned to me. "The Jaguar Knight just walked out of here," he said.

"The Jaguar Knight?" My mind, which had been focused on Eleuia's child, and on whether it might have been Neutemoc's, snapped back to the present. "Mahuizoh? The one who was visiting his sister?"

The Duality curse me. I'd forgotten to ask Neutemoc if he knew the man. He had to: there weren't that many Jaguar Knights in the city of Tenochtitlan.

"Yes," Ceyaxochitl snapped. "He said we had no evidence against him, that we had a perfectly good culprit in any case, and that he saw no reason to tarry here."

"So you didn't question him."

"Does it look as though I did?" Ceyaxochitl snapped. She rapped her cane on the ground. "I should have arrested him for disrespect. I'm getting too soft for this."

I didn't believe a word of that last sentence. She was still as harsh as she'd ever been: as harsh as she needed to be, to protect the Mexica Empire from wayward gods, stray underworld monsters, sorcerers and magicians…

"Why didn't you?" Yaotl asked, softly. He had a hand on his obsidian-studded macuahitl sword. "You had ample reasons."

Ceyaxochitl shook her head. "He's not guilty of any-thing, Yaotl. Warriors and arrogance go hand-in-hand, remember?"

I disliked arrogance as much as Ceyaxochitl, and Zollin's imperiousness was all too fresh in my mind. But Ceyaxochitl was right: warriors, especially Eagle and Jaguar Knights, were entitled to be arrogant, to dismiss us as of little consequence. It wasn't seemly be-haviour, but they had dispensation. They'd fought on the Empire's battlefields, taken prisoners to sacrifice to the gods, so that the world should go on, fed by the magic of living blood; survived gruelling battles and re-treats. Compared to this, we priests had an easy life.

"Do you know where he lives?" I asked Ceyaxochitl.

"No," she said. "But he's a Jaguar Knight. You can go ask at their House, tomorrow."

"Why not tonight?" I asked. "Neutemoc–"

Ceyaxochitl's lips pursed. "One night of imprison-ment isn't going to kill your brother."

"But I could–"

"You could not." Her voice was as cutting as obsid-ian. "One does not walk into the Jaguar House."

"I am High Priest for the Dead," I said, in the same tone she had used on me.

Ceyaxochitl's gaze told me all I needed to know: the Jaguar and Eagle Knights were the elite of the Empire, the warriors who kept us strong, and they had their own laws. "Acatl. If you go into the Jaguar House, and wake up sleeping Knights without their commander's permission, you'll be under arrest. And much good it will do your brother then."

"You're asking me to let go?"

"I'm asking you to wait until tomorrow. Daylight changes many things."

Yaotl's lips pursed. "And if you dress impressively enough, getting in shouldn't be a problem."

"Ha ha," I said. Even if I put on my full regalia, with the skull-mask and the cloak embroidered with owls, I'd still have difficulties entering the Jaguar Knights' House. "Do you think it's worth pursuing?" I asked Ceyaxochitl.

It was Yaotl who answered. "That Jaguar Knight was shaken," he said. "Very badly shaken, and trying hard not to show it."

Hardly a normal reaction. "You think he had something to do with it?"

"I'm having trouble seeing how he could not have had something to do with it," Yaotl said.

More suspects. On the one hand, this lessened the chances Neutemoc was guilty of more than adultery. On the other, what had looked like an easy case seemed to put forth additional complications with every hour.

"I'll go and see him tomorrow," I said.

Ceyaxochitl's eyes blinked, slowly; her face stretched slightly. I put my hand over my mouth to contain my own yawn.

"Anything else?" she asked.

I thought back to my interview with Zollin, and of the magic that had hung thick in her room. "You said you'd searched every room of the calmecac for the nahual. Did that include Zollin's rooms?"

Yaotl spoke up. "No supernatural jaguar hiding there, trust me. Although I've never seen someone less worried about Eleuia."

"I had the same impression," I said. "She seemed to polarise people."

Ceyaxochitl shrugged. "The beautiful often do, even if they're no longer young." She leaned on her cane, exhaling in what seemed almost nostalgia. Then she shook her head, coming back to more pressing matters. "The search parties are out. Yaotl will stay here and supervise them. You, on the other hand, should go to sleep."

I said, stung, "I don't need–"

"Sleep? Don't be a fool, Acatl. Dawn is in less than two hours. You won't be of any use to anyone, least of all your brother, if you can hardly stand."

My brother. Was I going to be of any use to him?

I hadn't dwelled on Neutemoc for years. Or perhaps it had started even earlier: when the calpulli clan's search party brought Father's drowned body to Neutemoc's house, and when we'd stared at each other across the divide, and known we'd become strangers to each other.

I didn't know. I didn't know what I ought to feel.

"There will be time, tomorrow," Yaotl said, almost gently. I must have looked really tired, if he was being solicitous to me.

"Was there anything else, Acatl?" Ceyaxochitl asked.

It was a dismissal: my last chance to get her help, instead of Yaotl's distant, ironic pronouncements. I said, finally, "I need the location… of a certain house in Tenochtitlan."

"A House of Joy?" Yaotl asked, his face falsely serious. "Feeling lonely in your bed?"

I was too tired to rise to the jibe. "Priestess Eleuia allegedly had a child, some years ago. I'm not sure it's significant, but I'd like to know if it's true."

Ceyaxochitl's eyes held me, shrewd, perceptive. I lowered my gaze. I didn't wish her to read my thoughts. But she had to know; she had to have guessed what I feared. "Yes?"

"I've heard whispers in the Sacred Precinct," I said slowly. "They say… they say that Xochiquetzal, the Quetzal Flower could not restrain Her lust, and charmed all the gods onto Her sleeping mat, one after the other. There is talk that the Duality expelled Her from Heaven for this sin, and that She now dwells in the mortal world, in a house which can be visited, if one knows its location."

Ceyaxochitl didn't blink, or give any sign of surprise. "Perhaps," she said. "You'd go to Her to know about the child?"

"Yes," I said.

I couldn't read her expression. But at length she said, "Priestess Eleuia belonged to Her. And she is Goddess of Lust and Childbirth, after all. Perhaps She'll know something useful. Go to bed, Acatl. I'll send the address to you in the morning."

So I couldn't go to the goddess's house now. They were both treating me like a newborn infant, which was worrying. Neither of them had shown any inclination to overprotect me before.

"Very well," I said. "You win. I'll go find some sleep before dawn."

"Don't worry. We'll take care of things," Yaotl said. His eyes glinted in the darkness. For a fleeting moment I thought there was more than amusement in his gaze – something deeper and more serious – but then I dismissed the thought. Yaotl was not my enemy.

I was too tired to think properly. I bade them goodbye and walked back to my temple, praying that they'd find Eleuia alive – that they'd find something, anything, that would exonerate Neutemoc.

## FOUR
## *The Midwife of Tenochtitlan*

My sleep was dark and dreamless. I noted, distantly, the blare of priests' trumpets that marked the return of Tonatiuh from His night-long journey – and then turned on my reed-mat, and went back to sleep.

When I woke up, sunlight flooded my house. I sat up, wincing as all the events of the previous night came back into my mind, as unforgiving as *peyotl* visions.

Neutemoc.

A child.

He had a wife and children of his own, and our sister Mihmatini under his responsibility. Even if Neutemoc was later found out to be innocent, the tarnish of his arrest and his attempted adultery would hang over them all for a long time. Huitzilpochtli blind him. Could he do nothing right?

I rummaged in my wicker chest for a clean loincloth, and took my grey cloak from the reed-mat where I'd left it. As I tied it around my shoulders, I thought of the last time I'd seen Neutemoc: of Mother's face, contorted in agony and anger as she accused me of cowardice; and of Neutemoc, standing frozen by her death-bed, unable to say anything.

He hadn't said anything as I walked out, later. He'd gone back to his wife and children, and I'd staggered through the city, trying to find words I could give Mother: reasons that would convince her that by entering an obscure priesthood, I hadn't wasted my life. I was needed: I kept the balance of the world; I gave the dead their rest. But not indispensable: there were plenty of priests – while there had been no one, save Neutemoc, to pay for the schooling and the feeding of my three sisters.

Enough worries. I had to make sure, first and foremost, that Neutemoc was truly innocent. I tried to ignore the voice whispering that he might well be the murderer Ceyaxochitl thought she'd arrested.

I walked out into the courtyard, under the lone pine tree, and exited my house. Outside, the hubbub of the Sacred Precinct filled my ears: vendors hawking their amulets and charms; a crowd of freemen in loincloths, coming to offer their sacrifices to the temples; a procession of priestesses, dressed in white skirts and blouses, singing their hymns to honour Toci, Grandmother Earth; warriors in embroidered cotton cloaks, striding arrogantly ahead.

Determined to start with the most unpleasant tasks, I went to the Jaguar House first: a squat adobe adorned with lavish frescoes of Knights trampling bound enemies underfoot, and of their patron Tezcatlipoca, watching the carnage with a slight smile across His striped face.

The House itself was always a centre of activity, bustling with Jaguar Knights and sacred courtesans, but today it was oddly silent.

There was a single guard at the gates, instead of the usual pair. He stared at me levelly as I approached. "Looking for something?" His pose and his voice exuded arrogance – not deliberately, but something that had become second nature to him. And yet he was a boy, impossibly young to have already been admitted into the ranks of the elite.

"I need to see a knight," I said.

"I have no doubt you do." His gaze lingered on me a little longer. In his eyes was the familiar contempt of warriors for priests. "That's currently impossible."

"Currently?" I asked.

His lips curled, in what might have been amusement. "They're at the Imperial Palace. There's a ceremony they have to practise for."

"All of them?" I asked, my heart sinking.

"All but me." He looked again at me, as if wondering what a shabbily dressed priest could possibly want of Jaguar Knights. Yaotl and Ceyaxochitl had been right; I should have put on my full regalia before coming here.

"When will they be back?" I asked.

He shrugged. "Tezcatlipoca only knows."

In other words, it was beneath his dignity to answer me. I bit back a curse. Antagonising the guard would bring me nothing but trouble.

"Noon?" I asked, insisting.

"They might be back then," the guard said. "You can try." His slightly mocking tone made it clear he believed I'd be thrown out of the House, regardless of whether the knights were back.

"I certainly will try," I said, determined not to let him get the better of me. "I'll see you then."

He didn't say anything as I walked away from the House. Privately, I doubted the knights would be back before a while. An Imperial ceremony was no small matter.

Curse it! Well, if I couldn't interview Mahuizoh, I could see about Xochiquetzal instead – not a pleasant thought, by any standards.

From the Jaguar House, it was but a short walk to my temple; and by the time I arrived there, most of the novice priests had already left for the market at Tlatelolco.

My second-in-command Ichtaca was in the courtyard, giving instructions to a handful of offering priests in grey-and-blue cloaks. As usual, he was acquitting himself so well I wasn't sure how I could have helped him. Why ever had Ceyaxochitl thought I'd make a good High Priest? I'd hoped to slip by Ichtaca undetected, but he was quite observant.

"Acatl-tzin!"

I suppressed a sigh. "Yes?"

"There's a message for you," Ichtaca said. "From Guardian Ceyaxochitl."

The location of Xochiquetzal's house, a message I'd hoped to recover discreetly. I nodded, and felt obliged, now that I was standing in front of him, to ask, "How are things going?"

He shrugged. "The usual. Two deaths in the district of Moyotlan. The examination revealed no trace of magic or other foul play, so I let the priests of the district handle it. A woman dead in childbirth in the district of Cuepopan. We'll have to supervise the burying rites, and make sure she's honoured properly."

As the woman had died struggling to bring a life into this world, her soul would already be flying upwards, to accompany Tonatiuh on His journeys; but the family's grief would be eased if the rites were said accordingly.

"I see," I said. "Well... I'll leave you to it."

Ichtaca looked at me. He seemed to be expecting something more of me, but I couldn't see what. Some orders? He had absolutely no need for that.

"I'll see that message," I said finally.

Ichtaca shrugged. Clearly, I had not given him what he had expected. "It's in the shrine. Come."

Before leaving, I detoured through the storehouse to take a parrot and a handful of marigold flowers: offerings for Xochiquetzal. Palli had been replaced by a younger novice priest, one whom I didn't know. He bowed to me, making me feel ill at ease.

Carrying the parrot's cage against my hip, I went to the address Ceyaxochitl had given me: a house on the outskirts of Moyotlan, the south-west district of Tenochtitlan. The city was on an island, of which the Sacred Precinct was the heart. Streets and canals snaked out from the central plaza, leading to the four districts – and further out, to the fields where we grew our crops. I walked away from the centre, into streets bordered by canals on either side. Small boats passed me by, ferrying their owners to their business: to the artisans' districts, to the marketplace, or an audience at a nobleman's house. The aqueduct canals were crossed at regular intervals by bridges. On each bridge stood a water-porter, ready to dip his bucket into the water, and to offer it to anyone who paid.

From the houses around me came the familiar grinding sound of maize pounded into powder, and the wet slap-slap of flatbread rolled onto the stones. That sound had woken me up every day when I was a child: Mother's daily ritual, making the food that Father would take to the fields. Long before I took the path to my humble priesthood, back when my parents had still been proud of my thirst for knowledge.

Lost in reminiscence, I finally reached my destination: a small, unremarkable alley, half street, half canal. At the back of the alley were the featureless walls of a huge house, one that seemed to waver in the morning light, even though there was barely any mist.

Magic hung thick around it: the familiar, bold strokes of Ceyaxochitl's spells, woven into a cocoon around the house, hiding it from the world. An uninitiated person could not have seen enough of that house to open its door.

The house had two storeys, a luxury reserved for noblemen. A lush garden of poinsettias and marigolds adorned its roof. In the courtyard, pines grew by the side of a stone pool, the water within, clear, cloudless, reflecting the perfect blue of the sky.

"And you would be?" a voice asked.

Startled, I turned, and met the eyes of a youth wearing the wooden collar of slaves – though he had jade and silver bracelets on his arms, and heavy amber earrings weighing down his lobes.

"No," I said. "I've come to see Xochiquetzal."

His face didn't move, save for some fleeting contempt in his eyes as he scrutinised me. "A priest, eh? I don't think She wants to see your kind."

"Someone's life is at stake," I said, more sharply than I'd intended.

He shrugged. "It's always the case. Life is cheap in the Fifth World, priest." He half-turned away from me, walking back into the building he had come from.

Life is cheap. My own brother's life, cheap?

My fists clenched of their own volition. Before I realised it, I was halfway through the courtyard, following him into the house.

What stopped me wasn't anything material – but rather a slow, prickling sensation running along the nape of my neck, and spreading to my entire back, like fiery embers touching my skin: raw power, coalescing in the sunlight. I had the feeling of being watched and dissected by something vast and unknowable, though there was no one but the slave and I in the courtyard.

The slave had turned. He watched me, his smile mocking me. "And you think this will solve anything?"

I struggled to find words, to mouth an abject apology, but could not bring myself to. "No. Nor will your arrogant attitude. I asked for an audience."

He spread his hands in a blaze of silver. "You did. And it's my right to refuse it."

"You—"

He shook his head. "Still not understanding? Defiance brings you nothing." He smiled again, displaying teeth as yellow and as neat as maize kernels. "But you're in luck. It has been a boring week. Wait here. And don't think you can look around. I'll know if you do."

I had no doubt he would.

He entered one of the rooms around the courtyard, the bells jingling as he pulled aside the entrance curtain. He came out again almost immediately. "My, my. You're definitely in luck, priest. She has nothing better to do, so She'll see you."

His arrogance was staggering, but I bit back the angry reply that came to me. I had already seen anger or despair would earn me nothing in such a house.

The slave pointed lazily to my obsidian knives. "Those will stay outside."

"My weapons?" I asked. He was observant: the knives, which were those of the temple, had been blessed by Mictlantecuhtli, and were saturated with His magic.

His smile was malicious. "Consider them payment for an audience. You'll get them back – maybe."

"I will get them back," I said, as I undid my belt and gave them to him. "Or else I won't be the only one hunting you."

He smiled an even wider smile. "Do you think you can touch me?"

I wanted, desperately, to try – to summon a minor deity from the underworld, to teach him fear and humility. But I knew I couldn't. He was Xochiquetzal's, and I'd already seen what kind of power She wielded.

Inside the room, it was dark, and cool: the fire in the three-stone hearth had sunk to smouldering embers, and yellow cotton drapes hung over the only window. The air smelled of packed earth, overlaid with copal incense. There was no need for light, though. The figure seated on the dais made Her own: a softly lapping radiance that played on the floor, on the frescoes of flowers on the walls, and on the backs of my callused hands.

In the silence, I knelt, laying the marigold flowers at the feet of the dais. Then I opened the cage and, using one of Xochiquetzal's own knives, slit the parrot's throat. Blood spurted out, covered my hands. I laid the bird by the side of the flowers and, bowing my head until it touched the ground, started singing a hymn to the Quetzal Flower.

> *"By the side of the roads*
> *And the steep mountain paths*
> *By the Lake of the Moon*
> *And on the faraway battlefields*
> *Grow Your flowers*
> *Marigolds and buttercups, flowers of corn and maguey*
> *Flowers to adorn the maidens' necks ·*
> *To be carried by amorous warriors*
> *Flowers to remind us*
> *Of Your presence everywhere."*

When I was finished, there was only silence. I dared not look up.

"Well, well," Xochiquetzal said, finally. "It's not often that I have visitors."

"My Lady."

"A priest, too. Although" – she sounded disappointed, like a jaguar that had missed its prey – "not one of my own."

I swallowed, wondering how much I could tell Her. "Your priests still think you in the Heaven Tamoanchan, my Lady Xochiquetzal."

The light over my head grew brighter, and in Her voice was the anger of the storm. I kept my gaze on the beaten earth. "They don't know because the Guardians have not seen fit to inform them."

And with reason. The last thing we needed was a religious war within Tenochtitlan. But I guessed it would have hurt, all the same, to be expelled from Tamoanchan by the Duality, for a mere sin of lust.

"I'm not a Guardian," I said, finally.

"No," She said. Her voice was toneless. "I can see that. You may rise, priest. What do you want?"

Carefully, I approached the dais, all my muscles poised to flee. Gods were capricious, caring little about the balance of the world – and one who had been expelled from the gods' company even more so. "I have come for a favour."

The Quetzal Flower smiled. She wasn't young, not any more. A network of fine wrinkles marred Her cheeks, and She kept rubbing at Her eyes, so often that the cornea had turned red with blood vessels. "You rarely come for anything else." She reached out, and took the parrot in Her hands. Something seemed to pass from the animal into Her: some light, fleeing the corpse and nesting under Her skin, coursing through her veins like blood. "Very well. Ask your question."

"My name is Acatl. There is a priestess," I said, slowly. "Eleuia–"

"I know who Eleuia is," Xochiquetzal said. "I may be fallen from grace, but I'm not completely powerless. What do you want?"

"She has disappeared, and we are looking for her."

The Quetzal Flower didn't move. "Eleuia," She said. "I don't know where she is."

"That wasn't–"

"What you needed? You would have asked for it, at some point."

"Why don't you know?" I asked, unable to resist my curiosity. "Isn't she your servant?"

The light dimmed, for a bare moment. Xochiquetzal said, finally, "I'm on earth. In a world where My body doesn't belong, where everything fights My existence. It takes its toll. No god can remain on earth and keep more than token powers."

"Except if they entrust them to a human agent," I said, thinking of Revered Speaker Axayacatl-tzin, and of the last time I'd seen him at the Major Festival: rising from the limestone altar of the sacrifices atop the Great Temple, his hands and obsidian knife reddened with human blood; his whole body brimming with the magic of Huitzilpochtli, the magic that kept the Mexica Empire strong.

Xochiquetzal smiled, and this time Her voice was bitter. "Not all of us are upstarts, ready to give our powers to anyone. Humans are unreliable. They have wishes and desires of their own. One day, what the Southern Hummingbird does will come back to haunt Him."

I said nothing. The affairs of gods were not my own; even less so those of the Quetzal Flower, whom I did not worship.

Xochiquetzal went on. "But it's the way of things. Huitzilpochtli rises to power, becomes the protective deity of your Empire. And We – the old ones, the gods of the Earth and of the Corn, We who were here first, who watched over your first steps – We fade."

The melancholy in Her voice was unexpected; and, because She was a goddess, it saturated the room, until my throat ached with regret for the days of my childhood. "You still have priestesses," I managed to whisper.

"Yes," She said, "but the greatest temple within the Sacred Precinct isn't Mine, and the sacrifices they offer Me are paltry little things, to keep Me amused. People believe in war and in the sun, more than they believe in rain or in love." She shook Her head, as if realising what She'd just said. "Enough. We haven't come here to wallow in My own misery."

"I just want to know…" I swallowed, trying to blot out the image of Neutemoc, grunting over the supine body of a shadowy priestess. "I was told Eleuia had a child. I want to know–"

"Whether it's true?" The Quetzal Flower didn't move.

"You know," I whispered.

"Of course. I'm a goddess of childbirth, among other things."

Goddess of love, of carnal desire; of lust and all the base instincts that made fools out of us. The Duality curse me, why couldn't I stop thinking of Neutemoc?

Xochiquetzal rubbed at Her eyes, absent-mindedly. "Eleuia. Yes, she had a child. Sixteen years ago. But it was stillborn."

"Stillborn?" I asked.

Her eyes slid away from me, focused on the jade flowers by Her dais. "Dead. She buried the umbilical cord on a battlefield, to ensure the child's safe passage into the afterlife."

That's not the custom, was my first thought. The second, which I spoke aloud, was, "Would you tell me

67

who the father was?" Not Neutemoc. Please, not Neutemoc.

Xochiquetzal shrugged. "I have no idea. Why does it matter so much to you?"

She was toying with me again, batting me to and fro, like a guinea pig between the paws of a jaguar...

"My brother is involved," I said at last. "I need to know–"

"Whether he had a child? How amusing, priest."

"Please," I whispered. Her radiance had become blinding.

Something landed at my feet, wet and soft. It took me a moment to realise, squinting through the strong light, that it was the body of the parrot, small and pathetic in its death, cast aside like a rag.

"One sacrifice," Xochiquetzal said. "One paltry, bloodless little bird. An insult. You're fortunate that I was inclined to accept it. I don't owe you anything more." She rose from Her dais – and, for a mere moment, She was every woman I had ever desired, passion and need searing through my bones at the sight of Her. Burning, my skin was burning, and I was on my knees before Her, scarcely aware of having thrown myself to the ground...

She laughed then: the sound of water crashing into underground caves. "Better," She said. "Much better." She walked by my side, even as I struggled to rise. I could have sworn Her radiance had grown stronger, sharper: deprived of the potency of blood sacrifices, did She now feed on simpler things, on fear, on abject obedience?

I rose on shaking hands, met Her gaze: ageless amusement, uncomfortably close to malice.

"You might yet be of some use," the Quetzal Flower said. She was back on Her dais, reclining on Her low chair like a playful jaguar. "You know the proper sacrifices for Me. Bring them here, and I may feel in the mood to give you more."

I knew what She wanted: offerings, proper worship offered before Her; not the distant sacrifices of Her priestesses, their smoke rising into the Heavens She'd been cast out of, but the blood of living animals, and perhaps of humans. I didn't have any hold over Her: certainly not here, on Her own ground, and perhaps not even in my own temple, with Lord Death's protection over me.

"I'll…" I struggled to find words. We both knew I had no choice.

She smiled again. "I'm sure you'll be back. Until next time, Acatl."

I left Xochiquetzal's house in a bad state. My hands would not stop shaking, and every time I thought back to Her, to the light enfolding Her as She rose from Her throne, my manhood would stiffen uncontrollably: something that hadn't happened to me since my calmecac schooling.

I walked through the first streets in a daze, barely seeing the boats in the canals; and it wasn't until I reached the temple of the Moyotlan district that I was able to collect my thoughts.

I hadn't expected Xochiquetzal to have such an effect over me. But then, every time I saw any of the minor gods of the underworld, coldness would creep up my spine, and I would remember that everything in the Fifth World would crumble; and that beneath my face lay a yellowed skull, beneath my skin the first hints of a skeleton, crinkling within the funeral fire.

With difficulty, I tore my mind from gods, and thought on what the Quetzal Flower had told me. I needed to focus on the investigation. Though, Tlaloc's lightning strike me, I had learnt precious little from the goddess. That Eleuia had a child now seemed to be a reality. But Xochiquetzal, like all gods, was capricious, and I didn't believe She had told me the truth when She'd said the child had been stillborn. No, he had to be alive. And if he was, then Eleuia had indeed had a serious affair with a warrior who could very possibly be Neutemoc.

Then another thought occurred to me: Eleuia's sudden interest in my brother. Had she thought he was worth courting, that his status as a Jaguar Knight made him powerful enough to be attractive?

I closed my eyes. Neutemoc might be a fool in thrall to his instincts, but I didn't think he'd abandon his responsibilities. The child, though... The Imperial priests would have means of determining his paternity, if he could be found. If Neutemoc was indeed the father, then the child was the proof of his illicit liaison: one that would get him expelled from the Jaguar Knights. The child, then, was a blackmail tool. Had Neutemoc seen through her, and summoned the nahual to put an end to the problem, never thinking of the consequences?

It sounded too much like something Neutemoc would think of. Far too much.

I walked back to my temple, to dress in my full regalia before going again to the Jaguar House – cursing Neutemoc all the while for putting our family in this situation.

I arrived at my temple, and found a man deep in talk with Ichtaca: a grizzled warrior wearing a blue feather headdress, and an armour of hardened cotton on which was drawn the fused-lovers insignia of the Duality.

Ichtaca gestured towards me when I came near. "That's the man you want," he said. Without another word, he walked away, towards the rooms to the eastern side of the courtyard.

The warrior bowed to me. "My name is Ixtli," he said. "I head the search parties."

"Oh, I see. Any results?" I asked, though he looked glum enough; wet and bedraggled, his eyes sunk deep into his face.

He shook his head. "No. I won't waste your time. I have twenty men out, combing the city. So far, not much."

Not encouraging; but then I had not expected a miracle.

Ixtli watched for a while, gauging me. "I'll go back to helping them, then." He sighed. "I'll have them spread out, to keep searching for as long as possible. But we're going to need some sleep, too."

I almost said no, told him to keep searching, no matter the cost. There had been blood in Eleuia's room – blood from deep wounds, scattered over the frescoes. She might be dying; and Neutemoc was still under arrest, while I had nothing to help him. But Ixtli had done enough, in an affair that didn't have personal stakes for him; and I couldn't afford to antagonise him in any case. "I don't think a few hours are going to make that much difference. Do what you can."

Ixtli drew himself to attention. "Yes," he said. "I'll see you again, then."

I climbed the steps to the shrine under the blazing morning sun. Inside, the nobleman's body had been collected from the limestone altar. On the cactus-paper registers, Ichtaca had noted in a steady hand: "In recompense for the wake of Acolmixtli, Keeper of the House of Animals: five quetzal feathers, one roll of cloth and ten quills of gold."

The nobleman's family had been happy, then, to give such a fortune to the temple. I still thought we had no use for such largesse, that it would be better for it to go to starving peasants, to those really in need of it.

I laid my cloak by the altar, under the hollow gaze of Mictlantecuhtli's statue, and went out on the temple steps to compose my thoughts.

I had to gather proper offerings for Xochiquetzal: a task I couldn't entrust to anyone but myself, for I feared the answer She'd give me. I also had to find the Jaguar Knight Mahuizoh, though the Knights wouldn't be back from their ceremonies for a while.

Who else did I have to see? Neutemoc, of course: I wanted him – no, I needed him to confirm that he had slept with Eleuia for a few nights – that they hadn't cared for each other, and that he hadn't been foolish enough to fall in love with her yet another time. Deep, deep down, I suspected what he would answer; and I couldn't bear the thought.

Impatient footsteps echoed on the stairs of the shrine. Startled, I looked down at the courtyard, which was still deserted. Someone, however, was climbing the pyramid's stairs.

A young warrior. He wore an orange cloak, its hem embroidered with scorpions: the mark of a Leading Youth, one who had captured a prisoner on the battlefield and thus ended his apprenticeship. His steps were quick, impatient. He reached the top of the stairs, and scrutinised me, as if unsure what to make of me. He couldn't have been more than eighteen years old; his face was smooth, still filled with the easy arrogance of youth; his gestures sure and fast, as if a great energy lay underneath them.

"You would be Acatl-tzin?" he said. In his mouth, the "tzin" was almost doubtful.

I nodded. "If it's for a wake–"

He shook his head, impatiently. "No. It's about the priestess."

At least he was direct. "Priestess Eleuia?" I asked.

"Who else?" He shook his head again, as if to clear a persistent ache. "The Guardian told me to go to you."

"Ceyaxochitl sent you?" Now I was curious. She had told me she couldn't provide help. Why send me a cocksure youth?

He was still staring at me, clearly unfazed by any notion of proper behaviour or respect. "Yes," he said. "She said I might be able to help." Again, he didn't sound convinced.

"I don't think I need help," I said, slowly. "From a warrior–"

"Because it would shame you?"

He was quick to take offence: overly sensitive, which was odd for a warrior, even a warrior this young. Why had Ceyaxochitl sent him? "No," I said, thinking of the coldness that seized my shoulder-blades every time the Wind of Knives – my counterpart in the underworld, He who dealt swift justice – materialised in my temple. "Because there are some things swords can't fight."

He stared at me, and for a moment I saw real fear in his gaze. But he clenched his jaw, and said, "No. But I'm not here to fight." Not yet, said everything in his stance. I couldn't fault him for his courage. Despite his inexperience, he was a warrior in every gesture, and in every mood. "I think I was the last one to see the priestess alive. Aside from your brother, of course."

So Ceyaxochitl had told him about Neutemoc. Just what I needed. What else did he know?

Focus. I had to focus. Ceyaxochitl meant to help me, however misguidedly. "When did you see her?"

"My name is Teomitl. I'm studying in the boys' calmecac."

Teomitl. Arrow of the Gods. He was well-named, as straight and as eager to spill blood as an arrow. I would have placed him in a House of Youth with the other novice warriors, not in a school. But of course the calmecacs didn't only educate priests: they also served as schools for the children of the wealthy. Given the richness of his garb, he could only be a nobleman's son.

"You saw Eleuia?"

He pursed his lips. For the first time, he looked embarrassed. "I– I was assigned to sweep the courtyards of the girls' calmecac ten days ago. As a penance." His gaze defied me to mock him.

I wasn't about to, though I guessed why they would send him to sweep the girls' courtyards. Some of that pride clearly needed toning down. "And you saw Eleuia?"

Teomitl nodded. "Often. She was…" His eyes unfocused for a moment. "Beautiful. Alluring, strong."

The Duality preserve us. Another man in love with Eleuia? Was there no end to her influence? I suppressed an inward sigh. "Her beauty doesn't have a bearing on what happened to her."

"It might," Teomitl said – a shrewder observation than I'd expected from him. "I was in the courtyard yesterday, before sunset. I saw her walk past. She looked nervous."

"Scared?" I asked.

Teomitl shrugged. "Maybe. She had a knife in her belt, and her hand kept wrapping around the hilt. But she'd been afraid for long before that."

"How long?"

"Seven days," Teomitl said. "Maybe more."

Afraid of whom? Of Zollin? Of Neutemoc? Of someone else? Huitzilpochtli cut me down, the suspects kept appearing, and I still had no lead that would explain anything. "And that's all you saw?" It was interesting, but surely not worth sending him to me?

"I saw other things. How they didn't know what to make of her. All the priestesses and the students, they tiptoed around her, because they'd never met her like. She was intense."

His eyes were glazed, and his face had softened imperceptibly. He had obviously been completely infatuated by her. Although I couldn't help feeling slightly suspicious. "What's your date of birth?" I asked.

He looked at me, blankly. "Ten Rabbit in the Year Ten Reed. Why?"

He could have been pretending, but his reaction sounded sincere. I debated over whether to tell him the truth, but I saw no reason not to. "Because nahual magic was used to abduct Eleuia. A jaguar-spirit."

Startled, he looked at me. "Surely you don't think–" The first stirring of anger, clouding his face.

"No," I said. "But I had to make sure."

Teomitl looked at me for a while. "You'll find her?"

"I don't know," I said. Deep down, I feared too much time had elapsed. "I can't promise anything."

"No," Teomitl said. "But…" He checked himself, started to speak again. "I'd like to help."

So that was why Ceyaxochitl had sent him to me: another pair of hands, ready to do my unsavoury work. But I just couldn't take on another apprentice, not another responsibility for another's life. "I don't think…"

He said nothing. He stood watching me. In his eager face I saw Payaxin, my first and only apprentice, for whom every spell had been a delight, every ritual a curiosity to be dissected. Payaxin, who had attempted a summoning without my help, and died for his failure.

I closed my eyes. I couldn't get involved again. It would have been unseemly for a High Priest; I had no time, nothing I could teach him, and I would only lead him into dangers he wouldn't be able to face.

"I can't–" I started, but the next words came unbidden. "Just for a little while, then." A small thing. A task of little importance, that will make him feel useful. And then no more. He wouldn't go the way of Payaxin.

Teomitl nodded.

I went back into the shrine, Teomitl in tow, and hunted around the chests for maguey paper and a writing-reed. Carefully, I wrote down the name of everyone I'd met or heard of, connected with Eleuia.

"Go to the registers," I said. "Check the birthdates of every one of those people."

Teomitl took the paper. He looked relieved, as if he'd leapt over a huge obstacle and found nothing but flat terrain after that. "To see whether they can summon a nahual?"

He was quick; eager to prove himself. He reminded me of Payaxin. Too much.

"Yes," I said. "Also–"

The entrance curtain was wrenched aside; a jarring sound echoed under the wooden rafters of the shrine's roof, as all the bells crashed into each other.

"Acatl-tzin." It was Ichtaca, his face uncannily grim.

"What's the matter?" I asked, a hollow deepening in the pit of my stomach.

"The novice priests have come back from the marketplace. I think there's something outside you need to see."

"Why?" I asked.

"Your brother has been formally charged with the murder of Priestess Eleuia. He's on display in front of the Imperial Palace now, awaiting trial."

In a heartbeat, I was up on my feet, and running out of the shrine.

# FIVE
## *The Caged Man*

It was past midday, and the usual throng filled the plaza of the Sacred Precinct. I had to elbow my way through the press of pilgrims and priests to make my way to the Northern Gate and the Tepeyaca causeway. What I had intended as a rush slowed down to a painful crawl.

As always when I passed nearby, I found my gaze drawn to the Great Temple. It was hard to ignore it: the bulk of its double pyramid towered over all the other temples. Celebrants were crowding on its platform.

Even from afar, it was easy to see the way of things. The right half of the platform, devoted to the God of War, Huitzilpochtli, was awash with noblemen, and the blood of numerous sacrifices had made the sacred vessels overflow. The left half of the platform, the temple to Tlaloc, God of Rain, was almost empty, with perhaps half a dozen priests shedding their blood.

*Things change*, the Quetzal Flower had said. *People believe in war and in the sun, more than they believe in rain or in love. And we – the old ones, the gods of the Earth and of the Corn, We who were here first, who watched over your first steps – We fade.*

As always, that sight inspired a complex mixture of feelings. My parents had both been peasants: but the true glory of life, they had always told me, lay in war. And wasn't it fitting that the God of War should reign supreme over the Fifth World? Yet I had chosen the path of a humble priesthood over that of the warrior, leaving the glory to my brother. Had it truly been the best choice I could make?

Enough. I couldn't afford melancholy at a time like this.

I tore my gaze away from the Great Temple. Unfortunately, I did so too late to avoid crashing into a group of priests flanking a sacrificial victim: a man with a chalk-whitened face, lips painted in grey. "Sorry."

The victim looked at me with a touch of annoyance, angry at being impeded on his way to a glorious death. The priests just nodded, as one craftsman to another. I resumed my crawl towards the exit.

Outside the Serpent Wall which framed the Sacred Precinct, it was easier to breathe: a clear area had been left between the wall and the first adobe houses. I ran east along the Serpent Wall, towards the Imperial Palace.

Emperor Axayacatl-tzin had built this massive, two-storey building on his accession: a sprawling mass of courtyards, gardens, tribute storehouses and noblemen's apartments, it extended over half the length of the eastern Serpent Wall. The Palace not only housed the Emperor and the high-ranking noblemen of the Mexica Empire, but also the tribunals for freemen, warriors and non-warrior noblemen.

A short flight of polished limestone steps led up to one of the entrances. To the right of the steps was a small platform where the prisoners waited for their trial, crouching in low wooden cages.

Neutemoc was in the first of those, still wearing his Jaguar regalia. His bloodshot eyes suggested he hadn't slept much in the previous night.

When I approached, he started to straighten up and almost banged his head against the ceiling of his cage. Something fluttered in my chest, some obscure guilt for failing him.

"Brother," he said.

I'd expected him to be furious, but he was obviously too weary for that. "Hello, Neutemoc. What are you doing here?"

He snorted. "Do I look as if I know?"

My eyes scanned the platform behind him. I finally saw Yaotl, coming towards me at a leisurely pace, smiling ironically, Huitzilpochtli blind the man. Ceyaxochitl was behind, deep in conversation with a magistrate and a priest I didn't recognise.

"I'll be back," I said, and climbed on the platform to meet Yaotl.

"Acatl," he said, bowing slightly.

I did not bother with pleasantries. "What's the meaning of this?" I didn't wait for him to answer, either. "You tell me I am in charge of this, you tell me I should get some sleep, and the moment I leave you start indicting him!"

Yaotl nodded. "Not much choice."

"Choice?" I looked at the priest with Ceyaxochitl. His blue-streaked face was unfamiliar; but his cloak was finest cotton, embroidered with frogs and seashells.

A priest of Tlaloc, God of Rain. And if he was not high in the hierarchy, he was close to someone who was. "I'm not sure I–"

"I think you do," Yaotl said.

Ceyaxochitl bowed to the priest and to the magistrate. The magistrate headed back into the Imperial

Palace, while the priest walked away, back towards the Sacred Precinct.

A priest of Tlaloc. Even if Huitzilpochtli was now the only guardian god of the Mexica Empire, the priests of the Storm Lord still wielded considerable political power.

"Politics." The word left a sour taste in my mouth. "Someone wants a culprit?"

Yaotl nodded. "It has to be solved, and fast."

I watched Ceyaxochitl walk towards me. "That priest forced you to do this?" I asked.

She had the grace to look embarrassed, but not for long. "I'm a Guardian, Acatl. I don't make the laws."

"You promised–" I started, and realised how childish I sounded. I settled for "Neutemoc can't be charged. He's innocent."

"You can't know that."

Sometimes, I hated her shrewdness.

"He's still entitled to a trial, Acatl." Ceyaxochitl leant on her cane, looking old and frail in the sunlight. Healing Emperor Axayacatl-tzin must have been sapping her energy. And yet she'd still stayed up last night to help me. "It's not over yet."

I turned, briefly, in Neutemoc's direction: sitting in his cage with his knees drawn together, he was the living image of the defeated warrior. "It's late for him," I said. "Very late. What's to say the magistrate won't have the same attitude as you?"

"He wouldn't dare," Ceyaxochitl said. "Penalties for corruption are severe."

She was deluding herself. If she, the Guardian of the Sacred Precinct, had given in to pressure, why should a mere magistrate resist? But I didn't say that. I simply asked, "Who's the priest?"

"His name is Nezahual. But he speaks for his master: Acamapichtli, High Priest of Tlaloc."

I'd thought so. "Acamapichtli wants a conviction?"

Ceyaxochitl shook her head. "He wants revenge, Acatl."

I mulled on this for a while. "He supported Eleuia's nomination as Consort, I presume." *Politics.* A word that could only be spat. Priests should serve the gods, not indulge in base power-grabbing.

It was a useless fight: every priest cherished the hope of serving at the Imperial Palace. I'd seen that, all too well, back in calmecac school; it had been one of the reasons why I'd turned my back on the most prestigious priesthoods, those of Huitzilpochtli or the Storm Lord, and chosen to make a living as a priest for the Dead, beholden to no one but grieving families.

Ceyaxochitl was watching Neutemoc. "High Priest Acamapichtli had an interest in her. He doesn't like losing pawns."

For some reason, Teomitl's face came back to me, shining with admiration for Eleuia. "I hope his interest was only political," I said, darkly. "She looked as if she was drawing attention, and not because of her talents."

"For some of them, at any rate," Yaotl said, with an amused smile. "You forget that she served the Goddess of Lust."

My fingers clenched of their own accord. "I don't find this funny."

"A shame," Yaotl said.

Ceyaxochitl banged her cane on the platform. I winced. Below the platform, a few passers-by had gathered to watch us: Eagle Knights in their feather uniforms, artisans carrying birds' cages and bars of silver, housewives with their ceramic wares on their back. "Enough, both of you," she said. "Acatl, I apologise for the discomfort, but I had no choice. And neither have you."

"It doesn't mean I'll bow down meekly," I snapped.

Her gaze was wryly amused. "I didn't expect you would. Have you made progress?"

She meant well, but I still didn't feel I could share information with her. "Yes."

Her lips tightened. "I see. We'll leave you to it, then."

"Stay out of it," I said, as calmly as I could. "No more interference."

"I can't promise that. I'm not the mistress of High Priest Acamapichtli," Ceyaxochitl said, clambering down from the platform. "You're intelligent enough to realise I cannot."

Yes. I didn't like it, but it was a given that once the High Priest of Tlaloc had started interfering, he wouldn't stop. If I wanted Neutemoc to have a fair trial, I needed to act quickly. I approached his cage, and knelt to peer through the bars.

"No improvement planned on my situation, I take it," Neutemoc said.

I sighed. "No. Not in the immediate future. How are you feeling?"

"You have some nerve," Neutemoc said. "You're the one outside, asking the questions."

"Yes," I said. "And I'm not the one who had a long-lasting affair with a priestess, not to mention a child."

"We didn't–" Neutemoc started, then fell silent.

"Neutemoc?" I asked.

His eyes gazed beyond me, towards the throng in front of the palace. After a moment's hesitation, I turned, and saw a tall woman making her way straight towards us, carrying a baby in a shawl tied around her chest.

Huei, and Neutemoc's youngest child, Ollin, born this last dry season. This was obviously not the moment to broach the subject of illegitimate children.

Huei walked towards the platform as if fighting her

way through a press of warriors. She wore a long, flowing tunic with an elaborate pattern of glyphs, and a skirt the colour of jade.

Her hair was brushed in the fashion of married women, in two braids, with the two ends of the braids raised to form two tufts on either side of her forehead, like small horns. Her face was grim, every step deliberate. Neutemoc was clearly going to have an unpleasant moment.

"I think I'll leave," I said.

Neutemoc's gaze didn't move, but his lips tightened. I couldn't tell if he was ashamed, or simply embarrassed. "Please, Acatl."

"It's private," I said. But Huei was already close enough to hear us.

"No," she said. "It's not private. Not once you're arrested and exposed like a common criminal."

Uh-oh. She was really furious, though I couldn't blame her.

"Huei," Neutemoc said.

Her gaze swept him, up and down. "What in the Fifth World did you think you were doing?"

"I know it's not a favourable situation–"

"It's not 'unfavourable'," Huei said. "It's a disaster, Neutemoc. Tell me what I should tell the children, when they ask me about their father."

"There's been a misunderstanding–"

"No," Huei said. "You were foolish enough to get caught bloody-handed in a priestess's room. I don't think I want to know why."

"Huei," I said. "I don't think this is the time."

"Then when?" she asked. "After they've strangled him, or crushed his head?"

She clearly knew what was going on. Those penalties she had mentioned were those for killing a woman, and for adultery.

"Priestess Eleuia isn't dead," I lied. "We'll find her, and she'll explain."

"Acatl." For the first time I saw pity in her gaze. "Don't lie to me."

"I'm not–"

But Huei had already turned back to Neutemoc. "I can't believe you've been such a fool," she said. Her hand rose: if the cage had had larger gaps between its bars, she'd have hit him.

Neutemoc said nothing. He looked through her, as though he'd already lost her. "I don't think you'd understand, even if I explained."

I glanced to the side of the platform. If my dispute with Ceyaxochitl had attracted some people, it was nothing compared to the crowd that gathered now: a throng of several dozens, men and women, freemen, noblemen and slaves, all staring quite shamelessly at the spectacle before their eyes.

"Why shouldn't I understand? Some words are so simple to say. Some feelings are easy to demonstrate." Huei lowered her hand slowly. "But then you could never do that, could you?" Her voice was bitter.

Hearing them, I felt... out of place, as if I'd tumbled into some other age of the world, where my brother, my successful brother who could do nothing wrong, was awaiting trial; where he and his wife were tearing at each other, oblivious to my presence.

Their marriage had always been happy; they'd had all I could lay no claim to... Hadn't they? The world, as in an earthquake, had shifted under my feet, and I couldn't mould it back into the right shape.

Neutemoc didn't answer Huei. They stared at each other for a while; finally, Huei said, "Acatl. Will you walk me home?"

I had known her for years, from the time she and Neutemoc had been engaged; and in her tense stance

I read, very clearly, that she wanted to speak to me, but not before her husband.

I glanced at Neutemoc, who owed me some explanations. But my brother was sitting, dejected, in his cage, not looking at me. Getting him to talk to me was going to be hard, not to mention painful for him. And I needed to be out of here. I needed to be alone, to have a place to breathe, to think.

"I'll come with you," I said to Huei.

She was quiet as we walked through the streets of Moyotlan. The baby on her back slept, wrapped in cotton cloth.

"I can't believe he's such a fool," she said, as we crossed over a canal.

The smell of cooked maize wafted from a street-food seller; my stomach growled.

"He was just in the wrong place–" I started, unwilling to cause her pain.

Huei looked at me, her wide eyes shining in the sunlight. "Do you really believe that?" she asked.

"No," I said, finally, and it was the truth. "I don't know what to believe in any more."

She laughed, bitterly. "That's two of us, then. I knew he didn't love me any more, Acatl. It's not hard to see."

Save, of course, if you had been distancing yourself from the family for years, as I had. "How long has it been going on?"

She shrugged. "Two, three years? It's always hard to determine. He's been such a good father," she said. "A good husband, better than anything I deserved."

"You deserved the best. And so did he."

Huei smiled. "Always such a liar, Acatl?"

I wanted to tell her it was only the truth – that the slender, shy girl my brother had brought home, so eager to learn everything she could about my own life, had deserved so much more than the taint of adultery – so much more than seeing her husband in a cage. But the words couldn't get past my lips.

She guessed them, all the same, and raised a hand to placate my protests. "No, I know you mean well. But you blind yourself. No marriage can last if there's no trust."

"I don't see any lack of trust," I said, though it was only a lie to comfort her.

We'd reached the pyramid temple of our family's calpulli, where a handful of novice priests were busy sweeping the ground with reed brooms, in preparation for the next sacrifice. A throng of people, most of whom I'd known in childhood, turned to stare at us as we passed. News travelled fast in Tenochtitlan. I had no doubt they knew about Neutemoc's arrest.

Huei sighed. "He'd go out at night, you know? He'd walk the streets, with the light and smell of parties spilling ahead of him. He told me he did it to remind himself of what he was."

"I had no idea he was lonely," I said.

"He shouldn't have been." Her voice was low, fierce. "I took care of him, of his household. Why, Acatl?"

"You think he killed Priestess Eleuia?" I asked.

She shrugged. "I think that he could have had the decency to keep his affairs private."

"But you don't like the idea of his having an affair," I said, wondering how bluntly I could go about the subject. Accusing her of murder in front of the calpulli clan didn't seem a good idea.

"What wife does?" Huei asked. "I'd be lying if I said it left me indifferent."

We'd reached a low, white-washed building adorned with frescoes of leaping jaguars: Neutemoc's house. The smell of spices, mingled with the sweeter one of copal incense, rose to my nostrils, a reminder of

86

a time I'd been a regular visitor here. "Come inside, will you?" Huei asked. "I know Mihmatini will ask after you."

"I didn't know she was back," I said, finally. Mihmatini was still in school: she and her comrades had left a year ago on a retreat on the slopes of Popocatepetl's volcano, a day's journey to the south of Tenochtitlan. I had visited her once or twice; but I had got the impression that once her retreat was over, she would join the clergy, not come back to Neutemoc's house.

"She came back a month ago," Huei said. "She thought you still in Coyoacan. As did we, to be honest."

What a family we made. Not even capable of keeping track of each other.

In the courtyard, I asked Huei, "What day were you born on?"

She looked surprised, but not totally disoriented by the question. "Eight Death," she said. "Why?"

"Nothing," I said.

"Not 'nothing'," she protested gently as we entered the reception room.

"Nahual magic," I said, curtly.

The reception room had changed in four years: all the walls were now covered with frescoes, depicting Huitzilpochtli, our protector God, in His guise as a young warrior. He trampled bound enemies under His huge feet, and a procession of lesser gods with bowed heads followed Him across the walls of the room. On the wicker chests were silver and jade ornaments, and jaguars' pelts covered the ground. An elaborate fan of green quetzal tail-feathers rested against one of the frescoed walls: an object worth at least two years' living for a poor peasant. Neutemoc had clearly earned a larger share of the tribute in the past years, and his family was enjoying the riches that came with his higher status.

Not for long, though, if he was disgraced. My heart tightened in my chest.

Huei set her baby in a wooden cradle. She unrolled a reed mat over one of the jaguar pelts, and sat on the ground. "I'll have the slaves bring some refreshments," she said. "Your sister is watching over the children. But I think you and I would rather wait until we include her in the conversation."

I said nothing. Huei had always been honest with me, which was one of the reasons we'd related so well to one another. "Very well," I said, finally. "Let's start with the awkward questions. Did you abduct or harm Priestess Eleuia?"

Her eyes flickered. "Through nahual magic? You know I can't use that."

No. Being born on the day Eight Death, she had no nahual. But her equivocation wasn't what I had expected, and it frightened me. "Huei, please. Can you answer the question?"

She didn't speak for a while. "I knew there was someone. It's obvious when you no longer have your husband's attention, and even more obvious when you see him acting like an infatuated child. But I didn't know her name."

I studied her for a while. "And if you had known?"

Huei spread her hands, carefully. "I – I don't know what I would have done." She sounded sincere. "But believe me, I wouldn't summon a nahual."

"How did you know he'd been arrested?"

"Calpulli gossip," Huei said. She picked up a wooden rattle – one of the children's toys – and flicked it between her fingers with a dry, hollow sound. "I came as soon as I could. Not that it changed anything, of course. The Storm Lord smite him," she said. "Didn't he realise that he'd lose everything? That we'd lose everything? I thought–" She paused, and her eyes glimmered in the light.

She was crying. "Huei…" I said, unsure of what I could do. I extended a hand halfway across the space that separated us.

Like Neutemoc, she was looking through me, as if I didn't exist. "He did things. He rose from his status of peasant to a respected warrior. He was going somewhere, and taking us along with him."

"I don't know what you mean," I said, as gently as I could. I felt as if I were intruding on some private grief: never a pleasant thought, and even worse when you knew the person as well as I knew Huei. "Going somewhere?"

"Making something out of his life," Huei said. "And then, all of a sudden, he realises it's not worth it any more, that he can throw it all into Mictlan."

"I don't think–"

"I know him, Acatl," Huei said. "He was driven."

And you? If he was driven, and making something out of his life, what did you think you were doing?

"And you loved him because of what he was?"

Huei said nothing, but she didn't need to. It was in her eyes: she loved him, and her anger at him was fear; fear that she would lose him to the executioner's mace.

"I'm sorry," she said after a while. "It wasn't meant for you."

I didn't know what to say. I just shook my head, feeling utterly useless. "I'm sorry."

Huei blinked, dispelling the last of her tears, though her voice still shook. Behind her, the gods in the frescoes watched, expressionless, uncaring. "You're not the one at fault. He is, unfortunately."

I said, "He might still be acquitted. I'm trying."

"But you don't believe in his innocence," Huei said.

"You don't either."

Huei's face tightened. "I believe he was sleeping with that priestess. I don't believe he killed her. He couldn't kill anyone, not in cold blood."

"He's a warrior."

"Yes, he is. But not an assassin, Acatl."

No. But a man used to making hard decisions, often in a short time. Huei wasn't the best judge of Neutemoc's character, being blinded both by jealousy and by love. And I still didn't know whether my brother had fathered Eleuia's child.

I said nothing for a while, thinking of all it would mean to her. I couldn't tell her about the child, or discuss my suspicions. It would have hurt her needlessly.

Huei must have sensed that I had run out of conversation subjects. She rose, went to the door, and clapped her hands to summon a slave. "Bring some chocolate," she said. "And tell Mihmatini to come, too."

She sat down again. "So," she said. "It's been a while since we last saw each other."

Four years, to be precise. Four years of minding my own small parish in Coyoacan – stopping, from time to time, to dwell on Huei and Mihmatini, but never gathering enough will to walk into that house again. The house where Mother had died; where Father's body had lain, untended to for hours.

"You haven't changed," Huei said. "Not really."

I shrugged. "I've come back to Tenochtitlan. But things are the same. I've been doing nothing much. The usual for a priest."

Huei's eyes narrowed. "You cheapen yourself," she said.

I shook my head. "You want success? Ask Neutemoc." Ask Mihmatini; ask Father and Mother. Ask them who had taken them in.

"Not any more." Her voice, loaded with terrible sarcasm, erased whatever I'd been about to say: we stared at each other in silence, until the noise of a shrieking child broke the awkwardness.

"Uncle Acatl!" A young child, whom I didn't recognise. Mazatl, I realised with a shock. She'd been much younger last time I'd been in this house, barely starting to piece sentences together.

Her brother Necalli was more dignified. I tried to remember how old he was. Eight, nine years old? His head was shaved; he wore the single lock of hair that marked the unproved warrior.

And behind him, my sister Mihmatini, grown from a gangly girl into a beautiful woman, blossoming in the calmecac like a marigold flower. She walked slowly, gracefully, her shirt swishing, revealing anew with every step the glint of jade bracelets at her ankles. Her hair, tied in a long queue at her back, shone like polished obsidian. My heart tightened in my chest.

"The lost brother comes home?" she asked, with a smile.

I shrugged. "Sometimes," I said. It had been too long since I had last seen her: my fault, for not finding the courage to walk back into that house in spite of Neutemoc's presence.

Mihmatini made a mock punching gesture. "Stop being so serious."

"It comes with the position, I'm afraid," I said.

She grimaced. "Sure, and I'm the Consort of the Emperor."

She sat down, with both children crowding near her. The toddler Mazatl, in particular, kept trying to climb into her lap, and Mihmatini gently pushed her off every time.

Slaves brought refreshments, and a light lunch: maize cakes, and frogs with chilli peppers, spread on the reed mat so we could each help ourselves from the ceramic dishes. I was famished. In fact, I realised with a shock, my last meal dated back to the previous evening. I'd been walking around the Sacred Precinct and the city on a completely empty stomach.

Mihmatini watched me gulp down a frog, and barely hid a smile. "I think someone's forgotten to eat today."

"Men," Huei snorted. "All the same."

I hurriedly swallowed, so I could answer. "Now you're being unfair."

Mihmatini raised her cup of chocolate to her lips, and inhaled the pungent aroma of vanilla and cacao. "Maybe, maybe," she said. She looked at Huei, obviously trying very hard to stifle a laugh.

I'd visited Mihmatini in her calmecac, but had never seen her so relaxed, so radiant. For all that she'd spent the last ten years away, she seemed to be utterly at ease with Huei and the children, so much more than me.

The rest of the meal was much the same: spent on pleasantries, listening to the two women mocking me, and carefully avoiding the shadow Neutemoc's arrest cast over both their futures.

Afterwards, I walked with Mihmatini in the court-yard garden, among the marigold and tomato flowers. "You look well," I said.

She grimaced. "I can't say the same about you." She poked me between the ribs. Surprised, I leapt out of her path, and she laughed again. "You're a priest for the Dead, not Mictlantecuhtli. The salient bones and skeleton look aren't compulsory, Acatl."

"Ha-ha," I said, trying to be serious. But in her company, it was hard to stay so, hard to remember all that waited for me outside. "I thought you were going to stay in that temple."

Mihmatini's face turned grave. "I thought so, too," she said. "The priestesses wanted me to stay. They said they had never had a student so gifted with magic. But..."

She shrugged. "In the end, it wasn't where my heart was. I wanted to go home, find a husband of my own, raise my own children."

All things that were forbidden to priests. "I see," I said. "And since then..." I started, wondering why she was still in Neutemoc's house, and not married.

She shrugged. "It will come, in time. I'm not desired."

"Surely, as Neutemoc's protégée–"

She blushed. "He's been busy lately."

My stomach contracted. What had Neutemoc done, again? "Too busy to look for a husband?"

"I'm young," Mihmatini said. "I can wait. It's going to take time for this to be sorted out, I expect."

"I hope not." Both for Neutemoc's sake, and for her own. She wasn't young. Eighteen was old, in a land where the first marriages were contracted when the girls were sixteen. She wasn't plain, or poor. But a husband would want a girl able to bear children; and the more Neutemoc and Huei waited, the more prospective alliances disappeared.

Mihmatini must have caught some of my thoughts. "He means well."

How could I answer that? "He's been busy, as you said." Busy quarrelling with Huei; busy giving in to the charms of a priestess. Great occupations, worthy of a warrior.

A thought occurred to me. "You sleep here."

Mihmatini pointed to a small opening, to the eastern side of the courtyard, its entrance-curtain adorned with leaping deer. "In that room. Why?"

"Do you know where Huei was yesterday night?"

She puffed her cheeks, thoughtfully, a habit neither Mother nor the calmecac had broken out of her. "Yesterday night? Pretty well. We played patolli all night. And a good thing we used tokens instead of cacao beans, or I'd be out of money."

I made a sweeping gesture, taking in her red-dyed cotton shirt, her wide skirt with its finely embroidered hem, and the jade necklace she wore around her neck. "Aren't you already out of money, owning all of that?"

She looked at me, her eyes widening in mock surprise. "Why, is that a joke, brother?"

It had to be written somewhere, on some divination priest's codex, that I'd never have the upper hand with her. "Very well. I'll stick to serious subjects, if that curbs your hilarity. Are you sure about the patolli? You didn't step out at some point?"

"For a very short time," Mihmatini said. "Huei couldn't have gone out and murdered the priestess, or whatever you think she did. She didn't have time."

"Hmm," I said. It all sounded solid. But still...

"You're calling me a liar?" Mihmatini said.

She might have protected Huei out of friendship or gratitude. But if that was so, my sister had changed much in the years since our childhood. I didn't think that was the case. "You might not realise the significance of something you saw, but–"

"I know what I saw," Mihmatini said. "Huei was with me the whole evening, Acatl. I'll swear to it in court, if it comes to that."

I hadn't really thought Huei was the culprit, in any case. She might have hated Neutemoc's lover, but one thing was sure: she truly loved her husband. Which didn't leave me with anything I could use to spare Neutemoc the death penalty.

# SIX
## *The Seekers*

I came back to the temple with a full stomach, intending to stay only briefly before I resumed my talk with Neutemoc. But I found Teomitl waiting for me at the entrance to the storehouse, chatting with Ezamahual: a lean, nervous novice priest, a son of peasants who couldn't believe he'd had the good fortune of entering calmecac. Given how captivated Ezamahual was by Teomitl's talk, I could have emptied the storehouse in front of him without raising the alarm.

Ah well. Youth would wear off at some point. I belatedly realised I wasn't so old myself: only thirty. But I felt old; out of place.

Teomitl didn't see me immediately, but Ezamahual did. He straightened up and Teomitl turned.

"Acatl-tzin. I've come back from the registers. I have what you asked from me." He was still filled with that coiled energy; it lay beneath every word, every short, stabbing gesture he made with his hands. "Out of all the names you gave me, only Priestess Zollin was born on a Jaguar day."

He gave me a quick account of the names: neither the dancers, Huei nor the other senior priestesses of the calmecac could have summoned that nahual.

There was one name missing from that recitation, though. "Mahuizoh?" I asked. "The Jaguar Knight? You couldn't find him?"

"I searched," Teomitl said, in what was almost an angry retort. I was starting to understand such a reaction was usual with him, and wondering if I had the patience to deal with that. "There are two Mahuizohs who are members of the Jaguar Knights."

"And?" I asked.

"Their birthdates?" I expected him to protest, but he surprised me by closing his eyes. "One Rain and Three Jaguar."

"I'm impressed," I admitted. "What about their age?"

"They're both around thirty-six," Teomitl said.

Tlaloc's lightning strike me. It didn't remove Mahuizoh from my list. Though it was significantly shorter now, with just the priestess Zollin, the Jaguar Knight Mahuizoh, and my brother Neutemoc left. I wished the search parties would find Eleuia, or, failing that, some evidence that would help me decide.

Teomitl was still standing, waiting. "You did well," I said.

"No." He sounded disgusted. "I was one hour at the records for six birthdates. That's hardly the pinnacle of efficiency."

"You're too hard on yourself," I said. An uncanny trait, when coupled with his staggering arrogance.

He shook his head. "Realist. Give me something else to do."

"I don't have–"

"You're in the middle of an investigation, and you're doing it alone." He must have seen my face, for he said, "The Guardian told me."

I wish I could tell Ceyaxochitl some words of my

own. "You're not giving the orders," I snapped. "That's the first rule you'll have to learn."

Teomitl smiled, and I knew why. I'd already given halfway in. "Tell me the others," he said.

I'd sworn I wouldn't take any apprentices, that I wouldn't hold out my heart to be torn apart. "You have no idea where this will lead you."

"The underworld?" he asked.

"You should have enough good sense to be afraid of Mictlan."

"Yes," Teomitl said. "I'm afraid. But don't the courageous go on, even in the face of fear?"

Again, an unexpected answer. There was obviously more to him than his arrogance, and that had to be the reason Ceyaxochitl had sent him to me.

But I still didn't know what to do with him.

"I can help," Teomitl said. "I can do better than this."

I was going to regret it. But still… "Very well," I said. "Go back into the girls' calmecac. See if you can find some trail, or someone who's seen something. That nahual didn't enter here through the main gate, and we still don't know how it left the building." What in the Fifth World had happened to that beast? At least, it would keep Teomitl busy for a while.

Teomitl nodded. If he was excited, he let nothing of that show on his face, just went rigid, like a warrior taking orders from his commander.

"I'll be back," he said.

As he walked past, a tendril of something brushed me. I narrowed my gaze, opening up my priest-senses. A slight, almost transparent veil of magic hung around Teomitl: not nahual, not underworld magic, but something tantalisingly familiar. Something…

The more I tried to bring it into focus, the more it slipped away from my mind.

"Teomitl!" I called.

He turned, halfway through the courtyard. "Yes?"

It was as if something had reached out, and brushed against his whole body, leaving an intricate network of marks over his skin. It didn't look harmful. Quite the reverse, in fact: it was an elaborate protection spell, one I had never seen.

"No, nothing. Be careful," I said, finally.

"He's an interesting man," Ezamahual said to me after Teomitl had left. "A bit abrasive, but interesting."

I nodded. "He must have stories to tell."

Ezamahual's lean, dour face lit up. "He's heard tales of the jungles to the south, and he's even met a merchant who went north, into Tarascan land. But he's not boasting. Just sharing." His unquestioning, almost boyish enthusiasm was endearing. In many ways, Ezamahual reminded me of myself at a younger age, when everything in the priesthood was still a wonder, opening pathways that radiated through the whole of the universe.

"I imagine Teomitl hasn't seen many things himself, though," I pointed out.

Ezamahual shrugged. "Second-hand accounts are better than nothing. And he's too young, in any case."

With a jolt, I realised that Teomitl had to be at least four years younger than Ezamahual: an adolescent, barely out of childhood. "Yes," I said, finally. "He's very young."

Ezamahual shifted position slightly. "He'll have time to see the world," he said, always pragmatic. "Warriors travel quite a bit."

They did. Most battlefields those days were further and further away from Tenochtitlan. Perhaps, one day, the fabled jungles, where the quetzal birds roamed free, would be part of the Mexica Empire. And Teomitl would have taken his place in their conquest.

None of my concern now. I had other things to do, like try to see Neutemoc and coerce him into admitting the truth about his relationship with Eleuia.

I walked back to the Imperial Palace on my own, under the light of late afternoon. Outside the Jaguar House, some sort of ceremony was going on. Three warriors and three sacred courtesans were going through the steps of a dance, to the piercing, slow tune of flutes: the jaguar pelts the warriors wore mingled with the courtesans' garish cotton skirts, weaving a pattern like a spell cast over the world.

Among the crowd that watched the dance, several faces stood out: a young girl of noble birth, her face flushed with lust, and a scruffy, ageless man, his face covered in grime, the wooden collar of a slave around his neck. His expression was hard to decipher, but I thought it was hatred. Odd.

I did not dwell on it for long: I elbowed my way out of the crowd, and made my way to the display platform in front of the Imperial Palace.

But when I arrived, Neutemoc was not there any more.

Stifling a curse, I paced up and down among the cages, drawing glances and a few jeers from the prisoners awaiting trial. My brother wasn't anywhere to be found.

"Excuse me," I asked one of Neutemoc's former neighbours in captivity. "The Jaguar Knight who was here…?"

The prisoner, a middle-aged freeman with a tattered loincloth, spat at my feet. I didn't step back. I had nothing to do with his case, and so could do little to him. And he knew it. Intimidation was the only strategy possible.

After a while, he shrugged. "They took him for questioning."

"They?" I asked, with the first stirrings of fear in my belly.

"The magistrate and some good-for-nothing, fancy priest."

Nezahual. The servant of the High Priest of Tlaloc, the one who wanted my brother convicted at all costs.

"Thank you," I said, and I climbed the rest of the steps into the palace.

Like the Great Temple, it was a huge complex: a maze of gardens, private apartments and sumptuous rooms. On the ground floor were the courts of justice and the state rooms; on the upper floor, the apartments of Emperor Axayacatl-tzin, and of the Rulers of Texcoco and Tlacopan, the other partners in the Triple Alliance that kept the Mexica Empire strong.

I headed straight for the military courts. The vast, raftered room was deserted: I made my way towards the back, and the patio opening on the gardens. Only one magistrate remained: an old man sitting on a reed mat and dictating notes to a clerk.

"And you would be?" he asked peevishly.

I didn't know him, but then my cases seldom came to a military court. "I'm Acatl. I'm looking for a Jaguar Knight."

The magistrate sneezed, turned to his clerk with his eyebrows raised. The clerk said, "He's being heard in the Imperial Audience."

*What?* It wasn't possible. The Imperial Courts were reserved for grave crimes that touched on the security of the Empire.

"It's not that serious," I said, when words came back to me.

The clerk shrugged. "It is, when the High Priest of the Storm Lord becomes involved."

I cursed under my breath, consigning politics and politicians to the depths of Mictlan. "Where is the audience?" I asked.

"Closed audience," the clerk said. He laid his writing reed on top of his maguey-fibre paper, and looked at me. "No one comes in."

"But I'm in charge of the investigation," I protested.

"Not any more, it would seem," the clerk said. He might have been sorry, though it was hard to tell. I wanted to scream, to tear something, anything to lessen the growing feeling of frustration in my chest.

"An important case?" the old magistrate asked. Beneath the rheumy veil, his gaze was still sharp.

I didn't want to discuss the details of the inquiry with a stranger. "Very important," I said.

He tapped his cane against the stone floor, in a gesture eerily reminiscent of Ceyaxochitl. "Supernatural case, eh? That's why you'd be involved. Though the High Priest…" He looked at me again. "I'm not without influence myself," he said.

Hardly daring to hope, I asked, "Can you get me into the Imperial Audience?"

He coughed. "No," he said. "I won't waste my influence on a guilty man."

"I don't know whether he's guilty. There's barely enough evidence," I said, a hollow growing in my heart. I didn't know what to think any more. I had few leads, and every time I seized hold of one, things seemed to become worse.

"That's not what I heard," the magistrate said. "It seems to be damaging, the situation they've found him in."

"Yes, but I don't…" I started, then caught myself. Whatever I admitted to couldn't make things worse. "He's my brother. I can't let him fall because of politics."

The old magistrate watched me, as unmoving as the statues of the gods in the temple. "The Emperor's Justice is swift," the old magistrate said. "But not that swift. It will take at least another three days of audiences for the Revered Speaker's representatives to reach a decision. If you have any evidence, you may bring it to me. Ask for Pinahui-tzin."

"What kind of evidence?" I asked.

"Proof of his innocence, or of someone else's guilt," Pinahui-tzin said.

"In a bare handful of days?" It was hope, of a kind, but barely within my reach, unless Chicomecoatl, Seven Serpent, saw fit to bless me with Her luck.

Pinahui-tzin rapped his cane on the floor: a parent scolding a disobedient child. "I'm no maker of miracles, young man. I offer you a chance. Whether you take it is your own problem."

I nodded. I had no real choice. But I prayed that Pinahui-tzin was right, and that Neutemoc would survive a few more days.

Otherwise I couldn't see myself telling the news to Huei, or to Mihmatini.

I did try to locate the Imperial Audience, but Pinahui-tzin had been right: the guards wouldn't let anyone in, not even me.

The Duality curse politics and politicians. If Neutemoc was innocent–

You don't know that, my inner voice pointed out to me.

No, I didn't. But let oblivion take me if I allowed Neutemoc to die because of priestly politics.

I left the Imperial Palace in a sour mood, and headed back to my temple. In front of the Jaguar House, the dance had ended and the dancers had left.

The scruffy slave was still there, though the two guards at the entrance pretended not to see him.

After my first aborted attempt at the House, I hadn't come back – if I thought about it, more out of fear than out of genuine reasons. But time was growing short for Neutemoc. Already the sun was low in the sky, and night would soon fall.

I walked straight to one of the guards and bowed to him.

He was dressed in full Jaguar regalia, in a uniform even more sumptuous than Neutemoc's. The jaguar skin covering him had no visible seams: it wrapped around him tightly, the jaguar's skin fitting tightly around his own head. A plume of red, emerald-green and blue feathers protruded from between the jaguar's ears; and his face between the jaguar's jaws was painted in an intricate red pattern. In one of his hands, the knight held a spear; in the other a shield covered with red feathers. He looked at me, puzzled, as if an insect had suddenly elected to speak to him.

Sometimes, I remembered why I hated warriors, and Jaguar and Eagle Knights worst of all. "I want to speak to a Jaguar Knight," I said.

The guard shook his head, and subtly moved to bar my way. Nothing unexpected, sadly. "Your kind isn't allowed in here."

"I know," I said, exasperated by the thoughtless slight. Only Jaguar Knights could enter the House. "But you can at least tell me whether he's here."

The guard looked thoughtful, probably deciding whether I would leave faster if he answered me than if he didn't.

"His name is Mahuizoh," I snapped. "I don't know his calpulli." From the corner of my eye, I saw the ill-kempt slave was leaning forward, suddenly interested.

The guard shrugged. "We have several of those."

"I know." Two, according to Teomitl's research. "Unfortunately…" I started, and realised that admitting to lack of knowledge would allow him to dismiss me. "He has a sister in the girls' calmecac."

"Mahuizoh of the Coatlan calpulli?" the slave said, his mouth yawning wide open. Half his teeth were missing – knocked out, by the jagged looks of the remains – and the others were stained as black as dried blood. He breathed into my face the rankness of someone who hadn't washed body or teeth for several days. I recoiled.

The guard slammed his spear on the ground. "Huacqui. Be silent."

The slave smiled. "I don't see why I should. The mighty Mahuizoh got me thrown out of the Brotherhood, didn't he?"

"Be silent," the guard said, raising his spear, but Huacqui leapt back, with more agility than I would have credited him with.

"Let me tell you about Mahuizoh and his high standards of behaviour. He gets me expelled from the Knights on a trifle–"

The guard growled, but he was clearly unwilling to abandon his post. "You stole from your comrades, Huacqui. That's an offence."

Huacqui cackled. "Yes, yes," he said. "But Mahuizoh… he enjoys his women, doesn't he?"

My heart gave a lurch in my chest. "What do you mean, he enjoys his women?"

"The talk of our clan," Huacqui said. "He has his own little prostitute in the girls' calmecac–"

"He has a sister," I said.

"A convenient excuse. He'd have found another if she hadn't been there. He's been sleeping with that priestess for ever." Huacqui stamped on the ground with both feet. "And he gets the honour and the glory, while I have to sell myself as a slave to earn a living."

"You were always too lazy for your own good," the guard snapped. "And there is no truth – none at all, do you hear? – in those rumours." That last was obviously addressed to me, but in the tense features of the guard's face I read the exact opposite of what he wanted me to believe.

"A priestess," I said to Huacqui. "Which one?"

He shrugged. "Priestess of Xochiquetzal. I don't remember her name. But he was jealous of all the men she kept flirting with, all the young warriors she'd eye like potential lovers." His face was sly.

Neutemoc had said that Eleuia had flirted with him, quite ostentatiously. If Mahuizoh had been her lover, and if he was indeed a jealous man, then he had motive both to kill her and to make sure my brother was indicted for her murder. "Priestess Eleuia?" I asked.

The guard winced; Huacqui burst out laughing, with a malevolent expression. "So it's come out, hasn't it? Yes, our dear little Jaguar Knight and his whore–"

The butt of the guard's spear caught Huacqui in the face, throwing him to the ground. "You – will – be – silent," the guard said, accentuating every word of the sentence. "You will stop spreading such filth, or I might just be tempted to do more than strike you."

Huacqui, lying on the ground with blood pouring into his eyes, just laughed and laughed. He knew the damage had already been done.

I knelt by him; I hesitated to grab him, as he was so filthy, but he pulled himself upward without my help. "Will you swear to that in court?" I asked.

He smiled, a truly unpleasant expression. "If it brings him down, I'll swear to anything."

"You've seen them together?" I asked.

He shook his head. "But I'll find you people who have."

I was afraid he'd bribe them, but I didn't think he was wrong about Mahuizoh's relationship with Eleuia. Mahuizoh had reacted far too strongly to her disappearance.

I drew Huacqui away from the Jaguar House, gave him a few cacao beans, and got his address. He also gave me a description of Mahuizoh, distinctive enough to recognise him if I saw him. It wasn't much, but it was more than I'd previously had.

Now I needed to see Xochiquetzal, and find out who the father of Eleuia's baby was. Hopefully, it wouldn't be Neutemoc. Please, Duality, let it not be my brother, I didn't need any more damaging evidence. I shook myself. I was making progress. There was hope for Neutemoc.

I just wished I could be sure that he was innocent of Eleuia's abduction.


I walked back into my temple in the gathering darkness, and headed straight for the storehouse. Ezamahual had gone, presumably to join one of the vigils, the death-hymns of which echoed through the courtyard; Palli had taken his place.

I needed suitable offerings for the Quetzal Flower, and I didn't remember what those would be. I could have asked the ever-useful Ichtaca, but I didn't want to lower myself in his esteem yet another time.

"Good evening, Palli," I said. "Watching the storehouse again?"

Palli shrugged. "I like it. It's quiet out here."

We had offerings, but not enough to tempt a thief; not when there were larger, richer temples within a spear's throw.

"I need to look in there."

Palli nodded. He wasn't going to question me, in any case. "Help yourself."

Inside, the storehouse was as dark and crowded as ever: owls screeched in protest as the light of my lamp fell on them; scuffling sounds came from the rabbit cages. The combined smells of copal, cedar oil and alum made my head spin. We'd have to sweep the place clean one of these days, before someone fainted in here.

Xochiquetzal… It had been a long time since I'd gone to calmecac, a long time since I'd learnt the hymns and proper offerings for all the gods. I remembered those for the gods I dealt with in everyday life: Mictlantecuhtli, Lord Death, and Mixcoatl, Lord of the Hunt. Xochiquetzal I'd never had many dealings with, for obvious reasons: She was hardly associated with death.

The light of my torch fell on an array of quetzal feathers, stacked near a pile of copal incense cones. Feathers? They were symbols of beauty, but they were not distinctive: I could think of a dozen gods who would accept that particular offering.

For Xochiquetzal, what I needed was some kind of flowers…

Palli's shadow fell across the doorway, casting me in darkness. "Do you know what you're looking for, Acatl-tzin?"

I shrugged, unwilling to admit to weakness. What a poor High Priest I made. "I'm fine," I started, and then thought of Neutemoc. Hmm. I changed my mind. "I need suitable offerings for Xochiquetzal," I said. "Would you remember what those are, by any chance?"

Limned by sunlight, Palli's face was unreadable. "For the Goddess of Beauty? Any flowers, but poinsettias are Her favourites."

A flower as red as the blood of sacrifices. I bit back on a snort. How unsubtle some gods could be.

"Anything else?"

"Butterflies," Palli said. "But we don't have those here. You can find the flowers in the temple gardens, but living butterflies... I could send to the market-place."

The animal marketplace would be closed, and wouldn't reopen until late tomorrow morning. "I'm not sure we have time," I said. "Anything else?"

"Jade earrings. And" – I heard Palli tap the mace at his side – "quetzals would do. Live ones, not feathers."

"Do you have any of those?"

"The jade earrings, yes. Quetzals... I think we have a pair somewhere at the back." He stepped into the storehouse with a torch in his hand. "Let me see. We got a rattle and drum from the vigil of that woman, four days ago. They're for Her Consort, but She's also patron of music, when the mood takes Her..."

He was going through the rows of aligned offerings with the ease of experience, picking up small items and discarding them after no more than a casual glance. I felt... not entirely useless, but close. I strolled back to the door of the storehouse and waited in the darkness.

Which was why I saw Ixtli, the head of the search parties, walk into the temple courtyard with a grim expression on his face.

My stomach sank. Whatever news there could be, it would not be good. I detached myself from the wall. "Ixtli!" I called out.

He bowed to me. "Acatl-tzin." In the gathering darkness, he looked even worse: his face drained of colour, his gnarled hands crooked like the claws of an animal.

"Any news?"

"Only bad." Ixtli shook his head, apparently annoyed. Suddenly he reminded me of an older Teomitl, still unwilling to forgive his own failures. "We searched all four districts of Tenochtitlan. Then we went further, into the Floating Gardens. But there was no track of that beast. It's as if it has vanished from the surface of the earth."

As it had vanished from within an enclosed calmecac. Something wasn't right about that nahual. What had I missed?

"I see," I said. "You found tracks near the calmecac?"

"No," Ixtli said. "No tracks. We were searching houses at random, on no more than instinct." He fingered the jade amulet around his neck, and said, "There was no chance we would find her."

"I see," I said. "Are you going to stop the search?"

Ixtli shrugged. "No, not yet. But I don't think you should depend on us."

No. I didn't think I should.

"The priestess," Ixtli said. "Do you think she's still alive?"

I shook my head. "I think it's too late."

His gaze held me, unblinkingly. "So do I. Will you be needing any more help?"

I searched my mind for something he could give me, but there didn't seem to be anything. "No, I don't think so. You can take off the jade amulets," I said. "Not much use against a nahual, anyway."

Ixtli smiled. "Better be safe. I'll go reassure my wife, and then I'll go back to the Duality House. Come there if you need us," he said, and then he turned on his heel and left.

Palli had gathered the offerings near the storehouse door. "You mean to go out again?" he asked.

I looked up at the sky. The night had well and truly

109

fallen this time: there would be vigils to take, and offerings to make at the proper times. The Quetzal Flower would certainly not want to receive me at this late hour; and I had seen already what would happen if I tried to enter uninvited. I did want to help Neutemoc; but angering a goddess was not going to arrange matters.

"No," I said, with a sigh. "I'll go tomorrow morning."

I was not, by any means, looking forward to the morrow. One interview with Xochiquetzal had been affecting enough; this one looked set to be even worse.

# SEVEN
## *The Chalca Wars*

The following morning, I woke up, made my offerings of blood to Lord Death, and went back to my temple. The priests seemed to have all disappeared. After a cursory search, I found them gathered in one of the largest rooms, watching Ichtaca examine the body of a dead woman: the older offering priests in front, the novice priests a little way behind – and, all the way at the back of the room, a handful of calmecac students, their pale faces fascinated.

"No blood," Ichtaca was saying, pointing at the livid face. "She's been in that position for a while…"

He'd be cutting her open next, if he wasn't satisfied, trying to determine if her death had been natural or provoked. It was a common enough event in the temple. I'd done a few such examinations myself, but thankfully I'd never had the whole clergy in attendance.

I withdrew quietly from the doorframe, and went to the storehouse to collect Palli's offerings. Then I walked back to Xochiquetzal's house.

In the courtyard, the same insolent slave was waiting for me, lounging against the trunk of a pine tree like a man who had all the time in the world.

"Back again, priest? You must really love Her."

I said, "I'd like to see Her, if it's not too much trouble." That last, because I couldn't quite contain my anger.

He shrugged, fully aware of my impatience, basking in it. "Probably not. But then who knows?"

He sauntered into the main room, closing the entrance-curtain behind him; and came back with a satisfied smile on his face.

"So?" I asked. The quetzal birds softly called to each other as the cage rocked in my hands.

He smiled, wider this time. "You may see Her, priest." His gaze took in the offerings I was laden with, and he pursed his lips. "And pray that what you bring is sufficient."

Inside, all was the same: the musky darkness, with the copal incense covering a rank smell that might have been, unsurprisingly, mingled sweat and sex; the goddess shining in the gloom, lounging on Her chair.

"Acatl," She said, and even my name on Her lips was alluring.

My fingers clenched around the handle of the cage. "I've brought you what you asked for."

She smiled. One of Her hands went, absent-mindedly, to rub at Her eyes, and something glistening fell to the floor. A tear, perhaps? But gods didn't cry. "And you thought you could just drop them on the floor and be done?"

I had hoped, but known it wouldn't be enough. "No," I said.

I laid the cage, the rattle and the wrapped jade earrings on the floor, and slowly divested myself of my cloak. Around my wrists hung bracelets of sea-shells: an odd feeling for me, since my usual worship did not include music. I tried to forget how foolish I looked –

Neutemoc, I did this for Neutemoc – and slowly started singing the words of the hymn:

*"You were born in Paradise*
*You come from the Place of Flowers*
*You, the only flower, the new, the glorious one*
*Dwelling in the House of Dawn, a new, a glorious*
*flower…"*

As I sang, I moved my wrists, so that the clinking sounds of the sea-shells accompanied the words I uttered, filling the silences with their voice.

*"Go forth to the dancing-place, to the place of water,*
*To the houses of Tamoanchan…"*

Xochiquetzal shifted on Her chair. Was it just my impression, or had She grown larger? Her eyes shone in the gloom, like those of a jaguar about to leap. And Her smile… Her smile was dazzling, revealing teeth as neat and as sharp as those of sharks.

*"Hear the call of the quetzal bird, o youths,*
*Hear its flute along the river, o women,*
*Go forth to the dancing-place, to the place of water,*
*To the houses of Tamoanchan…"*

She'd risen from Her chair, was walking towards me, growing larger and larger with each step, until Her shadow entirely enfolded me – and She kept smiling: the same smile that sent a thrill running through me – fear or desire I didn't know, I couldn't separate them, it was all I could do to keep singing…

*"Hear… it calling out to the gods…"*

And then She was by my side, kneeling to touch the cage of the quetzal birds. It burst apart in a shower of sparks, and the male ascended into the air, a streak of emerald-green and blood-red. It kept flying upwards, even though I knew it should have hit the rafters of the ceiling; but the room had changed, become vast and unknowable, its walls the dense undergrowth of the jungle, the dais a brackish pool, smelling of mud and fragrant herbs.

At the apex of its flight, the male quetzal folded its wings and plummeted downwards, its long green tail streaming behind it like the unbound hair of a courtesan. It sang as it dived: a hollow, high-pitched sound that seemed to meld with its descent, and that sent a thrill through my bones, as if I were the one courting the female, I the one with lust raging through my veins.

The female bird, still on the ground, raised its eyes. At the last possible moment, the male broke out of the dive and came to perch on the remnants of the cage, cocking its head questioningly. The female made a quick, nodding movement. And, in a blur of green and blue they were upon each other, mating with the desperation of butterflies about to die.

Nausea, harsh, unexpected, welled up in my throat. I turned my gaze away from the birds.

The Quetzal Flower was back on Her dais, smiling. In Her hand were the jade earrings: she tossed them up and down, unheeding of the stone's fragility. "An interesting display, Acatl."

The room hadn't reverted: we could still have been in the southern jungle, or in the Heaven of Tamoanchan, where all living things were born. The smell of muddy earth, mingling with the memory of copal incense, was overpowering.

I said nothing. In the face of who She was, all my words had scattered. The jade earrings went clink-

clink in Xochiquetzal's hands.

"Tolerable, I might say. Certainly a step in the right direction."

It hurt to… Gather my thoughts, I had to gather my thoughts. "You promised–"

She inclined her head, gracefully. "Did I? Only in exchange for proper worship."

"It – has – been – offered," I managed to whisper.

"Has it?" the Quetzal Flower asked. Her voice was sly. "Other things are expected of a worshipper."

A wave of desire swept through me, so strong I had to bite my lips in order not to cry out. I wanted Her as I'd never wanted any woman, any of my childhood loves, there could be no refusing her.

Was this, I thought, distantly, what Eleuia had had: some power that had drawn men to her like bees to honey?

Eleuia.

Neutemoc.

There was no time, not to let myself be battered into submission. "I gave – you – your due," I said, my voice breaking on each word. I felt like a fish, swimming up-river; like a dead soul, climbing the Obsidian Mountains, shards driven in hands and feet, a burning desire to yield, to vanish into oblivion…

Too easy.

"Give me–"

"Your answer?" Xochiquetzal sounded disappointed. "You could have so much more, Acatl."

"No," I whispered. "I – haven't come – here for illusions – for bliss–"

"Bliss is My dominion, Acatl," the Quetzal Flower said. But She had shrunk, become more human, if such a term could be applied to Her. "But if you reject it…" She made a sweeping gesture with Her hands, and the room, too, seemed to shrink.

"I… am not Your servant."

"No." Her voice was angry, or perhaps bitter? "You never were. Go bury yourself with the dead, Acatl, if you can't deal with what makes us alive."

"I–" I started, slowly, wondering why her accusation cut me to the core.

Xochiquetzal smiled, a sated cat once more; but I could feel the undercurrent of frustration in her stance. Next to me, the two quetzal birds had grown still, devouring each other with their gazes.

"The baby's father?" Xochiquetzal asked.

"Give me his name," I whispered. "The proper of- ferings have been made. The hymn was sung, and the dance was right, every step of it."

The Quetzal Flower let go of the jade bracelets. They crashed to the ground, shattered into a thousand pieces. I could have wept at Her casual rejection; but those weren't my thoughts, they were Hers. I was – a priest, first and foremost – a man with an indicted brother. I had no desires of my own: no lovers, no chil- dren, no mark on the world.

No.

Still Her thoughts.

"Give me his name," I said, again, articulating each syllable, letting the familiar sounds anchor me to the Fifth World.

On Her chair, the Quetzal Flower hissed. But finally she spoke. "His name? He was a man who loved her. A warrior she met in the Chalca Wars, and who un- derstood her like no one else could." She paused, rubbed at Her eyes, and She was no goddess, just a middle-aged woman with an ailment that wouldn't go away. "You never understood her, Acatl. You went right and left, and you think you can encompass her."

"No," I said, and it was the truth. "I know nothing about her. But there's no time. I need the father's name."

"There always is time," Xochiquetzal said, shaking Her head. And She went on as if I hadn't spoken. "Her parents had to sell her during the Great Famine, did you know? Because they were poor and couldn't feed her, they offered her to the first rich man who came along."

"I don't see what this has to do..." A name. I needed a name that I could give to Pinahui-tzin, so that Neutemoc would be free. A name, so that I could know the truth.

"He was a bully," the Quetzal Flower said. She shook her head. "He bought her because he needed a slave on whom to release his anger, and he beat her every time she did something out of turn."

"Slaves aren't treated that badly," I said. "She could have complained–"

"To whom? She was eight at the time, Acatl. She didn't know better."

"It's interesting, but–"

"She wanted to be safe," Xochiquetzal said. "After the Great Famine was over, and her parents bought her back, she swore to herself that her family wouldn't ever starve again, that she would have enough power to be sheltered from harm. But in this world, there's no such thing." She smiled. "She swore Herself to me, because priests never go hungry."

Safe. All that, to be hated and despised by everyone?

As if She'd read my thoughts, the Quetzal Flower said, "But a woman shouldn't grasp for power. It's unseemly, isn't it? Her superiors thought her over-ambitious. Her peers thought her obsessed. Her lovers – and she had many – thought her uncanny. Such is the price."

"Please..." I said. "There's no time..."

"In the Chalca Wars, she met a man. A warrior who made no claim on her, who didn't judge her. A good man, who would fight to see that the proper sacrifices were offered, although he was too hot-headed at times."

Neutemoc. It sounded far too much like Neutemoc. Please, Duality, no.

"She bore his child, and would have raised him, too, if he hadn't died at birth."

"Stop going around in circles. His name," I said. Her story was over. There was nothing else She could add. She had to give me his name, to banish my doubts.

She watched me, uncannily serene. "Mahuizoh of the Coatlan calpulli."

"He isn't here," the Jaguar guard said, angrily. "How many times do I have to tell you?"

The warrior of the Duality who headed my detachment – Ixtli, the same one who'd headed the unsuccessful search parties – put a hand on his macuahitl sword. "We have the right to search this house."

If the guard hadn't had both hands full, one around the shell-grip of his spear, one holding his feathered shield, he'd have thrown them in the air. "You can search all you want. What I'm telling you is that I haven't seen Mahuizoh come here. And I've been on guard duty since noon."

"So where is he?" I asked, intervening before matters turned sour.

The guard shrugged. "I'm not a calendar priest. I don't do divination. All I know is–"

"Yes. We understood that, I think." Ixtli turned to me. "Do you want us to search the House?"

I was about to nod, not caring overmuch about making enemies of the Jaguar Knights at this juncture. But someone interrupted us.

"What seems to be the problem here?" a voice asked, behind me.

I turned. My gaze met that of a Knight in Jaguar regalia, but somehow different. The plume behind the jaguar's head was made of emerald-green quetzal tail-feathers, enough to be worth a fortune; the sword at his belt was decorated with turquoise, carnelian and lapis in addition to obsidian shards. His hands, tanned and callused, bore several rings, all of good craftsmanship.

"This man wants to search the Jaguar House, Commander Quiyahuayo."

Commander Quiyahuayo, Head of the Jaguar Brotherhood, looked at me, thoughtfully. "The High Priest for the Dead?" he asked. "You'd be Neutemoc's brother, I take it."

I wasn't surprised at his shrewdness: to stay in his high position, he would need great intelligence, as well as political acumen. "Yes," I said.

The guard's face darkened. "The traitor's brother?" he asked.

Commander Quiyahuayo lifted a hand. "Not so fast, Yolyama. Guilt has not been established. What do you want?" he asked, turning back towards me.

I looked at him, trying to establish his feelings towards Neutemoc. He'd be of noble birth; how would he view the ascension of my commoner brother into the nobility?

"I'm looking for evidence," I said, non-committal.

"About your brother's case?" Commander Quiyahuayo asked. He scratched his chin. "I was given to understand that there were… complications."

"Yes." He missed nothing, and I had no time to fence. I decided to be frank with him. "Another of your Knights might be involved in this."

Commander Quiyahuayo raised an eyebrow.

119

"Mahuizoh of the Coatlan calpulli," I added.

Commander Quiyahuayo grimaced. "Mahuizoh," he said. His distaste was palpable. He hadn't reacted that way when I'd mentioned Neutemoc. "I see."

"You're surprised?" I asked.

Commander Quiyahuayo's face was too blank to reveal anything. "Surprise is a weapon," he said. "I try not to let it be used against me." He scratched his chin, again. "You want to search this House?"

"We're just looking for him," I said. "I need to ask him a few questions."

"We'll be discreet," the Duality warrior Ixtli added.

"I see," Commander Quiyahuayo repeated. "I have no objections. But make it fast, please. The sooner the Jaguar Knights withdraw from this sordid business, the better.

"Yolyama," he said to the guard. "Show them around, will you?" Without waiting for an answer, he turned and walked away.

The guard looked at me, then spat onto the ground. "You're lucky it was Mahuizoh you asked after," he said. "The commander's never liked him."

"Why?" Ixtli asked.

The guard's face closed. "Not your concern," he said. "The commander said you could search the House. That's all. Don't you expect more."

So there were factions, in the Jaguar Knights; and Mahuizoh was obviously not on the commander's side. I wasn't really surprised. It seemed to be the same everywhere within the Sacred Precinct. How secure was Quiyahuayo's position?

The search wasn't long, although it still felt like time wasted: by the time we exited the house, the sun was halfway down to the horizon line, and the light bathing the temples of the Sacred Precinct had turned as golden as ripe maize.

We'd seen rooms where the young Jaguar Knights – those still unmarried and without lands of their own – would spend the night; common rooms, filled with bored Knights playing patolli, focused on the rattle of the dice to the exclusion of everything else; courtyards where the recruits practised with spears and feather-shields. But no trace of Mahuizoh. Though I had never met the man, the slave Huacqui had provided me with enough a description to stop and question everyone who fitted it.

All wasn't lost, however: one of the Jaguar Knights had given us the address of Mahuizoh's house.

"I assume you'll want us to go there next," Ixtli said.

I nodded. "We have to find him." I still had no proof: just a fanciful story of a disappointed lover who might have turned to abduction and murder. It wouldn't hold before Pinahui-tzin, and certainly not before the Imperial Courts.

We had to find Mahuizoh; and we had to force him to confess where he'd hidden Priestess Eleuia.

Mahuizoh's house was a luxurious one, brimming with slaves, its roof planted with a lush carpet of marigolds and yellow tomato flowers. By its size, it must have lodged more than Mahuizoh's immediate family.

The slave at the door was certainly not expecting a dozen Duality warriors. "And you would be...?" he asked, trying to pretend unconcern. But his voice shook.

"We've come to see Mahuizoh." Duality, let him be home.

He looked doubtful. "I'll ask," he said and ducked briefly into the courtyard. I heard him call out to his fellow slaves; after a short time, he came back, and said, "The mistress will see you."

"Mistress?" Ixtli mouthed. "What in the Duality's name?"

I gestured for him to be silent. If Mahuizoh wanted to toy with us, handing us to his wife…

Ixtli and I left the warriors at the entrance, covering all possible exits, and entered the house.

The woman who received us in the house's reception room was even older than Ceyaxochitl: too old to be Mahuizoh's wife. Her seamed face had seen far more than a bundle of fifty-two years, and the stiff way she sat in her low-backed chair suggested acute rheumatism. By her side was a slightly younger woman: middle-aged, with a face that had sagged too much to remain beautiful.

"I hear you've come looking for my son," the old woman said.

Mahuizoh's mother, then. I nodded – and then, unsure of whether she could see me at all, said, "We're here to ask him some questions."

The old woman cackled. "The law finally caught up with him? Doesn't surprise me, doesn't surprise me."

"Auntie Cocochi," the younger woman said, sharply. "That's not what you wanted to say."

The old woman's rheumy eyes focused on her neighbour. "Did I? I always knew he would amount to nothing, that boy."

"He's sheltering you in his house," the younger woman said, shaking her head. By her tone, it was an argument she'd tried before, to no avail.

Cocochi snapped, "He still doesn't respect his elders. It was a different matter when Xoco was alive. She knew her place as my son's wife, she wouldn't speak unless spoken to. I've always told him he should have done the proper thing by his clan, that he should have remarried–"

"Please," I interrupted. "We really have to find Mahuizoh. It's urgent."

"Urgent? Ha!" Cocochi said. "Trouble again, mark my words. That boy was trouble from the moment he exited my womb."

"Do you," I said, slowly, trying not to show my exasperation, "know where Mahuizoh might be?"

"My cousin isn't home," the younger woman said. "He didn't come home last night, either."

"Sleeping out with his whores," Cocochi mumbled.

The younger woman's eyes went upwards, briefly. "He's not here." She lowered her voice and said, "If he was here, she'd know it, and she wouldn't leave him a moment of peace."

I didn't think Cocochi was deliberately trying to impede my inquiry. Though I dearly would have liked to tone down some of that acidity, it wasn't my place.

"Any ideas where he might be?" I asked.

"In the girls' calmecac?" the young woman started, and then covered her mouth. "His sister is there," she said, a little too belatedly.

I sighed. When having an affair, be discreet, which was obviously an art neither Neutemoc nor Mahuizoh had mastered. I was starting to think subtlety wasn't the hallmark of Jaguar Knights.

"I know about the calmecac," I said finally. "Any other ideas?"

"What's he saying?" Cocochi asked.

The younger woman shook her head, in answer to my previous question.

"Can we look around the house?" I asked.

She shrugged. "Of course," she said, with a tired smile. "It will give Auntie Cocochi something to harp on for days." And get the attention of Mahuizoh's mother away from her, which would surely be restful.

Again, not much. We searched room after luxurious room: most of them were occupied by Mahuizoh's aunts, uncles, siblings and siblings' descendants, but Mahuizoh himself was nowhere to be found. Not a trace of him, or of someone who might know where he was. Wherever was he keeping Eleuia? Why abduct her, rather than kill her, if he hadn't wanted something out of her – sex, abject excuses for her infidelity – something else entirely?

Disappointed, Ixtli and I went back to the Duality House. We settled in a small, airy room that served as the headquarters for his regiment. A map was spread out on a reed mat, depicting the four districts of Tenochtitlan, with the streets and the canals coloured in a different pattern, and small counters obviously standing for men or units of men. Ixtli looked to be a careful, meticulous planner.

Slaves brought us refreshments, and a quick meal of atole, maize porridge leavened with spices. I washed it down with cactus juice, enjoying the tart, prickling taste on my tongue.

"We're wasting our time," Ixtli said. "Why don't we just arrest everyone? We might just start with that awful old woman."

I shook my head, although I had the same sense of standing on the brink of failure. "Do you really think it will solve anything?"

"No," Ixtli said. "But it would be something. Are we going to run around Tenochtitlan another cursed time?"

I said, "I have no idea where to look, but…"

His face was grimly amused. "Wherever he's hiding, we can't find it."

"No," I said. But we needed to find him. We needed Eleuia, alive, and evidence to present to Neutemoc's trial.

Tlaloc's lightning strike me, how could I be so utterly ineffective?

"Can you ask around the city?" I asked Ixtli.

He shrugged, in a manner that implied he didn't have much hope. "The Guardian put us at your disposal. I'll do my work. But I'll warn you beforehand–"

"That you promise nothing. I know," I snapped, and realised how tired I was. It was late evening by now. The sun had set. Every passing moment lessened the light that filtered through the entrance-curtain, and we still had no trail. Nothing. "I'm sorry," I said. "It's been a bone-breaking day."

Ixtli looked at me much as Yaotl had, on the previous evening. "Go get some sleep, priest. You can't help here. We'll send for you the moment we find him."

Ixtli was right. They'd be more efficient without my hampering them.

I walked back to my temple in a tense mood, thinking of Neutemoc at the Imperial Audience. Duality, what was I going to tell Huei?

There was no vigil in the darkened shrine: a handful of offering priests were laying out marigold flowers on the altar, but the hymns wouldn't start for another hour. Frustrated, I found a small, empty room reserved for the instruction of the calmecac students, and closing my eyes, sat in meditation.

It didn't work. All I could focus on wasn't the safety of the Fifth World, but the missing Mahuizoh; the fate of my brother, hanging in the balance; and over it all, the shadowy shape of Xochiquetzal, unattainable, unadulterated desire.

The Duality curse us. Did I really need to dwell on the goddess now?

I changed approaches, and made my offerings of blood: drawing thorns through my earlobes, once, twice, three times, until the sharp, stabbing pain had drowned every one of my thoughts.

But I still couldn't banish the image of the Quetzal Flower. In my mind, it merged with that of Priestess Eleuia: everything a man could desire or aspire to, a woman who would suck the marrow from your bones and still leave you smiling.

I threw the bloodied thorns on the floor, exasperated. I needed to focus on Neutemoc, not on a goddess I didn't worship.

Go bury yourself with the dead, Acatl, if you can't deal with what makes us alive.

I wasn't a coward. I'd made my choice, entered the priesthood of Mictlantecuhtli, but I hadn't been running away from the battlefield. I hadn't been running away from life.

The Southern Hummingbird strike Her. I wasn't a coward.

"Acatl-tzin?" The voice tore me from my nightmares.

Ichtaca. Good, reliable Ichtaca, his thoughtful face an anchor for my sanity. "Yes?" I said, attempting to keep my voice from shaking.

If he heard it, he gave no sign of it, save for a slight tightening of his lips. "You have a visitor. It's late at night, but given how urgent the matter sounded..."

I shook my head. Ixtli. It had to be Ixtli, with news of where the Jaguar Knight Mahuizoh was. "No," I said. "Show them in."

Ichtaca's lips pursed again. "In here?" he said. His torch illuminated the whitewashed walls, the minimal furniture. "As you wish."

But the man who came behind Ichtaca wasn't who I'd hoped for, not at all.

"Acatl-tzin," Teomitl said. He radiated untapped energy: the magical veil around him absorbing it, pulsing like a beating heart. "I've done what you asked of me."

I tried to remember what task I'd found for Teomitl. Something that would keep him busy, that would keep him away from me. Searching the girls' calmecac school, wasn't it?

"I see," I said, trying not to let my disappointment show. Whatever Teomitl had found, it could have no bearing on the investigation.

"I was given something for you," Teomitl said. "By a young girl in one of the furthest courtyards."

The young girl with the nahual, the one who saw far too much for someone so young. I hadn't imagined she would contact me again.

"She says she found it in the bushes near the centre of the courtyard. Probably shaken loose when the beast leapt over the wall."

He was speaking too fast for me to follow: every word tumbled on top of the previous one, forming the basis of some arcane structure I couldn't comprehend. I raised a hand. "Slow down, Teomitl. What did she find?"

Teomitl smiled, and held out his hand. "This," he said.

It was the missing pendant from Eleuia's room. As I'd suspected, it represented the warrior alone, an exquisite miniature of an Eagle Knight in full regalia. The stone was obsidian, though strangely enough, it didn't shine in the torchlight…

No! This wasn't obsidian.

I reached out for the pendant. "May I?" I asked Teomitl.

He dropped it in my hand. "It was meant for you."

I rubbed my fingers on it, felt the familiar protective energy arc from the pendant to my heart, but far, far weaker.

Not obsidian. It was jade. Blackened jade.

And that in turn could only mean one thing: that I had been wrong. Only underworld magic could blacken jade so thoroughly.

## EIGHT

# *The Jade Heart*

"I don't understand," Teomitl said, as I tied my cloak around my shoulders. "What does it prove?"

It proved I had been mistaken. It proved Ceyaxochitl had been wrong. Incompetents. Accursed incompetents. No wonder we couldn't find a nahual. No wonder the beast had been able to leap over that wall: it had never been a jaguar.

I strode into the courtyard of my temple. A group of novice priests in grey cloaks, who had been talking among themselves, hurriedly walked out of my way. "It proves we need to change what we're looking for."

"It's not a nahual?"

I shook my head. To blacken jade... I wasn't sure, but it was probably a beast of shadows, summoned from the eighth level of the underworld.

Which meant two things: the first was that, since underworld magic was involved, I could track the beast after all. The second was that I didn't have to worry about the summoner: the underworld had its own justice. The Wind of Knives punished those who blurred the boundaries between the underworld and the Fifth World, and our summoner would soon find himself facing his own executioner.

All I had to do was find the beast and send it back to Mictlan. And rescue Eleuia. I was reasonably sure, though, that it was too late for the priestess. Whatever her abductor had wanted of her, they had it by now.

But first, I wanted to ascertain something.

At the door of the girls' calmecac, the priestess who was standing guard looked at me questioningly. "I have to check something in Priestess Eleuia's room."

"At this hour of the night?"

"It's a matter of life and death," I said. Behind me, Teomitl's footsteps slowed down. The priestess's gaze moved to him: a warrior wearing a white cloak embroidered with hummingbirds, and with an obsidian-studded macuahitl sword at his side.

"He's with me," I said, not wanting to discuss the matter further.

"You people," she said. "Go in, if that's what you want. But don't cause a fuss."

As we ran through the various courtyards, under the curious gazes of young girls, I reflected that a young warrior and a priest for the Dead had to cause some fuss within her school. Unless she had a different definition than I did.

Eleuia's courtyard was still silent: even Zollin's rooms were dark, no light filtering between the painted pillars of its entrance. The nahual's trail, subjected to daylight, had completely vanished. But what remained...

What remained was another kind of magic entirely: dark and roiling, and angry, the one that had given its flavour to the summoning. Underworld magic.

It was the faded trail of a beast of shadows, eager to feast on a human heart, to receive its promised reward.

"Two magics," I said aloud. I could have wept. Why hadn't I seen that before?

Teomitl had followed me into the courtyard; he stood, silently watching the pine tree at the centre as if he could extract some meaning from its twisted shadow. "Two spells?" he asked.

"I didn't think…" I attempted to make sense of what I'd seen. "Someone summoned a beast of shadows from Mictlan. And someone else – someone in this calmecac – added nahual magic on top of it, to cover the trail."

"I don't see the point–" Teomitl started.

"Beasts of shadows aren't common," I said. "You can track them." I could track it. I could find Eleuia. But a full day and night had elapsed since her disappearance. The beast, if it had not killed her, had had time to do whatever its summoner had wished it to.

"You couldn't track a nahual?" Teomitl asked, with faint contempt.

I shook my head. "Too many of them. And the magic dissipates in daylight. But using one magic to cover another…" That had been a masterful stroke; an uncommon idea that required a great knowledge of magic.

Who had captured Eleuia, and why? Was it Mahuizoh? I didn't know. But I didn't think he'd have the skill to cover his tracks, even if he had breached the boundary between the underworld and the Fifth World.

Anyone with the proper knowledge could summon a beast of shadows. But if I could find the beast, I would learn who its summoner was: a beast of shadows was imprinted with the few moments that had followed its entrance into the Fifth World. It would remember its summoner.

"I see." Teomitl's face was set. "Now what?"

"Now you go home," I said.

Teomitl shook his head. "No."

It was late; I was tired, and not in a mood to negotiate. "You don't understand," I said. "It's going to get dangerous. Very dangerous."

Impatience was etched into every feature of his face. "All the more reason for you not to go into this alone."

"I've been tracking beasts of shadows for ten years," I said.

"Yes," Teomitl said. "But you're tired."

I started. "How do you know?"

He shrugged. "I can read it. It's not so hard, Acatl-tzin."

Not only was I tired, it showed even to callow youths. "I don't need help," I said.

"But you might," Teomitl said.

"Look–" I started, and stifled the yawn that threatened to distort my face.

"I'll be careful," Teomitl said. "I know how to fight."

"It's not a warrior's fight."

"No," Teomitl said. "But it is still a fight."

"And you're that eager to get into trouble?"

"To prove myself." The hunger in his gaze was palpable: an obsession that was eating him from inside.

"Haven't you proved yourself already?" I asked. "You took a prisoner."

He snorted. "With my comrades' help. That's no feat of arms."

I sighed, and presented what I hoped would be a decisive argument. "Understand this," I said. "If you do help me, you can't breathe a word about it."

Most youths would have refused at that point. For what is the use of feats, if you cannot boast of them to your comrades? But Teomitl tossed his head, contemptuously. "I don't care about my peers' opinions. Is it a 'yes', then?"

I had exhausted my arguments; and time was running short. "You'll do as I say," I snapped.

Teomitl smiled widely. "Of course."

"And don't put yourself in danger needlessly. I don't need a death on my conscience." But he would not go the way of my apprentice, Payaxin, wouldn't die because of a mistake.

Teomitl shook his head, as if implying that needless deaths were utter foolishness.

"Let's go," I said, aware I'd just been played on, with the same skill as a musician on the flute. For all his arrogance, Teomitl was a shrewd judge of men. Too shrewd for his own good, perhaps.

Before Teomitl and I started tracking down the beast of shadows, I did take the precaution of sending someone to the Imperial Palace, to see if there had been any further developments in Neutemoc's case.

The offering priest – Palli, the burly nobleman's son who usually guarded the storehouse – returned as Teomitl and I were in the armoury of the temple, lifting throwing spears and arrows to find those tipped with magical obsidian.

Nothing further had happened. Everyone, High Priest Acamapichtli included, had gone to sleep. Lucky men. Fatigue was making my head light, and I had some trouble focusing on the objects Teomitl and I had spread on the ground: three spears with shell-grips, a batch of arrows still in their quiver, and two macuahitl swords, wooden clubs studded with razor-sharp obsidian shards. Everything shone, faintly, with the hues of underworld magic: a sickly light that seemed to diminish all it touched.

"I have a sword," Teomitl said, faintly annoyed. "A good one." His sword was well-made, but it would not be enough against the supernatural.

"You'll need one of those," I said, pointing to the swords on the ground. "To fight the beast. What do you know about beasts of shadow?"

A quick, fluid shrug. "Not much. They live on the eighth level of Mictlan. You need a jade bead to placate them."

I nodded. "They're made of shadows, of the darkness that lay over the world in the very first days. Jade will slow them down but not stop them. And they feast on human hearts."

Teomitl nodded. "Many things do."

"Indeed." The gods, the Celestial Women. Nothing was as precious as blood; and the most precious thing of all was the heart, which gathered all the blood and distributed it around the body.

"The beasts hate light," I said, curtly, picking up one of the sturdiest swords and hefting it. A faint touch of Mictlan's magic spread to my arm, stilling the blood in my veins, and numbing my skin. "Starlight won't bother them much, but moonlight or sunlight will weaken them. Sunrise might even destroy them."

"How do you kill them?" Teomitl asked.

"This sword has magical obsidian: Lord Death's gift to us. Stab their chest, and they'll die like any animal." I handed it to him. What I didn't say was that they were fierce fighters, more than a match for both of us.

"Hmm," Teomitl said. He was tense again, impatient to move on.

We repaired to one of the furthest rooms, after warning Ichtaca not to disturb us. The room was a simple, subdued affair, its only furniture a handful of wicker chests, its walls blank save for a spider-and-owl frieze running at head height. A small, discreet limestone altar was at the back, Mictlantecuhtli's skull symbol carved in its centre.

I knelt on the floor, feeling the coldness of the beaten earth through my bare knees. Before me, a wicker cage held a rabbit and a barn owl: a small bird with the sharp eyes of a hunter, blinking in the torch-light. On my left was a jade replica of a human heart, in exquisite detail. On my right was a jade plate, representing the journey of the soul through Mictlan, from the crossing of the River of Souls on the first level, to the ninth and final level, the Throne of Mict-lantecuhtli, God of the Dead.

I slit the throat of the rabbit with one of my obsidian knives, and carefully drew a quincunx on the floor: the four-armed cross with its fifth central point.

"Whatever happens, don't move," I said to Teomitl. He stood outside that quincunx, outside the underworld's zone of influence. "And don't step over the line."

He shrugged arrogantly. Who are you taking me for? he seemed to say.

Already, I regretted my decision to bring him with me. But I wasn't about to go back on my word.

*"In darkness they dwell*
*In darkness they feast*
*They eat, they consume their preys…"*

I reached for the owl and swiftly opened up its chest in a shower of blood. I retrieved its heart, and laid it on the jade plate: between the seventh and eighth level of the underworld, over a crude drawing of a shadowy beast. Blood seeped onto the plate, spread outwards like a scarlet flower opening its petals.

*"In darkness they feast*
*They eat, they consume their preys*
*All save one…"*

Shadows gathered around the room, pooled to fill the quincunx, until I knelt in absolute darkness. A wet, heavy breath blew down my neck: the breath of a huge animal, waiting for its food.

I didn't falter. I knew all too well the cost of failure. Death, if I was lucky; utter oblivion if I wasn't.

*"All save one*
*One is lost*
*One runs under the light*
*Under the light of stars and moons*
*One is lost…"*

I laid the tip of my obsidian knife against the jade heart, so that the remains of the owl's blood seeped into the stone. The jade grew darker, but it pulsed now, pulsed like a living heart.

*"A jade heart to find the eater of hearts*
*Who feasts on the living*
*Under the light of stars and moons*
*He comes to Mictlan, the Place of Fear, the Place of Death*
*A jade heart to find the eater of hearts."*

The jade heart went completely black. I reached out to enfold it in my hands, ignoring the searing pain that spread from the stone into my skin, and felt it beat under my fingers: a slow, regular rhythm that started in the rightmost ventricle and moved upwards, into my arm.

Slowly, carefully, I rose, keeping the heart in the same position. The beat didn't falter.

The shadows were gradually dispelled by torchlight; I could see Teomitl's shocked face, trying to reassemble itself into its usual haughty mask – and the body of the owl, blood pooling under it, the red flower blossoming on the jade plate.

Still standing within my quincunx, I turned to face each direction in turn. When I turned north, east or west, the beat of the jade heart went completely still. But when I faced south, towards the Itzapalapan causeway, the heart sprang to life under my fingers.

It had worked, then; and the beast we sought was somewhere in that direction.

Teomitl insisted on bringing a purse filled with medicinal herbs, as well as his new sword. He kept rubbing the weapon, as if its touch were subtly wrong. I couldn't blame him: the obsidian shards embedded in the wood were charged with enough magic to send anyone into oblivion. The veil hanging around him seemed to be weaker around the sword, as if the magics were fighting one another, but it did not appear to be serious – for which I was eternally grateful.

As we exited the temple and headed southwest towards the district of Moyotlan, I asked, "You do know about the magic?"

He looked puzzled. "Which magic?"

"Around you?"

The way Teomitl attempted to look at his arms and legs convinced me he hadn't known. But he didn't look happy about it: his face darkened, a change of mood that was visible even in the wavering light of his torch.

"A protective spell some fool laid on me without my consent," he muttered, darkly. "Nothing worth worrying about."

I did wonder, though: it was powerful magic, and I wasn't entirely sure how it would withstand the assaults of a beast of shadows – some spells just shattered, crippling the people on whom they'd been laid. "You'd better stay back," I said.

Teomitl shook his head and didn't answer.

Under my fingers, the heart beat at its steady rhythm as we ran through the deserted streets. The grand houses became smaller, turning from adobe to mud, the flat roofs replaced by high, tapered ones painted with abstract patterns; finally turning into the humble mud dwellings of peasants, ringed by fields of maize. We were almost at the lake shore.

Teomitl's hands held the torch steady as we ran out of the city altogether, and found ourselves in the midst of dried maize husks, crunching under our feet.

I turned the heart right and left; and it beat again, in the direction of a group of small, squat islands on the edge of the lake.

Teomitl saw the way I faced, and groaned. "Oh no. Not the Floating Gardens."

The *chinamitls*, or Floating Gardens, were artificial islands reclaimed from the lake. A mass of stones and clay, dumped at the bottom of the lake, served as a support for muddy, fertile earth. Over the years, the Floating Gardens had grown more numerous as well as closer to each other, and now formed a district of their own: a grid of fields separated by small canals, another city on the water.

"We need a boat," Teomitl was saying, his torch wavering left and right. "There." He all but ran to a small reed boat, moored to the bank ahead of us. "Let's take this one."

"It's not ours," I said, shocked. "At least ask for permission."

His eyes were wide in the torchlight. "Why?" he asked. "We'll bring it back."

"Before dawn?" I asked. "I can't guarantee that, and neither can you." A boat like that would be a family's sole means of transport, the only way to gather fish from the lake, to carry merchandise to the marketplace. To wake up in the morning, and discover it lost, to think it stolen… that would truly be disastrous. I scanned the banks: close by was the dark shape of a hut, its coloured thatch roof reflecting the torchlight. "Let's warn them."

"Acatl-tzin." Teomitl's voice shook on the verge of exasperation. "A life is at stake, and you worry about peasants?"

My own parents had been peasants. I had grown up in fields much like those we were walking in; and the weak were so easily overlooked in the scheme of things. Teomitl's attitude, while not unexpected, disappointed me. I'd hoped for more – intelligence? Compassion? "That boat is a family's living," I said, more sharply than I'd intended to. "I won't trample lives to save just one."

"But," Teomitl said, shaking his head, "you said you were looking for Priestess Eleuia…"

I was already walking towards the hut. With all the noise we were making, they would no doubt be awake.

A man dressed in a simple loincloth stood on the threshold of the dwelling, holding a trembling torch in his hand.

"We need to borrow your boat," I said.

His eyes focused on me, on my grey cloak, its colour uncertain in starlight, on the streaks of makeup that marked my face. I could have been anyone to him. But he saw that I was armed.

"Take what you need," he said. "But don't…" A sweeping gesture with his hands, encompassing the hut and those sleeping within.

"Oh, for the Duality's sake," Teomitl said. He threw something in the air. It glittered as it fell, and landed with the harsh sound of metal striking metal. "Buy a new boat with that, if we damage it. Come on, Acatl-tzin. Let's go."

The man bent down to pick up Teomitl's offering: quills of gold, tied together at the end, enough to ensure two months' living, if not more. Tossed casually into the mud, as if they were worth nothing at all: the quintessential warrior gesture. Some student. Obedience, like humility, was a foreign notion to him.

"Teomitl," I said as he untied the boat: an interesting feat, since he had one hand taken by his torch. "I thought I'd made things clear. You follow my lead."

He raised his gaze, briefly, to the sky. "You'd have stayed for hours arguing with the man."

"No," I said, stung. I knew how to handle such situations. "I would merely have eased things a little."

"Money eases things wonderfully," Teomitl said. He gestured for me to climb aboard.

The boat rocked as I stepped into it. My body, remembering gestures from more than twenty years ago, adjusted itself to the motion.

"Money won't buy him a better life," I said.

"No, but it will make the next months easier." Teomitl held out his torch to me, and I took it in my free hand, without thinking. "I'll row."

I watched him manoeuvre the boat into the canal, shifting my weight from leg to leg to compensate for the rocking. He had this natural authority, I guessed: something that made him hard to ignore when he gave you a command.

He also, quite obviously, had never rowed in his life. The boat spun to and fro in a haphazard fashion, and the jade heart in my right hand shifted from beating to still to beating again, as he directed us towards the nearest Floating Garden.

"Which one?" he asked.

"I have no idea," I said, annoyed, more because of the natural, insidious way he'd taken charge than because of his rowing. "If you kept us on course, I'd have an easier time."

"Not my fault," Teomitl snapped. "The thing won't stay still."

"It's a boat. They rarely stay still, The Duality curse you! Where were you raised? In the mountains?" Tenochtitlan was built on an island; every street doubled as a canal, and it was almost impossible for a boy to grow up without ever seeing a boat.

In the unsteady light, I felt his exasperation more than I saw it. "I'm doing my best, Tlaloc blind you! I'm just not used to this contraption."

The least that could be said. I sighed; and instead of holding the jade heart steadily in front of me, attempted to keep it on an even orientation. Not obvious, with only the starlight to go by. It kept becoming motionless without warning; but slowly, step by step, I managed to direct Teomitl to one of the furthest islands.

The boat ran aground in a spectacular fashion, scattering dried, slashing pieces of reeds over my legs. Teomitl leapt on the shore and snatched the torch from me. He stared at me, once more daring me to mock him.

I wasn't in a mood to reproach him, for the heartbeat under my fingers was faster than it had been on shore. "It's close," I whispered.

"Where?" Teomitl asked.

"On this island." I suddenly wondered why we were whispering. A beast of shadows would have hearing much keener than that of any jaguar on the prowl, and a sense of smell to match. It would sense me, a priest for the Dead, as it would sense the heart I carried in my hands. "Come."

This Floating Garden was, like most of them, a huge maize field. Dry husks crackled under my sandals, no matter how hard I strove to be silent.

The torchlight illuminated the small maize plants, poking out of the ground: it was the end of the dry season, and the maize had barely been replanted. In the night, the field seemed eerily desolate: every insect song echoed as if in the Great Temple, and every maize sapling rustle made me startle, and wonder if the beast wasn't going to leap at us.

The heartbeat grew faster still as we approached the hut at the end of the Floating Garden.

"In there?" Teomitl asked. "Can't we draw it out?"

I wished we could. "It's too canny for that. We'd just be wasting our time."

"I see," Teomitl said. "What an adventure." He didn't sound keen. I didn't feel so enthusiastic either. Inside the hut, we would have neither starlight nor moonlight, and fighting by torchlight was messy and ineffective. I looked up at the sky. The moon would rise soon, but we would be inside while it climbed into the sky. I didn't like that, but there wasn't much of a choice.

The heart went wild as I crossed the threshold. My hand dropped to the largest of my obsidian knives, and drew it from its sheath.

Nothing. No beast, leaping from the darkness to swipe at my chest. I released my hold on the knife; the hollow feeling in my stomach receded.

Teomitl stood on the threshold, his torch briefly illuminating the contents of the hut: walls of wattle-and-daub, embers dying on the hearth. And three bodies, face down on the ground, the sickening smell of rot and spilled entrails underlying that of churned mud.

The beat of the jade heart was frantic now, as if it didn't know where to start pointing.

I knelt by one of the bodies, lifted it to the wavering light: a man, his chest slashed open, and the heart missing. Of course. The beast of shadows had feasted on its preferred meal.

The other corpses were much the same, save that one of them was a woman. She could have been Eleuia. But I soon disabused myself: this woman was older than thirty-five, and wearing a rough cactus-fibre blouse and skirts, nothing like the clothes a priestess of high rank would have chosen.

"Acatl-tzin," Teomitl said, sharply. "There's something outside."

The heart was still madly beating, but it was useless at such close quarters. The beast could be anywhere. I rose from my crouch, drawing one of my three obsidian knives from its sheath.

"Stay where you are," I said.

A shadow passed across the threshold, knocking Teomitl off-balance. The torch fell: a brief, fiery arc before it was utterly extinguished. And in the interval before I gained my night vision, something huge bore me to the ground. Claws scrabbled at the clasp of my cloak – moving downwards, aiming for my heart.

# NINE
## Shadows and Summoners

I tried to roll aside, but the beast was too heavy. It breathed into my face the nauseous smell of rotting bodies, of pus and bleeding wounds. I wanted to retch. But I couldn't. I was pinned to the ground, my lungs all but crushed by the weight on my chest.

I'd dropped the jade heart, but my hand was still clenched around the obsidian knife. I tried to raise it, but the beast was blocking me. Its claws had shredded my cloak and were now digging into my chest, where the jade pendant was obviously giving it some trouble.

Good.

I heaved, felt the beast slide a fraction of a measure, enough for me to wedge the knife upwards and sink it into flesh.

The beast roared, but remained where it was, weighing down on my chest.

The Duality curse me. The jade amulet would slow it down, but at some point it would be entirely blackened – and thus useless.

I heaved again, to little avail.

Footsteps sounded in the hut. "Acatl-tzin!"

The beast roared, and turned away from me. I heaved again, sending it to the ground. As quickly as I could, I rolled upright.

My night vision was a little better, but not clear enough. Presumably, the two silhouettes hacking at each other in the hut were Teomitl, armed with his sword, and the beast, hissing like a frustrated ocelot. Teomitl's breath came in quick, heavy gasps, and he circled the thing in an awkward way: a wound, taken as he'd been struck down by the beast, must have hampered him.

Obviously, the beast had the upper hand. It didn't have the problem of inadequate night vision, and Teomitl's reflexes were no match for its rapid strikes.

But we had one advantage over it: because it was made of the deepest shadows of Mictlan, it hated light. Any kind of light. And outside the hut would be starlight, and the rising moon, steadily climbing into the sky. And a dense network of maize seedlings, which would betray the slightest movement.

I unsheathed both my remaining obsidian knives, feeling Mictlantecuhtli's power pulse deep within, and made my way to the door as fast as I could.

I closed my eyes, briefly, extending my priest-senses – and felt the beast, a black patch of raw anger and hatred, mixed with the deeper darkness of Mictlan. Not stopping to dwell on the consequences of failure, I took aim, and threw one knife at the combatants.

A howl informed me I'd hit the right target; I threw myself to the ground, and not a moment too soon. The beast leapt right over me, and landed in the maize with a dry, rustling sound.

The starlight limned its shape: a body half as large again as a jaguar's, a narrow snout, glittering fangs; and yellow, malevolent eyes that seemed to see right into my soul. That had to be what a deer felt, in the moment before the hunter closed on it.

No.

I had to–

I threw myself aside again, and the leap which had been meant for my chest caught my left arm instead. Claws sank deep into my skin. I stifled a scream as the searing pain spread through the bones of my upper arm. My hand opened, out of its own volition, and the obsidian knife, the only one I had left, fell to the ground.

The beast withdrew its claws. Its muscles bunched up, to snatch me and bring me closer to it. I did the only possible thing: I let myself fall to the ground. The beast's claws went wide. Frustrated, it shook its head, growling in a decidedly unpleasant manner.

I flicked my eyes upwards, glancing at the sky: the moon was steadily rising higher and higher, but it would be a while before its light fell on the Floating Garden.

Huitzilpochtli strike me down.

At the threshold of the hut, a shaking Teomitl had hauled himself upwards. He was attempting to raise his sword, but I didn't think he'd arrive in time.

There was no point in discreetly retrieving my obsidian knife. I simply dived for it, as the beast braced itself for another jump, straight in the direction I was going in.

The shock of its weight sent me sprawling to the ground, fighting not to scream as my left arm became a mass of fiery pain. Its claws scrabbled at my jade pendant and the thread holding it around my neck parted. The pendant fell to the ground with a clink. The beast roared in triumph and reared, both paws held high above my chest – with all their claws unsheathed.

"Acatl-tzin!" Teomitl bellowed.

The world turned to thick honey; everything seemed to happen more slowly than needed: the claws descending to slash open my chest; Teomitl's unsteady footsteps, rushing towards me, but too late, it was already too late; the glimmer of the obsidian knife, lying in the mud inches from my left hand.

My left hand.

I had to–

Focus. I had to focus.

I clenched the fingers of my left hand – I think I screamed, then, as the pain became stronger than anything I had endured in my noviciate at the calmecac – closed them around the hilt of the knife. The weapon felt alive under my touch, beating like a living heart. Power pulsed deep within: a smell of sick-houses and rotting bodies, hovering on the edge of becoming something far greater.

I didn't think. I couldn't afford to. In a quick, stabbing motion, I raised the knife, intending to sink it into the beast's chest before it opened mine.

The claws raked into my flesh before I could complete my motion. My hand clenched, convulsively, but I didn't let go. I screamed and writhed, but I still raised the knife. And, scrabbling for something, for anything that could save me, I instinctively opened myself wide to the power within the knife.

For a brief, timeless moment, the power of Mictlan seared through my flesh: the decay of every living thing, the loneliness and sadness of the dead, the dry smell of bleached bones and dust. For a brief, timeless moment, the pain was blasted away by emptiness. It was my hand and yet not my hand which pushed upwards, at an angle I would have been incapable of reaching with my wounded arm.

The beast, completing its downward motion, fell upon the blade I held up, and grew still. Its weight crushed my chest, slowly emptying my lungs.

The power of Mictlan slowly receded, leaving me exhausted: drained of joy, of hope. I had never had cause to draw on it that way. I had not even been sure it could be done.

I hoped never to do it again.

I lay, hardly daring to breathe. Every movement of my chest sent fresh waves of pain through my ribcage. My left arm would never be the same, either.

The moon's light struck the Floating Garden, throwing into stark contrast the bed of maize shoots, and the blood that was pouring onto it. My blood.

Someone – Teomitl – hauled the beast's corpse off me. "Acatl-tzin?"

I didn't move, just stared at him, watching him blur in and out of focus. His left leg sported an ugly gash, and he leant on his sword – but the spell around him was still tight, and his upright bearing was undiminished.

"I've been better," I whispered.

He pulled me upright, into a seated position. "Good thing we came well-prepared," he said, searching in the herb pouch he'd taken from the temple.

He pulled out a pad of dayflower and applied it to my chest wound. It turned dark; with a curse, he threw it away, and applied another one.

"Don't move," he said, when the bleeding had slowed down. "I think there were things in that hut that might help us…"

He was soon back, with a covered jar of clay that stank of alcohol. "Pulque," he said. "Unfermented maguey sap would have been better, but it will have to do."

When he poured it over the wounds, I thought I would scream again. But I'd had my fill of screaming. I clenched my teeth, and attempted to bring the world back into focus.

Teomitl tore my cloak into strips to make bandages; his gestures as he dressed my wound were cool, professional. "You're not – a – healer," I said.

He shook his head. "But I've seen my share of wounds, and my share of warriors whose wounds filled with pus and turned black. Stupid. Those things are easily cured, if you take them at the beginning."

"Your own wounds," I said, struggling to come up with something significant. My thoughts seemed to have scattered.

He shrugged. "Damaging, but not serious. I'll splint my leg after I'm done with you."

"Thank you," I said, when he was finished. My left arm was wrapped in maize leaves; my chest was covered in an array of cotton bandages soaked in pulque. The smell of alcohol was starting to go to my head, making me feel dizzy. I shook myself, and winced at the pain.

"Don't overexert yourself!" Teomitl snapped. He looked at his own wound, critically. "Mm."

I laughed, more sharply than I'd intended to. "The night isn't over. We still have to find who summoned the beast, not to mention Priestess Eleuia."

"Do you think I don't know?" Teomitl's voice was low, angry. "I'm telling you those wounds won't heal if you keep running around the city."

I rose, carefully. Even breathing hurt. Teomitl was pouring the rest of the pulque on his own wound, with an efficiency that made me suspect he didn't need my help.

"I'll go and search the hut," I said. I still needed to access the beast's memories, but that would be best done a little later, when I'd had time to catch my breath.

"By the way," Teomitl said, without raising his eyes. "You've got some nerve, throwing knives at me."

I shrugged. I hadn't liked doing it, but there had been no other choice. "I wasn't throwing it at you. I used my priest's senses to target the beast. Anyway, it missed you."

"It might not have."

"You'd rather have lost?" I asked, pointedly. "If you want to exchange wounds..."

He shook his head, sharply. "No. But I'd rather you didn't do it again."

"If it had been me fighting, and you outside, I'd rather take my chances with a thrown knife than with the beast's claws. But I'll remember."

Inside the hut, I carefully rekindled the dying fire, offering a brief prayer to Huehueteotl, God of the Hearth. The flames that rose between the three stones illuminated the walls, magnifying my shadow like that of a monster. The shards of the jade heart crunched under my feet.

With some difficulty, I turned the three corpses on their backs. In the sweltering heat of the marshes, they had already decomposed, flesh sloughing off, revealing the bones beneath. I'd seen too many dead people to be unsettled by the half-visible skulls, or by the strong smell of putrescence that hung in the air.

Their chests gaped open: an uncomfortable feeling, given how close I'd come to sharing the same fate. My wounds itched under Teomitl's bandages.

I whispered a quick litany for the Dead, brushing blood from my wounds over their rotting foreheads – the best I could do outside my temple and without much living blood of my own. Later, I'd make sure someone picked up the corpses and brought them back to give them a proper funeral.

> *"We leave this earth*
> *This world of jade and flowers*
> *The quetzal feathers, the silver*
> *Down into the darkness we must go*
> *Leaving behind the marigolds and the cedar trees*
> *Safe journey, my friends, safe journey*
> *All the way to the end."*

Dark splotches of blood marked the floor of the hut. I knelt, rubbed my fingers on one of them. It flaked. Completely dry, then. By the look of the corpses, they had been dead for some time anyway: at least a day, if not more.

There was something… A faint, very faint trace of magic within the hut. I closed my eyes. It was god-given, like the magic that had hung in Zollin's room, but somehow different. Less angry. More desperate. It seemed to emanate from the wattle-and-daub walls of the hut. Puzzled, I knelt to take a better look. In the blood was the faint imprint of a human hand; and faint scratches on the ground.

I picked up the fallen torch, started to dust it off, and gave up when I saw how much mud was clogging it. I teased a branch loose from the torch, cleaned it as best as I could before plunging it into the flames of the hearth. It took a long time for the fire to take hold. When it did, it was a small and sickly thing, pulsating weakly at the end of my improvised torch. I moved back to the hand imprint, shone the torch on the ground. By its side, the blood had formed patterns…

No, not the blood. Someone had started to trace glyphs for a spell. That was the reason the magic, spreading out from the incomplete pattern, had impregnated this area.

The glyphs, trembling in the torchlight, were the ones for "water" and "escape": both badly smudged, traced in a shaking, fearful hand, and the last one incomplete.

I closed my eyes. The beast had brought Priestess Eleuia here, after abducting her from the girls' calmecac. The attempted spell had to be hers, a desperate attempt to escape her abductor. But Eleuia was, quite obviously, no longer here.

My torch wavered, and finally went out. I bit back a curse.

"Anything?" Teomitl asked, shadowing me from the threshold. He was leaning on a crutch, his leg neatly splinted with dried branches.

"Blood," I said, with a sigh. "She was here."

Teomitl did the same thing I'd done: withdrawing a branch from the ruined torch, dipping it into the fire. He turned from one end of the hut to another, seemingly oblivious to the corpses. Of course, they'd only be peasants for him, not worthy of his attention.

"Mm," he said. "People came here."

"The peasants?" I asked.

"No," Teomitl said. "After the peasants were dead." He waved the torch towards the farthest end: outlined in blood were two footprints, of different sizes.

"At least two people?" I asked.

"With sandals. So probably not peasants," Teomitl said. "And it wasn't long after the peasants' deaths, or they wouldn't have left marks."

Eleuia had been there, too, while the blood was still fresh; otherwise she wouldn't have left a handprint.

"They took her?" I asked.

Teomitl shrugged. "Probably."

I glanced at the ground near the threshold, but we'd damaged too much of it with our battle. "And we still don't know where." Which was true, if frustrating. None of that would help me understand what was going on. "Very well. Help me out, will you? I have memories to access."

For the ritual, I needed a clean patch of land. One-armed and one-legged, Teomitl and I managed to drag the beast's corpse to the empty patch of earth before the hut. The wound I'd dealt it gaped in the moonlight, exuding faint traces of Mictlan's aura; of the magic that had coursed through me to bring the beast down.

I retrieved all my obsidian knives, and used one of them to draw a ragged circle in the earth. Then I withdrew to survey my handiwork. The circle looked as clean as I could make it. It would have to do.

Further away, in the field where the beast had fallen, its blood had shrivelled the maize, leaving a patch of emptiness oozing Mictlan's power. In that place, nothing would grow for many years.

Father, I thought uneasily, would have been angry at the way we'd damaged the harvest to come. The family might be dead, but the land would revert to the clan; and another married couple would soon cultivate this field, wondering why nothing would grow there.

Father wouldn't have tolerated this. But Father was dead. I had… I had run away from his drowned corpse, seeing in every feature of his face the disappointment that I'd turned out as I had. It was the single vigil I had never undertaken, and it still itched at the back of my mind.

Father was dead, buried into the bliss of Tlalocan, the Land of the Blessed Drowned. I had other things to worry about.

Teomitl's taut pose suggested the question he dared not ask: "And now what?"

"Stay out of the circle."

He made a quick, angry gesture. "Surprise me."

Ignoring Teomitl's taunt, I knelt inside the circle. With my good hand, slowly, methodically, I widened the wound in the beast's belly. The entrails came steaming out, exuding not the smell of bowels but the wet, musty odour of a grave long unopened.

I drew another gash, this time nearer the ribs, and went looking for the heart.

It was a small, pathetic thing when I finally pulled it loose: the size of a human one, as unmoving as the jade heart now was.

I arranged the entrails in an inner circle within the one we'd already cleared. Then I cut the small, stylised shape of a reed, my day sign, into the flesh of the heart. It barely bled, as if death had emptied the beast's veins.

Finally, I came to stand in the centre of both circles, holding the heart in my good hand. It was as smooth and as warm as the flesh of a young child.

"This is the day that saw me born, this is the name my father gave me," I whispered, and the heart twitched under my fingers.

I wrapped my hand around the heart, and went on,

*"I am the knife that severs life*
*I am the blade that stole this breath*
*Mine is the heart*
*Mine are the eyes that see in darkness*
*Mine the muscles and fangs that claim life."*

It was as if a veil had been lifted from the world: suddenly I saw the whole of the Floating Garden. In the hut were the corpses I had already feasted on. By my side was a young, impatient warrior whose heart beat so strongly: such a treat, it would be such a treat to open his chest and feast upon it. But I couldn't. I had other tasks to take care of.

*"Mine are the eyes that see in darkness*
*Mine the heart that longs for other hearts*
*Mine the memories of the true hunter."*

The world flashed, then went dark. When I opened my eyes I wasn't in the chinamitl any more but tumbling through an open gateway, into a house that was hauntingly familiar.

The sun hadn't yet set. I shied away from the light, growling softly, longing for the coldness of the Eighth Level, for the dry, clean smells of Mictlan. Here everything hurt, from the light to the sharp odour of maize wafting through the door.

A man laughed, high above me. I couldn't see his face: just a warm, beating heart with many years of life ahead of it. "Such a powerful one. A very impressive summoning, my Lady."

Another voice, deeper and graver. The heartbeat of this one was strong, brash. I salivated at the thought of devouring it. "Don't gape. It is adequate for the task."

A sullen laugh.

"My Lady, you know what we need," the voice said, turning to the third person, the one who hadn't yet spoken: an angry heart, all twisted out of shape by hatred. "Wait for night. And remember, do not kill. We need her alive."

"I know exactly what you need," the woman said. And the voice… The voice, too, was hauntingly familiar.

No. It could not be.

She knelt to grasp my head, raising my gaze towards her face. Her smell was intoxicating: anger and hatred and envy, all swirling around something else I couldn't name – and her heart... Such a young, delicate heart...

"This is what you will do," she said.

And there was no doubt left; none at all. For the voice, unmistakably, belonged to my brother's wife, Huei.

I must have closed my eyes. When I opened them again, I was lying in the middle of the circle, sprawled over the beast's body. My chest ached fiercely under the bandages.

Teomitl's scowling face entered my field of vision. "I told you–"

"Not to move around. I know," I said, taking the hand he offered me, and rising. Around us, the moon cast its light on the desolate Floating Garden: the place where I'd accessed the beast's memories was now nothing more than a circle of charred ashes, blackened earth which would take years to heal. Mictlan's magic was anathema to life; and the beast had been bursting with it.

More damage to the harvest. Just what I needed. I tried to remain focused on this – to forget what I had seen – but I couldn't.

Huei.

My brother's wife had summoned the beast.

Why?

She hadn't seemed... I shook my head. She had seemed sincere; but, then, like Neutemoc, she had moved away from me in four years. She was no longer my only ally in my brother's house, but something else entirely.

It wouldn't matter. A chill was working its way into my bones. Summoning a beast of shadows carried its own penalty. The Wind of Knives would soon appear in Tenochtitlan, to kill Huei for her transgression.

What would I tell Neutemoc, when he came home to find his wife dead? Neutemoc was innocent of everything save adultery; but that thought didn't bring me any relief.

No. There had to be some explanation. Something. Anything that would explain the utter failure of Huei's marriage.

"We need to get back to the city," I said to Teomitl.

He rowed me back to the shore in silence. As the oars splashed into the lake, I kept wondering when I would feel the first touch of cold on my spine. Seven years ago, I had merged my mind with the Wind of Knives to bring down an agent of Tezcatlipoca, the Smoking Mirror, and that mind-link had never quite died. When the Wind entered the Fifth World, I would know.

Teomitl was too tired to row farther than he had to. And I was not in a state to row either, with my injured arm. We left the boat at the edge of the Floating Gardens and walked north, back into the city of Tenochtitlan proper.

Teomitl didn't speak until we were walking once more on the familiar streets of the Moyotlan district, with the grand adobe houses of the wealthy rising all around us. "Where to?" he asked. He was leaning on his crutch, his face transfigured by eagerness. I hated to dash his hopes, but there were things I couldn't let him see.

"Home, for you," I said. I did not want to face the Wind of Knives; to face the darkness and the coldness, to plead for Huei's life even though I knew the

Wind could not be swayed. But this was something that I would do alone. I would not drag someone else into it. The Wind of Knives would merely cut them down like maize, dispassionately judging that they had no right to speak with Him.

"What?" Teomitl asked. "You promised–"

"No," I said, hating myself for my cowardice. "I allowed you to come with me. But what happens now is something you're not prepared for."

No, not prepared for. That while my married brother was busy courting a priestess, his own wife, Huei, plotted with shadowy figures to get her revenge.

"I'm prepared," Teomitl said, sullenly.

"You're in no state to fight."

I could have predicted his next remark. "Neither are you."

"No," I said. "But there are other ways to fight." Even magical weapons would shatter against the Wind of Knives, and nothing would stop or sway Him. How could Huei have been so foolish?

Teomitl was still watching me. "Go home," I said, as gently as I could. "I'll call on you the next time there is something, promise. But this isn't the right time."

"I don't see why," Teomitl said. But he looked down, at his splinted leg, and sighed. "You'll summon me?"

"Promise," I said, praying that the next time I was involved with the underworld, it would be safe enough for him to accompany me. "Go home, and take care of that leg."

"Very well," Teomitl said, grudgingly. "But I'll hold you to this, Acatl-tzin." He started limping towards the Sacred Precinct, then turned, a few paces from me. "And don't forget to be careful with those wounds!"

His attitude – thoughtless arrogance, the strange, buoyant mood that propelled him through life – was not only that of a warrior, but that of a nobleman's son. Where had Ceyaxochitl found him?

Left to my own devices, I walked back to Neutemoc's house. I made my way through the network of Tenochtitlan's canals – under deserted bridges, past houses lit up by late-night revelry, where snatches of music and loud laugher wafted into the street, a memory of what I couldn't have.

I prayed that there was still time left to avert the disaster.

# TEN
## *Mictlan's Justice*

Despite the late hour, Neutemoc's house was still lit, though the only sounds that pierced the night were the lilting tones of a poet reciting his latest composition. Cradling my bandaged arm in my good hand, I walked to the door.

"Yes?" the slave who was guarding the entrance to the courtyard asked. He was a burly man, with macuahitl scars on his legs: a veteran of some battlefield, though only the Duality knew how he had fallen low enough to sell himself into slavery. "What do you want?" His voice was contemptuous.

Only then did I realise what I must look like. My cloak had been torn to make the bandages that now covered my naked chest, and I stank of pulque alcohol like a base drunkard. In fact, it was a good thing I hadn't met a guard on my way through the city, or I'd have been arrested for drunkenness. And for a priest, that offence carried the death penalty.

"I'm Huei's brother-in-law," I said. "I need to see her."

"She has no time for–" The slave sniffed.

"Beggars?" I asked, infuriated. "I've looked better,

but I'm certainly not about to ask for her charity. Will you let me in?"

He didn't look as though he was about to. Luckily for me, someone crossed the courtyard to see what was causing all the noise.

"Acatl?" my sister Mihmatini asked. She wore a pristine dress of white cotton, with a simple embroidery of sea-shells along the hem, and her hair was impeccably combed.

I felt ashamed of what I looked like, compared to her. "Can you convince the guard here to let me in? I need to speak to Huei, quickly."

"Huei?" Her eyes widened. "Is it about Neutemoc?"

I shook my head. I still hadn't felt the familiar cold in my bones. But I was trying not to think of the old, old cenote south of Tenochtitlan, the fissure opening in the rock to reveal the stillness of an underground lake; and how the air above that lake would be growing darker and darker, as the Wind of Knives coalesced into existence at the only gateway He could pass through without being summoned.

"I need to talk to her," I said.

"If you wish, if you wish," Mihmatini said, sniffing. "He's with me," she announced to the slave, who clearly disapproved but didn't dare contradict her. "You're hurt," she added, to me, as I stepped gingerly into the courtyard. "What in the Fifth World have you been doing?"

"Later. Please."

Mihmatini grimaced, but she asked no further questions as she led me into the reception room.

It was almost deserted, though bearing the traces of a long banquet: remnants of food in clay dishes, left on the reed mats; the smell of copal incense thick in the air, barely disguising that of spices and chocolate; and feather-fans, left propped against the dais. Only

Huei and a few slaves remained – and the poet: an old man with a cloak of red cotton, and a headdress of yellow feathers, who turned to us with a hostile gaze as we entered.

"And what is the meaning of this?" he asked, drawing himself to his full height.

Too tired to bother with politeness, I merely jerked a finger in the direction of the entrance-curtain. "Get out."

"I am Icnoyotl, the Flower Speaker of Coatlan. I can't be dismissed like a slave boy."

"Actually," I said, marching towards him, "I think you can. Get out. Or I'll throw you out."

A doubtful argument, given my wounds, and he knew it.

Huei's gaze moved from me to the poet, and she said, "Icnoyotl, can you leave us alone? I'll pay you tomorrow."

"It's not about payment," the poet grumbled as he wrapped his cloak around his shoulders. "A man has his pride, you know. Professional pride…"

Huei also gestured for the slaves to step out. They scattered into the night like a frightened flock of birds. I didn't care. Not any more.

"So," Huei said when the poet had left, escorted by Mihmatini. Neutemoc's wife sat, gracefully, on the dais, wearing a skirt embroidered with running deer, and a matching shirt. Around her wrists were bracelets of gold and jade: Neutemoc's wedding gift to her, a token of their love.

A lie. Had there ever been love, in their marriage? Had she ever been truthful with me?

"What do you want, Acatl?" Her voice was frosty. "I hope you have a good reason for offending Icnoyotl."

I was too tired to exchange pleasantries with her. "How could you have been such a fool, Huei?"

Her hand went to her throat. "I don't understand you."

"You understand me very well," I snapped. "You summoned that beast. You asked it to abduct Eleuia, and you thought you'd never be discovered."

"You're insane," she said, her eyes widening slightly.

But I wasn't deceived. She'd already proved that she was a good liar.

"I'm not insane," I said. "One thing nobody told you about beasts of shadows: they remember the first moments after their summoning. And their memories can be accessed."

Huei shook her head. "You're lying, Acatl."

Couldn't she see? The Duality curse her, couldn't she see? "I'm not here to arrest you," I all but screamed, heedless of the slaves, who were now clustering at the entrance. "This is your life we're talking about. Don't you know the penalty for breaching the boundary?"

"Acatl…"

How could people be so ignorant of the boundaries that I maintained, of the price for dealing with the underworld – as if all that mattered was capturing prisoners and offering their hearts to the Sun God?

"*Death*, Huei. That's the price: an obsidian shard embedded in your heart, and the Wind of Knives carrying away your soul. What were you thinking of? You just can't play around with the boundaries!" A cold feeling was starting to work its way down my spine, but I couldn't tell how much of it I was imagining. He couldn't already be at the underground cavern, could He?

She said nothing. She was watching me, her face expressionless; and she still hadn't moved from her dais.

"How could you have been such a fool?" I asked, the question I'd been holding in my mind finally released. "You had everything. Why endanger it all?"

She inclined her head, a gesture as slow and stately as an imperial wife's. "You're the one who doesn't understand, Acatl." Her eyes were harsh. "Neutemoc was the one who gave us all of this: the house, the jade and feathers–" Her hands moved, encompassed the rich frescoes on the walls, the silver and jade ornaments on the wicker chests. "And he would have thrown it away for a whore's open legs. He was unhappy for a few months, and he'd take some ephemeral comfort, never seeing the consequences? I couldn't let that happen. I couldn't let him go."

"You loved him," I said, shocked. The coldness was halfway down my spine now. "You'd have killed him?"

Her hands clenched in a spasmodic gesture. "He wasn't supposed to be there, the Storm Lord smite him! He was supposed to be coming home." And for the first time I heard the emotion she'd been hiding beneath her haughty mask: not fear or anger, but despair. And it hurt me to the core.

"And finding you reeking of magic?" Some part of me knew that I was wasting time; that the coldness was all the way down my spine, and already a faint lament echoed in my ears. But I couldn't help it. I thought I had understood her, that we had trusted each other, and everything had been a lie.

"He would never have known," Huei said. "And he would have come back to me in time. The children would have been safe."

"No," I said. You couldn't rebuild on a canker. You couldn't go forward with a lie, any more than you could force maize burnt by Mictlan's touch to grow again. But she wouldn't see that. I couldn't make her see.

"Acatl?" Mihmatini's puzzled voice. "Can I have an explanation?"

I turned, briefly. She'd pushed aside the slaves with an authority I hadn't known she possessed. Suddenly, I remembered the stakes; and that I was standing there, wasting time arguing with Huei. "It's not the time," I snapped, more violently than I'd intended to. And, to Huei: "You still don't understand. The Wind of Knives is coming for you. To kill you."

For the first time, Huei looked uncertain. "I don't–" she started.

"You must have known the penalty," I said. "Please tell me you knew it."

And when she turned to look at me, her eyes widening in panic, I knew that she hadn't been the mind behind all of this. Someone had used her, and discarded her like a broken clay toy, knowing that she would die, putting an end to embarrassing questions. "You did not," I said. "Who told you how to summon the beast, Huei?"

I could feel the Wind now: a pressure in the back of my mind. He was moving north along the Itzapalapan causeway, gathering shadows around Him like shrouds. He was coming rapidly, covering in a few minutes what had taken Teomitl and me half an hour of running.

"That's my own concern." Huei was moving away from the dais, trying to get away from me.

I shook my head. "Not any more. Not from the moment you breached the boundaries. Who was it, Huei?"

Her smile was bitter. "And if I tell you... what then, Acatl? Will you protect me from the Wind of Knives?"

"I can't," I whispered, feeling the growing hollow in my stomach. I had been a fool to return here, hoping for answers, hoping I could safeguard my brother's perfect family, the pinnacle of achievement I couldn't reach. "I–"

"No," Huei said. Her voice was sad, but she held herself with the bearing of an Imperial Wife. "You've never understood, Acatl. I gave everything to this marriage, and Neutemoc repaid nothing to me. One grows tired of a hundred slights, of the casual gestures of indifference. One grows tired of wondering when one's husband will finally abandon his own household."

Every one of her words was a knife wound in my gut. Neutemoc couldn't have been so stupid. He...

But I had seen how much he desired Eleuia.

"Huei," I whispered, but she looked at me, straight and tall, and she didn't answer.

Mihmatini had been watching us, growing more and more horrified with each word. "Acatl," she said. "You don't mean..."

When she was younger, on my rare holidays from the calmecac, I'd shared with her the tales of the priests, trying to impress her with all the beasts we'd have to fight, deluding myself I could play the warrior. She knew about the Wind of Knives, and she knew why He was coming.

"It doesn't concern you," I said.

Her eyebrows shot up. "I live in the same house, don't I?"

"Look–" I started, but didn't go further. The Wind of Knives was in our district now, floating over the canals – reaching Neutemoc's house, passing under the gate, shadows trailing after Him.

I didn't stop to think. "Get out!" I screamed at both Huei and Mihmatini, and I ran outside, to face the Wind of Knives.

In the courtyard, the torches' flames had died down, blown out by the Wind's presence. The slaves, too, had scattered, gone back into their quarters, no doubt. And I couldn't blame them. The Wind's approach would have been heralded by darkness and the growing cold; perhaps by a few ghosts, flitting around the courtyard. Enough to make any sane man run away.

I supposed that I didn't count as sane, in any sense of the word.

The Wind of Knives stood under the tallest pine tree of the garden: a tall, humanoid shape made of obsidian shards, glimmering in the moonlight. In my ears was the keening of the wind, bringing to me the lament of dead souls, and the sharp, sickening smell of decaying flesh. Wherever the Wind went, He brought Mictlan with Him.

I didn't go to Him; I stood before the entrance-curtain to the reception room, feeling the cold work its way into the marrow of my bones.

"Acatl," He said. His presence in my mind was strong: it would have driven the uninitiated to insanity. But I was used to it – if one ever got used to the pressure in one's mind, the sense of standing on the brink of a vast chasm. "I have come."

"I know," I said, bowing to Him.

He shifted. Obsidian shards glittered, sharp, cutting, hungering for human blood. "Then let Me pass."

"I cannot."

He made a sound which might have been laughter, although I had never seen Him amused. "You are High Priest for the Dead. You keep the balance."

"I know," I said, but still I didn't move from my place.

He asked, "Would you break that compact? It is a dangerous game you play."

"I'm not playing a game," I said, thinking of Huei, thinking of my brother's radiant face when he'd announced his marriage. "I'm not playing."

"No," the Wind of Knives said. He moved, to stand in front of me. His hand reached out, stopped inches from my chest. Every finger was made of slivers of obsidian, as pointed as the end of a knife. My chest ached at the mere thought of another wound. "It's not a game, Acatl."

"She is my brother's wife," I said, slowly, not knowing what else I could offer Him.

"Should that make a difference?" the Wind of Knives asked.

"I don't know," I said, and it was the truth. Ceyaxochitl had been wrong. I couldn't be in charge of this investigation. I couldn't watch as the underworld tore my brother's family apart; as it tore my own fragile illusions apart.

His hand rested on my chest, inches above the heart, just as the fingers of my good hand closed around the first of my obsidian knives. Power pulsed within me: the familiar emptiness of Mictlan, rising to fill my soul.

The Wind of Knives made that half-amused, half-angry sound again. "You'd fight Me?"

"She had reasons–" I started, knowing how thin was the ground I stood on, knowing that He could not be swayed.

"There are no reasons," the Wind of Knives said. His hand closed. I recoiled, but His fingers only touched my bandages, cutting them away with the precision of an army healer. The bandages fell in a swish of cloth. Cold air ran over the wounds on my chest: a sting that made me hiss.

"This is what comes of dealing with the beasts of Mictlan," the Wind of Knives said. "Think on it, Acatl."

"Yes," I said. "But I still need to understand–" I needed to know who had given Huei the tools for her summoning; and if Priestess Eleuia was still alive.

"There is nothing to understand," the Wind of Knives said. "A transgression was made. Justice must be dealt."

Though He had been human once – a long, long time ago, before He swore himself to Lord Death and became the Wind – He didn't think like us any more. An eternity of watching over the passage of souls and of dealing with transgressors had moulded His mind into something else. Pity, or even reason, was alien to Him.

"There are other lives at stake," I said, raising my good hand in the air, as if to ward Him off. "I need to know who she was working with."

He watched me, unmoving. Moonlight outlined the shape of His head: huge and pointed, more akin to that of a beast of shadows than that of a human. "I do not investigate," He said.

"But I do," I said, and groped for arguments that He could accept. "She wasn't the only transgressor. There are others still at large."

He was silent for a while. At last, He said, "I end all transgressions. She was the only one to open the gate."

"But what of those who gave her the magic?" I asked, sensing an opening I could wedge myself into. "Aren't they as guilty as she?"

"Guilt is irrelevant," the Wind of Knives said.

"So, if I gave people the means to summon a beast, you would never kill me? That doesn't seem just."

He looked at me, lowering His head in a shimmer of blades. "I am justice," He said. "But not, I think, your justice."

"I can't accept–" I started.

"Acatl." His voice stopped me. "Do not lie to Me."

"I'm not lying." I still stood in the entrance; and He still did not strike me down, although it was only a matter of time before He grew bored with me.

169

"You are protecting her," the Wind of Knives said, "because she is of your blood."

"She isn't of my blood," I said. But as I said it, I realised that all I had given Him, all my reasons for His not killing Huei, were indeed just convenient lies. If I dug deep enough, the real reason didn't have anything to do with the investigation: it was that I couldn't face the thought of Huei's death. It wasn't just. There could be no exceptions. But I could not let Him pass. I could not let Him kill Huei. It went beyond reason.

I stood as tall as I could; and I raised the knife that Mictlantecuhtli had blessed, feeling the power of the underworld seep into my flesh. "I cannot let you pass," I whispered.

He came, again, to stand in front of me. Once more the wind keened into my ears; once more, I heard an endless lament for the dead, echoing in my mind.

"This knife?" He said. He reached out, plucked it from my fingers, and snapped it in two. "You're not Mictlantecuhtli's agent, Acatl. You have scraps of His power, but not enough to stop Me. And it is as it should be."

Before I could break out of my shocked stupor, He'd reached out again and enfolded me into His embrace. The obsidian shards dug into my flesh, each a source of fiery pain that spread outwards. I gritted my teeth not to scream and bit my tongue, so hard that blood flowed into my mouth.

He lifted me upwards effortlessly, gaining speed as He did so. In a brief, panicked moment, as I spun under the pitiless gaze of the stars, I saw what He was going to do: throw me out of His way like a sack of useless refuse.

I tried to grope for a hold, anything I could use to slow Him down. But my good hand closed only on cold, cutting shards, which I couldn't hold. His hands opened, releasing me. I fell, the lament of Mictlan's souls rising in my ears as the ground got closer and closer.

I had time to think on how thoughtless I had been, seconds before the Wind's hands closed again, catching me a hand-span from the ground. Pain blossomed everywhere He touched me, in my left leg, in my left hand, rising to meld with that coming from my chest.

Almost gently, the Wind of Knives laid me on the ground. "You serve well. But do not presume to interfere," He said, even as He walked away into the house.

I lay on the ground, amidst the discarded bandages. The smell of pulque rose to fill my nostrils. I struggled to get up. Blood ran down my chest: the beast's wounds had re-opened. Teomitl would be angry, I thought, with a short, wry laugh. But even that slight contraction of my abdominal muscles hurt. Every movement I made was constrained by pain. After one or two attempts, I gave up, and fell back onto the ground. I lay there, feeling pain rise within me like the steady beat of drums at the sacrifices.

He was in the house now, killing Huei. Things were as they should be, as He had said. I thought of Neutemoc in his cage – and of Huei's proud, bitter face as she told me about her family's future – and a different pain took hold in my chest.

What a fool I had been. The underworld's justice could not be swayed, or even delayed. In my mind, the familiar pressure of the Wind of Knives receded: giving way before the pain, I thought, dizzily.

"Acatl?" A familiar voice: my sister's, I realised. My head turned towards her, instinctively. Pain shot up my neck, but it was almost muted compared to the pain in my chest.

All I could see of Mihmatini were her sandals, and then her deer-embroidered skirt, as she knelt on the ground. "You're hurt."

"Tell me something else," I whispered.

She snorted. "Men! Why must you always be heroes?"

"I didn't–" My reasons were too much work to articulate.

"It looks like you did try," she said, then: "Can you bring some maguey sap?" I presumed she was speaking to a slave.

"What happened?" I asked. "The Wind–"

"He's gone, Acatl."

Gone? Then that was the real reason why the pressure in my mind had lessened.

Mihmatini's fingers ran over my chest, slowly, with the efficiency of a healer: gestures she'd probably learnt in school. For all that, I still couldn't help sucking in my breath as she probed the beast's claw-marks.

"Sorry," she said. "I'll go more carefully. Where in the Fifth World did you get those?"

"The beast of shadows," I said, curtly. "Huei."

"She's gone, too," Mihmatini said. "While you were outside temporising with the Wind, she left by the back door. The Wind is chasing her. She's slightly ahead of him; but she cast some kind of spell before leaving. It certainly seemed to slow Him down." She sounded halfway between horror and admiration. Her hands held me, effortlessly, as I struggled to rise. "Don't be a fool. You're leaking blood all over the courtyard. You won't go far."

"I need to–"

"You need some bandages, and rest." She sighed. "Knowing you, I'll settle for the bandages. Don't worry. We'll get you healed." More feet in my field of view: naked this time, with calluses. Slaves.

"Here," Mihmatini said.

That was all the advance warning I got: for the second time this night, maguey sap was poured onto my

172

wounds, and the pain that spread from the contact points was almost worse than before. Tears filled my eyes by the time they were finished applying the lotion.

"Here," Mihmatini said at last, and hands lifted me, propped me upright. "Don't move."

I wasn't planning on that.

She was silent as the slaves dressed my wounds and splinted my arm again: Teomitl's makeshift device had got broken in my aborted fall.

When they were finished, the slaves left. I was feeling more and more like a funeral bundle: bandages tightened around my whole chest, and spread downwards on my left leg. But at least I could move – not much, the bandages constrained me tightly – and I was ready to leave. Mihmatini helped me to my feet.

"Where did Huei go?" I asked. I realised I didn't need to ask the question. I closed my eyes, and felt, beyond the pain that filled my body, the familiar pressure of the Wind's mind. He was once again moving through the streets of the Moyotlan district, though He appeared bewildered for some reason. Huei's spell, surely. What had she cast? How had she known all that magic? "She's still in Moyotlan. He hasn't caught her."

Mihmatini squeezed my hand, briefly, and withdrew. "There's a boat outside in the canal. Oyohuaca will row for you. She's a competent girl," she said. "Go."

"I don't need–" I started, stubbornly.

Mihmatini shook her head, more amused than angry. "Help? Can't you accept, for once in your life, that you can't do it on your own?"

A groundless accusation: I had taken Teomitl's help. And then I thought, uneasily, of the way I'd summarily sent him home, getting rid of him before the climax.

Mihmatini watched me, silent – not judging, she'd never judged me. For her, I'd always be the brother who helped her climb trees, and brought her treats from the festivals. No, not quite; for the priestesses at the calmecac had changed her, moulded her into this coolly competent girl whom I hardly recognised.

"I'll take the boat," I said, finally.

Her face relaxed, a minute sag of her skin that made her less alien. "Go," she said.

"With not even a warning?" I asked.

"You know them all, Acatl. And you'll still ignore them. Go."

But, as I left the garden, she still called after me, "Try to come back standing on your feet, will you?"

Feeling even more broken than before, I limped out, bent on finding the Wind before he found Huei.

Given my present state, it was a hopeless undertaking, but I had to try. For Huei's sake, and also for my own.

# ELEVEN
## *Servant of the Gods*

In the canal before Neutemoc's house, Oyohuaca, a slave-girl clad in a rough maguey-fibre shift, was waiting for me in a long, pointed reed boat. I climbed in, wincing as my bandages shifted.

"Where to?" Oyohuaca asked, straightening up the lantern at the boat's bow.

I closed my eyes, feeling for the Wind's presence. He was a few streets away from us. He had slowed down, oddly enough, and was going in a slow, wide circle towards the south-western edge of the Moyotlan district.

"Left," I said.

She rowed in silence, with the easy mastery of one who had lived all her life at the water's edge. With each gesture, she whispered the same words, over and over like a litany for the dead. It took me a while to realise that the words were those of a prayer asking for the blessing of Tlaloc, the Storm Lord, God of Rain, and of His wife Chalchiutlicue, the Jade Skirt, Goddess of Lakes and Streams.

*"O Lord, Our Lord,*
*The people, the subjects – the led, the guided, the governed,*

*Their flesh and bones are stricken with want and privation*
*They are worn, spent and in torment—"*

There was something eerie about the sound of Oyohuaca's voice, floating over the canals in counterpoint to the splash of her oars. As we moved into deserted canal after deserted canal, it seemed to call up the mist, to trail after us. And something else trailed too, something dark and quiet that swam after the boat, biding its time.

Under the splash of the oars – in, out of the water, in, out – was its song: a quiet, hypnotic air that wove itself within my mind, melding with Oyohuaca's prayers until I no longer knew what belonged to whom.

*"In Tlalocan, the verdant house,*
*The Blessed Land of the Drowned*
*The dead men play at balls, they cast the reeds*
*Go forth, go forth to the place of many clouds*
*To where the thick mists mark the Blessed Land*
*The verdant house, the house of Tlaloc and Chalchiutlicue"*

For too long, it had bided its time at night, quieting its hunger with fish, with newts, with algae: the sustenance of the poor, the abandoned. But now it smelled blood: a living heart, so tantalisingly close. Soon, it would feast until satiation…

*"Let the people be blessed with fullness and abundance*
*Let them behold, let them enjoy the jade and the turquoise*
*– the precious vegetation*
*The flesh of Your servants, the Providers, the Gods of Rain*
*Let the plants and animals be blessed with fullness and abundance—"*

The song stopped; the oars fell against the boat's frame with a dull sound that resonated in my bones. "Acatl-tzin," Oyohuaca said, urgently.

With some difficulty, I tore myself from my reverie. "What?"

"Don't," Oyohuaca said. The slave-girl sounded frightened.

"I don't understand." The Wind was moving again, picking up speed, straight towards the edge of Tenochtitlan.

"An *ahuizotl*," I said, aloud. A hundred memories came welling up from my childhood. The water-beasts were Chalchiutlicue's creatures; they lived in the depths of Lake Texcoco, and would drag a man to the bottom, feasting on his eyes and fingernails.

Oyohuaca's face in the moonlight was drained of all colours. "Don't listen to its song."

"I didn't know they sang."

Oyohuaca shook her head. "They don't. Not unless they truly want you. Don't listen," she said, picking up her oars again.

I thought of Huei's spell, which had so bewildered the Wind. It certainly was possible she'd summoned the beast to cover her tracks, in case some more mundane agency attempted to follow her.

How in the Fifth World had she become proficient enough to know all of this?

Oyohuaca and I followed the Wind's trail across the canals of Moyotlan. As the night became older, the houses had become silent and dark, their thatch-roofs wavering in the light of the torch; and the only sounds that came to us were the distant shell-blasts from the Sacred Precinct.

Oyohuaca kept singing her hymn, but now I could discern its urgency: it was her only protection against the ahuizotl. It didn't cover its song, though. That kept

177

insinuating itself in my mind, whispering promises of happiness below the water – easy, it would be so easy to lean over the edge of the boat, lose myself in the Blessed Land of the Drowned...

I came to with a snap, sharply aware of how close I'd come to yielding. The smell of churned mud – and a faint, faint one of rotten flesh – filled my nostrils.

Don't listen, Oyohuaca had said. They don't sing. Not unless they truly want you.

The ahuizotls, like any magical creatures, would be drawn to power: to my own magic, embedded within the obsidian knives in my belt.

Focus. I needed to focus. I closed my eyes and thought of the Wind of Knives, of the dry emptiness of Mictlan, and how it would fill my skin and bones.

The song receded, fading to an insinuating whisper.

I opened my eyes. We were in one of the last canals in the district of Moyotlan. Beyond the houses on the right lay the open expanse of Lake Texcoco. There was no place to hide. Water wouldn't stop the Wind of Knives. Where in the Fifth World had Huei gone?

"Turn right," I told Oyohuaca.

We squeezed through a small canal between darkened houses, and emerged from the maze of Tenochtitlan's waterways onto open water. On the left was the Tlacopan causeway, its broad stone path snaking into the distance; on the right were more Floating Gardens: rows of fields bearing the crops that fed the city.

"And now?" Oyohuaca asked.

The Wind of Knives wasn't far away. No, not far at all. On the nearby bank was the familiar glimmer of obsidian. He wasn't moving. Was He waiting for something? I couldn't see Huei anywhere.

I pointed to the bank. "Leave me here," I said.

The slave Oyohuaca didn't look reassured. In fact, as soon as I'd managed to disembark, she rowed away from the bank, and waited in the midst of the water, away from us.

The Wind of Knives didn't move. Mud squelched over my sandalled feet as I climbed the muddy rise – as cold, I imagined, as the touch of the ahuizotl would have been on my skin.

"Acatl," the Wind of Knives said when I came near him.

I tensed, one hand closing on the hilt of an obsidian knife.

He did not move. He watched something below, in the Floating Gardens: a flickering light on one of the islands. "No need," He said.

"You–" I started.

"She is out of my reach."

"I don't understand–"

"It is a simple thing," He said, without irony.

"You are justice," I said, slowly, not yet daring to believe that Huei was safe. "You cannot be swayed, or set aside."

"Not by you," the Wind of Knives said. "But there are higher powers than I. Goodbye, Acatl. We shall meet again." He was fading even as He spoke, the obsidian shards receding into the darkness until shadows extinguished their polished reflections.

"Wait!" I said. "You haven't told me–" He hadn't told me anything. But He was gone, or perhaps would not answer to me.

I could summon him again, but I didn't have any of the proper offerings at hand. It would take time: more time than walking down the rise, towards the light that He had been watching.

I signalled to the boat again. After a while, the slave Oyohuaca rowed back. No doubt she had ascertained that the Wind of Knives was truly gone before she would approach again. She was a cautious girl.

"Can you row me to that Floating Garden?" I asked.

Oyohuaca spoke as I painstakingly climbed into the boat. "It's not a Floating Garden," she said.

But... "Then what is it?"

"A temple," Oyohuaca said, picking up her oars again. "To Chalchiutlicue, Our Lady of Lakes and Streams. It's where they host the sacrifices for Her festivals."

The flickering light turned out to be a torch, held by a priestess who kept watch over the temple complex.

It was a simple affair: a long building of adobe, firmly set onto a terrace of stone. Part of it appeared to be a calmecac for hosting the priestesses and the students; and another part of it – the part that hummed with a coiled power I could feel – had to be the shrine to the goddess.

There are higher powers than I, the Wind of Knives had said. It must have taken quick thinking on Huei's part to see that here, under the gaze of the goddess, was a place the Wind couldn't enter, and to reach it in time.

The priestess of Chalchiutlicue raised the torch when I approached. Her severe gaze swept up and down, taking in the whole of who I was. For the second time that night, I found myself wishing I had dressed better. Neutemoc's slaves and Mihmatini had done their best, but maguey-soaked bandages were nothing like the full regalia of a High Priest.

"Yes?" the priestess asked.

"I'm looking for my brother's wife," I said.

Her face shut, as if a veil had been drawn across it. "At this time of the night, the temple is closed to visitors."

"I don't think you understand," I said, slowly, although I suspected she did. "She isn't a student. She came here, about half an hour ago at most."

Her eyes didn't move. "No one came."

A lie. But I wouldn't disconcert her that easily.

"I am Acatl, High Priest for the Dead, and I speak for my temple and my clergy. Do you think it wise to stand against me?" I closed my good hand on the strongest obsidian knife, letting the emptiness of Mictlan well up to fill me.

Her face remained expressionless, though she had to see the power coursing to me. "I will talk to the Fire Priest. Wait here."

I did so. A breeze had risen over the lake, cold on my exposed skin. The mist would not dissipate. Was it just my fancy, or was something swimming in the water, near the bottom of the rise?

Two lights surfaced, briefly: yellow eyes, I realised with a shock. They were watching me with undisguised malice. The ahuizotl. It hadn't been there while Teomitl and I were on the lake, although Teomitl's warding magic might have kept it away. But it was the first time a water-beast had ever swum after me. Why wouldn't it go away?

I was wounded, smelling of blood, and reeking of the underworld magic I had been consorting with all night. To any magical creature, I would be a beacon.

But there was still something about it that made me uneasy. The ahuizotls belonged to Chalchiutlicue, and surely it was more than a coincidence that Huei had summoned them, and then found refuge in a temple to the goddess?

"Acatl-tzin," someone said.

Startled, I turned around. The priestess had come back with a man: a priest of far higher rank, judging by

181

his diadem of heron feathers and the drops of melted rubber that darkened his face.

"I am Eliztac, Fire Priest of this modest temple. I'm told that you seek someone." He exuded the same coiled power as the walls of his temple: a rippling light that seemed to be an extension of the starlight over the lake.

"My brother's wife, Huei," I said, giving him a brief description. Although, by the gleam in his eyes, he had no need of it.

"I see," Eliztac said, but ventured no comment.

"Understand this," I said, exasperated by yet another delay – by the knowledge that Huei was alive, so close to me – and yet out of my reach. "I know she came here, and I know she hasn't left. We can talk all night, or you can save some time and admit to having seen her."

Eliztac pursed his lips, thoughtfully.

"She has transgressed against Mictlan," I added, for good measure.

His gaze was disturbingly shrewd. "But is no longer, I think, your rightful prey."

"Why would you prevent me from entering?" I asked. I tightened my grip on the obsidian knife. The emptiness rising in my chest was almost comforting, a shield against all I couldn't face.

He sighed. "You're right. It's late. Let's not dance around each other like warriors on the gladiator stone. The person you want did come here – but you cannot see her."

"I still don't see–"

Eliztac raised a hand. "She has given herself to the goddess."

There could only be one meaning for this. But I still had to ask, to be sure. I might have misunderstood. "As a sacrifice?"

Eliztac nodded. "She is Chalchiutlicue's now. She's removed herself from the Fifth World. Neither you nor anyone else has a claim on her."

"When?" I asked plainly.

"When the proper stars are aligned and the proper omens have happened," Eliztac said. "It will take time. One, two years? Only the goddess knows."

One, two years. Huei still had time. But, as she learnt the dance, and the proper rituals for the sacrifice, she would never forget what was to come: the knowledge of her death would mingle with every moment she spent in the temple.

The Southern Hummingbird cut her down! How could she…? But, of course, once she had summoned the beast of shadows, she wouldn't have had a choice, not any more.

"I have to speak to her," I said.

Eliztac shook his head, forcefully. The heron feathers swayed to and fro, like white flags in the darkness. "She no longer belongs in this world."

"There are some things I need to know…"

"She fled from you," Eliztac said. "What makes you think she would talk to you?"

I said, "She's still family." In spite of everything, she was still the gangly girl my brother had brought home, all those years ago: the one who'd smile and shake her head whenever Neutemoc and I tried to make her take sides. The one who would die, drowned by the priests in order to bring the Jade Skirt's favour to the Empire.

Eliztac looked away from me, for a moment. "If you were her husband, it would be a different matter. But as it is, I can't allow it."

"Please," I said.

But he shook his head. "Forget her, Acatl-tzin. The goddess will take her as Her own, and lead her into the Blessed Land of the Drowned."

It was, I supposed, preferable to what would happen to Huei if the Wind of Knives took her. Lord Death dealt harshly with those who sought to use His powers.

I could have begged and pleaded with Eliztac, but it would only have demeaned me. He had made his decision, and I would gain nothing by attempting to make him go back on it.

Entering the temple without his permission was tantamount to suicide: in my present state, I didn't have the power to hide myself from Chalchiutlicue's magic, and I didn't want to know the fate the temple reserved to trespassers.

"Thank you," I said, and walked back to Oyohuaca's boat.

The ahuizotl watched me from the water, a dark, lean shape whispering its seducing song. It followed us all the way home.

Neutemoc's house was bathed in the grey light before dawn; and the slaves were already getting up to grind the maize flour. I found my sister, Mihmatini, in the reception room, playing patolli with one of the slaves. She was sitting on a reed mat, listlessly throwing the white bean dice on the board and picking them up again, but clearly making no effort to focus on the moves of her pebbles.

Mihmatini looked up when I entered. "Acatl!" Her gaze moved beyond me, focusing on Oyohuaca, who was waiting respectfully by the entrance.

"You didn't find her then," she said. Her disappointment was palpable.

I wondered what I could tell her. But if I started lying to my own sister, I had fallen very low indeed. "She's in Chalchiutlicue's temple."

Mihmatini frowned. She gestured for the slave to get out. He picked up the patolli board, dice and pebbles as he exited. "And you can't arrest her?" she asked.

I saw the instant the inescapable conclusion dawned in her mind. Her face, for a bare moment, froze into an expressionless mask. "Acatl," she whispered. "Please tell me she didn't–"

I couldn't lie to her. "I'm sorry. It was the only way she'd be safe."

"Safe for a month or so, until they drown her?"

I sat on the mat where her patolli partner had been, facing her. "The priests said a year or two. But yes. They'll drown her in the lake." I tried to tell it as simply, as emotionlessly as I could, but I couldn't quite hide the turmoil inside me. In just a handful of days, my comfortable world had shattered. But I, at least, was alive: not in a cage like Neutemoc, not awaiting death like Huei. "They won't let me see her," I said.

Mihmatini closed her eyes and bent her head backwards, in a gesture eerily reminiscent of Father when I'd displeased him. "I don't understand why she summoned the beast," she said.

"Do you think I do?"

She snorted. "You're the investigator."

"A poor kind of investigator," I said. "It seems I can't even get hold of my suspects."

Mihmatini said nothing for a while. Her eyes were on the empty place between both our mats, and her thoughts obviously further away. Finally, she said, "What about Neutemoc?"

What about him indeed. I'd been pondering the matter on the way home, and had some ideas, but nothing definite. "The judges will hear him today. Huei would have proved his innocence," I said.

"Chalchiutlicue's temple won't even let Imperial Investigators in?" Mihmatini asked. But she knew, as I did, that the investigators could drag the priests and priestesses out and do with them as they pleased, but that someone destined for sacrifice had already removed themselves from the flow of our lives.

I asked her, carefully, "Will you bear witness for me?"

"For Neutemoc?" she asked.

"He's in an Imperial Audience, and I need evidence to get him freed."

"I'm his sister," she pointed out. "They won't believe me."

"The slaves will support you," I said.

"A slave's testimony–"

"Is receivable before the courts, unless the rules have changed." Any man could become a slave; any one could fall so low they had no choice but to sell their freedom.

Mihmatini puffed her cheeks, thoughtfully. "But the rules have changed, haven't they? No one gets so quickly moved to an Imperial Audience."

"There are complications," I admitted. "Political matters."

Mihmatini snorted. "Politics. That alone makes me glad I'm a woman."

"Women take part in politics too," I said, thinking of Eleuia.

"Less often," Mihmatini said. "Anyway." She ran a hand on her jade necklace. "I'll say what needs to be said, but I don't think it's going to be enough."

I bit my lip, thoughtfully. "Huei received two men, two days ago, in the afternoon. Can you ask the slaves if they remember them?"

Mihmatini shrugged. "I can try. But I think they were all intelligent enough to make sure they wouldn't be witnessed."

"Maybe." It was a risk we'd have to take.

"Have you found the priestess?" Mihmatini asked.

"No," I said. I should have thought of sending to Ixtli, letting him try to find a trail from the Floating Garden. Duality curse me, I'd been too obsessed with what I'd learnt about Huei to even think of using Teomitl as a messenger.

It was too late now. I'd stop at the Duality House on my way to the temple, to see what could be done. "But I don't think she's alive any more," I said to Mihmatini.

"Then you'll never find her," Mihmatini said. "Few things are as anonymous as corpses."

She'd changed. She spoke like an adult, sure of herself. And yet her face was still that of the baby sister whose first steps I'd watched. It was unsettling. Had time passed so quickly, leaving me with nothing but my sterile priest's calling as my own?

"I know," I said, quietly, unwilling to delve deeper into the subject. "But at this moment, all I need to prove is that Neutemoc didn't summon that beast of shadows. We'll see about the rest later." Such as explaining to Neutemoc what his wife had done.

"Very well," Mihmatini said. "I'll come tomorrow. At your temple?"

"Tomorrow, at midday," I said.

She nodded. "You could stay here to get some sleep, you know. You're in no state to traipse through the streets."

I heard what she wasn't telling me: that the house without either Neutemoc or Huei would be huge, filled with slaves who barely knew Mihmatini. I wished I could comfort her; but I had to go back to my temple and gather all I could to get Neutemoc freed.

"I can't," I said. "Not tonight."

Tomorrow… tomorrow, if things went well and the High Priest of Tlaloc didn't have his way, Neutemoc would be home. He'd take care of her: she was blameless in the whole matter.

Mihmatini shook her head. "You're not walking home in this state. I'll get Oyohuaca to row you back to the Sacred Precinct."

I would have protested, but in truth I felt too tired for that. I rose, now used to the sharp pain that accompanied every one of my movements, and bade her goodnight. "See you tomorrow then."

"You fool," she said as I limped into the courtyard. But her voice was more amused than angry. "Give those wounds a chance to heal."

I did not answer, and left Neutemoc's house without giving her further incentive to tease me.

Oyohuaca rowed me back to the Sacred Precinct in silence and left me by the western docks. Flotillas of reed boats, each bearing the insignia of the temple to which they belonged, bobbed in the darkness. Somewhere at the back would be the large ceremonial barge reserved for the High Priest for the Dead, its prow painted the colour of bone, its oars carved with owls and spiders.

From the docks, it was but a short walk to the Duality House; but this left me so exhausted I was thankful to Mihmatini for insisting I take a boat back to the Sacred Precinct.

The Duality House was still bustling at this hour of the night, and Ixtli still wasn't sleeping. Did he ever sleep? He listened to my account, cocking his head from time to time. "Very well," he said when I was done. "I'll take some men and go to the Floating Garden. But–"

"I know," I said. The trail was old by now, and it was mundane, not magical. Whoever had come for Eleuia – whoever had instigated the whole affair –

had had the intelligence never to handle magic themselves. Even if they did find a trail, I wouldn't have results by the next afternoon. "Do what you can," I said.

I was about to leave the house when I saw a familiar figure ahead of me: Yaotl, Ceyaxochitl's messenger. He was striding ahead, not looking at me; but he did turn back when I called his name.

"Acatl," he said. "What a surprise. How goes your investigation?"

"As well as I can be," I said, tartly. "Where are you off to so fast?"

Yaotl shook his head, wryly amused. "To an interesting place, no doubt."

Huitzilpochtli blind him. He was as unhelpful as ever. "Let me guess," I said, more angrily than I'd intended. "The Imperial Palace."

His face grew thoughtful. "I might. But it doesn't concern you, does it?"

"It might," I said. "I'm planning to attend an Imperial Audience tomorrow."

"For your investigation?" Yaotl looked at me for a moment. Finally, he laid a hand on my shoulder, in a mock-brotherly gesture that made me uncomfortable. "I don't think there will be one."

My heart sank. "The Emperor is that ill?"

"I can't tell you more. But don't expect the Audience."

"What happens to the cases he was reviewing?" I asked, my heart sinking.

Yaotl shrugged. "Justice still has to move forward, doesn't it? I assume the High Priests will take care of them."

The High Priests. The twin powers at the head of the Empire's religious structure. The High Priest of Huitzilpochtli was theoretically the most important

189

one; but Ocelocueitl was an old man, tired by decades of overseeing the worship of the God of War.

Which left the other one: Acamapichtli, High Priest of Tlaloc: the same man who had been in such a hurry to have Neutemoc convicted.

## TWELVE

# The Imperial Audience

I returned to my house, lay down on my reed-mat, and fell asleep almost immediately.

My sleep was short, and disturbed: in my dreams, I stood in the boat of reeds with deep cuts in my arms and chest. Behind me was the dark shape of the ahuizotl – and I rowed and rowed, despite the pain that every gesture aroused in me. I had only to reach the end of the canal; to reach the temple of Chalchi-utlicue, where Huei was waiting for me, and everything would be made right.

But, no matter how hard I rowed, the boat never moved; and the yellow eyes of the ahuizotl broke the surface of the water; and it spoke, and its voice was that of the Wind of Knives.

*There are higher powers, Acatl. Fool.*

I woke up with a start. Outside, the sun had just reached its zenith. It hung, swollen, just over my courtyard. I felt as if I hadn't slept at all. Not the best state of mind to enter an Imperial Audience.

I covered myself in a clean cloak, trying to ignore the insistent pain from my wounds, and went into my courtyard. It was a modest affair, a patch of marigolds,

191

a pine tree and a small, covered well: nothing like Xochiquetzal's house, or even Neutemoc's. I sat cross-legged in the dirt before the well, thinking of what Yaotl had told me.

No Imperial Audience. That must mean that the Revered Speaker must be hovering at Mictlan's gates. The political infighting would now start in earnest. That was my only chance: that the High Priest of Tlaloc would be too busy plotting against his peers to worry overmuch about Neutemoc's fate.

I doubted it would be that easy.

I went back to my temple. In the courtyard, two priests were busy sweeping the ground, preparing for the afternoon's offerings; a further group were in one of the worship-rooms, in vigil for a dead woman.

I went into the shrine, where I dressed in my full regalia: the ivory skull-mask askew on my forehead, and the cloak of rich cotton, embroidered with owls, carefully tied around my shoulders.

Then I went down again, and settled into one of the furthest rooms: the same one where I'd given life to the jade heart, an eternity ago. I sat on the ground with maguey paper spread across my knees, dangling Eleuia's blackened jade pendant in front of my face.

What did I have?

Evidence that underworld magic had been behind all of this, and that someone as yet unidentified had summoned the nahual magic to cover Huei's tracks.

Mihmatini's testimony, as well as those of the slaves, would establish that the Wind of Knives had come for Huei, marking her as the summoner of the beast. If I was lucky, Mihmatini would also have a description of the two men who had come to see Huei in the afternoon.

Best not to rely on luck. Seven Serpent hadn't seemed to be on my side lately.

"Acatl-tzin?" Ichtaca's voice asked.

Startled, I raised my eyes. Ichtaca was standing in the doorway, lit by the midday sun. "Yes?" I asked. "I'm busy."

His gaze held mine, inscrutable. "So I see."

As usual, he made me feel like a child caught sneaking out of the house. "Yes," I said, testily. "Now if you don't mind, I have an audience to prepare for."

I'd expected him to go away; but he didn't move. "The Imperial Audience?"

"How did you know?"

He shrugged. "Rumours. Your brother was under question yesterday and the day before."

"Yes," I said, irritated. "And I intend to make sure he doesn't endure another day of this." Although the High Priest would want to do the exact opposite.

Ichtaca shrugged again, but said nothing.

"Acatl-tzin?" the offering priest, Palli, asked from behind Ichtaca. "Your sister is here."

I got up, wrapping the string of Eleuia's jade pendant around my wrist, and went out, bypassing Ichtaca without a word.

In the courtyard, Mihmatini was waiting for me, along with the burly slave who had stood guard at the gate when I'd arrived last night.

"This is Quechomitl," Mihmatini said.

He and I looked at each other, warily. This time, I was well-dressed. But from his stiff stance, Quechomitl hadn't forgotten the drunkard he'd almost thrown out on the previous evening.

"He saw the men you wanted," Mihmatini said. "But they covered their heads with the hood of their cloaks."

"Hooded cloaks?" I asked. Those were rare; but, as Mihmatini had said, it made sense that the men would cover their tracks. I asked Quechomitl, "What did they look like?"

Ichtaca was still in the courtyard, his rotund face thoughtful – battling with some decision, I could tell, but I didn't know which one.

The slave, Quechomitl, shrugged. "Men in their prime," he said. "Strong ones."

"You're sure they were men?" That eliminated Priestess Zollin, but not the Jaguar Knight, Mahuizoh.

Quechomitl nodded, obviously annoyed at my lack of trust. Well, it was mutual.

"There are complications," I said to Mihmatini, as we walked towards the temple exit, Ichtaca still trailing behind us. "The Emperor won't attend the audience."

"Then who will?"

"The High Priests," I said, grimly. "One of whom will be busy trying to condemn Neutemoc."

"Great," Mihmatini said. "Neutemoc always did have a talent for making enemies. So what do you plan on doing?"

"I think you're mistaken," a voice said, behind me. Ichtaca.

Surprised, I turned to face him. "What are you talking about?"

"The Imperial Audience," Ichtaca said, shaking his head. He was angry, I realised, though I didn't know why. "If the Emperor is unable to take his responsibilities, it's not the High Priests who will replace him."

"I was told–"

"Whoever told you was either lying or misinformed," Ichtaca said.

I didn't judge it pertinent to mention Yaotl's name. The two of them had long been locked in a battle of wills – possibly because Yaotl was a foreigner, and because Ichtaca was unwilling to admit that anything good could come from outside the Mexica Empire.

"Someone has to take charge of the hearings," I said.

Ichtaca nodded. "Someone will. The Master of the House of Darts, Tizoc-tzin."

The Revered Speaker's brother, and also the heir-apparent: the one who had the strongest chance of being elected to head the Mexica Empire, if the Revered Speaker died.

"Tizoc-tzin has his moods," Ichtaca went on. "But he doesn't like the clergy, and I don't think he'll want to favour any of the High Priests."

"How do you know?" I asked. I didn't want to point out the corollary to his portrayal of Tizoc-tzin: a man who didn't like the clergy would have no reason to favour any High Priest over any other – not even the High Priest for the Dead over the High Priest of Tlaloc. Our arguments would have to be very compelling.

Ichtaca smiled, grimly amused. "I attend court, most days."

"Why?"

"Because this temple couldn't survive without Imperial patronage."

The reproach in his tone was audible. "Because I don't attend, you mean?"

He shrugged. "Someone has to," he said. "If you won't, then I will."

But he was still reproaching me. "You're a better politician than me," I said, finally, knowing it was true. I couldn't manoeuvre through the maze of the Imperial Court. I neither had the capacities nor the heart to do so. If I did go to court, the Imperial patronage for our temple would soon wither. Ichtaca said nothing.

"We'll discuss this later," I said.

"As you wish." He bowed, though his anger was still palpable. "But I thought you might want the warning."

It was a welcome one, and I couldn't resent him for it, though I had the feeling some old grievance had just been laid out in the open. I would have to deal with Ichtaca at some point. "Yes," I said. "Thank you."

He bowed, low. "Pleased to have been of service."

"What was that all about?" Mihmatini asked, as we exited the temple.

"I don't know," I said, truthfully. "Come on. Let's go."

The crowd in the Sacred Precinct was dense: we had to fight our way past pilgrims and priests. The slave Quechomitl opened a path through the crowd for my sister with his arms, but let it close before I could follow. Clearly, he did not like me.

In the Imperial Palace, I headed straight for the military court, and asked for Magistrate Pinahui-tzin.

The clerk snorted in amusement. "He's taking a pause in the garden."

Pinahui-tzin was sitting in the garden of the military court, watching the water rise and fall out of a conch-shaped fountain. At the back of the garden was an aviary: huge wicker cages held parrots, eagles, and quetzal birds, their emerald feathers shimmering in the sunlight.

"Ah. The young priest," Pinahui-tzin said, when we arrived. "I was waiting for you." He rose, leaning on his cane, and turned to greet us.

"Those would be your witnesses?" he asked, looking at Mihmatini and Quechomitl.

I nodded. "I have evidence of someone else's guilt."

"Someone you should have arrested," Pinahui-tzin said.

Why was everybody reproaching me for the same reason? "I can't. She's given her life to the gods."

Pinahui-tzin made no commentary. "Let me hear the evidence," he said. "As quickly as you can. Your brother is already inside the Courts."

I had thought it might be the case: that High Priest Acamapichtli wouldn't want to wait to convict Neutemoc.

When I was finished, Pinahui-tzin pursed his lips. "Scant," he said. "Scant. But it will have to do, young man." He scrutinised me in silence. His eyebrows went up, in what I hoped was a show of appreciation. "Come."

The last time I'd tried to find the Imperial Audience, I had roamed the palace, asking the people I met the way. Pinahui-tzin, on the other hand, knew where he was going. His cane tapped regularly against the stone floor, as we walked through corridors filled with officials in feather regalia, towards the inside of the palace. Every courtyard we crossed was a marvel: ornate fountains, fabulous plants from cacao trees to vanilla orchids, and animals ranging from caged jaguars to the web-footed capybaras. All the wonders of the steamy south, enclosed in the sandstone mass of the palace like a stone set within an exquisite piece of jewellery.

Finally, we reached the gates of the Imperial Courts. No guards waited on either side of the entrance-curtain. But this was only the antechamber: the closed audiences would be taking place deeper within the Courts.

Inside was a wide, airy room, where clerks hurried from dais to dais, carrying piles of codices from magistrate to magistrate. One of the courts was hearing two prisoners, but the rest were still reviewing evidence: the magistrates on the dais thoughtfully tapping their writing-reeds against the papers they were holding, or making annotations in the margins.

Pinahui-tzin walked straight to the end of the room, where a curtain of turquoise cotton marked the start of the area reserved to the Emperor's close staff. The curtain was closed, and two guards stood on either side. But they let us through when Pinahui-tzin marched on them with his cane pointed like a sword at the level of the lead guard's chest. There was, nonetheless, a moment of hesitation on their part – and that was how I knew that Pinahui-tzin's influence stopped at getting us into the Imperial Audience.

Behind the curtain was a small antechamber where we divested ourselves of our sandals, for one went barefoot in the presence of the Revered Speaker, or of his substitute. A sizeable pile of sandals – mostly gilded, luxurious affairs – indicated we weren't the only ones to attend.

Then I pulled open the next turquoise curtain in a crystalline tinkle of bells, and we entered the heart of the Imperial Courts.

The room was much smaller than the first one, but it was crammed full of people. Underlying the hubbub were sounds from the Imperial Gardens, which lay on the far side: quetzal birds calling to each other, the grunt of capybaras digging into the earth. The air smelled of copal incense and honey.

In the centre of the room stood Neutemoc, his shoulders sagging, deep circles under his eyes. Two Imperial guards flanked him, though there was no need: he would never seek to escape.

On the dais facing him were three people, easily recognisable. On the left was the old High Priest of Huitzilpochtli, Ocelocueitl, wearing a luxurious feathered headdress, and with huge plumes hanging from his belt, spreading like the wings of a hummingbird. On the right, Acamapichtli, High Priest of Tlaloc, with a crown of heron feathers, the area around his eyes blackened to give an unsettling impression. And, in the centre, sat Tizoc-tzin, Master of the House of Darts, brother of Revered Speaker Axayacatl-tzin: a man in his mid-twenties, dressed soberly in a tunic of deep blue, and with a look of utter boredom on his sallow face.

The rest of the crowd, standing on the edges of the room, was mostly noblemen, no doubt of the Revered Speaker's close family: a dazzling array of vibrantly-coloured cloaks, and of painted faces under feather-headdresses, saturated with the magic of protective spells.

Tizoc-tzin's gaze turned to me as I entered, his face lighting up at the prospect of a distraction, in a way that was hauntingly familiar. His gaze moved from Pinahui-tzin to me. "Well, well," he said, in the sudden silence. "You bring exalted company, Pinahui. Our High Priest for the Dead, no less."

I walked to the centre of the room, close enough that I could have touched the first of Neutemoc's guards. Ignoring the shocked look that spread on my brother's face, I bowed low. "Your Excellency."

Tizoc-tzin made a dismissive gesture. "Let's not stand on ceremony. I have not yet had the pleasure of your presence at court."

I said, carefully. "My Fire Priest represents me at the Imperial Court. I am confident that he can speak in my name and in the best interest of my order."

I felt, suddenly, as if I stood on the edge of a chasm – a coldness creeping into my back worse than what I felt when summoning the Wind of Knives. With a word, Tizoc-tzin could send me to the farthest edges of the Mexica Empire, or elevate me to the highest echelons. He could topple our temple, or make it immensely rich.

"What an event, then, to see you here." Tizoc-tzin's voice was still bored, but I wasn't fooled: he was toying with me, relieving his annoyance at being stuck between the two High Priests. "To what do we owe this visit?"

Acamapichtli was the one who spoke, in a low, angry voice. "My Lord, he's come to defend his brother the traitor."

Neutemoc shook his head, but didn't audibly protest. He looked barely able to stand, let alone mount a coherent defence.

Anger flared within me, a sharp feeling that cut off my breath for a moment. Neutemoc and I might not be speaking to each other, but The Duality curse me if I let a worthless priest condemn him on false grounds. "Your Excellency," I said. "I was in charge of the investigation."

Acamapichtli shifted on his dais. "No longer." His voice was malicious.

I snapped, "No one relieved me of my functions. And a good thing, too. Otherwise we'd still have a beast of shadows loose in Tenochtitlan."

That got Tizoc-tzin's attention. "A beast of Mictlan?"

"Yes."

"I was given to understand this man's nahual had abducted Priestess Eleuia."

I shook my head, and gestured at Mihmatini. "It was a beast of shadows. And I can prove that Neutemoc did not summon it."

"Lies," Acamapichtli hissed.

Tizoc-tzin's gaze moved from him to me, and then to the old priest of Huitzilpochtli, who was blinking, still trying to understand what was going on. "We'll listen, priest," he said, and the hostile accent on the word "priest" was unmistakable. Why did Tizoc-tzin hate the clergy so much?

I held out the jade pendant. "This belonged to Priestess Eleuia."

Tizoc-tzin reached out, cradled it in the palm of his hand. "Jade," he said. "Blackened by Mictlan's touch."

He surprised me. With his apparent hatred of priests, I had assumed he'd know little about magic. Clearly, he'd taken care to inform himself on his enemies.

"Yes," I said. "By a beast of shadows. I tracked it to one of Moyotlan's Floating Gardens, and killed it."

Ocelocueitl spoke up. "A good thing. Mictlan's intrusions are always dangerous."

"Yes," Tizoc-tzin said, a tad impatiently. "I assume your wounds date from this point."

"Not entirely," I confessed. I feared Neutemoc's reaction, but it was necessary if I wanted to set him free. "I accessed the beast's memories, and found out the identity of its summoner."

For the first time, High Priest Acamapichtli looked uncertain. His gaze searched Neutemoc's face, trying to see a sorcerer in my brother's wan features. "Well?" Acamapichtli barked. "Out with it! Who harmed Priestess Eleuia?"

They all spoke of her, I noticed, as if she were already dead.

"Neutemoc had nothing to do with this," I said, carefully. "The culprit..." I closed my eyes. Neutemoc was going to kill me. "The culprit was his wife, Huei."

In the shocked silence that filled the room, Mihmatini's voice resonated like a trumpet calling the warriors to battle. "I will bear witness to that. The slaves and I saw the Wind of Knives come to kill Huei for her transgression."

Neutemoc's face had turned the colour of muddy milk. A hiss came from his mouth: my name, repeated over and over. "Acatl... Acatl..." His hands clenched and unclenched, as if to squeeze my heart into nothingness. "Acatl..."

"I see," Tizoc-tzin said. His gaze was on Neutemoc, lightly interested, like a man watching dissected insects writhe. "I see."

"He lies," Acamapichtli whispered. "He wants to save his brother, whatever the cost."

Tizoc-tzin's lips compressed into a thin line. "Be silent," he said to Acamapichtli, who immediately stopped speaking. "You lied to me. You spoke of nahual magic. You said this man's culpability was beyond doubt."

"There was nahual magic," Acamapichtli said, softly. His eyes shone with hatred, most of it directed at me. "He brings no solid evidence, my Lord. The testimony of his own sister and of her slaves. A jade pendant that might not even be Eleuia's – some leftover from his temple, maybe."

Mihmatini's face had whitened. I could tell she ached to fling an accusation into Acamapichtli's face. I laid a hand on her shoulder, squeezed hard. "Don't," I whispered. Acamapichtli would destroy her, as casually as he was destroying Neutemoc.

Acamapichtli was still going on. "He spins a fanciful tale of Mictlan's beasts, but he's a skilful man. As for his wounds... there are many ways to wound oneself."

Watching him, I remembered why I hated high-ranking priests: the perfidious insinuations, the sly smile on their faces as they attempted to lead you astray. Acamapichtli would do anything to enforce his power, even flout justice.

I laid a hand on one of my obsidian knives, felt the power of Mictlan pulse deep within the blade. The emptiness that filled me took away my fear; took away everything but my anger. "Go to Moyotlan, to the Floating Gardens," I said, softly, "and see the three peasants with their hearts missing. Ask them if the beast was real."

Acamapichtli wasn't about to give up so easily. "Words," he said. "Easy, cheap things, Acatl."

"No more than those you used to convict my brother," I snapped. "Do you want evidence? I can summon the Wind of Knives here, in this chamber, to give it to you. Will you accuse Him of being my accomplice?"

"You won't frighten me," Acamapichtli said, his face white with anger.

"Enough," Tizoc-tzin said. He was lounging on the dais, rubbing his fingers on Eleuia's jade pendant, an amused smile on his face. "It's unseemly for priests to argue."

An easy accusation: priests were supposed to be dignified at all times – a feat neither of us had mastered.

"You will go to be examined by a priest of Patecatl," Tizoc-tzin said. "He will ascertain the nature of your wounds. And we'll arrest the real summoner."

"Huei wasn't the only one involved," I said. "She only executed orders. Someone else gave her the knowledge, and that someone else is now holding Priestess Eleuia."

Tizoc-tzin did not move. "Who?"

"I do not know," I said, cautiously. Neutemoc's face had turned whiter.

"We'll interrogate the woman, Huei, and find out."

"I'm afraid," I said, carefully stepping away from Neutemoc, "that this isn't going to be possible."

Tizoc-tzin's face darkened. "You're telling me what I can or cannot do?"

I mentally reviewed several ways of speaking the next sentence. But I could find none that would spare me Neutemoc's anger. "She gave herself up as a sacrifice to Chalchiutlicue."

Tizoc-tzin said nothing. His anger at being thwarted by the gods was palpable. But not so palpable as Neutemoc's towards me.

"You let her?" Neutemoc growled. "Acatl? You let her do – this folly?"

Although it cost me much, I refrained from pointing out that Huei's little games had almost ended his life.

Tizoc-tzin watched us, again with that lightly interested expression, as if we were a spectacle to be enjoyed. "I see," he said, finally. "How convenient for her. Acamapichtli!"

"Yes, my lord?" the High Priest of Tlaloc asked with false meekness.

"Chalchiutlicue is your god's wife, isn't She? I'm sure you can arrange matters."

Acamapichtli shook his head with malicious glee. "Alas," he said, "the Storm Lord and His wife are separate. I have no influence over Her."

Tizoc-tzin snorted, sceptically. "Attempt something, will you?" He turned to me. "I will await the results of your examination before I rule on this case."

I bowed, inwardly relieved that Neutemoc would have some time to calm down before we met again.

It took time, more time than I had thought. After the priest of Patecatl was done with me, we had to wait until Tizoc-tzin's men came back with the bodies of the three dead peasants. Then the priest had to make a long, convoluted report to Tizoc-tzin.

Finally, after the priest was done, Tizoc-tzin pronounced himself satisfied. "Your story is consistent," he admitted. "But still no trace of the priestess."

Acamapichtli threw me a murderous glance from the dais. "No, my lord," he said.

Tizoc-tzin waved a jewelled hand. "Free the Jaguar Knight. The charges against him are obviously unsubstantiated."

If looks could kill, Acamapichtli's gaze would have already sent me into Mictlan. But it didn't matter. Neutemoc was free; his life was no longer in danger.

Unaware of this – or perhaps very much aware, and deriving secret amusement from it – Tizoc-tzin said to me, "The investigation will continue. Make sure you find her." It was half an order, half a threat. All I could do was bow down before him.

"Yes, my lord," I said. I took my leave, pausing on my way out of the palace to thank Pinahui-tzin for his help.

The old magistrate smiled, a wholly unexpected expression that seemed to light up his face. "Never could stand that arrogant priest," he said. "Good for you, knocking him down a peg, young man."

Neutemoc didn't say a word as we exited the Imperial Palace. He kept Mihmatini between himself and me – whether consciously or not, I couldn't say. I didn't complain in any case. His clenched hands and white face were ample testimony to how much restraint he was currently exercising.

We walked back towards the Atempan calpulli and Neutemoc's house in silence. It was late afternoon, but the air was still stiflingly hot: most people were inside, sheltering from the heat. The streets were deserted, and only a few boats bypassed us on the canals.

Neutemoc walked bent, with slow steps, like an old man – so unlike the Jaguar Knight who had been my parents' pride that something fluttered in my chest.

When we were within two or three streets of Neutemoc's house, I felt the air turn to tar.

What?

I span, my good hand on my obsidian knife. Neutemoc had felt it, too. His head snapped up and his muscles tightened. So it wasn't an illusion, or something I'd imagined.

The street was utterly empty, or had become so in the past few minutes. So were the canals. But the air pulsed with magic: a rhythm that was the rush of blood in my heart, the air exhaled from my lungs.

Something moved, at the corner of my eye, shimmering over the water of the canal. I couldn't get a hold of it no matter how I cocked my head.

But Neutemoc grunted and fell, a fresh wound blossoming on his thigh.

The slave Quechomitl rushed to guard his master, and whatever had felled Neutemoc also wounded him: marks appeared on Quechomitl's chest out of thin air, as if claws were being drawn across his skin.

Mihmatini screamed for help, but soon fell silent. It was quite obvious that no help would be coming. But what in the Fifth World was attacking us?

I closed my eyes, extending my priest-senses, and saw them, quivering at the edge of my vision: three shapeless beings with clawed hands, cackling as they crowded around Neutemoc. Their bodies were completely transparent, and only the glint of sunlight as they moved had betrayed them.

Keeping my eyes closed, I unsheathed one of my obsidian knives and, still one-handed, threw it. A good thing that my right hand wasn't the one in the sling.

The blade flew towards the nearest assailant but, somehow, the thing wasn't there when the knife struck. It cackled contemptuously, a sound like hundreds of insects skittering on a stone floor, and went again towards Neutemoc.

The Duality curse them and all their kind!

Mihmatini was kneeling on the ground, drawing a circle in the dirt with the knife in her belt. She was chanting as she did so. I couldn't make out all the words, but it sounded like a hymn to Huitzilpochtli, the Southern Hummingbird, in His incarnation as the Sun – a request for divine protection.

So far, Quechomitl was acting as a shield for Neutemoc. But Quechomitl was bleeding from a dozen wounds, and I didn't know how long he could hold on.

I withheld a curse and, drawing a new knife from my belt, slashed at what I could see of the creatures.

It was utterly ineffective. I could make them out, but not always. In the intervals when I couldn't see them, they would just shift out of the path of my blade, and I sliced only through air. It did not deter the creatures, which continued to converge on Quechomitl.

Quechomitl's face was growing paler and paler, and his grip on Neutemoc was slackening as his blood dripped onto the ground. His blood. Living blood: a powerful source of magic. Fool that I was!

I ran towards Neutemoc, snatching up my fallen obsidian knife as I did. Then I knelt by Quechomitl, closing my eyes again. The creatures were still crowding around him, trying to get past him – mindless, obsessed only by the idea of reaching Neutemoc. They paid little heed to me.

What in the Fifth World had my brother got himself into?

Mihmatini was opening her veins now, and pouring her blood on the ground. I dipped my hands in Quechomitl's blood and drew a sign on my forehead, calling on Quetzalcoatl, God of Creation and Knowledge, to grant me true sight.

*"Yours is the knowledge of the priests,*
*Yours is the knowledge of the stars wheeling in the sky*
*You find the precious jade, the precious feathers…"*

Fresh wounds opened on Quechomitl's arm, leaking blood in inexorable rivulets. The slave's face was pale, contorted in pain. I hurriedly finished my hymn.

*"You find the hidden things, the secret treasures*
*Grant us Your sight, the sight of the gods."*

The blood on my forehead went blazing hot, searing a mark into my skin.

A veil descended before my eyes, until the whole street went dark, the houses and the canals receding into faint shadows. Only the pulsing shape of Mihmatini's pattern retained some substance – that and the three creatures, hissing angrily at me.

With my eyes open, I reached towards the nearest one, letting the emptiness of Mictlan fill me, and sank the obsidian knife into it, where the heart would have been. This time, the blade went all the way in.

The creature hissed like a scalded jaguar and withdrew, but only a few hand spans. Numbness spread from the point of contact, up the hilt and through the obsidian blade – and into my hand, freezing my fingers into insensitivity.

Quechomitl grunted as three fresh wounds opened on his chest. His hand went slack and he started slowly, inexorably, to slide towards the ground.

The two others were already gathering around Neutemoc, in a frenzy to feed upon him. At Neutemoc's feet, his slave lay quietly emptily himself of the blood in his veins, his eyes already glazed, staring at nothing in the Fifth World.

With my awkward, frozen hand, I hefted my knife, trying to see where the creatures were coming from: if there was some thread of power I could follow to a summoner.

There was nothing.

Just a dying slave, and three creatures, gathering to feed on my brother.

Mihmatini. My sister's chanting reached a harsh, sibilant climax; her blood hissed as it filled the circle.

Light blazed, across the street, strong enough to dispel even my true sight. It spread in radiant wave after radiant wave, covering us, bathing us in warmth, growing in intensity with every passing moment. It was as if some covering of ice had slowly started to melt: as feeling returned to my injured hand, the creatures slowly melted away, with a disappointed hiss.

The light settled around Neutemoc and Quechomitl, seeping through every pore of their skin until they seemed to be made of it. It sank into me, too, hissing as it did so, leaving an itch against my hips when it encountered the knives in my belt, the magic of Huitzilpochtli conflicting with that of Mictlan.

I knelt, awkwardly, by Quechomitl's side. No more blood flowed from his wounds. When I groped, with a shaking hand, for the voice of his heart, nothing would beat under my fingers.

No. My fingers tightened on Quechomitl's skin, but there was no heartbeat. There would never be any heartbeat: never again, in the Fifth World or in the Heavens.

Mihmatini was helping a stunned Neutemoc rise. My brother was shaking, though I couldn't tell if it was from the wounds or from the sheer shock of the attack. I remained kneeling by Quechomitl's body, trying to understand how we had come here – how, on what should have been a simple journey back to Neutemoc's house, a man lay dead under my fingers, and for no reason at all.

I reached out, to close his eyes, but my hands shook so badly I couldn't. It took me three tries before the glazed gaze was hidden beneath his swollen eyelids.

Words came to me: the ones I said, over and over, for strangers. The only words I had:

> "You leave behind your fine poems
> You leave behind your beautiful flowers
> And the earth that was only lent to you
> You ascend into the Light, O Quechomitl,
> You leave behind the flowers and the singing and the earth
> Safe journey, O friend."

I thought of his soul, climbing towards the Heavens to meet the Sun-God – for he had died in battle like a true warrior, and the oblivion of Mictlan wouldn't be his lot. I thought of his soul, shedding the body like a worn-out shell, and I wondered what he had died for.

# THIRTEEN

# Funereal Thoughts

Between Mihmatini and me, we carried Quechomitl's body back to Neutemoc's house. Neutemoc himself trailed after us, still stunned and shaking. He hadn't spoken a word since thanking Mihmatini for saving his life.

In the courtyard, an old woman slave and Oyohuaca, the girl who had rowed me through the canals, were seated on the ground, waiting for us. When they saw Quechomitl's body, they gave a mournful howl.

"Master," they said, looking back and forth at Quechomitl's bloody husk, and at Neutemoc, whose Jaguar regalia were also covered in blood.

"Later," Neutemoc said. "Take him to the temple for the Dead. Give him a proper vigil and make the proper offerings." His voice shook at first, but gained in strength with every word.

Still oozing Huitzilpochtli's light, he walked, not into the reception room, but towards his living quarters.

I glanced at Mihmatini. "How long is your spell going to last?"

She shrugged. "Two, maybe three days? It's not going to be enough. Whoever got those to attack him will try again. And if they can't kill him, they'll try to harm those around him."

Like Quechomitl. "I know. Can you do something?" I asked.

Mihmatini puffed her cheeks. "I know a spell for warding a house against evil influences. It takes time to cast, but it's meant to last for a month."

"If you could…" I asked.

She nodded. "I'll go and get my materials. You talk to Neutemoc."

"I…" I didn't think I wanted to do that. When the shock wore off, Neutemoc was going to remember why his house was deserted, and who was to blame.

"Acatl." Her voice was stern. "You two have run away from each other for long enough. Go."

"When did you turn into Mother?"

She snorted. "All women turn into their mothers, Acatl."

And all men into their fathers. But I couldn't imagine myself as Father. I couldn't be that old, embittered man who'd never forgiven me for not supporting him in his dotage – and whom I'd repaid by refusing to undertake his vigil; a petty, useless gesture that would not change the grievance between us.

I found Neutemoc, not in his room, but in Huei's. He'd spread her jewellery on the reed mat, and was staring at it listlessly. The bloodstained jaguar head of his regalia rested against the wall frescoes, by a warrior twisting a noose around the neck of a fallen enemy.

When I entered, Neutemoc raised his gaze, but didn't speak.

I crouched on the other side of the reed mat, looking at Huei's jewels. Beautiful pieces, all: exquisitely sculpted jade in the shape of flowers and birds; polished necklaces with gold pendants; and a small

212

obsidian mirror, reflecting my brother's wan face. I reached out to pick up one of the necklaces. Neutemoc hissed.

"Don't," he said.

I withdrew my hand, slowly. I said nothing; just waited for him to speak.

After a while, he said, "You saved my life. It's the only reason I'm not throwing you out of this house. But I strongly suggest you get out, before I lose my calm and give you the thrashing you deserve." He clenched his hand. Blood oozed from one of his wounds.

"Mihmatini strongly suggested that I talk to you, after what happened."

I'd expected him to snort, but he didn't move. He was very angry, then. "You dragged our sister into this." He snorted. "Things still haven't changed, brother, have they? She's always liked you. I just can't see why."

"Neutemoc–"

His face contorted for a brief moment. "Our parents were right. You bring nothing but trouble."

"Our parents were wrong," I snapped. "I made my own choices."

"Leaving me to pick up the pieces," Neutemoc said.

"You had the means to," I said, more nastily than I'd intended. The "pieces" were Father and Mother, after they grew too old to support themselves.

"Yes," Neutemoc said. "But I don't see why I should have to pay for the choices you made. For any of your choices," he added, in case I hadn't understood the first reference.

"Look – this time, there was no other way."

"No other way? My wife gives herself up as a sacrifice victim, and you think this is a satisfactory outcome?"

I shook my head, wondering how I could calm him down. "She tried to kill you."

Wrong tactic. His face closed. "No," he said. "You imagine things that aren't. She's always loved me. More than I could bear."

You fool. "So you destroyed your marriage just because you 'couldn't bear it'? How convenient."

"We won't talk of my marriage here," Neutemoc said.

"Because it's not relevant?" I asked. "Don't you think your marriage got you here?"

Neutemoc's hand clenched again. "No. What happened to me…" His voice trailed off. He'd always been an honest man and a terrible liar, which explained how easily I'd flushed him out in my first interrogation. "Perhaps it had to do with my marriage," he said, finally. "But that still doesn't give you the right–"

"There was no choice!" I snapped. "For what she'd done, the sentence was death. Death at the hands of the Wind of Knives, or at the hands of the Guardian's warriors – whoever found her first."

Neutemoc spat. "And your solution was…?"

"My solution?" I asked. "She made her own choices, Huitzilpochtli curse you! She was the one who went to Chalchiutlicue's temple and offered herself to Her," I said. "I couldn't stop her." How could he not see what Huei had got herself into: something far greater than her, which had ultimately swallowed her whole? How could he not see?

Neutemoc's hands clenched. "So you had no part in this? How convenient. That was also your excuse for not becoming a warrior on exiting the calmecac, wasn't it: events beyond your control. Not good enough, Acatl."

He had always known how to find the least of my weaknesses. His argument was, almost word for word, the reproaches Mother had kept addressing to me. "Leave the calmecac out of this, will you?"

He smiled. "Because you think this had nothing to do with the calmecac, and what you've made of yourself? The brother I used to play with would have given his life rather than harm me, or any of mine."

It was so patently unfair it didn't shame me. All it did was infuriate me. I raised my good hand, pointed at the wounds on my chest and on my arm. "You see these?" I asked. "I asked the Wind of Knives to spare her, Neutemoc. I pleaded for her life – I, who'd never allowed anyone to sway me – I made a fool of myself trying to sway a divinity that cannot be swayed."

Neutemoc's lips tightened in grim amusement. "Yes. I know how unbending you can get." He rubbed his face, but didn't speak further.

"I did all I could," I said. "But she ran away from the Wind of Knives, to the only refuge she could find."

Neutemoc stared at me. At last he said, "A poor refuge." And, with a shock, I realised that the glimmer in his eyes were tears.

"I…" I started, not sure what to say. Neutemoc had always been a strong man: going on, regardless of the circumstances. Even when he'd been arrested, he'd never broken down. "You can go to the temple, talk to her."

"It won't bring her back to me, will it?" Neutemoc said.

I could have lied to him; but I, too, had never been a good liar. "No," I said. "The temple is the only place where she's safe, both from the Wind of Knives and from the Imperial Guards."

Neutemoc didn't speak. His eyes were closed and he breathed slowly, heavily, swallowing his tears. His hands toyed with a small, broken obsidian pendant, heedless of the thin line of blood the edge of the stone was drawing on his palm.

"Neutemoc," I said, "she made her own choices, and you can't go back on any of them. And one of her choices was to summon that beast."

Neutemoc opened his eyes. "Tell me something," he said.

"Anything you want," I said, and it was a lie. There were some things I would be incapable of telling him.

"Did you know she was a sorceress when we married?"

I hadn't expected this question, and it took me a while to understand what he was asking me. "No," I said, shocked. "You're mistaken. Huei was never a sorceress."

"Then how did she summon that beast?"

I sighed. "People came to the house. They gave her the means."

Neutemoc's face hardened. "The same people who abducted Eleuia?"

"Yes," I said. Possibly the same ones who were trying to kill him, although I didn't understand why anyone would take my brother as a target.

Save for Acamapichtli. But the High Priest of Tlaloc wasn't a fool. He'd wait until Tizoc-tzin's attention was no longer on Neutemoc before striking.

Neutemoc took a deep breath. He was obviously wrestling with a difficult decision. At last he said, "I want to join your investigation, Acatl."

If anyone deserved to, it was Neutemoc. He'd suffered much in this, but I wasn't sure I could bear his ongoing hostility towards me. On the other hand... I'd allowed Teomitl to take part; I couldn't in all honesty deny Neutemoc for my own comfort.

I laid my hands on the reed mat, a hand-span from Huei's jewels. "You're sure?"

"Yes," Neutemoc said tersely.

"Then you'll have to be honest with me."

His eyes flickered. "I will. After all, I have nothing to hide any more. Or to lose, indeed." His voice was bitter, and cut me to the core.

"Very well," I said. "You can help."

He nodded. "Thank you." But he didn't move to touch my hands, and the set of his jaw said, clearly, that he hadn't forgiven me: that we were temporary allies, to avenge Huei and Eleuia and Quechomitl, but that we were not, could never be reconciled. And I wasn't sure I could ever be on friendly terms with him: not when his own foolishness had been the canker at the heart of his marriage, turning Huei into a stranger to both of us.

"Do you know," I asked, "why someone would try to kill you?"

"Apart from our friend the High Priest?" Neutemoc asked.

"I think he's more crafty than this." The least you could say about the attack was that it lacked subtlety.

"Then no," Neutemoc said.

"Any enemies?" I asked, and thought of Mahuizoh. I'd forgotten about him in the rush to defeat the beast of shadows; but he had a prime motive for wanting Neutemoc dead.

"Not that I know of."

Neutemoc appeared sincere, but I still asked, "Among the Jaguar Knights?"

"The usual resentment that I was elevated, not born into the nobility. But not, I think, enough to justify such determination."

"Hum," I said. I would definitely have to meet Mahuizoh, if he ever came out from wherever he was hiding. But, if Mahuizoh was a sorcerer of such powers, how come no one at the Jaguar House, or within his own household, had ever mentioned it? "I'll enquire. Mihmatini is putting wards around the house, in addition to the protection she already put on you. It should keep you safe."

"Safe," he repeated wryly. "Whenever did my own sister turn into a powerful priestess?" He didn't sound unhappy, but rather deeply puzzled, as if this were a wholly unexpected outcome.

I shrugged, feeling as dislocated as he was. "When she started eating maize gruel, I suppose." It had been an ongoing joke in the family that Mihmatini had screamed whenever Mother attempted to switch her diet from milk to gruel.

Neutemoc smiled, a tight expression that didn't reach his eyes. "I suppose," he said, and the moment of shared reminiscences was past.

"I'll go to my temple," I said. "I've got some unfinished tasks." Such as speaking to Ichtaca before matters between us festered beyond recovery.

Neutemoc nodded. "I'll join you later."

I toyed with the idea of telling him to get some sleep, but decided in the end that only Mihmatini could afford that kind of remark. I didn't want to tear our fragile understanding.

As it turned out, I didn't go to my temple immediately, because Mihmatini caught me in the courtyard, and insisted on my getting a proper meal. Despite my protests, I somehow found myself sitting next to her and the children, and facing a pale, angry Neutemoc who no doubt wished Mihmatini would stop trying to reconcile us.

The dinner was brief and perfunctory. Despite the sumptuous dishes aligned on the table – fried newts, white fish with red peppers and tomato, agave worms and sweet potatoes – I ate little, my stomach roiling at the mere thought of receiving food. I tried to avoid Neutemoc's gaze as much as possible, and focused instead on what I needed to do. Many, many things, including having a heart-to-heart talk with Ichtaca.

But Mihmatini forestalled me again, insisting I spend the night at the house.

"I have other things–" I started.

She drew me aside, exasperated. "They're going to come back. You know that. Do you really want to leave us undefended?"

"You're good," I said. Better than me, I suspected. The spell of protection she had cast on Neutemoc – and now on the whole house, removing us from the sight of any foes – was intricate, and mastered by few. I was incapable of casting it.

She shook her head. "I'm not good enough to keep him safe."

My first, shameful thought was: Then let him die. Let my parents see that he's no better than me. But I couldn't hold that thought for long, not without remembering how I'd already let Father down by not undertaking his vigil. I couldn't do it a second time.

"He's not going to be happy," I said.

"Then let him brood," she said. "It will keep him alive."

I didn't know what Mihmatini said to Neutemoc. She talked to him in a low, urgent voice, making a couple of stabbing gestures with her hands. He said nothing when I unrolled a sleeping mat in one of the spare rooms.

Sleep was a long time coming. I kept seeing Huei's bitter, resigned face, moments before the Wind of Knives arrived; and in my dreams it turned into the wrinkled face of the ahuizotl, its eyes yellow and malevolent.

Finally, darkness came and swallowed me whole.

• • •

The following morning, Mihmatini badgered us all into having breakfast together again: Neutemoc, the children and I.

We were sipping some cacao laced with vanilla and spices when the young slave, Oyohuaca, came into the room. "Acatl-tzin," she said. "There is a man outside to see you."

The man outside turned out to be Yaotl, who smiled widely when I entered the courtyard, followed closely by Neutemoc.

"Acatl," Yaotl said. "I hear you've been having considerable success at the Imperial Court."

"Ha ha," I said, unwilling to start yet another war of words. "Are you here to congratulate me, or to drop further obstacles into my path?"

"Neither," Yaotl said. "I bring you good news." He checked himself. "Well, 'good' in a certain meaning of the word, of course."

I was fighting a rising sense of frustration. "Can you get to the point, instead of taunting me?"

"My my, we're in a bad mood today," Yaotl said. "Mistress Ceyaxochitl sent me. We've found Priestess Eleuia's body floating near Chapultepec."

As expected, Neutemoc accompanied us. Yaotl made no comment; he spoke with me as if Neutemoc were not there.

Chapultepec was a small town at the end of the Tlacopan causeway, west of Tenochtitlan. Sitting on the banks of the lake, the town comprised mostly peasants working the fields of the Floating Gardens, and a sizeable community of fishermen. It was with one of those – a grizzled man in just a loincloth, his face deeply tanned by the sun – that Ceyaxochitl was speaking. She and the fishermen stood by the edge of the lake. I couldn't see Eleuia's body at first; but then

I made out the white shape floating in the fisherman's net.

"You see," the fisherman was saying, "I get up this morning and go pull up the nets like I do all my life, except that they won't come up so easily. A big fish, is what I tell myself. A fish big enough to feed the whole family, sons and cousins and uncles and aunts." He barely stopped between two sentences, obviously proud of his find.

Ceyaxochitl nodded from time to time, but didn't interrupt him.

"So I pull harder and harder, and when the net finally surfaces, there's this white thing in it. A fish, I still tell myself, but then I see her hair trailing behind her, and then I continue pulling, I see her face and I know I have to tell someone…" His voice trailed off.

"You did well," Ceyaxochitl said. "Ah, Acatl. You see what we have." The fisherman, curtly dismissed, stepped away from us.

"Not yet," I said. I walked closer to the net. Neutemoc was standing behind me, frozen in shock. "Can we get it out of the water?" I asked.

"I was waiting to know if you could see anything," Ceyaxochitl said.

I extended my priest-senses, but felt only the everyday setting: the wide expanse of the lake, the peasants tilling the fields, the anchor of the earth beneath us. I shook my head. "Easier to see if you're on dry land." As Neutemoc and Yaotl started hauling the body of the net, I asked her, "I thought you'd be at the Imperial Palace?"

Ceyaxochitl's eyes were on the muddy banks of the lake. Further away, boats ferried peasants with hoes and baskets from the town to the Floating Gardens. At last Ceyaxochitl said, so softly that no one but I could have heard, "There isn't much that can be done any more."

No wonder the noblemen had been so numerous at the Imperial Audience. The succession of Revered Speaker Axayacatl-tzin grew closer and closer, and Tizoc-tzin would be in a prime position to claim it. "How long?" I asked.

"A few months, if the Southern Hummingbird's protection holds. In reality... considerably less, I'd say."

"I see." Neutemoc and Yaotl were laying the body on the bank; I went closer to take a better look at it.

In life, Eleuia might have been strong and alluring, drawing men to her as peccaries will draw jaguars. In death, she was small and pathetic, her beauty extinguished. The lake's currents had torn her clothes off: her skin was as white as the new moon, and clammy, as unsettling as the touch of a Haunting Mother. Multiple bruises had formed on her arms and legs. Algae had twined with her hair, and her face... Her face was the worst: empty eye-sockets gazed at me, still encrusted with dried blood. Small scratches, like those made by tiny claws, spread around the place where the eyes should have been.

I didn't need to take a look at her hands to know what kind of claws had pawed at her eyes, probing until they detached. "An ahuizotl?" I asked Ceyaxochitl.

She nodded. "Yes. Her fingernails are also missing."

I closed my eyes, remembering the monster that had tracked me across the canals. Too many coincidences. What was Chalchiutlicue's part in this?

I looked at the body again. The last thing we knew about Eleuia was that Huei's mysterious allies had taken her. They might have released her, although it sounded unlikely, and I didn't think Eleuia would have gone to the town of Chapultepec. She'd have tried to go back to her temple.

Which left the second option: she had been dead by the time she entered the water, and the ahuizotl had only feasted on a corpse.

I could have cast the same spell as before, back in the calmecac, to see if Mictlan's gates had opened on the lake-banks – but that spell worked best in confined spaces. Here, sunlight and the passage of numerous fishermen and peasants would lessen the traces of Mictlan's magic. The results would be misleading at best. No, better to take the easier choice and examine the body. There would be time for spells later, if the examination wasn't conclusive.

"I need to make sure what she died of. We'll take the body back to my temple," I said. "It will be quieter for a full examination."

Neutemoc bent, stiffly, to lift Eleuia's left hand. He stared at the wrinkled skin of her hands, at the incongruously pale skin revealed by the absent fingernails. His face was rigid, washed of all emotion.

"We leave this earth," he whispered, softly, slowly: the beginning of a hymn to the dead. "We leave the flowers and the songs, and the maize bending in the wind. Down into the darkness we must go, leaving behind the marigolds and the cedar trees..."

I hoped Eleuia had indeed drowned. Drowned men and women went, not into the oblivion of Mictlan, but into Tlalocan, the Blessed Land of the Drowned: a place where flowers blossomed all year round, and where maize never lacked; where Father would be, tilling the eternal fields, blissfully unaware of me. I prayed that Eleuia, who had suffered so much during the Great Famine, would at least have this consolation.

To us, the living, would be left the task of finding out what had happened to her.

• • •

Yaotl and Neutemoc carried Eleuia's body back to my temple. As we walked on the Tlacopan causeway, the macabre load elicited more than a few startled glances. But the presence of a Guardian deterred people from approaching us.

Ichtaca was descending the shrine steps when we entered. He took a look at the body in Yaotl's arms, and a long, darker one at me. "You'll be needing one of the examination rooms, I take it?"

I nodded. I really needed to speak with Ichtaca about the running of the temple, before whatever grievance he had festered into something incurable; unfortunately, time was hard to find.

I sent the others to follow Ichtaca, while I stopped by the storehouse to recover a wooden cage with an owl. I might not need magic to examine the corpse, but one never knew.

The examination room was a simple affair: a stone altar with grooves to evacuate the blood; a wooden chest holding a collection of obsidian knives; and at the back, a smaller altar of polished ivory dedicated to Mictlantecuhtli. I set the owl's cage on the floor, near the altar.

I recovered a small, sharp obsidian blade from the chest, and made my offerings of blood to my god: three quick slashes across the back of my left hand, blood flowing onto the altar. "We come for the truth," I said, softly. "Blind not our eyes; deceive us not. We come for the truth."

I touched the tip of my obsidian knife to the altar. A small jolt passed from the handle of the knife to my palm: a sign that some of Mictlan's magic had suffused the blade.

Yaotl and Neutemoc had already laid Eleuia's body on the stone altar. Bluish blotches marked her stomach: the same place as the stretch-marks of her childbirth.

224

Ceyaxochitl's cane tapped on the stone floor, until she found her place. She watched me like a vulture awaiting carrion.

I put the tips of my fingers on Eleuia's purple lips, and gently forced them open. The touch was cold, numbing. Froth had adhered to the inside of her mouth. Not sufficient – many things other than drowning could cause the foam – but a good start.

I retrieved a clean cloth from the chest and wiped off the foam. Then I pressed down on her chest, forcing her to exhale.

Foam bubbled up, replacing what I had removed. So Eleuia had drowned: she had been alive before entering the water. Interesting. I would have expected her captors to throw her dead body into the lake, not for her to be dragged down by the ahuizotl.

"Well?" Ceyaxochitl asked.

I shrugged. Not much to say at that point. "She died of drowning. The ahuizotl is most likely what killed her."

I turned my attention to the bruises. They were by no means abnormal: as the body bumped against branches and other obstacles, it was bound to gather quite a few of them. But something about their pattern...

I felt them, carefully. The skin was bluish-black and swollen, resilient to my touch. But bruises inflicted after death didn't swell, and they seldom turned blue-black.

Not all of the bruises were the same age. I stepped back, lifted one of Eleuia's arms. There was... a gradation: some of them were blue-black, bordering on a greenish colour, some of them were barely turning blue; and a few were still red marks on the skin.

My stomach churned. She'd been beaten up, consistently and regularly: in three days, the oldest bruises had had time to start discolouring, but the most recent ones were only burst vessels, the blood barely coagulating.

"Someone tortured her," I said, slowly.

Neutemoc's face turned white and harsh, like a shell.

"They took her, and then they beat her, again and again."

"What for?" Ceyaxochitl asked.

I shook my head. "I don't know. I thought – she had a child, in the Chalca Wars." Even though I didn't see what the child would have had to do with all of this. Unless Eleuia had tried to blackmail Mahuizoh?

"Yes," Neutemoc said. "I remember." His gaze was distant. "But it was stillborn, Acatl."

"That's what Eleuia told you."

Neutemoc said, "I was there, Acatl. I saw her bury the body. Trust me. He could never have lived."

"You're sure?" I asked.

Neutemoc's lips were two dark lines in the oval of his face. "Yes," he said. "I'll bear witness to that, if you wish."

"No need," I said. Huitzilpochtli strike me down. The child had sounded like too great a thing to be ignored – and Eleuia herself not above doing whatever she had to do to ensure her future. But if he was dead…

What could her abductors have wanted from Eleuia?

I ran my fingers on the bruises. Perhaps I was mistaken. But no, there were too many of them, and they were too large to have been caused by random objects dragged by the currents. The way they were spread, too: few parts of Eleuia's body weren't covered in them. It spoke, not of rage, but of a cold-blooded method, from the summoning of the beast to Eleuia's deliberate, methodical torture. My stomach churned again. Who were those people?

Mahuizoh? He had loved her, if I believed my witnesses, or at any rate, had had affection for her. Surely he wouldn't...

My fingers, probing, found a raised area on Eleuia's cheek: a smaller bruise, barely old enough to have discoloured.

It was the pattern of an object that had hit her, engraved into her flesh: a wound that dated from not too long before her death. I knelt, and stared at it. Unfortunately, the blood had spread and partially erased the contours. It had a shape: hints of curves, of stylised lines meeting to form the point of something else...

"Neutemoc?" I asked. "Does this mean anything to you?"

Neutemoc turned Eleuia's face to the light; carefully, as if afraid she'd crumble under his touch. He stared, for a while, at the eyeless hollows, at the small pattern on her cheek. His face was expressionless but his fingers had clenched into fists. "There was no reason," he muttered. "What kind of man...?"

I knew what he was thinking, because I felt the same nausea welling up in me, tightening until I could barely breathe. "Neutemoc."

At length, he shook his head. "No," he said. "That mark is too badly damaged, Acatl."

Ceyaxochitl's cane tapped on the stone floor. "Let me see," she said.

Neutemoc stepped aside, without a word.

Ceyaxochitl, unlike Neutemoc, probed Eleuia's flesh like a buyer investigating the fitness of a dog. A faint trace of magic hung in the air: she was calling on the power of the Duality to aid her sight. "Hum," she said. "It is very deformed."

"Spreading blood," I said. "She was alive for some time after that bruise."

"How long?" Ceyaxochitl asked.

"Not very long," I said. "So?" I felt sick. In my years as a priest for the Dead, I had seen death; I had seen cruelty. But never had I seen it so methodically applied.

And yet they had released Eleuia, or she had escaped. Unless... unless they had summoned the ahuizotl to kill her, thinking to hide their crimes. Possible. It was a risk – no one summoned the Jade Skirt's creatures without paying a price – but possible.

Ceyaxochitl stared at the mark for a while. "I have seen something like it. But I can't remember where."

"Can you find out?" Neutemoc asked.

"Yaotl will take a copy of it," Ceyaxochitl said. "I can't guarantee I'll remember, but maybe someone at the Duality House..."

Neutemoc said nothing while Yaotl sketched a copy of the mark on a maguey paper. He was watching Eleuia like a man dying of thirst, as he must have watched her while she was still alive. I couldn't help thinking of Huei's anger; and how, ultimately, it had been justified.

# FOURTEEN
## *Two Knights*

Ceyaxochitl and Yaotl left soon after that, claiming pressing business at the palace. Neutemoc remained where he was, staring at the corpse, in what seemed to be a particularly bleak mood.

I stopped Ceyaxochitl at the door. "I don't suppose you could summon someone from Tlalocan?"

Her eyes held me, expressionless. "From the Blessed Land of the Drowned? You want to summon Eleuia?" Finally, she sighed. "No. The Duality is the source and arbiter of all the gods, but They have no power over where the dead go. And you…"

I could summon the dead, but only those who belonged to my god, Mictlantecuhtli. Eleuia, who had drowned, belonged to Tlaloc, and I couldn't summon her without the Storm Lord's blessing. But there was another way. "If she won't come to my call, I could go to her."

Ceyaxochitl raised her eyebrows. "Risky."

In a god's world, I would be an exile, my magic diluted, my body weak. And there was a risk, no matter how insignificant, that I would meet Father's soul: a small thing compared to the stakes, but not something I was looking forward to, by any means.

"I know," I said. But Eleuia would know why she had died, and who had abducted her. It was the most direct way to find out the truth.

"I really have to be at the palace," Ceyaxochitl said. "But if you're not back in three hours, I'll know what happened."

I nodded. By trying to enter Tlalocan, I would subject myself to Tlaloc's whims. If I hadn't come back in three hours, there wouldn't be much Ceyaxochitl could do, except perhaps succeed where I had failed.

After Ceyaxochitl and Yaotl had left, I went back into the room. Neutemoc was still staring at Eleuia's body, with a naked hunger that made me sick. He obviously hadn't been listening to a word we'd said, and what he was thinking of was quite obvious. It rankled. Here I was, endangering my life, and all he could think of was Eleuia? Not even Huei, or his children, or his family?

I asked, angrily, "This is what you'd have destroyed your marriage for? This flesh?" I made a sweeping gesture towards the altar, encompassing Eleuia's small, reduced body: the whitened flesh, the wrinkled fingertips… the missing eyes.

"It wasn't about carnal lust," Neutemoc snapped.

I walked to face him, words I couldn't hold any more welling up in me. "Wasn't it? You had everything, Neutemoc. It's not my fault if you tried to throw it all away."

"You can't understand."

"No," I said. "You're right. I can't even start to fathom it." I knelt on the ground, and gently traced the outline of the glyph for "water" on the stone: the mouth of a jug, out of which issued the serpentine shape of waves.

"What are you doing?" Neutemoc asked.

I shrugged. "You'll see." I retrieved the owl's cage from the altar, set it in the centre of the room, and withdrew the cloth that was covering it. A deafening, angry screech came from the bird in the cage.

"You're going to do magic here?" Neutemoc said.

I didn't answer.

"Acatl!" he said.

I raised my eyes briefly. "Yes," I said. "And I'm going to need you here, watching out."

"What for?"

I went back to the altar, and picked the jade plate and the spider carving. "I'm going to enter the World Beyond. To speak to Eleuia."

"Can't I come?" Neutemoc asked.

Gods, could the man think of nothing else but his would-be mistress?

"No," I said, curtly. That would be risking two lives instead of one. "You stay here."

I withdrew the owl from its cage and slit its chest. Blood spurted out in a rush of quiescent magic, its pungent animal smell mingling with the bittersweet odour of decomposition from Eleuia's body. I retrieved the owl's heart, and set it on the jade plate, above the First Level.

*"Every year Your banners are unfolded in every direction*
*Every year you turn again to the place of abundant blood*
*Coming forth from the place of clouds*
*From the verdant house, from the water's edge…"*

Magic blazed, closing the water-glyph pattern. It was if a veil had been thrown over the room, hiding Neutemoc and the altar, and the stone walls. The ground under my feet shifted, started to become mud.

*"Coming forth from the beautiful place*
*From the misty house, from the verdant house*
*From the bliss of Tlalocan…"*

Beyond the water-glyph, meadows were coalescing into existence, covered with the whiteness of maize flowers, lit by the warm afternoon sun. Somewhere, children were laughing, with such careless innocence that my heart ached.

*"Coming forth from the water's edge*
*From the verdant house, from the bliss…"*

Something pushed at me: two cold, dripping hands laid upon my shoulders. Startled, I lost my balance within the water-glyph and set one hand outside of the line of blood.

The meadows wavered, and were lost. The children's laughter slowly faded into insignificance. The golden light lost its warmth and colour, turning instead into a harsh, white radiance that outlined the bones under my skin. No. No. There was nothing left now; nothing of innocence, nothing of comfort. I could have wept.

The veil across the water-glyph hadn't returned either. Puzzled, I looked around me. I'd expected to return to the temple if my spell failed; but this was clearly no Fifth World place. Under my feet, the earth was black, and utterly dry. In fact, it wasn't earth. It was dust.

"Acatl," a voice said, behind me. "What a surprise."

Trying hard to contain the frantic beat of my heart, I rose and turned.

The harsh, white radiance came from a dais made of bones: skulls, arms and legs, ribcages poking out at odd angles. And on the dais… Mictlantecuhtli, Lord Death, and His wife, Mictecacihuatl, watching me as one might watch an unworthy insect.

I wasn't in the Fifth World at all. Somehow, I'd found my way into the deepest level of Mictlan.

Because there was nothing else I could do, I bowed. "My lord. My lady. I wasn't expecting to be here either."

Lord Death smiled: an eerie expression, stretching across His sunken cheeks. "Understandable. But one place leads to another."

"Tlalocan?" I asked.

Mictlantecuhtli crossed both arms over His skeletal ribcage. "The dead all take the same path. It's only the end of it that differs."

"That still doesn't explain why someone pushed me out of Tlalocan."

He smiled again. "You seem to have lost the Storm Lord's favour, if you ever had it."

There was an obvious reason. "I annoyed His High Priest recently," I said.

Mictlantecuhtli shook His head. "By the look of it, I would say it's an older offence."

"I don't see which one," I said, finally. But it was a lie. I knew why. I knew the only vigil I hadn't undertaken; I still remembered Father's drowned body, lying in the emptiness of the temple for the Dead – and of how I'd run away, unable to face the reproach still etched in every one of his features. Some things I just could not find the courage for.

Lord Death said nothing. He wasn't a god who judged, after all. He just received all the dead no other god had claimed. He wasn't fussy.

"There is no way in, then?" I asked.

"Not into Tlaloc's dominions," Mictlantecuhtli said. "If you've lost His favour, it's likely you've also lost Chalchiutlicue's."

I'd never been a worshipper of the Goddess of Lakes and Streams, and She wouldn't forgive my unfulfilled vigil. Father, after all, also belonged to Her.

"I was trying to find a priestess. Eleuia," I said, finally. Mictlantecuhtli, after all, was my patron. He would perhaps be inclined to offer hints. "Something is going on."

"In the Fifth World?" He asked. "Something is always going on. But it doesn't concern Us."

"It concerns the other gods."

"The Old Ones?" Mictlantecuhtli said. "And the newer ones – the upstart?"

"Huitzilpochtli."

Mictlantecuhtli ran His bone-thin fingers on the fibulae and femurs that made His throne. "Yes. The Imperial upstart and Tonatiuh, His incarnation as the Sun-God." He sighed, an uncannily human sound, although not a feature of His death-head's face moved. "My dominion is here. My power is here. Why should I look elsewhere? Let the others squabble over the Fifth World. I see no need to."

"So you don't know?"

"No," Mictlantecuhtli said. "I don't know what Eleuia would have known, or why she died. I presume that's what you want."

"Yes," I said. "But–"

He smiled again. "All I can offer is My knives, and some advice. Be careful of what you meddle in, Acatl. Cornered animals have a way of turning on you."

"I don't see what this has to do with anything," I said slowly, not daring to question him further, not in His dominion.

Lord Death shook His head. "Perhaps nothing. Perhaps everything. I think you can find your own way back, Acatl."

I'd never been this deep into the underworld, though I had caught glimpses of Mictlantecuhtli Himself before. I knew, theoretically, the path I would have to follow: back through the City of the Dead, the

Plain of the Shadow Beasts, and through every level, until I could cross the River again and go back into the Fifth World.

"I–" I started.

I could feel Their amusement. "The gate is that way," Lady Death said, Her bony face stretched in a rictus grin. She gestured, and a cold wind blew around us, raising the dust at Her feet. Underneath was stone: cold, unyielding. And as the dust lifted, it revealed the carved pattern of a quincunx, pulsing with magic.

I stepped towards it but Mictecacihuatl caught my arm in a grip as unyielding as the embrace of death. Her bony hands probed my flesh, cold, unresponsive. I tried not to wince as Her pointed fingers slid into my wounds.

"You've bled much," She said. "Mostly in Our service."

I didn't speak. I was trying not to let Her see my pain.

Mictecacihuatl smiled: a grin that revealed yellowed teeth, as clean as animal-picked bones. "I suppose that after going all the way down here, you deserve something for your pain."

Light blazed around Her, sinking under my skin. Something tightened, impossibly compressing my bones, pressing my flesh against my rib cage – stretching me thin, as if on a funeral altar. The smell of rot grew strong, and then faded into the dryness of crumbling bones, of the dust at my feet. My wounds were closing one by one, not so much healing as being drained of pus, of blood, and each wound closing hurt worse than it had opening. I struggled not to scream.

When She released me, I crouched, panting, by the side of Her quincunx. I was unmarked again, even though my skin tingled, as if blood were returning to every vein in my body at the same time.

Lady Death was smiling again. "A fitting gift, I should think."

Standing where I was, in the deepest level of Mictlan, there was nothing I could answer to this; nothing beyond a croaked "Thank you, My Lady", which rang insincere. It had been a healing, but I almost wished it had not taken place.

"My pleasure," Mictecacihuatl said. "Go, now."

I did not need to be told twice. I stepped into the quincunx; and I welcomed the blurring of the world with relief.

When everything coalesced again, I was in the examination room, my wounds still tingling: an unpleasant reminder of what I had just undergone. Neutemoc, who had been kneeling by the altar, jumped up with a start.

"I thought you'd never come back," he said.

"How long has it been?" I asked.

"Two hours or more."

It had felt much shorter, but the time of the gods wasn't our own.

"Did you see her?" Neutemoc asked.

I shook my head. "I couldn't enter." I was too ashamed of myself to go into details.

"But–"

"It all depended on the Storm Lord's goodwill. And He wasn't very co-operative, to say the least."

"So you couldn't find her." Neutemoc sounded disappointed. I wanted to scream at him to stop being obsessed by her; to do something about his own wife, his own family. But all I would achieve was to set him further against me.

The smell of blood was strong, sickeningly so. My water-glyph had all but vanished, absorbed in the aborted passage to Tlalocan, but the smell had insinuated itself everywhere. "No, nothing learnt. I'll go and see if I can get something to clean the room," I said.

Neutemoc was watching Eleuia's body again, and didn't answer me.

When I came back with a reed broom, I found Teomitl in the courtyard, obviously waiting for me. His crutch was gone; his wounds were healed, far too quickly to be natural. I presumed his family – clearly noblemen, judging from his attire – would have had access to spells to facilitate his recovery. Teomitl himself was still as lean and as sharp as a jaguar on the prowl, still bursting with that boundless energy.

He bowed when he saw me: the sketchy gesture of one unused to obeisance. "Acatl-tzin," he said. "How are you?"

How was I? Angry – at Neutemoc for being such a fool; at Huei for being so easily manipulated; at myself for being blinded by my old illusions. And frustrated at being unable to enter Tlalocan. Although I didn't know what I would have done, had I met Father there. "I've been better," I said, curtly.

"You freed your brother," Teomitl pointed out.

"Hmm." I didn't feel inclined to talk about Neutemoc in front of Teomitl. Searching for another subject of conversation, I remembered that he had been one of those besotted by Eleuia. "We found Eleuia's body."

Teomitl's face froze, minutely: disappointment, carefully masked. "Can I see her?"

Inside the room, Teomitl knelt by Eleuia. He noted, I was sure, the bruises and the missing eyes and fingernails, but giving no hint of any expression whatsoever. He whispered something to her, but I couldn't hear his words. Something he likely didn't want me to hear.

I busied myself with the broom and some cold water, and energetically scrubbed the ground clean. When I finished, both Neutemoc and Teomitl were still watching Eleuia's body, with the same hunger in their eyes.

The Duality curse them both. What had they seen in her?

After Teomitl was done, he walked out again and stood in the courtyard, watching the sunlight play on motes of dust. He was silent, uncannily so, seemingly hunched in the shadow of the frescoed walls. He breathed slowly, evenly, his eyes unfocused.

"I should have known," he said. "They always die."

"Who?" I asked.

He shook his head. "They're always the same, haven't you noticed? They walk as if the world had no hold on them. But the gods catch them, sooner or later."

I was beginning to suspect that he wasn't talking about Eleuia, and that I had misjudged him. He hadn't been infatuated with her, but with someone else. "Teomitl—"

He straightened up as if I'd struck him. "I came with news, Acatl-tzin. You were looking for Mahuizoh of the Coatlan calpulli."

"Yes," I said, tearing myself from my questions about Teomitl with some difficulty. Mahuizoh. I still needed to interview him: I still needed to find out who had tried to kill Neutemoc.

"He has come back into Tenochtitlan," Teomitl said.

"How do you know?"

Teomitl shrugged. "Rumours make their way, even into the calmecac."

Was he still sweeping the courtyard of the girls' calmecac? His manners, at any rate, had not improved. He still had the same unthinking arrogance that chafed

238

at me: a glimpse of what I might have become, if I had chosen the path of war at the calmecac. But that was irrelevant.

"Do you know why he left the city?" I asked. It sounded far too convenient.

Teomitl shook his head.

I sighed. "Come. Let's go see him."

We extracted Neutemoc from his moody vigil over Eleuia's body. While we strode to Mahuizoh's house, I told him what he needed to know.

"Her lover?" he asked, plainly crestfallen.

Sometimes, my brother could be such a child. "Yes," I said, stifling another sigh. We were talking about a man who had a good motive for wanting Neutemoc dead, and all he could think of was that he'd had a rival.

Teomitl walked by our side, not saying anything. In the afternoon sunlight, his skin shone. Seeing him side by side with Neutemoc, it was easy to know what Teomitl's protection spell was: a much stronger version of the one Mihmatini had cast on my brother. Huitzilpochtli's protection, a fitting spell for a warrior. Teomitl's eyes went from Neutemoc to me; but clearly he was still thinking on Eleuia. Not, not on Eleuia – on whomever he'd really been infatuated with.

At the entrance to Mahuizoh's house, no slave tried to stop us. When I'd come with the Duality warriors, they'd been fearful. But to receive a Jaguar Knight in full regalia was an honour, judging by the way they bowed to Neutemoc.

"The master is at home," the slave said. "He'll be delighted to see you."

Mahuizoh received us in the reception room, sitting on the same dais as old Cocochi. He was dressed, not in his Jaguar Knight uniform, but in a simple loincloth, with a cape of white cotton falling down his shoulders. For a man in his mid-thirties, he was still going strong: the flesh of his arms firm, his face almost as smooth as that of a young man.

"I gather some of you attempted to visit me earlier," he said, after I'd introduced everyone. His gaze was curious, not hostile: the hostility was reserved for Neutemoc, who was blithely unaware of it. But I wasn't fooled. Mahuizoh was a clever man. He had to be, to balance both his affair with Eleuia and his belonging to the Jaguar Knights – two utterly incompatible things.

"We were looking for you," I said. "To ask some questions."

"Indeed?" His gaze still didn't reveal anything. And yet he had to know the reason we were here. "If you must."

The only way I'd get something out of this man was by shattering his composure. "We found a body this morning, near Chapultepec. It belonged to Priestess Eleuia."

He stared at me, for a while. Blinked, slowly, very slowly. "I see," he said, finally. And then, more softly, "I see." He was shaking.

"It was suggested that you slept with her," I added.

Mahuizoh looked at Neutemoc, the hatred on his face unmistakable. "I wasn't the only one, was I?"

Near me, Teomitl shifted. "The Imperial Courts cleared Neutemoc of wrongdoing."

Mahuizoh smiled. "I see you're not even brave enough to defend yourself," he said to Neutemoc. "You send pups to sing your praises."

Teomitl went still, one hand on his macuahitl sword, tightening around the hilt. "You call me a pup?" he asked.

"An unbloodied pup," Mahuizoh said. His teeth

were as white and as sharp as the fangs of a jaguar. "Anyone can see that."

"I took a prisoner," Teomitl said.

"What a feat," Mahuizoh said, his voice mocking. "One man against… how many of you untrained youths? Four, five?"

It was a deliberate insult, for Teomitl wouldn't have been a Leading Youth unless he had captured a prisoner by himself. His face paled: he couldn't tolerate such an blow to his pride.

"Leave him alone," Neutemoc said, stepping between them with both arms extended, as if to fend off an enemy. "We both know I'm the one you want."

Mahuizoh laughed, bitterly. "Do I?" he asked. I finally realised what he was doing: his anger was all that kept his grief at bay.

"She loved both of us," Neutemoc said. Given Eleuia's propensity to take lovers, that was a singularly foolish thing to say. Mahuizoh didn't fail to rise to it.

"No," he said. "You're wrong."

"Because you had her longer?" Neutemoc asked, his voice shaking in anger.

Mahuizoh smiled. "No," he said. "Because she only loved one person in her life."

"You?" Neutemoc asked, stepping closer – just as I said, "Herself."

Mahuizoh's gaze moved from Neutemoc to me. "You're perceptive, for a priest," he said, surprised.

The "priest" carried the slight tone of contempt warriors always put on it. I said, slowly, not about to be outdone by a proud Jaguar Knight, "But you, on the other hand, loved *her*."

Mahuizoh was silent for a while. He stared at me; and, when he spoke again, his voice shook. "Yes," he said. "She was the only one who made me feel alive."

"She could be like that." Teomitl still had his hand on his sword. He was still glowering at Mahuizoh.

"You met her," Mahuizoh said. "Whenever you met her, you'd remember. Because there was so much anguish in her, so much desire to live."

I remembered the Quetzal Flower's description of Eleuia: a woman who would do anything rather than know hunger again. I began to believe that Mahuizoh had indeed loved her. He had known her, better than Neutemoc or Teomitl.

"And you couldn't bear the thought of sharing her," I said.

Mahuizoh laughed, a sickening sound. "Sharing?" he asked. "Let me tell you something," he said, turning to Neutemoc. "If she flirted with you, it's because you had something she wanted."

A house of her own. Rooms filled with riches, and a status that would make most men and women envious. All she had to do was take Huei's place, or convince Neutemoc to take her as a second wife.

On the other hand... Mahuizoh himself had all of that. Why hadn't she asked him for that?

"You never married her?" I asked.

Mahuizoh shook his head. "I asked. She didn't want to. She had ambitions, you see."

"Higher than being the wife of a Jaguar Knight?" Teomitl asked.

Mahuizoh smiled. "She wanted her own power, not something that was dependent on a husband."

Hence the drive to become consort of the god Xochipilli. It explained Eleuia's life, but still not why someone was trying to do away with my brother. And not, either, why mysterious men would abduct and torture her. Eleuia's ambition had been unsuitable for a woman; but surely that offence warranted no such punishment.

"Do you know why someone would want to kill her?" I asked.

Mahuizoh shook his head.

"She had a child," I said.

His eyes flicked. "Possibly."

"And you were the father."

He looked genuinely surprised this time. "No," he said. "Wherever did you get that idea?"

"From a reliable source," I said, wondering exactly how much I could trust the Quetzal Flower. No more, I guessed, than I could trust Mahuizoh.

"I didn't father any child with her," Mahuizoh said, curtly. "Whoever told you this was mistaken."

"And you didn't attempt to kill Neutemoc?"

Mahuizoh looked at Neutemoc. My brother wasn't even paying attention, absorbed in thoughts. Mahuizoh's face, for a bare moment, twisted into a mask of hatred so frightening that I recoiled. "No," Mahuizoh said. "I didn't make attempts on his life."

But he had taken far too long to answer. And his jealousy of Neutemoc, in spite of everything he had said, was obvious.

"Why did you leave the city?" I asked.

He blinked, slowly. "Am I forbidden to go where I wish?"

"No," I said. "But with an investigation going on—"

"An investigation," Mahuizoh said arrogantly, "that I have nothing to do with."

A patent lie. "So you deny you had a part in this?"

"Abducting her? Torturing her? Yes."

"How do you know she was tortured?" I asked.

He shrugged. "I heard the rumours."

A convenient reason. Too convenient, maybe? It had only been half a day since we'd found Eleuia's body. How could he have known about its state?

"Who told you?"

243

Mahuizoh smiled. "It was all over the Jaguar House. Probably the Eagle House as well."

"I see," I said. Though I was suspicious, I couldn't think of anything more to ask him. I turned to Neutemoc to see if he had any more ideas; but my brother was still deep in thought.

With a sigh, I took my leave from Mahuizoh.

Neutemoc was still thinking as we walked back to the Sacred Precinct. "He's right, you know," he said.

"He's a liar," Teomitl snorted. "A liar and an honourless man, who thinks nothing of insulting his peers."

"Yes," Neutemoc said. "But still…" He spoke to no one in particular. He refused to look at me, or even to walk near me. "She was cold when she first saw me. I had to remind her of the Chalca Wars before she'd pay attention to me."

"And?" I asked, unable to resist a small jab. "She'd been through so many men she didn't remember you."

"She remembered my name," Neutemoc said. "But it wasn't until we talked together…" He shook his head. "I wonder if he was right, and I had something she wanted." It appeared to bother him immensely. And no wonder, since it showed Eleuia in a wholly different light.

"She wanted power over you," Teomitl said.

"What did you talk about?" I asked.

Neutemoc shrugged. "I don't remember exactly. Mostly about bygone times – the thrill of the battlefield, and how you'd wager every bit of your future, going into combat." The nostalgia in his voice was palpable: a raw hurt. Was this what he'd tried to regain with his affair: the sense that everything could be won or lost?

We walked the rest of the way in silence. In the temple courtyard, Neutemoc asked, "What now?"

I glanced at the sky. It was late afternoon, high time for lunch. "Let's get something to eat," I said. "And then I need to visit your home." I wanted to know if Mihmatini's wards still held, if the creatures had come back and tried to attack the house while Neutemoc was still protected by the Southern Hummingbird.

Neutemoc's eyes blazed. "I told you—"

"Never to darken your doorstep again. Yes, I know that. But do you really want yourself or Mihmatini to be attacked again?" I asked.

Neutemoc shuddered. "No," he said. He wouldn't look at me. "You can look at the wards. But—"

"I know. I won't stay more than I have to."

Teomitl had obviously been fidgeting the whole time we'd been talking. Now he said, "Well, if you're in this for a while, I'll go back to the calmecac."

"Won't they worry about your absence?" I asked. For a calmecac student, he was leading a remarkably careless life, never noticing the strictures the school was meant to impose on one's days and nights.

Teomitl shrugged. "I'll get another penance," he said, with a smile. "Good day, Acatl-tzin."

And, as he turned to go away, the golden light of the sun hit him full on the face – highlighting the hawkish profile, the high cheekbones, until the features that I had seen many times turned into something else. Tizoc-tzin's face.

"Teomitl!" I called.

Halfway through the temple gates, he turned, and there was no doubt. The resemblance with Tizoc-tzin was so marked it was hard to believe I'd missed it before.

Imperial blood. That explained the unthinking arrogance, as well as the spell hanging around him. As a young member of the Imperial Family, of course he'd be under Huitzilpochtli's protection. Who was he to Tizoc-tzin, to Revered Speaker Axayacatl-tzin? A nephew, a distant cousin?

Teomitl was watching me, his head cocked, impatient to move on.

"Who are you?" I called, because I couldn't help it.

Teomitl looked at me with incomprehension. "A warrior."

"No," I said. I couldn't stop the shiver that ran through me. Who had I taken into a hunt for a beast of shadows? Who had nearly been killed by my carelessness? "Who are you? Tizoc-tzin's cousin?"

Neutemoc's head jerked up. He stared at Teomitl with widening eyes.

Teomitl's gaze moved from Neutemoc to me. His face was expressionless.

"I'm his brother," he said. And, turning on his heel, he walked away into the crowd of the Sacred Precinct.

Neither I nor Neutemoc had the courage to stop him.

## FIFTEEN
### *Food of the Gods*

In Neutemoc's house, I found Mihmatini in the children's room, cradling Ollin against her chest. The baby rocked with her, making small, unhappy mewling noises.

"He misses his mother," she said.

"I know," I said darkly. Neutemoc wasn't about to let me forget that.

"Is Neutemoc with you?"

"In the reception room, I suppose." After Teomitl had left, Neutemoc had been silent, not even venturing a word on the way back. And I... I couldn't afford to think of Teomitl, not now. I couldn't think of how I'd almost lost the Emperor's brother, because I hadn't been suspicious enough of who Ceyaxochitl was sending to me.

"How was your day?" I asked Mihmatini, to clear my thoughts.

She shrugged. "I took care of the house, and of the children. They weren't very happy at being kept inside. But how else can I protect them? A good thing most of them are in calmecac. Can you imagine my keeping control over five shrieking children?"

I shook my head. "Three is enough." Mazatl and Necalli were both in the courtyard, helping, with the intent seriousness of children, to water the flowers.

Ollin had fallen asleep. Mihmatini laid him in his cradle, humming a lullaby. She'd make a good mother. If only Neutemoc would start seeking a husband for her. Unlikely, given his present state of mind.

"The wards?" I asked. For, after all, it was the only reason Neutemoc endured my presence.

Mihmatini smiled, bitterly. "Come and see them," she said.

The last light of the afternoon, golden, already fading towards evening, illuminated the buildings around the courtyard, throwing into sharp relief the painted frescoes of pyramid temples and star-constellations. The buildings should have blazed with the presence of magic; but almost nothing shone.

I ran a hand on the adobe: the magic pulsed weakly under my fingertips like the heartbeat of a dying man.

"They came back?" I asked. "The creatures?"

Mihmatini stood a few paces from the wall, her arms crossed over her chest. "I suppose so. The wards kept fading every time I looked, and that's not normal."

I suppressed the curse that came to my lips. "You should have–"

"Called for you? You can't spend your time guarding us," Mihmatini said. "You have to stop whoever is doing this, not exhaust yourself fighting pointless battles." She'd inherited Father's pragmatism, although not Father's bleak moods, for which I was eternally thankful. "Speaking of which, any progress?"

"No," I said. The only thing I was sure of was that Chalchiutlicue was involved, somehow. It couldn't be directly: for She couldn't act in the Fifth World without an agent. But I still didn't see why the Jade Skirt would want to kill Eleuia or Neutemoc.

248

"Mm," Mihmatini said. "I'll rebuild the wards again."

I sent to my temple for hummingbirds, birds sacred to Huitzilpochtli. It was with their blood that my sister rebuilt the wards, layer after layer. When she was finished, the house shone in my priest-senses like a small sun; and night was upon us.

"You should stay here tonight," Mihmatini said.

"I don't think Neutemoc would appreciate it."

"Neutemoc is going to appreciate waking up tomorrow morning, and finding his children and servants safe," Mihmatini snapped. "Honestly, you two are worse than calmecac students."

"It's not that simple," I started, unwilling to involve her in our quarrels.

Mihmatini snorted. "It's always simple, Acatl. You're the only ones who can't see that."

Neutemoc, forced by Mihmatini, accepted that I stand guard, but in the courtyard, nowhere near him.

I took an ornate reed mat from one of the spare rooms, and laid it under the shadow of the pine tree. Then I sat in the darkness, and watched Metzli the moon climb into the sky. The air was hot, humid; the rainy season wasn't far away.

Behind me, the house was silent, a far cry from the joyous place I remembered, the place of riches and warmth I'd envied Neutemoc so much. Once, I would have felt glad of my brother's downfall, but that was when both our parents had still been alive. Now... I didn't know what to think. He had ruined his own marriage – leading, ultimately, to Huei's impending death, and the destruction of the haven they'd both created for my nephews and nieces – and that I found hardest to forgive.

The wards Mihmatini had traced shone brightly in the night. But, as the moon rose higher and higher and the dampness of the night worked its way into my bones, I became aware of a scratching noise behind the walls: like claws, scrabbling at the adobe.

I rose, and laid my hand flat on the wall of the nearest building. Under my palm was the deep, familiar pulse of magic; but it was erratic, rising and fading to the rhythm of those scratching claws. And each time it faded, it rose a little weaker than before.

Mihmatini had been right: whatever was on the other side of that wall was depleting our wards.

I withdrew my hand, and unsheathed one of my obsidian knives. I knelt in the dirt of the courtyard and opened my veins, saying a prayer to Quetzalcoatl:

*"Yours is the knowledge of the priests,*
*Yours is the knowledge of the stars wheeling in the sky*
*You find the precious jade, the precious feathers..."*

A darkness deeper than night swept across the courtyard, extinguishing the moon and the stars in the sky. The buildings around me slowly receded into indistinct shadows, leaving only my pulsing blood, shining on the ground.

The walls, too, became shadows interlaced with the network of our wards. Through those, I could see the creatures. They were, without a doubt, the same shapeless things that had attacked us on the previous day. This time, though, there weren't three, but at least ten of them.

Eyeless, mindless, they swarmed around Neutemoc's house, scooping up the essence of our wards with their claws. They made a small, huffing noise as they did so: something that could have been breathing, were it not obvious that they had no lungs.

In my time as a priest, I had seen many things – Haunting Mothers returned from their graves, beasts of shadows tearing out hearts, gods smiling as we shed our blood – but nothing, nothing was quite so eerie as these creatures' mindless insistence. I had no doubt that, in time, they'd whittle down our wards to nothing.

What were those things?

I knelt again and cut open my veins once more, to draw another quincunx, this time for an invocation to Mixcoatl, God of the Hunt:

> *"You who come forth from Chicomoztoc, honoured one,*
> *You who come with the net of maguey ropes*
> *The basket of woven reeds*
> *You who come forth from Tziuactitlan, honoured one…"*

Power blazed across the quincunx, wrapping itself around me, sinking into my bones. The usual dizziness was made worse by my spell of true sight. I barely managed to rise after completing the invocation.

I looked at the creatures again. They were still clawing at the walls, pressing against each other to feed on our wards. I couldn't help shuddering. Their mindlessness, their relentlessness didn't seem to belong in an ordered world.

From their centre issued a thread of white power, so faint it was almost transparent. The threads joined, high above the creatures, in some sort of complicated knot: a spell of control. After the knot…

I narrowed my gaze to see. Beyond the knot, the threads merged into one, and hurtled back towards the earth. I couldn't see where the spell ended. To do that, I'd need to go outside, to walk past those creatures. In principle, the spell of protection Mihmatini had cast on all of us the previous afternoon should keep me from their sight. In principle.

I guessed they would pay no attention to me: they hadn't done so when they'd attacked us, not unless we stood between them and Neutemoc. But there were guesses, and then there was truth. There were blustering boasts – and there was Quechomitl's body, lying on the ground, draining itself of blood through his wounds, drop after drop, going deeper into Mictlan with every passing moment.

I closed my eyes. Did I want to do this? For Neutemoc? For my brother, who could only fling the reproaches of the past into my face?

No. For Huei, who had let herself be dragged into this. Who had let someone manipulate her, not knowing the price. Someone would pay for this. There would be justice: the only thing I could give her.

I went to wake up Mihmatini.

She was not happy. "You want to do what?" she asked, when she'd finished rubbing at her eyes.

"Find the source," I said, pointing to the wall. "And you–"

"Yes," Mihmatini said, curtly. "I should keep watch." She puffed her cheeks, thoughtfully. "I'll renew Huitzilpochtli's wards on you, just in case."

I watched her trace a quick circle on the ground – Neutemoc was never going to forgive us for the mess in his courtyard – and start a hymn to Huitzilpochtli.

> *"Coming forth in the garb of our ancestors*
> *You led them forth from Aztlan, the White Place*
> *You led them forth from Colhuacan, the Place of Deception*
> *You led them forth into battle…"*

Radiance blazed across the courtyard, as strong as sunlight. It sank into my skin, tingling with warmth, hissing as it came into contact with Mictlan's knives at my belt. I waited for the feeling to subside; for the protection to be complete.

Mihmatini looked at me critically. "Hum," she said. "It's not really taken hold, has it? It's already skittering away."

Unlike Neutemoc, I wasn't a devotee of the Hummingbird; quite the reverse, in fact. Mictlantecuhtli and Huitzilpochtli were opposites: the dry, wizened God of Death and the youthful War God could hardly be compatible. "How long do I have?" I asked.

Mihmatini shrugged. "A couple of hours. I'd tell you to be careful, but I know when I'm just wasting my time. Do try to come back without leaking any blood."

I made a mock punching gesture; she sidestepped, gracefully, smiling. "You're getting better at this whole humour thing," she said.

I didn't trouble myself to answer that.

As I passed the gates with a lit torch in my hand, three of the creatures turned towards me: a quick, lithe movement that put me in mind of snakes or pikes. I held my breath, knowing with a cold spike in my belly that I was lost if they decided to attack me.

But the spell worked: they didn't pay attention to me. They merely turned to the wall, and started feeding again, huffing. It might have been, I realised with a chill, my brother's name they were breathing out, over and over.

I turned away from Neutemoc's house, and followed the rope of magic that issued from the creatures. It snaked, leisurely, through the wide streets and canals of Moyotlan: past the houses with the sweet smells of banquet food wafting out into the night, past the groups of warriors going into the Houses of Joy, laughing among themselves.

Here, alone in the darkness, I was in my element – not High Priest, not brother or son to anyone – but tracking a wrong in the fabric of the universe. For the first time in days, I felt at peace. A strange kind of peace, tinged with the awareness that it couldn't last, but it still soothed my heart.

The trail snaked south, towards the Itzapalapan causeway, the same direction we'd taken when hunting for the beast of shadows. I walked through the deserted streets, thinking on the case. Moonlight shimmered on the canals to my right and to my left; and the reed boats at anchor bobbed up and down, as if on the rhythm of some unseen breath.

Someone had tortured Eleuia; and someone was now trying to kill Neutemoc. It might be for the same reason, in which case they both had knowledge of a secret. But Neutemoc had sounded sincerely ignorant of anything useful. Or, it might be two different groups, trying to achieve different aims.

But still, what vital information could Eleuia have possessed? Despite everything Neutemoc had said to me, my instincts told me that it had to do with Eleuia's child. But why, if the child was indeed dead? Unless Neutemoc had been deceived. Unless, blinded by love, he had seen exactly what Eleuia wanted him to see.

I walked past the fort at the gates of Tenochtitlan. The warriors on duty, standing outside with their feather-shields and throwing spears, gave me a cursory glance, and dismissed me as harmless. The trail was still following its leisurely path along the Itzapalapan causeway. My heartbeat quickened. Could it be so easy to find who was behind the summoning of the creatures?

Alas, it was not to be. For, as the trail went over the third of the wooden bridges in the causeway, it plunged downwards; and faded into nothingness. Huitzilpochtli curse the summoner and all his ilk. Once again, they'd planned ahead, and their trail was well hidden. I'd endangered myself for nothing.

I fumed all the way back to Neutemoc's house, indiscriminately consigning to the depths of Mictlan the summoners, Huei, Neutemoc, and the goddess Chalchiutlicue – though I still couldn't see Her part in this. She'd had nothing to gain from Eleuia's death. But still… I couldn't quite shake the impression that I was missing something, and that the key was Neutemoc.

At the gates of the house, the creatures were still crowding and the wards were much weaker than they had been an hour before. Mihmatini was on her knees in the courtyard, going through the last stages of re-newing them again. She nodded grimly at me.

It was a blessing the creatures still couldn't reach Neutemoc. But Mihmatini was right. We couldn't pro-tect him and his household for ever.

I woke up early: a few moments before dawn, at a time when the first of the kitchen slaves were pound-ing maize into flour. The rhythmic thump of the pestle against the mortar filled the courtyard as the sky light-ened – bringing, as always, memories of a childhood I couldn't come back to.

In silence, I made my offerings of blood to Lord Death. The courtyard was still deserted. The slave who guarded the gates had obviously not been replaced since Quechomitl's death. I checked Mihmatini's wards, cursorily. The creatures were still scratching at the wall; but the wards had held. I kept seeing Teomitl's face, that moment before he turned and walked away from Neutemoc and me.

Who are you? Tizoc-tzin's cousin?

*I'm his brother.*

This wasn't going to be a good day.

I managed to get some spiced maize gruel from the kitchen, and ate it sitting under the pine tree, as the light flooding the courtyard turned from pink to white.

"I thought I might find you here," Ceyaxochitl said.

Startled, I looked up. She was standing over me, leaning on her cane.

My first reaction wasn't exactly joy. "What in the Fifth World–?" I asked, pulling myself to my feet.

"You haven't been at your temple lately."

"No," I said, curtly. The Southern Hummingbird blind me if I had to explain myself to her. "I've been busy."

"I've heard," Ceyaxochitl said. She leaned on her cane, looking for all the world like an old woman enjoying the morning sun. I wasn't fooled. "You have some interesting things outside, as well."

"You saw them?" What a foolish question. She was Guardian of the Sacred Precinct, agent of the Duality in the Fifth World. Of course she'd see them.

"Yes," Ceyaxochitl said. "Persistent little things. A marvel of creation."

"Creation?" I asked.

"Someone made them," she said, as if it was obvious.

"A sorcerer?" I asked.

She shook her head. "I think not. Though they might well have summoned them."

"A god, then?" I asked. Chalchiutlicue had created the ahuizotls, after all, to keep watch over Her waters.

"Maybe," Ceyaxochitl said.

The last thing I needed was gods thinking They could play games with our lives. Xochiquetzal and Her kind weren't much interested in the Fifth World, as a rule. But I guessed pliant toys were always irresistible.

"I take it that means you have no idea how to kill them?" I asked, unable to restrain my sarcasm.

Ceyaxochitl shrugged. "Nothing is invulnerable. I can look into it, if you wish. Though I didn't come here for that."

"No," I said. "What for, then?"

"My warriors trawled through Lake Texcoco. We've found some of Priestess Eleuia's things."

"What things? Clothes?" Clothes would be carried by the current, and hard to find again. Heavy things, on the other hand, would sink to the bottom.

"A purse," Ceyaxochitl said. "And an obsidian knife in its sheath. Teomitl confirms that it belonged to her."

"Teomitl," I said, not without bitterness. "What were you thinking, sending him to me?"

She looked at me – for once, genuinely surprised. "It seemed obvious, Acatl. The boy needs guidance, badly. Ever since the death of his mother he's grown up like a wildflower."

"And I was to train him?" I asked.

"I don't see what there is to be angry about." Her voice was infuriatingly reasonable.

"You don't?" I asked. "I almost got him killed by a beast of shadows, and you ask what the problem is?"

"He's a grown man," Ceyaxochitl said. "He can take his own risks."

"No," I said. "A grown man can, but the brother of the Emperor?" If he had died under my responsibility, the Imperial Guards would have arrested me immediately.

"The Emperor has many brothers," Ceyaxochitl said. "Not all of whom reached adolescence."

I was shaking, badly. "Then tell me this: how far away is he from being Revered Speaker?"

"Tizoc-tzin will be Revered Speaker when Axaya-catl-tzin dies in the next few weeks." Ceyaxochitl said "when", not "if".

"And when Tizoc-tzin is crowned?" I asked. "What will Teomitl be?"

She had the grace to look away. "Master of the House of Darts, if he has proved himself."

Master of the House of Darts. Commander of the greatest arsenal in Tenochtitlan, all the paraphernalia of war. Heir-apparent to the Mexica Empire.

If he had proved himself. My task was all too obvious. "I won't be his training ground," I spat between clenched teeth.

"Why?" Ceyaxochitl's voice was genuinely curious. "Think of the influence you'd have over him – a man who will one day be Emperor, the Duality willing."

"I'm a priest. I don't meddle in politics."

"Acatl." There was pity in her voice – all the more worrying because she seldom showed compassion for anyone. "Priests thrive on politics. If you wanted a life free of them, you should have been–"

"A warrior." I knew. I also knew that I could never have been like Neutemoc, that I didn't have the courage to enter the battlefield, or the relentless will for combat that kept warriors going. And I also knew how much it hurt.

"If you won't take part in politics," Ceyaxochitl was saying, "politics will be the death of you."

"I'll keep my head down."

"Your head down?" she laughed. "You're High Priest for the Dead. There's no hiding place any more."

"I never asked to be High Priest," I said. "You got me into this." It was all too easy to fling the accusation into her face.

She didn't move. She didn't rise to the bait as Neutemoc or Teomitl would have done. After a while, she said, tapping her cane against the ground, "You can't remain small all your life, Acatl."

"What if it's the only thing I want?" I asked, knowing that it was true. My place had been in Coyoacan, with my small parish – not in the grand temple of the Sacred Precinct, where I was as ill at ease as a fish on dry land.

She still wouldn't look at me. "Everyone has to grow up and take responsibilities," she said, in an unusually quiet voice. "Even small, humble priests."

"Not everyone," I said. She was wrong. I wasn't made for any of the things she wanted me to do – neither for managing the politics linked to Teomitl, nor with my temple. Ichtaca would take care of that, much better than I could ever hope to do.

Ceyaxochitl made a small, annoyed gesture. "Very well. Let's focus on the investigation, then. Do you want to see Eleuia's things?"

"How far is it?" I asked.

"Not far. They're at the Duality House."

I didn't think anything would come of it, but I didn't want to leave an avenue unexplored. "Let me warn my sister," I said.

Ceyaxochitl was looking at the walls, cocking her head left and right. "Your sister. The family's youngest, if I remember correctly. I assume she set the wards?"

"Yes."

She nodded. "She's good, Acatl."

I smiled. "But not, I think, bound for priesthood or guardianhood."

Ceyaxochitl shrugged. "Life has many paths," she said. "Anyway, with all those… things eating away at them, they're not going to last long, no matter how strong. Let me give you a hand to set up something more durable."

Mihmatini did not take to Ceyaxochitl; but even she had to admit that the Guardian's work was impressive. By the time Ceyaxochitl was finished, the house shone as brightly as the sun, moon and stars combined. The walls were covered by an intricate network of shimmering lines, anchored between the underworld and the Heavens, and taking its strength from both.

At a guess, this would last for days.

"There," Ceyaxochitl said. "Let's go now."

In a small room of the Duality House, Yaotl had spread out Eleuia's possessions on a reed mat: an obsidian knife with a hilt in the shape of a warrior and an ornate sheath; the closed purse, soaked with water. I fingered the knife – a sharp, deadly thing, but without a hint of magic – and its sheath of cured leather, with its straps cut open.

"You haven't opened it?" I asked, touching the purse.

"No," Ceyaxochitl said. "I kept it aside for you."

Gently, I loosened the strings and tipped the contents of the purse onto the reed mat. Soggy cacao beans tumbled out; and dark-green discs, half-eaten by rot.

No. Not discs. Plants.

I picked up one, ignoring the mouldy smell that wafted into my nostrils. It had been sliced off with three expert knife-cuts. In the centre was a lighter circular area, no larger than the tip of my finger.

"Peyotl?" I said, aloud. "I didn't know the priestesses of Xochiquetzal partook of it." Peyotl, collected from the top of a cactus, was a powerful drug that allowed some priests to enter a divinatory trance. One of its first effects was nausea, and a sense of dislocation from the world.

Ceyaxochitl shook her head. "They shouldn't, but it's not forbidden."

Something about peyotl was troubling me. Something about Neutemoc. It wouldn't come back, though. I sighed. "Not much of interest."

Ceyaxochitl did not bother to comment.

"And the mark on Eleuia's body?" I asked.

"Yaotl has been making enquiries. I'll let you know when we have something."

As I walked out of the Duality House, she added, "I'll look into the creatures and help your sister with the wards, if they don't hold. But if I were you, I'd get your brother out of Tenochtitlan for a while."

"Why?" I asked.

"Someone is summoning them," Ceyaxochitl said. "They can't be far from their creatures, or they'd lose their hold. Remove yourself from the scene, and there is a strong chance they won't follow."

"I see. Thank you," I said. How in the Fifth World was I supposed to convince Neutemoc that he had to flee the city?

I went back to Neutemoc's house, to see about the wards – and because if I didn't go to him, he'd never know where I was. On my way there, I stopped by a street vendor to buy a chocolate, and sipped it while I walked. The pleasant, pungent taste of vanilla and spice soothed my nerves. In fact, all I could taste was the vanilla and spice, the chocolate being drowned underneath.

I kept seeing the sheath on Eleuia, its straps cut by the rocks and the branches the body had bounced against. It had been of small use to her, in the end.

I closed my eyes for a brief moment. I hadn't been paying enough attention to the sheath. Three straps, distributed evenly along the length of the blade. This wasn't a belt sheath: it was made to hide the knife against one's ankles or calves.

Instants before she disappeared, Eleuia had been carrying that knife. But she had also been safe within her rooms, in the process of seducing Neutemoc. It didn't fit. If you intend to take a man into your bed, why would you need to keep your knife? Unless…

The peyotl. I remembered Neutemoc's words on our first interview: *She poured me a glass of frothy chocolate,*

261

*with milk and maize gruel – good chocolate, too, very tasty. That's the last thing I remember clearly. Then the room was spinning, and...*

The room was spinning – not because of the beast of shadows, but because of the peyotl Eleuia had put into his chocolate. No wonder Neutemoc had been over-turning the furniture by the time the guards had arrived: he must have been hallucinating, hardly aware of what he was doing.

*If she flirted with you, it's because you had something she wanted,* Mahuizoh had said. She had wanted some-thing out of him: his silence. And, if she could not get it by flirting – because Neutemoc was still a funda-mentally honest man – then she'd make sure he didn't speak.

It was a monstrous hypothesis. But it fit the facts, and the character of Eleuia, all too well.

But why had she thought Neutemoc was a danger to her? What had made it so important to her, to the point of driving Mahuizoh, her steadfast lover and support, furious with jealousy?

Neutemoc's words came back into my mind, with agonising clarity: *She was cold when she first saw me. I had to remind her of the Chalca Wars before she'd pay attention to me.*

Neutemoc had to know something he hadn't told me yet. And it all dated back to the Chalca Wars.

Suddenly all became clear. I was tired of running away; of reacting to events forced upon me by others. It was time to take my own initiatives. I had to get Neutemoc away from Tenochtitlan? Then we'd go to-gether to see the battlefields of the wars, and the place where Eleuia had supposedly buried her dead child.

# SIXTEEN

## *Setting Forth*

"You're mad," Neutemoc said, flatly. He was sitting in his room, on a reed mat, looking up at me as if I'd just offered him a chance to witness the birth of the Sun God.

It wasn't wholly unexpected; but it still grated that he'd dismiss everything I said, as if I had no intrinsic value.

"Look–" I started.

"There's no 'look'. Do you seriously expect me to believe those lies about Eleuia?"

"The peyotl was real."

"And the rest are your own delusions." Neutemoc's voice was cold.

That stung. But the conversation had been going on for a while, in much the same fashion, and I was beginning to see that I'd never convince Neutemoc of Eleuia's guilt. He might have accepted the fact that she might have had an ulterior motive for seducing him, but not that the motive was silencing him. That was too great a setback.

But I'd thought of other arguments to convince him. "Come into the courtyard, will you?"

I'd already traced a quincunx on the ground. Neutemoc stared at it. "There had better be a good reason," he said, his face darkening.

"It's not going to be long," I snapped. "Are you going to listen to anything I'm saying?"

"I'm not sure," he said. But he still let me put him in the centre of the quincunx. He did recoil when I dabbed my blood onto his forehead – a slight movement anyone who didn't know him would have missed – but he didn't say anything.

When I finished casting the spell of true sight on him, he stiffened and stood still as the world went dark around him. I knew what he would be seeing: my blood pulsing at his feet and, behind the shadowy walls of his house, the creatures, frantically crowding to leach the magic from the wall.

Even imagining them nauseated me. Whoever had made those things had a sick, sick sense of what constituted life, or a very good idea of what could frighten men.

Neutemoc stood still. His lips moved, without sound. Then, in a heartbeat, he crossed the courtyard, and crouched by the wall. He watched them as he must have watched enemies before an ambush.

"Those are the things that killed Quechomitl?" he asked.

"Yes."

"How long have they been there?"

I shrugged. "Two days. The only reason they're not getting inside is because Mihmatini is frighteningly good at what she does."

Ordinarily, Neutemoc would have reacted. He would have made some wry comment about Mihmatini. But he didn't. He just crouched there, one hand resting on the hilt of his macuahitl sword. His eyes had narrowed to slits.

"What do they want?" he asked, though he had to know.

"You," I said. "Your household, very possibly."

"My children?" His voice was flat, deadly.

For once, I was glad the anger wasn't directed at me. I didn't actually think the creatures were clever enough to draw Neutemoc out by attacking his children. They'd just kill anyone who might protect him. But I had to get him out of Tenochtitlan, and to Chalco, to know why his house was under siege.

I said – not quite a lie, but not quite the truth either: "Anyone close to you. There's a powerful sorcerer behind them. And trust me, they won't give up."

He was silent for a while. "And this has to do with Eleuia?"

"Yes," I said. The chance that it didn't was minuscule. "You know something," I went on. "Something that's dangerous to someone. And Eleuia did, too."

Neutemoc didn't turn. "I told you already. I don't know anything relevant."

"You may not think you do. Why not come with me to Chalco? It's one day's journey at most."

Neutemoc shook his head. "To Chalco, yes. But that's not the place you want to see, Acatl. Most of the battles of the Chalco Wars took place near Amecameca, at the foot of Popocatepetl's volcano. That's two days. And I really think there are better times to leave the city."

"When you're under siege by creatures you can't fight?"

"I never asked for that." His voice implied, quite effectively, that he held me responsible for this state of affairs.

It wasn't the moment to start another fight. I held my silence, though I chafed inside.

Finally Neutemoc said, "Two days to go, two days there, and two days to return. Not more, Acatl."

Six days away was both not enough and too much. Not enough, for we had no idea what we were looking for. Too much, because of the unknown sorcerer who was currently besieging Neutemoc's house – for all I knew, he might turn his attention away from my brother, and to some other part of the city, and that wasn't a pleasant thought. All I could do was pray that the Seven Serpent would grant us Her fickle luck, for the journey to be fruitful, and the city to remain safe.

"Very well," I said. "Six days."

Some things couldn't be put off forever. I went to my temple to collect some of the things I'd need for the journey – and found Ichtaca, waiting for me in the courtyard with his arms crossed over his bare torso.

"Acatl-tzin." His voice had the edge of broken obsidian.

I'd been putting our discussion off ever since the Imperial Audience, but I couldn't in all decency continue to ignore him. "Let's find a quiet place," I said.

The quiet place turned out to be the same room where I'd prepared for the hunt of the beast of shadows. Dried blood still stained the ground: the faded remnants of my quincunx, not completely subsumed into the earth.

Ichtaca sat cross-legged on the ground, looking up at me, but saying nothing.

"You wanted to speak to me?" I said.

Ichtaca didn't move. I sat cross-legged in front of him; and we watched each other like a pair of jaguars after the same prey. Finally Ichtaca sighed. "Things have to change, Acatl-tzin."

"You've been angry at me," I said. "For not attending the Imperial Court?"

Ichtaca didn't speak for a while. He lowered his eyes to the ground, traced a line in the earth with his index fingers. "No," he said. "At least, not in the way that you would understand it."

That was more words than we'd ever exchanged. "You wanted the temple," I said, groping for reasons for his iniquity. "To be High Priest yourself?"

Ichtaca smiled. "You should know, Acatl-tzin. A Fire Priest for the main temple, no matter how competent, doesn't rise to that level – not so quickly, not without favour."

"I still don't understand–" I said, feeling more and more ill at ease.

"I'm Fire Priest of this temple. I see to its daily business," Ichtaca said. "I know my place. But you do not."

Whatever I'd expected, it wasn't such a reproach. "You–"

"You're High Priest," Ichtaca said. He raised his eyes, to look directly at me. "Head of the whole order. But you pass through this temple like a shadow."

What was he talking about? "I'm not sure…"

Ichtaca put both hands on the ground. "Listen to me," he said. "Then you can expel me from here, if that's what you want."

He and I both knew I couldn't really demote him. Ichtaca was only half-lying when he said his appointment hadn't been political: one did not become Fire Priest of a temple in the Sacred Precinct randomly, or even through talent. "Go on," I said, although I liked this conversation less and less.

"You have priests," Ichtaca said. "They serve, and do the vigils and the proper sacrifices. In return, they expect something from you."

I still didn't see what he wanted.

"You're High Priest," Ichtaca said. "Responsible for all of them. I run this temple, but you keep it together."

"I can't–"

"If you don't know the proper ways, I or someone else will show you, or replace you. If you don't want to attend the Imperial Audience, I can go. But you cannot detach yourself from what we do."

"I do the vigils," I said finally, still surprised that he'd judge me. I had not paid enough attention to him, seeing him as part of responsibilities I didn't want to accept. My mistake.

Ichtaca shook his head. The conch-shell around his neck clinked, softly, against his necklace of jade. "This isn't about vigils. It's about–" He pushed both hands into the ground, obviously frustrated at his inability to find the right words. He said, finally, "Someone has to stand for what we do. Someone has to make us into more than individual priests: into the clergy of Mictlantecuhtli."

"I'm not a leader," I said.

"Then be a figurehead," Ichtaca said. He sounded – not angry, but desperate. "Most priests in this temple haven't even seen your face. You keep to your house. You keep to yourself. It can't work. If all you wanted was this, you should have stayed in Coyoacan."

"Understand this," I said, annoyed now. "I didn't ask to be posted here. I wanted to stay in Coyoacan." Doing what I had always done: caring for the small, the forgotten; those who could not attain the glorious ends of warriors, but who would still be mourned.

Ichtaca made a grimace. Plainly, he didn't believe me. "It's a political appointment."

"Yes," I snapped. "The Guardian campaigned for it."

"You had to–"

"Refuse? How do you refuse an Imperial Edict?"

He knew, as I well did, that you couldn't.

Ichtaca was silent for a while. "You may not have wanted it, but it doesn't change anything. Everyone needs someone to look up to, and you're not filling this space."

"I can't," I said. "You know I can't."

Ichtaca's face tightened. "Be there. In this temple. Know what goes on. Speak to everyone, offering priest or novice priest. I can do the rest."

"And that's all you want?"

"No," Ichtaca said. "I want you to lead us. But it will have to do, for the time being."

"That's not…"

"It is possible," Ichtaca said.

"Not right now," I said, obscurely embarrassed. "I have to leave on a journey."

Ichtaca's face didn't move, but I knew the expression. Disappointment. Anger. It was the one Father had borne all his life; and even in the blankness of death I'd still seen it engraved on his face.

"When I come back…" I said.

Ichtaca smiled, half-sadly, half-angrily. He didn't believe me. And I couldn't blame him. But I'd never been meant for this place, for this function. Everything in this temple confirmed that I was just a fraud.

If only I could resign. But it wasn't a possibility.

"I'll be gone for six days," I said.

Ichtaca smiled, though there was no joy in it. "On an official journey?"

"No, not quite," I said, embarrassed. "It has to do with Priestess Eleuia."

Ichtaca pursed his lips. I didn't like the light that had come into his eyes. "It's an official journey, then. Take two of the priests with you."

"But–"

"I won't let it be said that our High Priest has no escort when he goes on temple business."

He looked at me: like Teomitl, waiting for me to defy him, to contradict his authority. Knowing that I couldn't. "Very well," I said. "I'll take the priests. We'll talk about the rest when I come back."

I was once more avoiding confrontation, but there was no other way. Huei had to be avenged; and I had to understand who was threatening Neutemoc, who was threatening Mihmatini and my nephews and nieces.

Because they were the only priests I knew, I asked Ezamahual and Palli to come with us. Both of them looked surprised by the request. In fact, knowing their taste for staying inside the temple, I would have expected them to refuse. But of course, no one could refuse their High Priest.

"Where are we going?" Ezamahual asked.

"Chalca. And then to the foot of Popocatepetl's volcano."

"I'll take some supplies," Palli said.

He also took along Ezamahual, who as a novice priest was beneath him in the hierarchy of the temple. When they both came out of the storehouse, Ezamahual was burdened with equipment: he carried several cages containing macaws and owls, and a heavy bag that Palli would not let me open. "You never know what you might need, Acatl-tzin."

We went back to Neutemoc's house. My brother was waiting for us in the courtyard, with one slave by his side: a tall, dour fellow by the name of Tepalotl, who carried my brother's bag.

"Priests?" Neutemoc asked, looking sceptically at Ezamahual and Palli.

Palli bristled. "The High Priest's escort," he said.

"I see," was all Neutemoc would say. "Mihmatini said she had something to give us."

My sister finally emerged from the house, with a bundle of maize flatbread. "You'll need that," she said, handing it to Palli. The smell of spices wafted from her callused hands – and for an eerie moment she was the image of Mother, standing in the courtyard, watching Father go out to the fields, in those bygone days when Neutemoc and I had still been children, daring each other to dive in the lake.

I shook my head, still hearing Ceyaxochitl's voice. *Everyone has to grow up, Acatl.*

"Anything wrong?" Mihmatini asked.

She'd always been perceptive. Too much, perhaps. "No, nothing. Thank you," I said.

"I'll put more wards up," Mihmatini said. "That might just fool them into thinking Neutemoc is still here."

It might. It couldn't hurt, in any case. "Don't overexert yourself."

She shrugged. "I can handle it."

Neutemoc and Tepalotl were already outside, waiting for me, not speaking. With my spell of true sight still on Neutemoc, he'd had some misgivings about stepping so near the creatures. But Mihmatini's protection still held: the creatures approached, but could not see him, and soon lost interest.

We walked the first section of the journey in silence, Palli, Ezamahual and Neutemoc's slave in tow. I kept looking back, to see the creatures still frantically attacking the walls of Neutemoc's house. I feared they'd follow us, that one of them would turn and see my brother. But they didn't. Our protection spell hung firm, and we were soon out of sight.

We went south on the crowded Itzapalapan causeway, looking for the nearest boat to Chalco. Women from the southern suburbs passed us, going to the Tlatelolco marketplace to sell the wares on their backs: woven cloth of maguey fibres, ceramic bowls and tanned leather skins.

The Itzapalapan Causeway was the largest of all three causeways linking the mainland to Tenochtitlan. It forked near the shore: depending on the path you chose, two or three hours' walk would lead to Culhuacan or Coyoacan. On the fork was a fort manned by warriors with the Imperial insignia and, a little further down, a harbour where Palli bargained with a fisherman for passage to Chalco.

Ezamahual stood at my side, watching his fellow priest. "He's always been good at this," he said, with an encouraging smile at me. Trying to draw me out, I guessed – and was grateful to him for the attention.

"So I see."

"He's the one who trades at the marketplace for the storehouse."

Palli finished his bargaining, and handed the fisherman a small purse. "There you go," he said. "A day's journey."

The fisherman's reed boat was larger than the ones our temple owned, and the small one in which Oyohuaca and I had chased Huei through the canals. We fitted, quite comfortably, in the front, even with Ezamahual's load of equipment.

As the fisherman pushed away from the shore, Neutemoc turned towards the city of Tenochtitlan, outlined in the morning sun: the gates leading to the southern districts of Moyotlan and Zoquipan; and the shadow of the Great Temple rising above all the pyramids of the Sacred Precinct. His face was a mask, and he did not speak a word.

In silence, we went south, leaving Lake Texcoco for Lake Xochimilco and the maze of Floating Gardens that sustained Tenochtitlan's agriculture. Even though it was daytime, I kept my eyes out for ahuizotls; but there was nothing in the water but weeds and algae. The steady splash of the oars was the only noise punctuating the journey: the boat, navigating unerringly between the rows of artificial lands, passed from Lake Xochimilco into Lake Chalco – before leaving us, late in the evening, at the limestone gates of the city of Chalco.

Before the gates, soldiers in feather regalia manned a fort much like the ones at the exit of Tenochtitlan. They had throwing spears and feather-covered shields, adorned with an upright coyote. They watched us with a bored air: we were only the last of a steady stream of travellers seeking passage through the city.

There were inns for travelling merchants, but Neutemoc had no wish to mingle with those he saw as his social inferiors. He was being ridiculous, and I argued with him about this, but he wouldn't budge. We ended up camping in a field, some hundred measures away from the city's first houses.

The air was warm, saturated with the promise of rain. The dry season was still upon us: Lake Chalco had sunk to low levels, revealing the woven mat-and-branches structure of the numerous Floating Gardens in the vicinity.

Neutemoc sat against a wizened tree, his whole body tense. He had spoken few words during the journey, sinking into a silence I wasn't sure I liked.

"Acatl?" he asked.

I raised my head. "Yes?"

"Can you see whether those – things – are here?"

"They haven't followed us," I said.

"Is that a guess, or an observation?"

I had been keeping a watch, but had relaxed it on the last leg of our journey. "How would they come here?" I asked.

"So you're not sure."

He had some nerve asking me this, after seemingly not caring about staying in his besieged house. "No," I snapped.

"Can you see?" Neutemoc asked again.

I was tired, and the last thing I wanted was to draw more of my blood to fuel a spell. But it was clear Neutemoc was going to work at me until I gave in.

I turned to Ezamahual, Palli, and Neutemoc's slave Tepalotl, who had been watching this in silence. "Can you do a spell of true sight?"

Palli shrugged. "Not a problem. What are we looking for?"

"Anything suspicious," I said. I described the creatures as best as I could.

In the waning light, Ezamahual's face became pale, leached of colours. "They don't sound very friendly," he said.

Palli was already rummaging in Ezamahual's pack, withdrawing a caged owl and a purse of what looked like dayflower. "Come on," he said. "Let's go."

Neutemoc said, "Take Tepalotl if you're going far away from the camp. You'll need some kind of protection while you cast those spells." His lips were pursed: clearly he didn't believe in their fighting abilities.

Neutemoc's slave Tepalotl followed my two priests in silence, leaving both of us at our improvised campsite. Neutemoc and I unpacked the maize flatbreads and the flasks of water, preparing the small meal we would eat. Kneeling in the mud, we looked at each other for a while, the same thought on our minds: could we start a fire here?

Neutemoc was the first to shake his head. "Too damp," he said. "Unless you have a spell."

"You don't summon gods for trifles," I said.

Neutemoc smiled, briefly. "Then we'll just be damp, won't we?"

Palli, Ezamahual and the slave Tepalotl were walking back towards us. Ezamahual was carrying the limp body of the owl in his hands, and looking puzzled.

"Nothing," Palli said, curtly, when they reached the camp. "Not a trace of anything magical."

"Good," Neutemoc said. He inclined his head a fraction. "Thank you."

I couldn't help feeling relieved. It was one thing to have Ceyaxochitl's assurances that all would be well once we left Tenochtitlan, and another to actually see it happen.

Palli, Ezamahual and Tepalotl took their share of food, and drew back from us: my two priests at the edge of the camp, talking quietly among themselves, and Neutemoc's slave a bit further, standing guard in the darkness.

Neutemoc didn't speak for a while. He reached for one of the maize flatbreads, and cradled it in the palm of his hands, staring at the darkening skies.

"It brings one back," he said at last. "All of this."

I swallowed a bite of my flatbread. If he was in a talkative mood, I'd be a fool not to draw him out, to understand why someone was threatening him. Although I feared it was going to cost me. So far, I hadn't seen much to explain why he'd behaved in such a spectacularly foolish fashion. "It must have changed in sixteen years."

"Not that much," Neutemoc said. "Places don't change. People – that's another story." His voice was bitter.

"Eleuia?" I asked.

Neutemoc didn't answer for a while. "Let's not bring her up, shall we? We'll disagree. And I wasn't thinking about her."

He was in a melancholy mood tonight. "About whom, then?" I asked.

He smiled, a flash of white teeth in the growing darkness. "There was a time when all I wanted was

275

the certainty that I would live until the morrow."

"War is that way." I felt like an impostor. I'd never been to war, after all.

Two days ago, Neutemoc would have risen to the bait, taunting me with what I'd failed to accomplish with my life. "Life was simpler, back then," he said.

"Yes." I thought of my small temple in Coyoacan, of comforting the bereaved, tracking down underworld monsters. Simple things. But life, it seemed, was no longer that simple, either for Neutemoc or for me.

Neutemoc finished the last of his flatbread, and wiped his hands clean. "Things change. You grow stale, complacent. Sometimes, you deserve your own fall."

Stale? Yes, stale. His growing indifference to Huei had certainly done little to close the growing breach between them. As for his attempted adultery with Eleuia…

He went on, "When I first came here with the army, I used to go for walks at night, to think on the following day's battle. One night, I met an old peasant carrying a basket of maize kernels. He asked what I wanted to do with my life. I told him of my dreams – to earn fame and fortune on the battlefield; to have a grand house, and a loving wife, and to move through the Imperial circles."

The story's familiarity pulled me from my angry thoughts. "And?" I asked, though I suspected where the story was going.

"He just smiled. 'You will have all of this and more, young warrior. But remember: I always hold the dice.' And he was gone as though he'd never been."

I nodded. "Tezcatlipoca." The Smoking Mirror, God of War and Fate: He who controlled the destinies of men.

"Whoever he was, he was right." Neutemoc sighed. "Life is just another, vaster patolli board on which the gods move us at Their whim. The things you have, you can lose so easily. They're just not worth holding."

"You're a warrior," I said, finally. "You're not supposed to wallow in your own misery."

Neutemoc's eyes flashed in anger, but he didn't answer. "We need someone to stand guard," he said, rising. He walked to where Palli and Ezamahual sat, and said something to them in a low voice. They nodded.

Neutemoc came back, and lay down on the ground, ready to sleep. "They'll take turns," he said.

I nodded, not feeling inclined to talk further with him.

"We'll reach Amecameca tomorrow at noon," Neutemoc said. "There's a hill where Eleuia buried the body of her child. You'll see for yourself that he's dead."

I shrugged. "Maybe." Even if my instincts were wrong, and the child had nothing to do with this, something had happened in the Chalca Wars: something that Eleuia had wanted to hide so badly she'd been ready to kill for it.

I woke up at dawn, my clothes soaked by the mud and the morning dew. Neutemoc was already up. He was going through some exercises with his macuahitl sword, hacking and slashing at cacti as if they'd personally offended him.

Palli, Ezamahual and I withdrew from the camp, making our offerings of blood to Lord Death. The sky was cloudy, and the sun nowhere to be seen: a gloomy, wet pall stretched over the marshes, clinging to everything it touched. I hoped it wouldn't rain today. There were few more unpleasant things than finding oneself without shelter on marshy ground.

We ate one of the flatbreads, waiting for Neutemoc to finish killing innocent plants.

"Feeling frustrated?" I asked.

He didn't even rise to my jibe. "Let's get this over with, shall we?"

We walked the rest of the way to Amecameca, with the snow-capped heights of Popocatepetl's and Ixtaccihuatl's volcanoes looming ever larger over us.

The land became drier, the lakes forgotten behind us, and the ground deepening into valleys and hills, with grass and conifers gradually replacing the sparse marsh vegetation.

Neutemoc didn't speak much. From time to time, he'd point out a place, and say things such as, "This is where we fought the first Chalca regiments." But he was again sunk into that melancholy mood he'd shown in Chalco, reliving the past and the carefree days of his youth.

Towards mid-afternoon, we reached Amecameca, a small town nestled at the foot of a hill. Neutemoc pointed to the heights above us. "That's the place," he said. "The hill of Our Mother."

I craned my neck. At the top of the hill was a small, ornate adobe building with red flags: a shrine to Teteoinan, Mother of the Gods.

"We took it sixteen years ago," Neutemoc was saying. "A hard-fought battle."

"That's where Eleuia buried her child?" I asked.

"You'll see," Neutemoc said.

It was a small hill, dwarfed by the much larger volcanoes behind it. The ascent wasn't long. A steady flow of pilgrims came from Amecameca to make their offerings at the shrine: peasants, with their hands full of maize and feathers, and a procession of merchants leading a woman slave in a white cotton tunic, who would be sacrificed to the goddess.

278

Neutemoc stopped halfway up the hill, on a grassy knoll. Not knowing what else to do, we stopped as well.

"Let's see," he said. He closed his eyes for a moment, and a fleeting expression of nostalgia crossed his face. "That way," he said.

He walked to a place in the middle of the knoll, and stopped. "Here."

"You're sure?" I asked. Not that I disbelieved him. But still, it had been sixteen years.

Neutemoc pointed to a handful of rocks, arranged in a circular pattern. "I remember those." He knelt, rummaged within the grass, and gave a small grunt of triumph. "Her marker's still here."

Eleuia's marker was a small rock, engraved with two fragmentary glyphs: one for "water", and one that might have been "blessing" or "luck". They looked much like the ones she'd tried to draw in the Floating Gardens – while she was held captive by the beast of shadows, waiting for those who would torture her and push her into the lake. Odd. It wasn't any spell I recognised; and no magic that I could see hung over the tomb.

I turned to Palli. "Can I see the contents of that pack?"

The young offering priest smiled. "Of course, Acatl-tzin."

He'd brought many things: obsidian blades, herbs to heal wounds, to curse a man; a variety of containers for blood, their shapes ranging from eagles with an open beak to chac-mools, small men holding a blood-stained bowl in their outstretched hands. Among them, I finally found what I was looking for: a small, pointed shovel, which I withdrew from the pack. "Thank you."

"Do you need help, Acatl-tzin?" Ezamahual asked.

I shook my head. "There's only one shovel, and it's not a large grave. I'll work faster if I do it alone." I whispered a brief prayer to Mictlantecuhtli and to the Duality for what I was about to do – disturb the rest of an innocent child – and hoped They'd understand, if not forgive.

I hoped my instincts didn't turn out wrong about this.

It was harder than I'd thought: the ground was mostly rocks, mixed with a little soil. I had to go carefully in order not to break the bones, which would be small and fragile. Neutemoc had stepped away with a stern, disapproving face, and didn't offer any help.

At last, I overturned something that was neither earth nor rocks: a cloth with faded colours, sewn closed at both ends. I withdrew it from the hole, and brushed the earth from its folds, gently. Then, using one of my obsidian knives, I sliced through the threads.

Small, yellowed things spilled into my hands: the pathetic, familiar remnants of someone who hadn't had a chance at life.

"Bones," Palli whispered, by my side.

Yes, bones. But they felt wrong. Deeply, fundamentally wrong. They were the right shape, they had the right touch. But my skin was crawling, and the longer I held them the more ill at ease I felt.

"Neutemoc?" I asked.

My brother turned, saw what I was holding. "You've found what you wanted," he said, flatly.

No. I hadn't. They were wrong, subtly wrong, but I couldn't see why.

"You were with her when she buried them?" I asked.

"Yes," Neutemoc said. His gaze said, "I told you it was a waste of time."

"Did she do anything particular?" The bones were still in my hand, and everything in me wanted to throw them down.

"Particular?" Neutemoc looked at me as if I were mad. "No," he said. "She sewed them in that cloth, buried them, and carved the marker."

"That's all?" I asked. What was wrong with those bones?

Neutemoc said nothing for a while. "She went into a cave to say a prayer to the Duality," he said. "The same one where she gave birth."

"A cave?" I laid the bones down in the clothes. The uneasy feeling on my skin abated, but didn't cease. Nausea welled up in me, sharp, demanding – I struggled to focus through it.

A cave was a good shelter to give birth in with impunity, especially in this arid country. And praying to the Duality for a child wasn't extraordinary, since They watched over the souls of babies. But the Duality was worshipped in the open air, or on pyramid temples. I'd never heard of such a temple in a cave.

I took the baby's bones and wrapped them back into their cloth. "Can you take us to the cave?" I asked.

It was further away than Neutemoc remembered: we had to go down the hill to another one. Shelves of rock rose around us as we trudged on the steep path. The air was cold, crisp with a bitter tang that insinuated itself into my bones.

The cave had a small entrance, half-obscured by a fall of debris. Faded paint stretched on both sides, and traces that might have been bloody handprints, weathered away by the rain. A wet, pungent odour like that of a wild animal rose as I ducked under the stone ceiling.

Inside was only darkness, the sound of our own breathing – and, in the distance, the steady sound of dripping water. "Is anybody here?" I called.

No answer.

"Some place," Palli said behind me.

I paused for a moment to light a torch with some flint and dry kindling from Palli's ever-useful bag. The flame shone over moist rock walls, reflected in a thousand shards of light.

"It must have been abandoned some time ago," Neutemoc said, defiantly.

"If it ever drew large crowds," Ezamahual said. He sounded sceptical. "Everything looks faded here."

"I know," I said. I shone the torch towards the back: the cave narrowed into a rock corridor. Having no choice, I headed straight ahead.

My footsteps echoed under the stone ceiling: a deep, faraway sound, as if the place had been twice as deep. And as I made my way deeper into the cave, a sense of wrongness slowly crept up my spine. It was the same thing I'd felt when holding the baby's bones, but much, much stronger: a growing disquiet, an impression that the world around me wasn't as it seemed – a sense of a cold power coiling around me like the rings of a snake.

"Neutemoc," I whispered, but there was only silence, and the feeling of something immense, barely contained within the walls. Something that hadn't yet seen any of us; but that might, at any moment, turn its eyes our way.

"Acatl-tzin," Palli whispered, and I heard the same fear in his voice.

I reached towards the knife at my belt, with agonising slowness – and closed my hand on the hilt. The dreary, familiar emptiness of Mictlan rose: a welcome shield against whatever lay in the cave. It wasn't strong, and it waned with every passing moment. But it would have to do.

"Use your knives," I whispered to the two priests behind me. "Mictlan's magic will ward us."

Neither of the priests answered. I pushed ahead, stubbornly, and heard their footsteps behind me, more hesitant. They were falling behind.

The corridor ended in a circular place, filled with the sound of water dripping onto the rock. There was a pool at the centre, with barely enough water to reflect the light of my torch; and small tokens, scattered around the rim: dolls of brightly-coloured rags, fragments of chipped stones and seashells.

Offerings. This was – had been – a shrine, till not so long ago.

I shone my torch around the room: the paint had run, but frescoes still adorned the walls. The sense of disquiet, of wrongness, was rising, slowly drowning out Mictlan's rudimentary protection. I had no intention of remaining in that cave any longer than I had to. Close by, the frescoes were hard to identify. Characters in tones of ochre moved across a narration in smudged glyphs: fighting each other, or perhaps handing something to each other?

"What is this place?"

I started. I hadn't heard Neutemoc for so long that I'd almost forgotten that he was there. He stood by the pool, looking ill at ease. Neither his slave, Tepalotl, nor my two priests were anywhere to be seen.

"You should know," I said, more angrily than I'd intended to. "You took Eleuia here."

"No," Neutemoc said. He sounded angry as well. "I waited outside. I've never set foot in here."

"Well," I said sombrely, "the one thing we can be sure is that this isn't a shrine to the Duality." I held my torch up to the frescoes again, hoping for a clue, for anything that would allow us to get out of here and leave behind that great, sickening presence. But the glyphs were too smudged by the incessant fall of water, and the details of the frescoes similarly erased.

I walked away from the pool, fighting an urge to scratch myself to the blood.

The frescoes on the furthest wall were also badly damaged, but some details had survived better. One character appeared constantly in the vignettes: a being with dark skin, brandishing various objects: a fisherman's net, a rattle, and several bowls holding offerings.

I knelt by the oldest of the frescoes, peered at the details. The eyes were dark, accentuated by black marks, and a plume of heron feathers protruded from His head.

*Tlaloc!* Eleuia had given birth in a shrine to Tlaloc, God of Rain.


We met Palli, Ezamahual and Tepalotl halfway out: they had been unable to push past the sense of uneasiness. Tepalotl, being a slave, didn't look as though he cared much one way or the other; but my two priests were sheepish.

"We could have followed you, Acatl-tzin," Palli pointed out, once we were safely outside.

Ezamahual said nothing. He was clenching and unclenching his hand around his obsidian knife, frowning. "I scarcely feel anything," he said.

"The magic is here," I said, finally, not knowing what else I could tell him. "It takes some practise to open to it, that's all."

Ezamahual looked doubtful. "I suppose," he said.

"Acatl-tzin would know," Palli said, looking at his companion severely.

Ezamahual said nothing. I could tell he wasn't completely convinced. He should have had confidence in me, but I hadn't been capable of proving my abilities to him.

Huitzilpochtli curse me.

"It doesn't matter," I said. "We have what we need."

"We do?" Neutemoc asked, behind me. "I, for one, haven't understood anything."

I didn't react to his sarcasm. I weighed the baby's bones in my hands, thoughtfully. After the shrine, the small feeling of wrongness was almost restful. "Neither have I." But one thing was sure: the Storm Lord wasn't a god of childbirth. There had been no reason for Eleuia to go into that shrine to give birth unless something else was going on. "But I don't think Eleuia's true allegiance was to the Quetzal Flower."

"And that solves the matter for you?"

I shrugged. "If she was to become Consort of Xochiquetzal's husband, she couldn't afford the worship of another god." Hence the need to silence Neutemoc, who might remember the child; who might remember this place and cause someone else to realise what Eleuia had done.

Neutemoc said nothing, but he didn't look convinced. That wasn't what bothered me. The bones that I held in my hand, however... What kind of child had Eleuia given birth to?

It's dead, my conscience pointed out, reasonably. Whatever happened, she didn't carry it to term. But that wasn't enough to dispel my growing feeling I'd missed something.

## SEVENTEEN
### Confrontations

We came back to Tenochtitlan two days later, at dawn.
Fog hung heavily over the canals and the streets, clinging in wisps to the houses even after sunrise. The air
was humid and sweltering. Overhead, there were no
clouds yet, but the rain would not be long in coming.

I sent Palli and Ezamahual back to the temple;
Neutemoc, his slave Tepalotl and I went back to
Neutemoc's house.

Mihmatini was waiting for us in the courtyard, wearing a creased dress of cotton, embroidered with
butterflies. Her face was as wan as the moon, and dark
circles underlined her eyes. I had never seen her so tired.

"You shouldn't be up so early," I said.

She shook her head. "If I sleep, they'll eat the
wards." She glanced at Neutemoc. "And your protection is almost gone. I need to renew that for you."

"I thought you and Ceyaxochitl had everything
under control when we left?" I asked, slowly, afraid of
what she would answer me.

Mihmatini gave me a tired smile. "They're either
more powerful, or more numerous. Either way, I'm
losing this battle."

"You can't stay here," I said to Neutemoc.

He shook his head, angrily. "And whose fault is that?"

"Neutemoc," Mihmatini said.

I bit back on a wounding retort. "Can we argue about responsibilities later? I need to get you and your household to–"

I contemplated the possibilities. Most temples weren't warded, except perhaps for the Great Temple. But half of that belonged to Tlaloc. And, given what we now knew of Eleuia's ties with that god, I wasn't eager to find refuge there.

"We'll go to the Duality House," I said, at last. "That's large enough to hold us all." At least, while I worked out what I did next. I'd have to go back to the Jaguar House, and ask Mahuizoh about Eleuia's ambitions.

"The Duality House?" Neutemoc asked, incredulous. "My whole household? Acatl, it's one thing to take me on a fruitless journey–"

I cut him off, with no effort to be civil. "That wasn't fruitless, unless you want to deny what happened in that so-called shrine to the Duality. And I'm not taking risks."

He stared at me: weary, cynical, angry. "Priests hide and run away. Warriors don't."

Warriors and priests. Why in the Fifth World did it always have to come to the same thing?

I'd had enough of that. I said, sharply, "You can stay here if that satisfies your pride. I'm not seeing Mihmatini and your children die like Quechomitl."

"He died because you involved him in this," Neutemoc snapped.

I shook my head. "He died because he defended you. That's all."

"He would have had no need to defend me if you hadn't interfered."

Interfered? I'd risked my career to prove him innocent, and that was all he could find to say to me? I said, "I wasn't the one who drove Huei against you. You did that yourself."

This, as I had expected, wounded him. His eyes narrowed; his muscles tensed, readying for a leap in my direction. I laid a hand on one of my obsidian knives, feeling the emptiness of Mictlan well up.

Mihmatini gave a snort of disgust, and stepped between both of us. "Enough. A pity Mother isn't here any more. You're behaving like children, both of you."

"Neutemoc," she said, firmly.

He turned to her. It must have been something in her voice, so reminiscent of Mother's flat, deadly tones. "Yes?"

"Come here. I'll renew the spell on you. And then we'll pack." She threw me an angry glance. "As to you… don't think I'm on your side, Acatl."

"You don't sound as if you are," I said, but she was already fussing around Neutemoc.

I almost went to lean against the wall, until I remembered the creatures, hungrily pressing themselves on the other side.

So I settled in the middle of the courtyard, watching Mihmatini draw a circle on the ground. I stood, trying to empty my mind of everything. But I couldn't. In the bag at my back were the baby's bones, so subtly, so incomprehensibly wrong. What had Eleuia tried to do with the baby – and was it for this failed attempt that she'd died?

We drew many curious glances as our small procession crossed the Sacred Precinct, heading towards the Duality House. Even at this early hour, priests were already out: through the fog, I thought I caught a glimpse of Ichtaca in his headdress and spider-embroidered cloak, leading a handful of black-clad offering priests back to the temple for the Dead.

Getting inside the Duality House required some negotiation: the guards weren't willing to let in two dozen people. They sent for their superior – who turned out to be Yaotl, Ceyaxochitl's personal messenger. I wasn't sure whether his smug smile was an improvement on the situation. His eyes took in the slaves, Neutemoc, and Mihmatini, with Ollin sleeping in a wicker basket at her back, and four year-old Mazatl in her arms.

"I'm sure there's a good explanation for all of this," Yaotl said.

I wasn't in the mood to provide much of anything to anyone. "There is," I said. "I'll give it to you once we're inside."

"I suspect I'd rather have it now," Yaotl said.

I sighed. "Your walls are solidly warded. Is that good enough?"

Yaotl glanced at the adobe walls, and finally shrugged. "Warded against what?" he asked.

"Against things that might be trying to kill us," I said.

Neutemoc was standing to the side, glowing with Mihmatini's protection, brooding like a jaguar over lost cubs. He wasn't talking to me, and he was avoiding Mihmatini, too. But then, we both were, after the verbal flaying she'd given us on the way there.

Yaotl looked again at the walls. "Protection. It's irregular–" he started.

"You care about irregularities now?"

He smiled. "Possibly. However, you come at a good time. Mistress Ceyaxochitl wanted to see you. I suppose we'll count all the others as your retinue."

"Ha," Neutemoc said.

"The sense of humour runs in your family, I see," Yaotl said, as Neutemoc's slaves all gathered in the first courtyard of the Duality House. Neutemoc found himself an isolated place, from which he could glare at me in peace.

"No," I said, "I can't say I ever had much of one." I gathered my priest-senses, and felt the solidity of the Duality wards, woven into the very foundations of the walls by generation after generation of Guardians. This was a safe place, the safest haven magic could devise. The surest prison, also. I could well imagine how Neutemoc would chafe within those walls.

Mihmatini was laying Mazatl on the ground, wrapping a blanket around him with the help of an old slave woman. Then she settled down, and started rocking Ollin against her chest, singing a soft lullaby.

"Come," Yaotl said. "They can get settled without your help."

Ceyaxochitl was waiting for me within the Duality shrine: a vast, open space at the top of the central pyramid, with a limestone altar, a carved piece of stone, as flat as the surface of a still lake. There were no grooves to collect the blood, either on the altar or on the platform; for the Duality only took bloodless sacrifices such as fruit or flowers.

"I wasn't expecting you so early," she said. She was leaning on her cane as if rooted to the ground. Her face, like Mihmatini's, was wan and tired. Above her, heavy clouds were gathering: the rains were coming, and would start soon, thank the Duality.

"He's not alone, either," Yaotl said, with some satisfaction.

Ceyaxochitl raised an eyebrow. "Not alone?"

"He's brought a whole household."

"Your brother's?" Ceyaxochitl asked, quick to see the point. "I take it the creatures are still there."

"Yes, and it's getting worse. Your wards are down."

Ceyaxochitl tapped her cane on the floor, thoughtfully. "They shouldn't be. I'll have to look into this. When I have priests to spare."

"Hum," I said. "I'd rather you focused on these." I handed her a bundle of cloth, containing the bones of Eleuia's baby.

Ceyaxochitl held it in the palm of one hand, and carefully started unwrapping it with the fingers of her other hand. "What is this?"

"Bones," I said. "The bones of Eleuia's child."

"Mm," she said, poking at them with one finger. "Odd bones, you mean."

"Yes," I said. "But I'm not sure if it's relevant."

Ceyaxochitl looked at them for a while. "They feel wrong. But I'm not sure why. I need to think."

She was exhausted, it was obvious: this promise was likely all I was going to get. But I could not force her, in any case. "Why did you want to talk to me?" On the way there, I'd entertained the notion that she'd found a way to kill the creatures – even that she'd have found the sorcerer, and that both Neutemoc and I could go our separate ways. But it didn't look to be the case.

Ceyaxochitl's face was grave. "I have news, Acatl."

Bad news, judging from her solemn voice. "The Emperor?" I asked. Though, if Axayacatl-tzin died and there was political upheaval, Ichtaca would deal with the consequences of that.

Then I remembered, with a twinge of unease, the conversation we'd had. I didn't need further conflict between us.

Ceyaxochitl was shaking her head. "Yaotl?" she asked. "Can you make sure we're alone?"

Now she was frightening me.

Yaotl came to stand near the top of the only stairs leading to where we were, his hand resting on the hilt of his macuahitl sword. Ceyaxochitl moved towards the altar – on which, I suddenly noticed, lay a piece of maguey paper.

She took it in her free hand before I could read it. "I haven't been idle while you were away."

"I didn't think you would," I said, finally. "Why all the secrecy?"

Ceyaxochitl handed me the piece of paper without another word.

There wasn't much to see: it was just a drawing in red ink, and another in black ink, superimposed upon it. Together, both sets of lines formed a stylised figure: an animal, suggested by its claws and the shape of its maw.

"I don't understand," I said.

Ceyaxochitl sighed. "The red pattern is the one Yaotl took from Eleuia's cheek."

"And the black?" I asked, a hollow deepening in my stomach. Missing lines. If you added the black lines to the red, you had a complete pattern.

Ceyaxochitl raised a hand. "Promise me you're not going to do something foolish about it," she said.

She was really, really worrying me. Was the overall symbol some Imperial seal? "I can't promise that until you tell me," I said.

She was silent, for a while. "It was badly smudged," she said. "Barely recognisable. But Yaotl has a good memory."

"And?" I hated that she was toying with me, holding her answer at arm's length.

She turned, to lay one hand on the altar, as if drawing strength from the stone. "It's a ring," she said. "A ring of engraved turquoise."

My stomach twisted. Turquoise was an Imperial colour. "Who wears that ring?" Tizoc-tzin? Or – and my heart missed a beat – Teomitl?

"Only one man," Ceyaxochitl said. "Quiyahuayo, Commander of the Jaguar Brotherhood."

Commander Quiyahuayo. I'd met him, was my first, incredulous thought. He hadn't sounded like… Like a sorcerer. Like a ruthless man, ready to sacrifice Neutemoc for the Duality knew what aim. Was I such a fool as not to recognise a sorcerer?

"That's not possible," I said. "Someone made a copy…"

Ceyaxochitl shook her head. "That would be going to a lot of trouble for not much. We had so much trouble tracing that ring, I don't think it was meant to mislead us."

"I don't understand," I said, stupidly. But I did. The Jaguar Knights were privileged warriors, heavily connected to the Imperial Family – especially their Commander. Ceyaxochitl was telling me that Quiyahuayo might be behind the abduction of Eleuia; but that I would have to tread carefully.

I thought of the bruises on Eleuia's skin; of how no part of her had been left undamaged; of how Quiyahuayo had left Neutemoc to rot in his cage for days; of how he'd induced Huei to betray her husband and put her own life in danger; of how, because of him, she was now condemned to death. A cold anger crystallised in my chest.

I crumpled the paper between my fingers. "Thank you," I said, and walked out before she could stop me.

Yaotl joined me as I reached the outer courtyard of the Duality House. "You're about to do something foolish," he said, flatly. For once, he didn't sound amused or ironic.

"Do you have any other solutions?"

"Mistress Ceyaxochitl can appeal to the Imperial Courts–"

"That's not a solution," I said. "That's just delaying things."

"Sometimes, it's the best thing," Yaotl said. "Quiyahuayo has more influence than you believe."

"No," I said. I wasn't there to dally in politics. I wasn't there to be thrown left and right by events out of my control. I wanted justice.

Yaotl started to say something, but then met my gaze. He sighed: an unusual, uncharacteristic gesture. "It's your choice," he said. "Don't say we failed to warn you this time."

I shook my head. If my destiny was to rush in, like a fool, then so be it.

I was almost all the way to the doors of the Jaguar House when I realised someone had followed me. Neutemoc.

"You're not safe here," I snapped.

He stood, some paces away from me, stubbornly unmoving. "I heard you. It's my Brotherhood, Acatl. My commander. I think I deserve an explanation."

He still shone, faintly, with Mihmatini's spell: a soft light, barely visible to my priest-senses, which spilled on the beaten earth under us. The rising wind whipped at his cloak, giving him the air of an uncanny monster.

I looked at the bulk of the Jaguar House, throwing its shadow over us – at the guards at the entrance. For company, I could do worse than Neutemoc: he might hate me, but he'd guard my back, if only because I was family and because his brotherhood had betrayed him.

"Very well," I said, finally. "Come on."

He walked some paces away, which suited me. I had no desire to start a long conversation. When we reached the Jaguar House, though, I saw the faces of the guards darken.

"You shouldn't be here," the first guard said to Neutemoc.

A faint, dangerous smile stretched Neutemoc's lips. He spread his hands, palms up, as if to show he had no weapon. "I'm still a Jaguar Knight," he said. "And I'm entitled to be here."

The second guard growled. "You haven't set a foot in here since your arrest, and now you come back."

"It's the coming back that matters," Neutemoc said. He was hiding his anger, his sense of betrayal, very well, but I saw it in the slight tremor of his hands. "I want to see the commander."

The first guard laughed, his fingers tightening around the shell-grip of his spear. "As if he'd see you at this hour?"

Neutemoc's voice was slow, deadly. "Ask him," he said.

The second guard looked at Neutemoc, clearly trying to decide whether he was jesting.

"Ask him," Neutemoc said, "about Priestess Eleuia."

I had been carefully folding the crumpled maguey paper into a small square. By the guards' blank faces, they'd obviously not been involved in Eleuia's abduction. Time to pass a discreet message to Commander Quiyahuayo, then. There was no reason to drag the guards into the shame of Eleuia's murder.

"Tell him we found this on her body," I said, handing my folded paper to the first guard.

He wasn't long gone. When he came back, his face was set in a frown. "He'll see you," he said.

The Jaguar House was almost deserted at this early hour: a few Knights were playing patolli in one of the courtyards, and all the unmarried Knights were in

295

their dormitories – some, by the noises wafting through the entrance-curtains, still engaged with various courtesans.

Neutemoc didn't speak until we were a long way in. "I'd hate to be trapped here," he said.

I shrugged. "You shouldn't have come, then." The dice were all Quiyahuayo's in this House, anyway. At least, if I didn't come back, Ceyaxochitl and Yaotl would know who held me.

It was a meagre consolation, but it sustained me until we reached Quiyahuayo's room.

A delicate entrance curtain, adorned with images of the great Tezcatlipoca slaughtering the enemies of the Mexica, opened to reveal a wide room lit by two braziers. Lord Death and His wife faced each other in the frescoes on the walls. The god and His consort sat on Their thrones of linked bones, with the Wind of Knives a small, sharp shadow in the background. It was... wrong. They shouldn't have been there. It wasn't their place.

The only furniture was a reed mat, and four large wicker chests. One of the chests, I saw, held piles of folded codices, laid on top of each other. Even from this distance, I could tell what they were: books of prayers to Mictlantecuhtli, detailed indexes to the minor gods of the underworld, spells to summon them and bind them to one's will.

Altogether, it painted a picture of a man's obsession with Mictlan: a trait ill-suited to a commander of the Jaguar Knights, a man who should have been sworn to the Hummingbird. It was clear, though, why he had chosen to use a beast of shadows to abduct Eleuia.

Commander Quiyahuayo, in full Jaguar regalia, was sitting on the reed mat, surrounded by discarded codices and by broken writing reeds. He held a clay tablet, which he used as a support to write on maguey paper. His gestures were slow, but precise.

He raised his eyes when we came closer. "My late-night visitors," he said, seemingly amused. "Leave us, will you?" he asked the guard – who nodded, and exited the room.

Commander Quiyahuayo put down his writing reed, and tilted the tablet towards us. He'd been writing on the paper I'd sent him: he had drawn a circle around the symbol, like the shape of a signet ring.

He knew.

I glanced at the entrance-curtain. The guard was standing just behind it. I couldn't tell with certainty, but there was probably a second guard as well. No choice, then; no way back; but I had known that before entering the room.

"So," Commander Quiyahuayo said. "Do sit down."

Neutemoc had been watching him with a mixture of horror and fascination. "Going through your pretence of politeness?"

Commander Quiyahuayo bowed his head. The quetzal tail-feathers on his headdress followed his motion, bending like stalks in the wind. "The proper gestures, at the proper time," he said. "Incidentally, don't even think of trying to attack me, physically or otherwise." He said the last with a quick nod in my direction, having seen my hand tighten around one of my obsidian knives. "It would only make things more painful. And believe me, I have no wish to do so."

He sounded sincere, and in many ways that was the worst. "More painful than you made them for Eleuia?" I asked.

"Ah," he said. "Eleuia. Do sit down," he repeated.

"I'd rather remain standing," Neutemoc snapped. "Since you judge that what happened to me was just an inconvenience?"

"A minor thing," Commander Quiyahuayo said. He set his clay tablet aside carefully. "Compared to the stakes."

"What stakes?" I asked, wondering what kind of man would speak of human lives as if they were part of some vast game. Not a man I would like.

Commander Quiyahuayo's smile was ironic. "Why, the Fifth World. What else do we play for?"

"I don't understand," I said, just as Neutemoc snapped, "Are you going to toy with us all night? Or just do to us as you did to Eleuia?"

Commander Quiyahuayo's smile slowly faded. "You still care for the bitch," he said, surprised. "Why? She tried to kill you."

If Neutemoc was shocked at this, he didn't show it. "So did you," he said.

Commander Quiyahuayo shrugged. "Hazards of combats."

This was obviously leading nowhere. Neutemoc was right: Commander Quiyahuayo was toying with us until he became bored. "What's your interest in Eleuia?" I asked. "Does it have anything to do with her child – the one she had in the Chalca Wars, in a temple dedicated to the Storm Lord?"

Commander Quiyahuayo recoiled visibly, though he soon recovered.

"Tell me what is going on," I asked. "We know about the child. We unearthed his bones. We know something is wrong with them." I couldn't help shivering as I said this.

"You've been busy, I see," the commander said.

"Yes," I said. "But I still don't–"

He cut me with a frown. "You're a priest, Acatl. Don't you know what those bones are?"

Eerie, was my first thought. I remembered the feeling I'd had when holding them, the same feeling as in Tlaloc's shrine. "Powerful," I said.

Commander Quiyahuayo shook his head. "Power."

"I–"

Gently, Commander Quiyahuayo rested his hands on the reed mat. "Power incarnate."

"The Storm Lord's power?" I asked.

He shrugged. "The gods' powers are constrained in the Fifth World. That's why They find human agents." He probed at the clay tablet on the ground as it were an aching tooth. "But agents are tricky. Unreliable. They have a will of their own. Some gods desire a vessel that is more... pliant, shall we say?"

I stared at him, my contempt forgotten. Surely... "Tlaloc made a child?" I asked. "He fathered a child with Eleuia?"

Commander Quiyahuayo smiled with the pleased expression of a teacher who had just managed to pass on knowledge. In the flickering light of the braziers, the fangs of the jaguar maw framing his head shone: a second, far more dangerous smile. "The Storm Lord wanted a child who would hold the full extent of His powers. To create life with those constraints is hard, more so when one is a god with no idea of where to start." His voice was grim. "Hence the stillbirth."

It was a fascinating story he was telling me, but I couldn't trust him. Every one of his words was a lie. This was the man who had arranged Eleuia's abduction. "Why should I believe you?" I asked. "You tortured her. You killed her."

"I didn't kill her. The bitch escaped." Commander Quiyahuayo sounded angry. "As to why you should believe me... That, I'm afraid, is your own problem. If you don't, it won't change many things for me."

He was right: either way, he had us at his mercy. I ought to have felt frightened. But I'd entered the Jaguar House knowing what I was doing. I wanted explanations.

Commander Quiyahuayo spread his hands. "Think of Eleuia. Of the kind of woman she was."

The problem was that for a lie, it rang true, too much in keeping with Eleuia's character. Bearing a child would earn her the Storm Lord's favour: an easy way to rise through the hierarchy, borne on the god's powers. And what better way to be safe from hunger than to have the favour of the God of Rain – He who made the maize flowers bloom?

"I still don't understand," I said slowly, to give me time to compose my thoughts. "The child is dead. Whatever Tlaloc wanted to do, it wouldn't have worked."

From outside came shouted orders and the sound of footsteps, running in the distance. Commander Quiyahuayo shook his head in distaste. "My, they're noisy tonight. Pay no attention. Where were we? Ah yes. The child." He smiled. "You see, there was a second child. And this one survived his birth."

I stared at him, incredulous. "That's why you tortured her?"

The shouting had moved away from us, and the sounds of running men were gradually dying down. A breeze stirred the curtain. Neutemoc cursed, and moved away from the draught.

"No," Commander Quiyahuayo said. "I knew there was a child, made jointly by Xochiquetzal and Tlaloc, and borne in Eleuia's womb. I know that it was given to a family of peasants, to raise as their own."

By Xochiquetzal and Tlaloc. Of course. Xochiquetzal had brought the expertise about childbirth; and the Storm Lord the raw power. That was why the Quetzal Flower had lied to me about Mahuizoh and Eleuia. What a fool I'd been.

Commander Quiyahuayo went on, "And I also knew this: that this year is the year the child comes of age. The year Tlaloc can transfer His powers into him. What I wanted to know from Eleuia was where she'd hidden him."

A god-child. A child invested with immeasurable powers, loose in Tenochtitlan, with no constraints placed on his magic. The living extension of the will of a capricious, angry, cruel god...

I shivered.

"I fail to see what the Storm Lord could want," Neutemoc said. He was clearly uncomfortable with the thought of the gods directly interfering in the Fifth World.

I was more used to the idea. And there was only one thing that Tlaloc could want. Xochiquetzal Herself had told me.

*He moves up into the world, becomes the protective deity of your Empire. And We – the old ones, the gods of the Earth and of the Corn, We who were here first, who watched over your first steps – We fade.*

Xochiquetzal and Tlaloc had both been displaced by Huitzilpochtli's rise to power.

"They want revenge," I said.

"Not revenge," Commander Quiyahuayo said. "Faith."

Another draught lifted the curtains, and spilled rain onto the floor – and the world seemed to grow still.

"Acatl," Neutemoc said, sharply.

Commander Quiyahuayo was still sitting on the reed mat, but now he was staring at two bloody gashes opening on his chest. Even as I turned

301

towards him, more wounds opened, blossoming like obscene flowers.

Even without the true sight, I could guess at the mass of shapeless, frenzied things that would be fighting to reach his veins. The creatures were back.

# EIGHTEEN
## *Season of Rain*

As Commander Quiyahuayo stared back at us, his blood dripping on the reed mat, pooling in meaningless patterns, Neutemoc pulled at my cloak.

"Come on," he said, dragging me towards the door. "Let's get out of here."

I threw a glance at Commander Quiyahuayo. His eyes were glazed. The terrible numbness of the creatures' wounds would already be coursing through his whole body. He'd stay there, helpless, until they'd fed to satiety. And then the Duality knew what they'd do. Turn on us?

"I–"

"There's nothing you can do for him," Neutemoc snapped. "Remember? We can't kill those things. Besides, he's a murderer."

I wasn't so sure about that. Commander Quiyahuayo had admitted to torturing Eleuia easily – indeed, as if it didn't matter at all – and I didn't think he'd lied when he said he hadn't killed her. It did leave open the question of who had killed Eleuia, and why.

With a terrible knot of guilt in my stomach, I sprang to my feet. Neutemoc was standing near the entrance curtain. "Come on!" he said.

The air seemed to have turned to tar. I ran towards Neutemoc, but it seemed to take an eternity for me to reach him.

"Let's leave." Neutemoc opened the curtain: outside, a thin drizzle veiled the courtyard. A blast of wind splattered rain into my face.

There had been guards, I thought, struggling to think. There had been...

The guards lay in the muddy earth, their faces drained of colour, their jaguar uniform rent open to reveal chests criss-crossed with claw-marks. I remembered the noises of men running, and of fighting, moving away from us. Not, it seemed, moving away from us: merely ending with the death of all the fighting men.

The Jaguar House was all but silent. Only the soft patter of the rain on the terraces broke the terrible stillness. Rain. The Storm Lord's rain.

"He's come into his powers," I said.

"Because you believed that bastard's lies?" Neutemoc screamed. He was running towards the courtyard's exit. His face through the drizzle was that of a man who realises the ground has shifted under him, bringing the yawning chasm that much closer.

Commander Quiyahuayo's story had sounded too complicated to be invented on the spur of the moment; and it fitted, chillingly, with the evidence we already had. "Why else would someone kill Commander Quiyahuayo?" I asked.

Not someone. Something. The creatures, the same which had tried to kill Neutemoc. The servants of Tlaloc.

Neutemoc didn't answer. He was ahead of me now, making his way through the maze of courtyards and rooms as if they were his own home. Of course, this was the House of his Brotherhood. Everywhere, the same stillness: the patolli boards abandoned on the ground, pelted by rain; and the bodies beside them, pale and unmoving.

Through the open door of a dormitory, I caught a glimpse of a warrior lying in a courtesan's arms: both bloodless bodies curled together in a grotesque parody of life. The same sense of wrongness as in the cave was rising in me, slowly, steadily, like a vessel filling up. I looked up at the rain, and felt the magic coiled at the heart of the clouds, coming down with each drop. The rain wasn't normal, either. As if we needed this.

"They're catching up," I said. I couldn't keep up with Neutemoc. I'd lost track of how many courtyards we'd run through.

"I know!" Neutemoc shouted, without turning around.

Would Mihmatini's spell protect him – or would it would yield under the creatures' repeated assaults?

A child. Nausea was rising in me, sharp, demanding. A living child, somewhere in the teeming mass of Tenochtitlan, sending the creatures like puppets to destroy Commander Quiyahuayo and his men, who might still have thwarted the Storm Lord's plans.

At the entrance, the two warriors no longer stood guard. But the gates were wide open; and beyond them, sharply outlined through the curtain of rain, lay the pyramids of the Sacred Precinct, and the safety of the Duality House.

Neutemoc was already running through. Not being as agile or as lithe as my brother, I did my best to follow him. As I passed under the gates, something clawed at my cloak: the cloth tore with a ripping sound, and flapped loose in the wind.

I didn't turn. I wouldn't see anything. I just ran on. But the next claw-swipe went for my back. A fiery trail opened on the left side of my spine. Numbness spread from the wound, slowing down my rush of panic until I felt nothing at all. Just the wounds, opening one by one, and the strange, pleasant feeling of drifting away...

At the edge of my vision, Neutemoc had stopped, wondering why I wasn't following.

I had to... Grimacing, I forced myself forward. It was like moving through thick honey. I lifted my leg, laid my foot on the ground – once, twice – but neither the gates nor Neutemoc grew closer.

More wounds, in my back. Blood, trickling down, a warm, steady flow washed away by the rain. But everything was as it should be: I would be at peace for ever in Tlalocan, and I would have no need to prove myself any more...

Light blazed across the gates: a radiance so strong it hurt my eyes. For a moment, I hung suspended in time, the numbness burning away like paper crinkling in the fire, before slamming back into my own body.

Every wound in my back hurt. But it was pain; it was keeping me alive...

I tottered forward. My feet slid into the mud, and somehow I found myself on one knee, fighting dizziness.

"Acatl-tzin!"

Hands steadied me, dragged me upwards. Blinking, I managed to bring Teomitl's face into sharp focus.

"You..."

"Later," Teomitl said. He was blazing: Huitzilpochtli's power streamed into the night, a warmth in my bones and on my soaked skin. I'd been wrong: he wasn't Payaxin. He was much tougher than my dead apprentice, much more adapted to survival. "We have to find some shelter."

• • •

The shelter turned out to be a room in the Duality House, where Mihmatini tended to my wounds with an exasperated sigh. My cloak was ruined; my belt had frayed in the battle, and my knives were gone: the obsidian blessed by Mictlantecuhtli had disintegrated in the rush of the Hummingbird's magic.

"Acatl," Mihmatini said, shaking her head.

Teomitl was leaning against one of the walls, watching me. "Ceyaxochitl thought you might need help getting out of the Jaguar House," he said.

Imperial help. The words were on my lips, but wouldn't get out.

"There," Mihmatini said, tying the last of the bandages into place. "I've put a minor spell of healing on it, but it won't hold if you overexert yourself." She stared curiously at Teomitl. "And thank you for getting him out of trouble."

Teomitl's smile was radiant. "My pleasure. I am Teomitl." He bowed slightly.

"Mihmatini. I'm his sister." She rolled her eyes upwards. "And designated healer, obviously. Sometimes, I wonder why I bother. You're a priest, too?"

"Not exactly," Teomitl said. "I'm training to be a warrior. I hope to be a worthy one."

Mihmatini smiled at him again. "I'm sure you will." There was an uncomfortable silence.

No, not quite uncomfortable. I realised, with a shock, that she and Teomitl were both staring at each other with an interest that was obvious, and my presence here was superfluous, except as a chaperone.

I cleared my throat, startling both of them out of their trance. "We should join Neutemoc."

He was waiting for us in the next room, seated on a reed mat. Mihmatini hesitated on the doorstep, staring at both of us. Finally she shrugged. "I'll see you afterwards," she said to Teomitl, smiling again.

Teomitl bowed to her. "I hope so." I shook my head, amused in spite of myself.

Slaves brought us hot chocolate. I cradled the clay glass in my hand, feeling the warmth dissipate the last of the creatures' numbness.

Teomitl sat cross-legged between Neutemoc and me, taking on the role of shield without realising it. Neutemoc's hands rested in his lap; clenched into fists. "What is happening, Acatl?" he asked in a tone that clearly implied I should be able to explain everything.

"I don't know," I said. Rain was pelting the roof above our heads. But it was more than rain. Each drop that fell down was mingled with magic: a bittersweet tang that I could smell, even from inside. "Tlaloc is coming," I said.

For revenge. For faith, Commander Quiyahuayo had said.

A brief tinkle of bells, soon muffled, heralded Yaotl's arrival. He leant against one of the walls, his back digging into the stylised frescoes of fused lovers.

Beside me, Teomitl was silent for a while, pondering, an uncharacteristically mature expression on his face. "My brother is weak," he said. "And as his health wanes, so does Huitzilpochtli's ability to protect us."

Neutemoc stared at his glass of chocolate as if it held deep secrets. He said, finally, "I'd much rather believe that you're both mad."

Teomitl said nothing.

"But something is going on. Something unnatural," Neutemoc went on. He looked at me. Despite his grievance towards me, still believing that I could set right anything magical.

"Tlaloc," I said. "His child – the one he and the Quetzal Flower fashioned, the one Eleuia bore within her womb – the tool for His coup. But we're not strong enough to find him. Ceyaxochitl…"

She was the agent of the Duality in the Fifth World. She would have some powers, constrained by her human nature, but hopefully still enough to do some damage.

Yaotl spoke up. "She's at the palace. I don't know about what you're saying. But Mistress Ceyaxochitl agrees with you: this isn't normal rain."

She was the Guardian for the Sacred Precinct. How could she be away when such a thing happened? "She has to know–" I started.

Yaotl shook his head. "She felt it, Acatl. But she has to remain where she is."

"Why?" I asked, at the same moment as Neutemoc said, "The Emperor."

Of course. The ailing Emperor: the last remnants of the Southern Hummingbird's power, our last defence against Tlaloc. If he died, nothing would protect us.

From what? Would one god replacing another really be that disastrous? After all, Huitzilpochtli had done nothing in particular for me or mine. I thought of the creatures, mindlessly gorging on power, and of Jaguar Knights lying dead in their own Houses. The Storm Lord's rule would not be gentle.

Teomitl was watching me, his gaze disturbingly shrewd. "The Southern Hummingbird protects us. Tlaloc is one of the Old Ones. He brings drought and floods on a whim."

"He brings famine," I said, remembering how Eleuia had suffered during the Great Famine.

Teomitl said, "Do you want to gamble everything on the Storm Lord's gentleness?"

On a god's... humanity? "No," I said. "I would rather keep the old order." To gods and goddesses such as Xochiquetzal, we'd always be toys: easily subjugated, easily broken. "But we're still nothing compared to His powers. And you forget: we don't know where the child is."

Obviously not at the palace, or the panic would be stronger than that. Commander Quiyahuayo and the Jaguar Knights had known. But they were dead now, all of them.

"How long do you think we have?" Neutemoc asked.

I stifled a bitter laugh. Who could tell what went on in the mind of a god?

Yaotl detached himself from the wall. His scarred face was thoughtful. "Still some time, I'd say. If everything had been ready–"

"Yes," I said. If everything had been ready, and the attack launched on the Imperial Palace, there would have been no need to kill the Jaguar Knights. If the creatures had done so, it was because Commander Quiyahuayo still posed a danger to them. Because the child was still vulnerable.

"We have to find him," Teomitl said, voicing what we both thought. I wasn't sure what Neutemoc thought: if he still believed we were crazy to impugn Eleuia, to imagine wild stories of gods taking over the world.

Yaotl's voice was grave. "Easily said."

"Commander Quiyahuayo knew..." Neutemoc started, and then he shook his head. "He died in battle. He'll be in the Heavens, won't he? Out of your influence."

"Yes," I said. And I wasn't fool enough to attempt another summoning without divine favour. "We need–" Help. We needed help, and from someone who both had some idea of what Tlaloc was up to, and who would be favourable to us. We needed divine powers on our side, no matter the price we had to pay. "We need to find a god," I said.

Teomitl nodded. "Which one?" he asked, simply, never thinking of what the price or the difficulty would be.

Not Huitzilpochtli: He was as weak as the dying Emperor, and as ignorant. Not the Quetzal Flower: She was on Tlaloc's side, and without Ceyaxochitl we would get no answers from her. Not Lord Death: my patron had made it clear that He would take no part in the Fifth World's affairs.

Who would stand against the Storm Lord?

I remembered Commander Quiyahuayo's words: *I didn't kill her. The bitch escaped.*

An ahuizotl had killed Eleuia, dragging her down into the muddy depths of the lake, and feasting on her eyes and fingernails. An ahuizotl: a creature of Chalchiutlicue, Tlaloc's wife. His wife. And Tlaloc's child, which wasn't Hers, but Eleuia's. I doubted the Jade Skirt would have been happy about the whole affair.

"I think I know who we can try to see," I said. "Chalchiutlicue."

"The Storm Lord's wife?" Teomitl asked. "Why not?"

Neutemoc grimaced. "You have no idea how to summon Her, do you?"

I shook my head. "To ask a favour of a god, you don't summon. You go into Their territory." I wasn't looking forward to that: men were weak enough in the Fifth World, but in a god's land... We would be as helpless as Xochiquetzal was on earth. Perhaps even more so.

"Into Her territory," Teomitl repeated. "Lake Texcoco?"

"No. Into Tlalocan." The Blessed Land of the Drowned, where Chalchiutlicue had Her gardens.

It was also Tlaloc's country; but I was hoping that the god would be too busy with His child to pay much attention to us.

Neutemoc snorted. "And you know how to get there?"

Tlalocan, as I had seen, was closed to me. But the way might yet be opened for us, by someone who had the Jade Skirt's favour.

"I know a priest," I said. Half a lie. Eliztac hadn't been helpful last time I'd seen him. But he was the only priest of Chalchiutlicue I'd had dealings with. I tried, resolutely, not to think of Huei. Surely, if I could appeal to Huei...

But it wasn't my place. "You and I can go to see him," I went on.

Yaotl nodded. "Teomitl and I will stay here, to inform Mistress Ceyaxochitl when she gets back."

I visited, briefly, Ceyaxochitl's storehouse: a low, pillared room with row upon row of magical objects – everything Guardians had thought might be useful in the event of an emergency. At the back was a box made of glued human bones; and inside I found what I was looking for: ten obsidian knives pulsing with the magic of Mictlan. I withdrew three from the box, and put them into the sheaths at my belt, to replace those I had lost.

Under the thatch awning of the courtyard, I packed ceramic bowls and polished maguey thorns into a new bag. I was almost finished when footsteps echoed under the awning.

"Acatl-tzin?" Teomitl's voice asked.

I raised my eyes, briefly, knowing why he was here. "Yes?"

"I–" He looked at me, biting his lips. "Let me come with you and Neutemoc."

"It's too dangerous. I've already put you in danger too much as it is."

Teomitl shook his head, half-exasperated. "I won't be coddled. I'm a warrior, not some old-woman priest..." He stopped, his face hardening. "I'm sorry."

At least he had the honesty to voice the warriors' prejudice aloud. "You're heir-apparent to the Mexica Empire."

"My brother isn't dead," Teomitl said, fiercely. "Tizoc is still Master of the House of Darts."

"He's very ill," I said. "Lord Death waits for him. And when that moment comes–"

"It hasn't come." He held himself straight, impatiently. "I have to prove myself. You'd deny me that?"

Ceyaxochitl had asked me the same question. I made him the same answer. "I'm not your testing ground," I said.

"I'm not asking you to be," he snapped. "Just to let me have my chance. You heard Mahuizoh. 'An un-bloodied pup'. That will be all they think of me, at the Imperial Court. By your doing."

The accusation, as unfair as it was, didn't ring quite true in his mouth. "It's not the Court you're trying to impress," I said. "Nor was it the Court you thought of when you followed Eleuia."

Teomitl said nothing. He watched me, one hand on his macuahitl sword. "No," he said. "But it doesn't concern you."

"Doesn't it?" I finished packing my bag, and laid it aside.

He met my gaze squarely. "Let me come. Or I'll be as nothing."

"To whom?" I asked.

"To her," he snapped, throwing the pronoun into the air like an offering to a god. "Who else?"

I didn't move. I simply asked, "Her?"

"Huitzilxochtin," Teomitl said. "My mother." When I still didn't speak, he said, "She was strong and she fought to the end, but it was all for nothing. She died bearing me. And I–" His voice was bitter. "I am nothing. I have no great battles behind me, nor feats of arms."

"Battle isn't the only way to prove yourself," I said, finally. But in my mind were my parents' voices, whispering about how wrong I was, how there was no glory, no honour outside the battlefield. About how I'd failed. "And where we're going… That's no battlefield."

Teomitl smiled. "There are battles everywhere," he said. "You just have to know where to look."

I'd forgotten the ease with which he could take control of a conversation. "That doesn't change anything. I can't risk your life."

"It's not yours to risk," Teomitl said. He didn't sound as angry as he'd been. Just thoughtful. "It's mine, and I do what I want with it."

"I–" I said.

"Is it so hard? You let me come, when you thought I was a calmecac student. Nothing has changed. We're still the same."

Why couldn't he see that everything had changed? "I can't be your testing ground," I repeated. I couldn't face the repercussions of taking him with us. What if Axayacatl-tzin died tonight, and Tizoc-tzin became Revered Speaker? I'd have endangered the life of the heir-apparent.

Teomitl watched me for a while, his brown eyes shrewd. Behind him, in the courtyard of the Duality House, the rain fell in a steady patter – the Storm Lord's magic slowly, steadily seeping into the earth. "Why? It's a simple thing."

He was wrong. Things were never that simple. "I can't. Let someone else…"

I met his eyes – my apprentice Payaxin's eyes, eager to do what was right – and I realised what I was saying. Let someone else shoulder this burden. Let me go on as if nothing had changed. It was fear that made me say that: fear and nothing else. But I was no coward. No warrior – there were some things for which I would never find the courage – but no coward.

"Very well," I said, finally. "You can come."

We stopped to see Mihmatini briefly. She'd followed Neutemoc's household into one of the Duality House's vast rooms. Reed mats were spread on the floor; both Mazatl and Ollin were already asleep. Mihmatini sat cross-legged against the wall. Over her was a fresco depicting the Duality's Heaven. Under the gaze of the fused lovers, a tree grew out of the waters, the shadowy souls of babies clinging to its trunk as if to their mothers' breasts. Dead babies: the Duality's Heaven was the only place that would receive the souls of unweaned children, preserving them until they could be reborn.

Dead babies. I was reminded, uneasily, of the bones in Ceyaxochitl's possession, and of the god-child we were seeking.

Mihmatini, oblivious to my thoughts, smiled tiredly at me. I couldn't help noticing, though, that her brightest smile was reserved for Teomitl, who had followed us into the room.

Neutemoc stopped to stroke Ollin's forehead: the baby's face shifted, and settled into a pleased smile. Neutemoc's face, a careful mask, cracked. He knelt by his son's cradle, and watched him sleep, his lips moving to whisper a mournful lullaby.

Sweat had stained Mihmatini's cotton shirt, and the dark circles under her eyes were, if anything, more accented.

"Get some sleep," I said. "Don't worry."

"I am worrying," Mihmatini said, tartly. "You'd have to be a fool not to, with that rain."

"It's dangerous," Teomitl said.

"You can feel it?" I asked Mihmatini.

She shook her head. "I'm not sensitive enough. Yaotl told me."

"Yaotl," I said, not quite over my rancour yet, "interferes with what doesn't concern him."

She smiled. "Don't we all?" Without waiting for my answer, she turned to watch Neutemoc, who was still kneeling by Ollin's cradle.

"He tries so hard to be a good head of his household," she said, with a sigh.

Something unnameable shifted in my chest, until I could hardly breathe. "Yes," I said, finally. "But the way he behaved towards Huei…"

Mihmatini didn't answer at once. Her face had grown dark. "Let's forget Huei for the moment."

I couldn't. "We'll be going out again," I said, finally.

Mihmatini shifted. "Then I'll renew the protection spells on you. Although they really don't hold on you, Acatl. And you–" She looked at Teomitl. "You definitely don't need me to cast a spell on you."

Teomitl's face fell. "You're sure?" he asked. "Another kind of spell, perhaps?"

Mihmatini suppressed a smile. "Men," she said, shaking her head, but she didn't sound angry. Quite the contrary, in fact.

There would be time to work this out later, if we survived.

Once Mihmatini finished casting the spell, we went back into the streets. By then, it was raining heavily. Storm clouds had drowned the sun, and the light falling on the Sacred Precinct was as weak as that of evening, even though it was barely noon.

Teomitl took the lead, filled with his boundless energy. In the gloom, his spell of protection shone like a beacon: a much, much stronger construction that the ones Mihmatini had laid on us.

As we walked, raindrops fell on our clothes, mingling with our hair. With each drop, the protection lessened. I could feel it fading away, a vanishing itch on my skin. Teomitl's protection, though, did not show any sign of corruption. Here, if nowhere else, Huitzilpochtli's power ran strong. We went south, towards the district of Moyotlan and the temple of Chalchiutlicue, making a wide loop to avoid Neutemoc's house and the creatures that would be congregating there.

Finding a boat to take us to the temple was a simple matter: even with the pouring rain, the fishermen were used to taking worshippers to the island. The rain fell unceasingly, until the world above and below seemed to be made of water: an opaque curtain that joined the murky lake under the boat to the clouds above our heads. And every drop, charged with magic, burnt like acid.

"A good time for sacrificing to the goddess," the fisherman said.

"Yes," Neutemoc said, curtly.

Teomitl's face was set in a grimace; he stared at the water. "A good time to remember the old gods."

I had no wish to join the conversation. I sat at the prow of the boat, keeping an eye on the waters of the lake. There was something swimming by our side: something sleek and dark, with a tail that spread out, opening like a flower... As the waters parted under the boat's keel, I heard, with a growing horror, the song of the ahuizotl, rising from the depths of the lake.

*"Go forth, go forth to the place of many clouds*
*To where the thick mists mark the Blessed Land*
*The verdant house…"*

No. I threw myself away from the edge. The boat rocked alarmingly, almost sending us into the water, towards the yellow eyes waiting for us.

With a curse, Neutemoc steadied the craft. "What in the Fifth World are you playing at?" he hissed. "We almost fell into the water."

I knew. The Duality curse me, I knew. I could still see those eyes at the bottom of the lake; and that oddly shaped tail, lashing out towards me. Even through the murk, I'd seen it clearly. It had had the shape of a small, clawed hand: the same hand that had left the scratching marks near Eleuia's empty eye-sockets. My eyes itched, and I felt sick.

The fisherman looked at the water, then back at me. "Leave him be," he said to Neutemoc. "There's evil afoot today."

How perceptive. Ahuizotls. My heart was beating madly in my chest. Well, we didn't have to worry about the Jade Skirt. She knew we were coming.

## NINETEEN
# *The Drowned Ones*

The ahuizotl remained in the lake, though its dark shape followed us as we walked around the shore to enter the temple.

To my surprise, there was no priest on watch at the temple entrance. But, in the courtyard, Eliztac himself was waiting for us, his soaked plume of heron feathers drooping on his head.

He grimaced when he saw us. "You shine like wildfires. I presume you're not here to pay homage to Chalchiutlicue."

"In a manner of speaking," I said, cautiously. "We need help."

Eliztac's eyes wandered from Teomitl to Neutemoc. My brother wasn't in Jaguar regalia, but his rigid stance could only belong to a warrior. And the Duality knew what Eliztac made of Teomitl, who currently radiated light like Tonatiuh Himself.

"I think I already told you–" he started.

"We're not here to see her," I said.

As I'd foreseen, Neutemoc stiffened. "Acatl," he said, warningly. "Don't tell me–"

"It was the closest temple," I snapped. And, without waiting for his answer, I said to Eliztac: "I need to get into Tlalocan, into Chalchiutlicue's Meadows."

His eyebrows rose. He looked upwards, at the rain. "Magical water. A bit of an odd season," he said. His gaze was shrewd. He had to see how each drop attacked our protection. "I presume you're seeking guidance."

"In a manner of speaking," I said, again. "But it's urgent."

Eliztac's gaze was sarcastic. "What isn't?" he said. "Very well. If you'll swear to me you're not here to see her, I'll let you in."

It was Neutemoc who spoke. "No," he said. "I won't swear to that." His face was pale, leached of all colours by the darkness, and the rain fell on his cheeks like tears.

Eliztac started to say something; but Neutemoc forestalled him. "I'll see my wife," he said. "And don't think you can prevent me."

Eliztac took us through a first courtyard, and then into a smaller one, closer to the heart of the building. Everything, from the painted adobe walls to the beaten earth under our sandals, shimmered with magic: a thick covering of wards against which the raindrops slid, and became normal water again.

Teomitl had also noticed it. "It's different in here," he said.

Eliztac barely turned. "This place is under the gaze of the goddess," he said. "This way."

At the far end of the courtyard, he stopped before the door of a room, its entrance-curtain decorated with a heron in flight and patterns of seashells.

"I can make my own way," Neutemoc said.

"I have no doubt you can," Eliztac said, gravely. "But I can't leave you alone here."

Neutemoc drew himself up. "Do you think I'll try to take their dues from the gods?"

"I have seen many men do many things," Eliztac said. "Not all of which contributed to the continuation of the Fifth World."

Neutemoc's face darkened. "You–"

He hadn't been in a good mood for a while. I could understand why, but it might all have ended badly if someone hadn't lifted the entrance-curtain. The tinkle of bells spread between Neutemoc and Eliztac, stopping them dead.

It was Huei, as I had never seen her: her face painted white, lips greyed, her unbound hair falling onto her shoulders in a cascade of darkness. Her shift, too, was white, as if it had already been time for her sacrifice.

My heart tightened in my chest.

"Neutemoc." She turned, slightly, towards me. "Acatl. What a surprise." Her voice was ironic. Behind her, a green-clad attendant closed the curtain and moved closer to her, in protection.

Neutemoc's hands had clenched into fists. "You had to know I'd come."

"I'd almost given up hope that you'd make it out of your cage." Under the white makeup, her face was expressionless; but in her eyes shone tears. "But I'm sure you're not here for my health."

"Why, Huei?" Neutemoc asked, the question bursting out of him before he could hold it back.

"No one can be cheated of their dues," Huei said. "Gods, goddesses, wives…"

I felt embarrassed, as I had when they'd started quarrelling in front of me; as if the masks had fallen, revealing the faces of mortals instead of gods. Standing between them wasn't my place. It would never be. "I think we shouldn't be here," I said, pushing Teomitl away from Neutemoc.

"Do stay," Huei said, and the irony in her voice was as frightening as any ahuizotl. "You're involved, after all, aren't you?"

Teomitl and Eliztac, luckier than me, were discreetly withdrawing to the other end of the courtyard. I spread my hands, trying to contain my frustration. "I didn't cause anything that you didn't already start. You should have known the consequences of what you did." Both of them.

Huei said nothing for a while. "They didn't tell me."

"The commander?" I asked.

She looked at me, surprised. "Yes. He and his second-in-command. How did you know?"

"He told us," I said, curtly. "And he's dead now."

Huei's hands clenched into fists. "I see. It doesn't matter." She said to Neutemoc, in a lower voice, "But you couldn't see what was happening, could you?"

He looked at her, for a while. His face was unreadable. "The gods give, and the gods take away."

"Still your old excuse?" Huei crossed her arms over her chest. "Everything dies, Neutemoc. That's no reason to detach yourself from what's yours. That's no reason to abandon me or your children."

Neutemoc's face was white. "You've seen how easily everything can tumble."

"Then things are all the more precious, aren't they?" She shook her head. "You can't armour yourself against loss, Neutemoc. That doesn't work."

"I've seen," he said, stiffly. "But still—" His voice was low. "I almost lost you to childbirth. Twice. How can I love what can't last?"

"Everyone does," Huei said. Her voice was sad. "And lust won't make you forget."

"No," Neutemoc said. "It will not. We agree on that, if on nothing else." His lips tightened around an unseen obstacle.

Huei looked at him for a while. "No matter," she said, with a sigh. "What's done is done. I have no regrets."

"You sought to kill him," I said, softly, not knowing what else to say.

"Yes," she said, defiant. "Because he left me no choice."

Feeling more and more of an intruder, I started slowly retreating. Neither of them made a gesture to stop me.

Neutemoc didn't move. He shook his head, once, twice. "The children miss you," he said, finally.

Huei stood, tall and proud, as she had in her own household. "I've made my choices."

I joined Eliztac and Teomitl at the other end of the courtyard. If Neutemoc said something more to Huei, I didn't hear it. How could they both have been so foolish – too blind to see the consequences of their acts, in spite of what Huei had blithely affirmed?

Once it had been established not only that I hadn't been there to coerce Huei into leaving but that I'd brought her husband to see her, Eliztac became more helpful. He probably thought our request to go into Chalchiutlicue's Meadows was a crazy endeavour: two warriors – a far cry from the peasants the Storm Lord and his wife favoured – and a priest of Mictlan, whose magic was anathema to life. The equivalent of mice trying to walk through an eagle's eyrie. But, after all, as he said, our lives were our own.

He led us into a smaller room, with a discreet altar to the Jade Skirt. The room was dark, illuminated only by the flames of a brazier, and filled with the wet, earthy smell of churned mud. A limestone statue of the goddess stood behind the altar: a woman with braids and a shawl with green tassels, opening out Her hands to encompass all of the Fifth World.

Eliztac knelt before the altar, whispering a brief prayer. Then he withdrew from a wicker chest a small figurine of the goddess, which he set on the altar, within a ceramic bowl.

"Stand this way," he said, pointing to a carved pattern on the floor: a huge water-glyph, still bearing traces of dried blood. And, to me: "I'll open the gate, but you'll have to complete my spell with your own blood offerings."

I knelt within the glyph, running my fingers on the smooth stone. "I'm used to it," I said. There was a slight draught that raised goose bumps on my skin: an air current running from behind the altar to the door. There must have been a hole somewhere in the wall.

"Our blood, too?" Teomitl asked. He was watching the statue of Chalchiutlicue as if it might come to life at any moment. Despite the accumulation of magic in the room, I didn't think this was possible.

Eliztac shook his head. "Acatl's blood should be enough."

Neutemoc wasn't speaking. He stood inside the glyph in his appointed place, but he was sunk in one of his moods again.

Eliztac began chanting: a repetitive hum that started low, and gradually rose until it resonated in my chest:

*"You created the Third World*
*The Age of Water, the Age of Streams and Oceans*
*The Age of Your unending bounty*
*Giving Your essence to us..."*

Gently, he set the figurine within the brazier. The fire flared black for one moment, before the flames began eating away at the statue. It burnt, not like wood, but with the mingled, acrid smells of resin and copal, creating a black smoke that fled towards us. The magic in the room intensified.

I knelt and opened three slashes on the back of my hand with my obsidian knife. Blood dripped out, settling in the grooves of the glyph.

*"You destroyed the Third World*
*The Age of Water, the Age of Streams and Oceans*
*The Age of Your unending bounty*
*Water burst from the ground, from the deepest caves*
*Water to cover the earth, to drown the fields…"*

The smoke, billowing around us, grew thicker and thicker until only the area within the glyph was left clear. I couldn't make out Eliztac; his voice, singing the end of the hymn, receded further and further away.

Through the pungent smell came another: that of wet earth, mingled with the faint, heady scent of flowers. The smoke swept through the glyph, wrapping itself around us until I could no longer see anything. Copal and resin invaded my lungs. A cough welled up, irrepressible, and I found myself on my knees, struggling to breathe.

Light blazed, across the glyph. The smoke slowly vanished, revealing, as far as the eye could see, a land of marshes and deserted Floating Gardens. The air was saturated with magic – not the feeble makings of humans, but something far more primordial: the magic of a goddess, unconstrained by any mortal concern.

I stood up, carefully. My sandals squelched: the lines of the glyph were traced in the mud at my feet, and filled with water instead of blood.

Neutemoc and Teomitl were still on their knees, clearing the last of the smoke from their lungs. I stood, looking around the pools. It was a quiet, peaceful land. But I wasn't fooled. We weren't welcome here, and never would be. The more quickly we got out of here, the better.

## TWENTY
## *The Goddess' Will*

Knowing where we had to go wasn't difficult. A path opened, though the heart of that marshy land: an area of drier land snaking between brackish pools and stunted trees, leading towards the silvery surface of a lake. Behind us was the shimmering shape of Eliztac's gate, the only way back into the Fifth World.

Neutemoc grimaced, but he still went ahead, soldiering through the mud as if it were a march. Teomitl followed, casting a glance in my direction from time to time.

I was last, keeping a wary eye on the magic swirling around us. This wasn't our territory but Chalchiutlicue's, and She had known perfectly well that we were coming.

A splash in the water made me start. I turned in its direction; and saw two yellow eyes, at the bottom of one of the pools. Two eyes that followed me with naked hunger. Huitzilpochtli curse them. Couldn't we ever leave the things behind, even in Tlalocan?

"What is it?" Teomitl asked. Neutemoc was halfway to the lake by now, unconcerned by the mud that sucked at his gilded sandals.

I shook my head, irritably. "Nothing."

Another splash. I turned towards the ahuizotl – and, with a fright, saw that it was crawling out of the pool.

It was black, as sleek as a fish; but instead of fins, it crawled on four clawed hands. Its wrinkled face was vaguely human: not that of an old man, but that of a child that had stayed for too long in the water; and the eyes were those of eagles or pikes, round and un-blinking and filled with frightful intelligence. Its tail was long and sinuous, ending in a small, clawed hand that kept clenching on empty air, a motion that was oddly sickening.

"Acatl-tz…" Teomitl started, behind me, then stopped. He must have seen the ahuizotl too.

Two more splashes of water: two other beasts, crawling out from other pools. And then a fourth, and a fifth, until the path was crowded with a dozen of them. They moved towards us, blocking our way. Their tail-hands clenched, unclenched in a swaying motion. I tried in vain to forget Eleuia's empty eye-sockets, and the claws that had scrabbled at her face to tear her flesh.

"Acatl," Neutemoc said.

I didn't move. I couldn't move.

Two handspans away from us, the ahuizotls stopped. Their eyes shone with the desire to drown, to rend, to maim. But they didn't come any closer.

"What do we do?" Teomitl asked.

"Move," I managed. I cleared my throat. "Forward. Move." The message, after all, was clear enough.

Neutemoc resumed his march towards the lake; so did Teomitl and I. A dry, rustling sound came from be-hind us: the ahuizotls were following. No going back.

The path went straight towards the lake, and plunged into it. I didn't think we were expected to go underwater, though. Neutemoc stopped at the water's edge. He didn't say anything, but his whole stance radiated impatience. Where do we go now, Acatl? You who always have the answer to everything…

I turned, as slowly as I could. The ahuizotls had spread out in a ring, their wrinkled faces turned toward the lake. Waiting. For what? A signal to leap upon us?

The ground shook, under my feet. Magic surged from the mud, arcing through my back in a flash of pain. Water fountained from the lake, forcing its way into my hair, my clothes, into my bones.

When I managed to raise my gaze again, the goddess stood in the middle of the water.

No. She was the water: it flowed upwards, turning into Her translucent body – and then, higher up, solidifying into brown skin with opalescent reflections. I could see algae and reeds in Her skirt; and, far into the depths of Her lake, small shapes that might have been fish, or very young children, still swimming in the waters of their mother's womb.

"Visitors," Chalchiutlicue said. Her voice was the storm-tossed sea, the gurgling of mountain streams, the wind over the empty marshes. "It is not often that you brave My World." In one hand She had a spindle and whorl; in the other, a small flint cutting axe.

I went down on one knee, keeping a cautious eye on Her face. "My Lady," I said. "We have need of Your help."

The Jade Skirt laughed, and it was the sound of water cascading into pools. "And how may I help you, priest?"

"I…" I started, but Her eyes, as green and as opaque as jade, held me, silenced me. They were wide, those eyes, with small, black pupils inset like obsidian – wide open, and I was falling into Her gaze, a fall that had neither beginning nor end.

She was inside me, rifling through my mind with the ease of an old woman sorting out maize kernels. Memories welled up, irrepressible: Mother's angry face on her death-bed... Neutemoc's smile as he urged me to run after him in the maize fields... Mihmatini, as a baby, snuggling against my chest with a contented sigh, her heartbeat mingling with mine – a feeling I'd never experience with a child of my own... The clan elders, bringing my father's body back for the vigil – and I, standing at the shrine's gate, not daring to enter and make my peace...

Chalchiutlicue slid out of my mind, leaving a great, gaping wound. I stood once more on the shores of Her lake, struggling to collect myself.

"So small," She said with a satisfied smile. "So filled with regrets and bitterness, priest. Shall I summon the past for you? Shall I summon forth the spirits of the dead?"

I knew who She wanted to summon – who had drowned in the marshes: Father. "You have no such power," I said, shaking inwardly. "The dead don't belong to you."

"Is that so?" Her smile was mocking. "The drowned are my province, and my husband's. And some others, too. Tell me now, shall I call up your father's soul from the bliss of Tlalocan?"

Father here, seeing me, seeing Neutemoc and knowing what I had done... She couldn't do that. She was powerful, but not capable of doing that. She just wanted to see me squirm. It was an empty threat. "No," I whispered. "No."

Her smile was even wider. "So small, priest." She reached out. Her huge hands folded around the knives at my belt, lifting them to the level of Her eyes and flinging them downwards into the mud. I could have wept. "Carrying your feeble magic as if it could shield you."

"We came for help," I whispered, struggling to turn the conversation elsewhere. "There is a child–"

Her face didn't move. "How convenient. And tell me: why should I help any of you? You," and She pointed to me, "with your allegiance given to another. And you and you, serving the upstart, Huitzilpochtli?"

Neutemoc hadn't intervened. So usual of him. He'd done the same when Mother had died. But now, with the goddess's finger still pointed on him, he came forward. "Your husband puts the Fifth World in danger."

The Jade Skirt laughed again. "Why should it matter to Me? I have seen five ages; and I ended the Third World. We'll start anew. We always do."

"Not so soon," I said, softly, knowing it wasn't an argument which would convince Her. "This isn't the proper time, or the proper way."

If She had been human, She would have shrugged. Instead, She made a wide, expansive gesture that made all the water of the lake spout upwards – and then fall back again, like an exhaled breath. "The proper way? Doesn't Tlaloc do what We've all wished for? Tumble the Hummingbird from His place in your Empire, and give Us back the worshippers He took from Us?"

She was, like Tlaloc, like Xochiquetzal, one of the Old Ones: the gods who had been there before Huitzilpochtli, before the Sun God. But She was also Tlaloc's wife – and the Storm Lord had cheated on Her to make His agent child. As Neutemoc had cheated on Huei. I needed to find the words…

Huei. What would have I told Huei? I closed my eyes, for a brief moment, and then said, as softly as I could, "Is this truly the way You would have wished this to go?"

Chalchiutlicue's jade-coloured eyes blinked, once, twice. "You don't always choose your way, priest."

"No," I said, thinking of Huei, who was at this moment waiting for her sacrifice. If only things could have gone another way. "Nevertheless…" She smiled again, but said nothing. "That child should have been yours," I said, softly. "But it's not."

She shook Her head, slowly, but didn't make any gesture to stop me. I took that as an encouragement. "He slept with a mortal," I said. "Instead of asking you."

When Chalchiutlicue spoke again, Her voice was lower: the soft sound of water, welling up from the earth. "It couldn't have been Mine," she said. "Any child of gods would be a god, and subject to the same limitations. But you are right in one thing, priest. He didn't ask me."

"Then–" Neutemoc started, but the Jade Skirt cut him off.

"In truth, I care little for your petty struggles. If you choose to make the Southern Hummingbird supreme, then you'll reap what you've sown. I have already had a world in which every mortal worshipped Me, where everyone gave their life's blood to sustain My course in the sky." She smiled, and this time the nostalgia was unmistakable. "Tlaloc had His world, too. But the Storm Lord has always been greedy for more."

"Don't you want revenge?" I asked, softly.

Chalchiutlicue's eyes were unfathomable. "I told you. I care little either way. Huitzilpochtli will tumble, without any need for Our intervention."

"Is there nothing that will persuade you?" I asked. "So much is at stake…" The Imperial Family. The safety of Tenochtitlan. The balance maintained by the Duality.

Laughter, like storm-waves. "You would sacrifice something to Me, priest? Your endless regrets? Your pitiful virginity, so carefully preserved? Your first-born

332

child?" Her voice turned malicious. "But of course, that's something you've given up on."

Every word of Hers dug claws into my heart, and slowly squeezed, until the world blurred around me. "I–"

"Your allegiance?" She said. "You're sworn to another, and Mictlantecuhtli doesn't let go of what's His. You have nothing to give Me."

Neutemoc's face was white, but he didn't move. He stood as if paralysed. It was another who broke the silence.

"No," Teomitl said. "He has nothing to give. But I have." His face was transfigured by a harsh joy. Here was what he had been waiting for, all along: a chance to be useful, to prove his valour.

Chalchiutlicue turned towards him; the invisible claws around my chest opened one by one, freeing my heart. "One of the Southern Hummingbird's devotees? That's an amusing thought." Her eyes narrowed. "You're–"

"Yes," Teomitl said. He'd thrown back his warrior's cloak, revealing a simple glyph of turquoise on his chest: the colour of the Imperial Family. "Will you accept my allegiance?"

The goddess's face was a mask, and I could almost hear Her calculations. Was this a trap? An opportunity She couldn't ignore? "Your god is also jealous," She said, finally.

"But not careful," Teomitl said. "He has hundreds of devotees over the land."

Chalchiutlicue's eyes narrowed again. "But there would be no gain, would there?"

Teomitl shrugged. "I've always thought the Great Temple was disharmonious. There should be rooms for more gods, shouldn't there? For the peasants as well as the warriors; for the waters as well as the battles."

333

"Don't lie to Me. You're a warrior," the Jade Skirt said. "All that matters to you is glory on the battlefield."

Teomitl shook his head. "No," he said. "The only glory comes from winning battles. But there are many battlefields."

"In My realm?"

"Fighting currents," Teomitl said, simply. "Struggling not to capsize in a storm. Swimming ashore with the ahuizotls surrounding you, eager for your eyes and fingernails…"

She regarded him for a while. By Teomitl's shocked, blank gaze, She was probing into his mind, as she had into mine. "You are sincere," She said, finally. "When you become Revered Speaker – will you re-establish My worship?" She didn't, I noticed, say "if", but simply assumed it was certain that Teomitl would succeed Tizoc-tzin – who in turn would succeed Axayacatl-tzin.

If Teomitl noticed that, he gave no sign. "Should I ever become Revered Speaker, I'll make You and Your husband a worthy temple: a building so great that everyone will prostrate themselves on seeing it, so magnificent that it will be the talk of the land…"

Chalchiutlicue laughed, but it was amused laughter: waves lapping at a child's feet, a stream gently gurgling over stones. "Will it?" She asked. "That would be something to see indeed, child of the Obsidian Snake. I should wait for it."

"Will you accept my allegiance, then?" Teomitl asked, impatient as ever. Someone was really going to have to teach him forbearance, or he'd never survive at the Imperial Court.

The Jade Skirt watched him for a while, perhaps weighing Her choices. "That would be interesting," She said. "Amusing, if nothing else. Yes, child. I'll take your offer."

Power blazed from the heart of the lake, welling up from the earth in an irresistible geyser. It wrapped itself around Teomitl like a second mantle, sank into his skin until his bones echoed with its ponderous beat. He fell to his knees in the mud, gasping for breath.

Neutemoc, finally finding some energy, took a step towards him. I laid a hand on his shoulder. "Wait," I said. Intervening would just make things worse, both for Teomitl and for us.

Teomitl's head came up, in a fluid, blurred gesture that had nothing human about it. His eyes were the colour of jade: a mirror of Chalchiutlicue's triumphant gaze. His mouth opened; but all that came out was a moan, a shapeless lament.

"Feel it," Chalchiutlicue whispered. Her voice made the ground tremble under our feet. "Feel it, child of the Obsidian Snake..."

Teomitl closed his eyes. His head fell down again; his back slumped, as if under a burden too heavy to bear.

In the silence, all we could hear was his breath, slow and laboured. Something cold and slimy bumped against my legs: one of the ahuizotls, creeping closer to Teomitl. I bent down, instinctively, to recover my obsidian knives from the mud into which Chalchiutlicue had flung them.

"No!" Her voice was the thunderclap of the storm. "He made his choice, priest. Let him bear the consequences."

In the eerie silence of Chalchiutlicue's Meadows, the ahuizotls converged towards Teomitl. They formed a wide, malevolent ring, circling him like a flock of vultures, and their hypnotic song rose, slowly, faintly, ringing in my chest like a second heartbeat:

*"In Tlalocan, the verdant house,*
*The Blessed Land of the Drowned*
*The dead men play at balls, they cast the reeds…"*

The clawed hands over their heads clenched, un-clenched, a sickening counterpart to the rhythm of the song. I couldn't hear Teomitl's breathing any more.

Slowly, ever so slowly, Teomitl rose from his kneeling position. He raised his head, and every one of the ahuizotls around him did the same.

Nausea welled up in me, sharp, uncontrollable.

Teomitl's eyes weren't jade any more; but yellow, the same colour as the beasts surrounding him.

"Acatl," Neutemoc whispered. I said nothing. I waited for Teomitl to say something, anything that would prove he was still human.

Teomitl sucked in a breath, and then another – slow, deliberate. "It… hurts," he whispered. "It…" And, for the first time, he wasn't a warrior or an Imperial Prince, but just a boy, thrust into responsibilities he'd never been meant to have.

Chalchiutlicue smiled. "They'll come to your call," She said.

"And the child?" Neutemoc asked.

Teomitl shook his head, as if to clear his thoughts – which must have been moving in another place, far from the Fifth World. The ahuizotls' heads moved slightly; but they seemed more to be following him than mimicking his gestures. I didn't know whether that was an improvement. Everything about the ahuizotls made my hackles rise. But the Jade Skirt was right: Teomitl had made his choice, and couldn't go back on it.

"The child–" Teomitl whispered. "I can feel him," he said. "Everywhere…" His face twisted. "In the rain, in the waters of the lake… Like a wound in the Fifth World."

"My husband placed a spell of concealment on the child," Chalchiutlicue said. "He was given to a family in the Floating Gardens in the district of Cuepopan, to raise as their own." She opened Her hands wide. Within them lay a small, translucent jade figurine of a baby, shining with an inner light. She blew on it: the baby scattered, became dust blown into Teomitl's face. "That is where you'll find him."

Before going back, I retrieved my knives from the water, and put them back in my belt. They still pulsed, but the emptiness of Mictlan was somehow different, tainted with Chalchiutlicue's touch.

The ahuizotls followed us on the way back: an escort I could gladly have done without. Teomitl was silent, his eyes lost in thought. The veil of protection I'd always seen on him was still there. But it had subtly changed, shimmering with green reflections. Like my knives, Chalchiutlicue's magic had altered it.

Neutemoc, too, was silent. Brooding again, probably. I could only hope I wasn't at the forefront of his thoughts.

When we reached the remnants of the glyph through which we'd entered the Meadows, the world spun and spun, and coalesced into the small room where we'd started our journey.

Eliztac stood watching the brazier, in which the last remnants of the copal and resin figurine were consuming themselves. He looked up when we stepped out of the glyph. "You've returned, I see." His gaze froze on Teomitl. "She's made you Her agent?"

Teomitl said nothing. His eyes were still unfocused.

"There's no time," I said. "We have to go to the district of Cuepopan. Can you lend us a boat?"

Eliztac's eyebrows rose. "Always in a hurry, I see."

"It's the rain," Teomitl whispered, and his voice echoed, as if Chalchiutlicue were speaking through him. "It's all wrong, can't you see?"

Eliztac said nothing. He had to have seen. "This temple has many boats," he said. "But few boatmen who will be ready to brave the goddess's anger."

"I'll row," I said at the exact same time as Neutemoc, who glared at me, defiant. Of us both, he'd always been the faster rower; but it had been many years since he hadn't had a slave rowing for him.

Eliztac smiled. "I'll take you to the docks, while you decide."

When we did reach the docks, there wasn't any discussion: Neutemoc settled himself into the boat, taking the oars and glaring at me. Quarrelling would have been futile, so I let him be. In any case, I was more worried about Teomitl, who looked at the boat blankly, as if he had forgotten what it was.

"This way," I said.

Teomitl sucked in a breath and exhaled slowly, as if it had hurt him. "We have to hurry," he said. Around him, the rain fell in a steady curtain: magic shimmering around us, chipping away at our wards.

When our wards were gone... I didn't want to think on what would happen, but it was a fair bet the creatures would be close.

"I know," I said. "Get in."

Teomitl laid an unsteady hand against the boat's edge. "I–" he said. He breathed in, again. "I'm not used to it."

I'd never been a god's agent, but the Wind of Knives' powers had been invested in me, for a very short while. "It will get easier as time passes."

Teomitl snorted. "A good guess," he said. He climbed into the boat; Neutemoc stilled its rocking effortlessly.

"I'll guide," Teomitl said.

There was still a chance we would find the child before the full measure of His powers manifested; before he became much harder to kill. But Teomitl was right. We had to make haste.

The streets and canals Neutemoc rowed through were deserted: the unexpected, unrelenting rain seemed to have sent everybody indoors. At one intersection, a woman stood watching the water level under a bridge, her face creased into a frown. I could understand her worry: all of Tenochtitlan was an island, and the lake was our foundation. A flood would be a disaster.

But there were other, deeper worries: the Fifth World would not last if Tlaloc tumbled Tonatiuh, the Sun God, from the sky. Everything would once more be plunged into the primal darkness.

"This way," Teomitl said, as we reached the first of Cuepopan's Floating Gardens. He steered Neutemoc from island to island with small gestures; my brother said nothing, only rowed like a man who had nothing to lose any more.

The Floating Gardens were silent. With the rain, no peasants planted seeds, or tilled the fields. It was as if everything had withdrawn from the world, save for the steady patter of rain on the water, and the regular, splashing sound of Neutemoc's oars, leading us ever closer to our goal.

And a couple of other splashing sounds. Without surprise, I saw two dark shapes in the water, trailing after the boat like an escort.

"You can feel them?" I asked Teomitl.

He shook his head. "I could tell them to go away."

I was tempted. The ahuizotls frightened me; but we weren't there to be subject to my whims. And against a god-child, any weapon could prove useful. "No," I said. "Let them be."

They followed us, whispering of the Blessed Lands, of the dead gathered in Chalchiutlicue's bosom. Of Father, still unaware of how much I mourned him.

"This one," Teomitl said.

There was nothing remarkable about the Floating Garden he singled out. Like the others, it was a mass of earth and roots, anchored into the mud of the lake by poles and woven reed mats. A single house, perched on an artificial rise, dominated it: a small affair – and yet, as in my parents' house, it would host hordes of children; old people; and a couple of peasants, struggling to feed them all.

I laid a hand on one of my obsidian knives, feeling the emptiness of Mictlan within my chest, mingling with the bitter tang of the Jade Skirt's magic. This wasn't the time for reminiscence.

Neutemoc moored the boat near the edge of the Floating Garden, where we all disembarked. I couldn't help remembering the last time I'd done this, when Teomitl had run us aground. At least my brother was a decent oarsman.

"And now what?" Neutemoc asked.

I shrugged. "We go see what's inside."

The rain, though heavy, didn't yet hamper our vision. I wasn't confident the situation wouldn't change, though, if the god-child grew into his powers. Hopefully, it wouldn't happen. Hopefully.

Wordlessly, we crept up the small rise. Neutemoc was in the lead, his sword drawn. I was right at his back, Teomitl trailing some way behind us. The ahuizotls remained in the water – for which I was grateful.

Inside, it was dark and cool, but the air was saturated with magic: the same deep, pervasive sense of wrongness that I'd sensed at Amecameca. Here, however, it was strong enough to choke the breath out of me. "I… I don't think I'm going to last for long."

"What's the matter, Acatl-tzin?" Teomitl asked.

It hurt to breathe, even to focus my thoughts. Wrong, it was so wrong. Teomitl had had it right: it was like a wound in the fabric of the Fifth World, a wound that kept widening, spilling its miasma to choke us all.

"Who comes here?"

By the extinguished hearth crouched a wizened figure, wrapped in a tattered shirt, its clothes torn to shreds and stinking of refuse.

"Huemac? Is that you?" the figure asked.

An old, old woman, her face seamed with the marks of many seasons, blind gaze questing left and right, still trying to see us. She didn't look threatening, though the magic pervaded her, soaking through her skin, outlining the pale shapes of her bones. Wrong. All wrong.

"We're not your son," Neutemoc said.

"'We'?" she asked. "How many of you are there?"

"I'm not sure that's relevant," Neutemoc said, nonplussed.

"This is a small house," the old woman whispered. "A small, small place, my lord. We have nothing worth your time."

Even without her sight, she could still distinguish the confident tones of a warrior's voice.

"We're not here to attack you," Teomitl said, finally. "We're looking for your… grandson?"

"I have many grandsons." Her voice was sly. "Many, many children of my own; and many fruitful marriages."

Teomitl closed his eyes for a bare moment. "He's young. Six, seven years old, no more. His hair is as black and as slick as dried blood, and his skin the colour of muddy water." He spoke as if he could see the child. And perhaps he could, indeed; perhaps that had been part of Chalchiutlicue's gift.

"Chicuei Mazatl," the old woman whispered. "My sweet, sweet Mazatl." She crooned, balancing herself back and forth on her knees. "Mazatl. A deer, a strong child like his father; born to be a hunter…"

I didn't know what was worrying me more: the wrongness that crushed my chest, or the chilling fact that this old woman was completely unanchored from the Fifth World.

"Mazatl." Neutemoc's voice was flat. His own daughter was called Mazatl – simply after the day she had been born, like many children – but he would see the parallels. "Where is he, venerable?"

"Not here," she cackled. "No, not here. The deer has fled into the forest, into the trees. Not here…"

Teomitl knelt by the fire, and took her hands. "Look at me," he said.

Her blind eyes rose towards his face, and stopped. Slowly, hesitatingly, she extended her right hand in his direction. Teomitl didn't move. He let her touch his skin and recoil, as if she'd burnt herself. "You shine, like a sun, like the sun at the beginning of the world. You – who are you?"

"Ahuizotl," Teomitl said, softly. "He who bears Chalchiutlicue's gift."

"Ahuizotl. It is a strong name," the old woman whispered. "Will you protect me? They've left, they've all left, taking their reed mats and the last embers, and the altar of the gods, and the ceramic bowls. Gone…"

"I see," Teomitl said. His voice was soft, with the edge of broken obsidian. "Do you know where?"

"I–" Sanity returned to her face, for a brief moment. "They'll kill me if I tell. They said they would. They never lie, you see."

Teomitl's hands tightened around hers. "I never lie, either," he said. "I'll protect you." He surprised me; I would have expected him to dismiss the old woman, as he'd dismissed the peasants on our last hunt together. But Chalchiutlicue's gift had moulded him into someone else entirely.

"From what is coming?" Her voice was fearful.

"As best as I can. But you have to tell me."

The old woman didn't speak for a while. "You'll remember me," she said. "Ahuizotl. You'll remember me."

"Yes," Teomitl said. And although he spoke in a low voice, the whole hut vibrated with his power, and for a moment the wrongness coiled within the walls abated. "I'll remember you. Where did Mazatl go?"

"It's the day," the old woman said. "The day he leaves his childhood name behind. The day to enter the House of Youth, you see."

I didn't think there would be a House of Youth. What Mazatl needed to learn about war and his place in the world, he'd be told by his father.

"Yes," Teomitl said. "The day he takes his true name."

"Yes, yes," the old woman said.

Neutemoc, although he hadn't said anything, was clearly growing impatient. I was growing worried. Mazatl and his foster parents had obviously been gone for some time. Whatever preparations they needed to make would be near completion.

"Where did they go?" Teomitl asked.

"You'll protect me?"

"I'll protect you," Teomitl repeated. "Look." He blew into her face, gently: his breath became a shimmering cloud that wrapped itself around her, making Tlaloc's magic recede. "That way."

"You're strong," the old woman whispered. "You'll keep your word, won't you?" She shook her head.

"They went to the heart of the lake. To the place where they plant the tree of the Star Hill, the place where Spring is reborn."

Neutemoc and I looked at each other. "The Great Vigil," we both whispered.

One month after the start of the rainy season, a tree was brought from the Star Hill, where our first Emperor had built a temple to his father, Mixcoatl, the Cloud Serpent. Scores of warriors hoisted the tree upwards, and planted it into the mud at the centre of Lake Texcoco. A girl was sacrificed and her blood poured on the trunk, and into the water; and thus the Storm Lord would grant us His favours for another year of growing maize.

There would be no tree: by now, it would have rotted down to nothing. But something of that yearly sacrifice would remain, some power that could be tapped into.

"I see," Teomitl said, gravely. He blew again on her, gently. The shimmering cloud of his breath expanded to cover her from head to toe. It sank into her bones, one magic to replace another. And as it did so, the old woman faded slightly, as if she stood at a remove from the Fifth World.

"Such strength," she whispered. "Such unthinking strength. Thank you."

Teomitl clasped her hands, and did not answer.

"Let's go," Neutemoc said.

Outside, it was easier to breathe, although the rain hadn't abated. If anything, it was stronger: a veil, gradually falling across the land; the endless tears of the Heavens, filling the lakes and canals to overflowing.

"It's transformed you," I said to Teomitl. "Her gift. Once, you wouldn't have looked twice at that woman."

"It–" Teomitl shook his head, unable to describe what had happened to him. "It – changes you. To the bone."

"So much?" I asked. I couldn't help wondering if Chalchiutlicue had had some other motive in making Teomitl Her agent, if Her gift had had some thorns we hadn't seen.

Teomitl was looking at the lake. "No," he said. "But that woman in the hut… she felt so wrong, yet it wasn't her fault."

"No," I said, finally. When this was all over, we'd have to see that old woman, to make sure she would survive after Teomitl's protection had cut her off from her family.

The ahuizotls were waiting for us near the boat, their heads half out of the water. They appeared more curious than hungry. But The Duality curse me if I trusted those beasts to do anything more than obey Teomitl.

"It's not so far," Neutemoc said.

I snorted. "Not so far. It's at least one hour from here. And I don't think we're doing the right thing."

"What do you propose we do, then?" Neutemoc asked, sarcastically.

"I think we'll arrive too late," I said.

"I don't agree," Neutemoc said.

"Then you can go ahead with Teomitl, and scout. But I'm going back to get reinforcements."

"We don't need–"

"Oh? You can defeat a powerful god's agent, and his creatures, all by yourself? Last time I saw, you were busy being wounded."

"Don't toy with me," Neutemoc said.

"I'm not toying," I snapped. "I'm telling you to be careful for once. Or is that not a warlike virtue?"

"You know nothing of war," Neutemoc said, softly. "Don't presume to judge."

"What other choice is left to me?" I asked, angrily. "You won't judge yourself."

"I don't think it's quite the right time for this," Teomitl said. He was sitting in the boat, lounging in the back as if it were a comfortable chair.

Neutemoc's face was closed. "Maybe not," he said. "But things have to be clear, don't they?"

"Enough," Teomitl said. Again, he didn't raise his voice, but it cut through every word I might have thought of. "Reinforcements are probably going to be useful. Duality priests?"

I shrugged. "Whatever I can find." I hoped it would be Duality priests, though I'd have preferred Ceyaxochitl and Yaotl at my side, even over a dozen of them. But the priests were fierce fighters.

"Very well," Teomitl said. "We'll leave you in Tenochtitlan, and go on to the tree and see what's going on." He raised a hand to forestall my protest. "We'll be careful, never fear. I don't intend to get killed before I get a chance to strike."

Neutemoc said nothing. I wasn't so sure he wouldn't rush, but at least he'd have Teomitl to control him. It was amazing how persuasive the boy could be, when he applied his mind to the conversation. A boy who would one day be Emperor. Better not to think about that – not right now.

# TWENTY-ONE
## *The Great Vigil*

When I arrived, the Duality House was all but deserted.

"The priests?" the warrior at the gates asked. "I'm not sure if there are any left inside. You can look, though."

My heart sank. "The Guardian?"

The warrior shook his head. "She hasn't come back from the palace."

The Southern Hummingbird blind me. I had counted on Ceyaxochitl not being there, but not on all the priests leaving.

I found two priests in one of the rooms at the back: an old man and an old woman, who sat with Mihmatini, sipping hot chocolate.

"Greetings," I said. "I was looking for help."

The priests acknowledged my presence with a nod of their head. "I'm not sure you're in the right place," the old priestess said. "We're somewhat depleted at the moment."

"Help? What kind of help?" Mihmatini asked.

"Against creatures of Tlaloc."

The old priest nodded, sagely. "There's been trouble all over Tenochtitlan. The waters rising, and people mauled by things they couldn't see."

The creatures. Neutemoc had been wrong: the child had come into his full powers, and he wasn't shy about using them either. This wasn't good. Not good at all. "That's where all the others are?"

The old priestess nodded. "Emergencies. We're – ah, staying here as a precaution. Keeping the wards up."

The priest took a sip of his cup. "But if it's urgent..."

It was urgent. But Mihmatini was in the Duality House, as well as Neutemoc's whole household. Two old priests wouldn't make that much of a difference against what was coming. "No," I said. "Given how badly things are turning out, it's more urgent to keep a safe place. I'll – find help somewhere else."

Mihmatini had been relatively silent until now. "I'll come with you," she said.

I shook my head. "Stay here."

"Because you think I'm too weak to fight?"

The Duality preserve me, why did everyone take what I said badly? "No," I said. "Because you're not putting yourself in danger."

Mihmatini set her cup aside, but didn't speak.

"Do you really want to fight those creatures again?"

"They frighten the soul out of me," Mihmatini said, finally. "But my wards–"

"Won't last in this rain," I said. "And it takes you too much time to draw them. Stay here. You'll be safe. No need to endanger your life."

Mihmatini puffed her cheeks, with a familiar thoughtful expression. "Is there need for you?" she asked.

I stared at her for a while; trying to imagine myself ensconced in the safety of the Duality House. But I couldn't. "It's my place," I said. "No matter how hopeless things are."

I couldn't read her expression. "Your place," she said. She shook her head, as if exasperated. "You're impossible, you know. You and Neutemoc, come to think of it."

I felt embarrassed; though I didn't know why.

Mihmatini shook her head. "I'll stay here," she said. "The children are frightened, in any case. And you – you're not leaving until I set new wards on you."

I made a mock-frightened face. "As you wish."

Mihmatini snorted. "What did I say? Impossible, both of you."


On my way out of the Duality House, I stopped in the barracks, looking for Ixtli. I found him supervising a mock-battle in one of the larger rooms. Three of his Duality warriors were taking on another three, hacking at each other with their macuahitl swords, the harsh sound of wood striking stone echoing under the carved rafters of the ceiling.

"Acatl-tzin?" Ixtli asked, surprised, when I came in.

"I need help."

Ixtli glanced at his warriors. "What kind of help?"

"Fighting men. There's a god's agent loose in Tenochtitlan."

Ixtli raised his eyebrows. "The rain, eh?" he asked at last. "I thought something was wrong. But we're not priests, Acatl. We don't deal in magic."

I shook my head. "I know. But I still need swords, and men to wield them. Your armoury has magical obsidian." I'd borrowed some of Mictlan's knives from it.

Ixtli sighed. He looked at the warriors again: only two men were still fighting. "I can spare two dozen men," he said.

It wasn't much, but it would have to do. "Can you gather them in the barracks? I'm going to find some priests to put on our side."

Ixtli smiled. "That would be good. We'll gather our weapons and get ready."

I left the barracks and stood in the rain outside the Duality House. Each drop slid on my skin, trying to replace my protections with the Storm Lord's magic.

That wasn't the most attractive prospect: I only had to think of the old woman in Mazatl's house, and of the suffocating sensation of wrongness emanating from her, in order to know the consequences of such an event.

The Sacred Precinct was deserted: a deeper, subtler sense of wrongness. There should have been pilgrims. There should have been priests, and the dull thud of sacrifices' bodies, hitting the bottom of the pyramid's steps. Instead, there was only the soft pattern of rain, drop after drop falling like tears, sinking into the muddy earth.

Through the veil of rain shone the twin lights of the Great Temple: one for Huitzilpochtli, one for Tlaloc. There, I would find help. But the priests of Tlaloc weren't on my side, and the priests of the Southern Hummingbird would be at the palace, defending the Imperial Family.

My protection was dwindling with every moment I spent outside. Both Neutemoc and Teomitl would be waiting for my purported reinforcements. I had to make a decision, and soon.

The Duality House was empty; the Jaguar Knights were dead. I could go to the Eagle Knights, but even assuming they weren't at the palace, they had no magic to help. The temple of Tezcatlipoca shimmered in the moonlight – but His priests were closely associated with the Imperial Family, and they would also be at the palace.

That left…

I turned right, towards the weakest light: that of my own temple.

I wasn't looking forward to the next few moments. But there was no choice. The more time passed, the more Teomitl and Neutemoc would grow impatient. And, knowing them, they'd then rush in, without any regard for danger.

I walked through the gates of my temple – and, as Tezcatlipoca's Fate would have it, met Ichtaca under the arcades, rising from a kneeling position. At his feet were the remains of a quincunx, the magic already fading. He had no wards, and the rain had soaked into his bones, into his skin, seeking to twist his whole being out of shape. Teomitl had been right: the Storm Lord's rule wouldn't be gentle, but rather make us all into what we were not.

"Acatl-tzin." His voice was lightly ironic. "I had an idea you might come. Can I help you?"

I stared at him – at the drawn eyebrows; brows, ready for a further rebuke; at the faint smile on his lips. And he was right. I had stolen through the temple like a beast of shadows among men, taking what I needed and never giving anything back. I had no claim on Ichtaca, nor on anyone within the temple – and I would never have one, for I wasn't ready to be what he wanted.

I had been wrong. It wasn't in my temple that I was going to find help. "No," I said, finally, "I don't think you can help me. How do things go?"

His face didn't move. "As well as can be, considering." He raised his gaze to the grey skies. "The rain isn't natural, is it?"

Surprised that he'd turn to me for answers, I blurted out, "Why do you ask me?"

He smiled. "You look like you might know."

I sighed. "No, it's not natural. Now, if you'll excuse me…"

Ichtaca looked at me for a while; and at the remnants of his quincunx. Then he said softly, with the edge of a drawn knife, "Running away again, are we?"

How dare he? "I have no time," I said.

"Haven't you? You came for something, didn't you?"

"There's no need for it any more," I snapped. If I tarried too much, Teomitl and Neutemoc would lose their patience and rush in. I had no time to fence with Ichtaca. I needed to find some other place for reinforcements…

Ichtaca's face was a mask of weariness. "I think there is. Again – what did you want?"

Exasperated, I flung into his face, "I came to ask for help against creatures of Tlaloc. But you were right. I have no claim on this temple, or on anyone within."

Ichtaca was silent for a while, but some of the irony was gone from his features. "That's not what I told you," he said.

"No," I said. "But I can't do what you want. I'm no leader of men."

Ichtaca traced the outlines of his quincunx with the point of his sandal; staring at the ground. "No," he said. "But where will you find your help?"

"There are other places," I said, knowing that there weren't.

"I don't think you'd have come here if there had been." Ichtaca finished retracing his quincunx, and looked up. "I'm no fool, Acatl-tzin. Whatever the rain is, it's not on our side. And a spell of this magnitude can only mean one thing: that the Fifth World is in danger." His lips had tightened to threads of pale pink. "I'm no fool," he repeated. "Whatever I think of you can have no bearing on our duty. If you need help, I won't deny you."

"You don't understand," I said, still trying to take in what he was saying. "I have no guarantee–"

"That we'll survive." Ichtaca's face was grim. "Do we ever have one? Lord Death takes whom He pleases, when He pleases."

"Then–" I could hardly believe what I was hearing.

Ichtaca smiled. "But there is a price to pay. There is always one."

"More involvement in the temple's affairs?" I had no taste for it. But with Neutemoc and Teomitl's life at stake, not to mention the fate of the Fifth World, it didn't matter.

Ichtaca's face was a carefully composed mask. "No," he said. "You'll be the one who explains to them why they have to follow you."

"I can't–"

"You forget." His voice was soft, but it cut through the patter of the rain. "You are High Priest of this order. They'll listen to you. They'll obey." He smiled again, mirthlessly. "And, perhaps, if you speak well enough, they'll do so with their hearts instead of with their fears."

Ichtaca was efficient: within less than half an hour, he had most of my twenty priests gathered in the greatest room of the shrine. He wasn't a fool, either, to cause anyone to stay under that rain any longer than they had to.

I stood by the altar, under the lifeless gaze of Mictlantecuhtli, Lord Death. The gaunt cheeks and the yellow skin all contributed to lend Him an amused expression. The priests, though, weren't looking at the frescoes or at the dried blood in the grooves of the stones, but at me, whispering among themselves. I couldn't tell whether their expressions were hostile.

They had settled in an order that seemed immovable: the senior offering priests in front, the younger novice priests in the middle; and at the back, closest to the entrance curtain, two calmecac students, thirteen years old at the most, looking far too young to be involved in this at all.

I knew some of those priests, such as Palli and Ezamahual, by name; some by sight; and some I had never seen. Perhaps, after this was over, I'd have time…

It wasn't the time to think of it, or to make endless plans for the future. Some of those priests wouldn't survive the night. All of them might not, if we failed and Tlaloc took His revenge on our clergy. I bore more responsibilities than just my own life.

Ichtaca clapped his hands together, and, in eerie simultaneity, every priest fell silent. "The High Priest has an announcement to make," he said.

If I'd felt ill at ease before, now I wanted to hide. I'd never been a speech-maker like Neutemoc or even Ceyaxochitl. Others navigated the world of politics through their silver tongues. I couldn't. But there were Neutemoc and Teomitl; and Huei, caught by mistake in an ageless struggle and literally sacrificed upon its altar.

*Even small priests have to grow up, Acatl.*

I took a deep breath, and said, slowly, "I need your help. All of you. I…"

They watched me, silent – not yet disapproving, but surely it would come. I caught Ichtaca's grimly amused gaze, and wondered why I'd been fool enough to think this easy. Surely all I had to do was give them an order?

I…

If I did this, I admitted, once and for all, that I was what Ceyaxochitl and the Emperor had made of me:

a High Priest, head of my clergy, and responsible for its well-being. I admitted that the days of my youth and solitude were past. And I...

Above my head, the rain fell in a steady patter, like hundreds of footsteps on a causeway.

This wasn't, had never been about me. This was about the dead Jaguar warriors and the dying Emperor; about the peasants in their flooded fields; about the myriad small priests who didn't engage in politics, but sought the well-being of their flock.

"You have seen the rain," I said softly. "There is a child in Tenochtitlan: a child who is no more a child, but the living embodiment of Tlaloc's will. He seeks to remake the Fifth World in His image."

Once I had started, the words came easily, jostling each other for release – and if I saw the faces of the priests, I wasn't focusing on their expressions any more.

"He has creatures with him. You cannot see them without Quetzalcoatl's True Sight. The knives of Mictlan will slow them down but not kill them. They feed on magic, and whittle down wards to nothing. But somehow, we have to get past them. We have to kill the child and put an end to this madness.

"I tell you all this because... because I need your help."

When I finished, there was silence again. Then a growing whisper, as some of the priests turned to discuss with their neighbours. I couldn't read their faces; I couldn't hear what they were saying.

Someone – Palli, I realised – detached himself from the crowd. "Are you ordering us?"

I shook my head. "I can't take up a command I haven't earned. I'm asking you. I'm asking you to go into danger."

"For the sake of the Fifth World." That was Ezamahual.

"Yes," Ichtaca said, to my left. "Doing what we have always done."

"We didn't pledge ourselves to suicide," one of the offering priests said: a thin, coyote-like face I vaguely remembered from vigils. "We say the funeral rites. We call up the Dead to comfort the living. Even if the world were in danger, that wouldn't be our responsibility."

"Is that what you think?" Ichtaca asked, softly. "That this is a sinecure, an easy path to the circles of power? Then you can leave right now, Chimalli. Being a priest is laying your life in the hands of our god, even more so than the ordinary people."

Chimalli fell silent. But I could see that he had his following: a group of three young novice priests with embroidered cotton cloaks, probably sons of nobles – enjoying the riches of their fathers, without feats of arms to their names. Teomitl would have had no end of harsh words for them.

In the silence, someone spoke again. Palli. "I've seen you work, Acatl-tzin. Where you go, I'll follow." He stepped further away from the crowd, almost close enough to touch Ichtaca. Chimalli's friends sneered.

I said, my eyes on Chimalli, "If you don't want to come, you can stay where it's dry. You can stay safe. No man can fight if they don't believe in what they're doing."

There was silence. Then Ezamahual spoke. "We're not cowards," he said, with a pointed look at Chimalli. "We may not be warriors, but we won't stay safe while the world breaks apart."

Chimalli snorted. But when he didn't move, the other priests did. One at first, slowly; and then they came by groups of twos and threes, gathering around Palli and Ezamahual.

On the other side of that invisible line were Chi-malli, his clique – and the two calmecac students, looking frightened out of their wits.

"We're not cowards," Ezamahual repeated. "Tell us what we have to do."

Beside me, Ichtaca's face was grim, but I could guess that he hadn't expected me to have this much success.

But then, neither had I.

"We haven't much time left," I started.

Because the true sight hampered one's ability to see the Fifth World, I decided to lay it only on half of the priests, trusting that they would see enough to warn the others. I included myself in this half. I also sent word for Ixtli and his men to join us at the temple docks.

I had just finished laying on the true sight on myself when Palli came back.

"We have rabbits, and owls, and a handful of hummingbirds," he said. In the gloom of the Feathered Serpent's sight, Palli shone like the moon: cold, harsh, the veins of his arms and legs contracting and expanding to the rhythm of his heart. He carried two magical knives in his leather belt, one for each hand.

I finished my spell, and carefully brushed my hands clean, praying that Neutemoc and Teomitl would have had the good sense to wait before launching an attack.

I said to Palli, "Whatever you've found will have to do. I'm not sure we'll have time for real blood-magic." Sacrificing an animal and doing a full ritual required preparation. In the midst of a battle, I didn't think we'd have time for this.

Palli said, "Ichtaca is sending messengers to the palace, to request the Guardian's help at the Heart of the Lake."

"He sent Chimalli?"

Palli shook his head. "No," he said, grimly amused. "The two calmecac students, the ones that were frightened by the whole prospect."

"You're not frightened?" I asked, remembering how he'd preferred storehouse duty because of how quiet it was.

"When I stop to think about it. But then, it doesn't change anything, does it?"

He looked and sounded disturbingly like Teomitl: like a warrior, uncaring of his own life. I finished erasing my quincunx, and rose in turn. "No," I said. "It doesn't change anything. Come on. Let's get to the boats."

The boats were the flotilla of the temple, moored on the boundary between the southwest district of Moyotlan and the northwest one of Cuepopan, beyond the Serpent Walls. We had a dozen sturdy reed boats, which the priests took on their errands throughout Tenochtitlan.

Ichtaca was already in the second largest of those, with a novice priest holding the oars, and two clustering at the back. He pointed, wordlessly, to the largest craft, the one reserved for the High Priest. It bore the spider-and-owl design of Mictlantecuhtli, and shone with the wards accumulated on it.

Ixtli and his Duality warriors had their own boats: long, thin vessels holding nine warriors in a single line, with two rowers, one at the back and one at the prow. Ixtli raised his hand to me in a salute; I nodded to him, and climbed aboard my own boat. Palli took the oars; and Ezamahual positioned himself at the prow.

Every temple boat, including ours, was full of covered cages. It wasn't so much the cages I saw with the true sight though, but the light cast by the animals they contained: the rabbits huddled against each other, and the hummingbirds flitting against the covers in a whirr of wings.

Palli pushed the boat away from the shore in a splash of oars, and gently directed us south.

The docks were on the western edge of Tenochtitlan; the tree of the Great Vigil on the eastern side of the city. Even though the town was crisscrossed by canals, the fastest way to go east wasn't through Tenochtitlan, but around it, passing south under the Itzapalapan causeway and swinging back in a north-easterly direction.

The rain fell steadily around us, but there was something different about it. Something distinctly hostile. In the semi-darkness of the true sight, I could see nothing, but the sense of disquiet increased. The oars splashed in the water, on the left side, then on the right – and back on the left, like a slower heartbeat.

I turned around, briefly, and saw the city, a mass of huddled houses enclosed by the rain. Light spilled from the Sacred Precinct, beacons in the growing darkness: the temples of Mictlantecuhtli; of Mixcoatl, God of the Hunt; of Tezcatlipoca, God of War and Fate. And towering over it all, the blazing radiance of the Great Temple.

Something about the last light was wrong. I watched it for a while, as Palli's rowing got us clear of the causeway. Something about the light, which kept flickering.

The light wasn't strong any more, but tinged with the green of algae. With every passing moment, the green grew stronger. And, crowding around the twin shrines atop the pyramid, were the half-distinct shapes of Tlaloc's creatures, swimming through the air like some sick imitation of fishes, sinking into the stone of the stairs like transparent blood.

"It's fallen," I said, aloud.

"What's fallen?" Palli asked.

Ichtaca, whose forehead also bore the mark of the true sight, was watching the same direction. "Not yet," he said. "Huitzilpochtli is stronger than you give Him credit for."

"He's weak," I said, watching as the light flickered.

"So is Tlaloc's child, for now," Ichtaca replied. And, to his oarsman: "Faster."

Palli's gestures quickened, as if he'd been the one given the order.

Faster, faster, I thought, listening to the splashes of water on either side of me. In the darkness, all I could see were the beacons of the temples – and the creatures, slithering in and out of the Great Temple. Faster...

The Itzapalapan causeway faded behind the veil of rain; the creatures, too, until the whole world seemed to have turned to water. Around us was the vast expanse of Lake Texcoco, the shores so far we couldn't make them out in this stormy weather; above us, the rain-clouds unleashing their fury on us. Thunder rolled overhead, and lightning flashes tore the heavens: the Storm Lord's full anger, finally unleashed.

And ahead...

It should have been an artificial island isolated in the middle of the lake, with an altar where the Revered Speaker would sacrifice to Tlaloc.

But it wasn't, not any more. Or rather: the island was still there, surrounded by a group of boats I couldn't identify from this distance. But at its side was something that drew one's gaze.

The tree offered at the Great Vigil, sixteen months ago, had indeed rotted to nothing. But something had taken its place: an after-shadow of a trunk, a silhouette outlined by the lightning flashes, with half-transparent branches reaching up to join the black rain-clouds with the surface of the lake. Magic pulsed from the roots and the branches, joining in the middle to form a tight knot of light.

Around the tree were more of the creatures, attached to the trunk like leeches, gorging on Tlaloc's bounty, growing fat with every passing moment.

I couldn't repress the shudder that ran through me, or the rising nausea that always came when I saw so many of those creatures.

Behind me, someone – Ichtaca? – let out a string of curses. A more sensible answer than mine, I guessed.

As we got closer, the situation became clearer: in the group of boats were two dozen priests dressed in the blue-and-black garb of the Storm Lord, their blackened faces filled with the light of magic. They watched us come without a word.

At the centre of the island, the altar to Tlaloc was overwhelmed with creatures. They passed through the stone as though through water, their clawed hands moving to and fro. They looked like brothers to the ahuizotls, with the malevolence but not the intelligence of Chalchiutlicue's beasts. They seemed to be guarding something. A young child, I suddenly realised. I caught a glimpse of a childhood lock, sweeping over a face the colour of cacao beans, and of wide eyes, as green as algae.

Mazatl. The god-child. And, by his side, lying in the mud, were two adult bodies. My heart sank. They had to be Mazatl's foster parents.

Below the altar were more of the creatures, gathering around two silhouettes, one of which stood knee-deep in the water, magic streaming out of him. Teomitl – and the ahuizotls, gathering around him, snapping at the creatures with their jaws, reaching out with their claws. And beside Teomitl…

Neutemoc, the wards of Huitzilpochtli shining weakly in the dim light of the true sight, hacking and slashing at the creatures, even though it seemed to make no difference.

Trust my brother to get into the heart of trouble. Although I couldn't see what else he could have done. I'd misjudged. Given the configuration of the place, there was no way to approach discreetly. I glanced again at the priests of Tlaloc. They had made no move, trusting the creatures to dispatch both Neutemoc and Teomitl. But now that we were approaching, they detached themselves from the island, aiming towards us with the sureness of cast spears.

"Faster," I whispered to Palli – and, to the boats behind me: "Prepare yourselves!"

Ixtli's boats swung around us, blocking the path between us and the priests of Tlaloc: an unequal fight, on an element belonging to the god Himself. Teomitl had His wife's protection, but no one else did.

There was no choice.

I laid my hand on the smallest of my obsidian knives, and felt the emptiness of Mictlan fill me, so strong I could have gagged. Chalchiutlicue's touch had definitely changed those knives, although I wasn't sure it was for the better.

Teomitl went down on one knee; and two more of the creatures leapt past him, towards Neutemoc.

Faster…

## TWENTY-TWO
### *The God's Child*

Palli grounded the boat ashore. At the moment the dried reeds came into contact with the mud of the island, a sense of growing unease crystallised into me, almost strong enough to fill Mictlan's emptiness.

I had felt this before: in the Jaguar House, and in Tlaloc's shrine in Amecameca. There was no cure for it.

I leapt from the boat onto the shore, fighting a rising wave of nausea. Beside me, several of the priests were on their knees on the ground, retching and retching, although no bile came up.

No. You have to fight it. You have to… Ichtaca's face was a mask of disgust; but he at least didn't double over. And then the creatures were upon us. Within the true sight, they shone, their squat bodies exuding algae-tinged light, their clawed hands reaching for us. I threw myself aside, and a claw-swipe narrowly missed my forearm.

"Huitzilpochtli cut me down," Palli whispered, beside me. "How do you fight them?"

I wish I knew. Beside me, one of the novice priests was down on one knee, bleeding from a wound, his face already going slack, in an expression sickeningly like Quechomitl's.

Another creature launched itself at me. The Duality curse us, the things had grown more powerful, capable of ignoring Mihmatini's wards. Without conscious thought, I threw myself aside, but too late: the claws were going straight for my chest...

Another clawed hand batted them aside; I looked into the yellow, malicious eyes of an ahuizotl – I had time to wonder, dimly, absurdly, if it was the same that had maimed Eleuia – and then Tlaloc's creature, hissing, was retreating, while the ahuizotl's slimy skin pressed itself against mine. Forcing me leftwards, I realised: towards the shore, and Teomitl, who stood with water halfway to his knees, his face creased in concentration.

I half-walked, half-ran towards him. One creature detached itself from the pack that was engaging the priests, and glided lazily towards me. I quickened my pace. The ahuizotl's jaws snapped at its midriff, and the creature engaged it instead of me.

I had no particular wish to see who would win; and I couldn't bring myself to cheer for the ahuizotl, despite the fact that it appeared to be on our side.

"Acatl-tzin!" Teomitl called out. He stood in a circle of emptiness. The Jade Skirt's light spilled around him, creating a barrier the Storm Lord's creatures prowled around, but were unwilling to bypass.

When I approached, they turned their attention to me, hissing with an eerie joy.

I did the only thing that made sense: I ran, and threw myself at Teomitl's feet, into the water.

I rose, coughing up algae, to peer into Teomitl's amused gaze. "Some reinforcements," he said.

I turned around, to survey the battlefield. On the water, Ixtli's men were engaging the priests of Tlaloc, trying to bring their boats close enough to strike at their exposed enemy. Meanwhile, the priests were also trying to get within range, though their spells did not require contact to be cast.

One priest in particular seemed to be their leader: a tall, lean man with green paint smeared across his face, standing at the back of one of the largest barges. It wasn't Acamapichtli. No matter how hard the High Priest of Tlaloc had worked to indict Neutemoc, it appeared he was quite blameless in the matter of the Storm Lord's child. I wasn't sure whether I ought to have been disappointed.

On the island, Ichtaca had a cage with two hummingbirds at his feet. He was busy drawing a circle in the mud, whispering the words of a prayer to the Southern Hummingbird. I recognised a much stronger version of Mihmatini's warding spell, directed not only at Ichtaca, but at every human being in the vicinity.

It might possibly dispel the creatures, but that spell would take time to cast, time we were running out of.

Next to Ichtaca, two offering priests swiped at the creatures – failing to do any damage, but still keeping them at bay. As I watched, one of them slipped in the mud, and one of the creatures' claws opened up a wound on his arm. He fell, a vacant smile stretching across his face.

*No!*

An ahuizotl welled up from the water, and leapt to take the priest's place. Neither Ichtaca nor the other priest did anything more than nod tiredly. Any help was better than none.

Palli was down on one knee, but otherwise unharmed, and Ezamahual was busy protecting two of his fallen comrades, his harsh face transfigured by battle frenzy.

The least that could be said was that the battle was not going in our favour.

"Where is–" I started; and saw Neutemoc. He had somehow managed to evade the creatures, and was steadily fighting his way towards the top of the rise – no, not fighting, more weaving his way between claw-swipes, each of which could mean his death.

"He's insane," I said, though not without a touch of jealousy.

Teomitl shrugged. "Don't you recognise it? He has nothing to lose any more."

An image of Huei rose in my mind: of her standing in the reception room, bitter and sad, and I, refusing to understand her until it was too late. I quelled it. It wasn't the time. "Are you wounded?" I panted.

Teomitl shrugged, although every feature of his face was drawn and wan, like a man drained of blood. "I'll go on."

I stared at Neutemoc, and at the child Mazatl, still standing before the altar. "We have to help him to reach the altar," I said. "Close enough to strike."

Teomitl grimaced. "Will the child die?"

I shrugged. My experience of god-children was, thank the Duality, fairly limited. "He's human. If he wasn't, he couldn't wield so much magic. He'll die."

Teomitl didn't look convinced; and I wasn't completely, either. But it was a fair chance. "Worth a try," he said. "Distract the creatures, then?"

I nodded. At least until we found a way to kill them. I hefted an obsidian knife with my left hand, feeling the slight twinge from old wounds, and stared at the creatures, bracing myself to leave the circle of Teomitl's protection.

Over the water, some of Ixtli's men had managed to get close enough to the priests: they were hacking and slashing, their boats swaying under them. The priests, though, were casting spells: darts of green light that wounded as much as if they had been metal. As I watched, one of Ixtli's men, struck in the chest by three darts at the same time, stood shock-still at the prow of his boat – and keeled into the lake. He did not move. Blood stained the water, lazily spreading over the fluid shapes of the ahuizotls.

With a sigh, I lifted my knife to strike; and felt the emptiness of Mictlan fill me, a hundred, a thousand times stronger than it had ever been. The wind in my ears was the lament of the dead, and the water lapping at my ankles cold and unforgiving, like a drowned man's kiss – and even Teomitl's voice was the rattle of a dying man.

I had felt this, once before, when fighting the beast of shadows. But it had never been this strong, never altered the shape of the Fifth World.

Those were not my knives.

Within me, Chalchiutlicue was laughing. *A gift, priest*, she said, and Her voice was terrible.

Gasping, I stepped away from Teomitl, straight into the path of one of the creatures.

Its clawed hands snaked, lazily, to strike me. One of the ahuizotls leapt up from the water, snarling, but it was too late – the claws sank into my skin – and numbness spread from the wound, that terrible numbness that marked the end of the fight.

I was dimly aware of sinking to one knee; of someone – Teomitl? Palli? – screaming in a faraway land; of the creature rushing in to gorge on my blood. With sluggish hands, I raised my knife – held it against my chest to defend against the claws – and the creature, too eager to exploit my weakness, impaled itself on the blade.

Within me, the numbness of Tlaloc's wounds met the growing emptiness of Mictlan: two huge waves clashing against each other and breaking, sending their aftershocks into the depths of my soul. Visions of Eleuia's empty orbits mingled with the image of Father's body – and Mother's face, contorted in anger, held the fervent gaze of Commander Quiyahuayo. My limbs would not stop shaking.

Chalchiutlicue laughed and laughed in the empty rooms of my mind. *A gift, priest. For My husband.*

Far, far beyond me, the Storm Lord's creature screamed: a thin, reedy cry like a strangled new-born. As the visions slowly faded away, I came to myself, in time to see the creature withdraw from my blade as if scalded; and with each passing moment it grew fainter and fainter, still screaming in that pathetic way that tore at my guts.

And then the creature was gone. Stillness spread from the place of its death like a shroud thrown over the Fifth World. Everything in its wake paused or slowed down: Ichtaca's harsh chanting, Neutemoc's macuahitl-swipes, the ahuizotls' clenching tail-hands, the priests' dart-throwing, the Duality warriors' strokes. But the worst affected were the other creatures. They came to a standstill, as if sharing in the death of their comrade.

Time slowly returned to normal, it seemed, and my heartbeat finally slowed back to a more leisurely rhythm.

"How in the Duality's name did you do this?" Teomitl asked, beside me. His face was still taut, contorted on the edge of pain.

"I didn't," I said, curtly. The creatures were markedly slower, and more reluctant to approach me. "Thank your protector."

Teomitl said nothing. I kept my hand near my knife, but not actually touching it; and saw Neutemoc evade the last of the creatures, and run towards the child at the altar.

For a brief moment, they faced each other: Neutemoc's face, contorted in the battle-frenzy, and Mazatl's, his green eyes expressionless. Then Neutemoc's sword swept towards the child, biting into the exposed flesh of his neck.

I'd expected some struggle, or some vast display of magic. But Mazatl simply crumpled, like a felled gladiator at the combat-stone: the knees first, then the chest, and the small head with its childhood lock, sinking into the mud by the altar, small and forlorn in death.

Beside me, Ichtaca's chanting paused, and Tlaloc's creatures turned towards the altar, watching their master's death.

Over. It was over.

Then why didn't it feel like it?

I glanced at the ghost tree: it still stood, rooted in the water of the lake, filled with creatures growing fat on magic. The rain falling over us was still gorged with Tlaloc's magic, and none of the other creatures had gone.

Laughter, bright and terrible, echoed over the lake. It was the sound of a lightning strike, earthing itself in a peasant's skin; the wild roar of heavy rains; the sound of wind, tearing away cacti and trees from the land.

"Did you think it would be that easy?" a voice asked.

It came from the roots of the ghost tree, I realised with a shock: from a small silhouette, radiating power as the sun radiated heat.

I looked again at Neutemoc, who was kneeling by the body of the boy he'd just killed, his face frozen in shock.

I remembered the old woman's words: *I have many, many grandsons.*

It was the wrong child: one of Mazatl's foster brothers, casually sacrificed as a decoy. The wrong child.

*Did you think it would be that easy?*

In the terrible, heavy silence, magic flowed from the branches of the ghost tree: threads of raw power, plunging into the creatures' bodies, filling their featureless shapes with magic the way one pumped water into the earth. The creatures made a soft, hissing sound; and turned back towards us, filling the air with their mindless glee.

Over the water, three priests of Tlaloc had died, but over half of Ixtli's men would never see the Fifth World again. And atop the altar, Neutemoc was surrounded by creatures, mindlessly crowding each other to drink his blood.

*Did you think it would be that easy?*

One of the creatures leapt at Teomitl, passing through Chalchiutlicue's circle of protection as if through flimsy cotton. Teomitl raised his macuahitl sword. But it was too late. The claws had already bitten into his flesh. He sank to one knee, gasping.

I ran towards him, but two more creatures blocked my path, their featureless bodies undulating, as if they tasted my scent from the air. My hand tightened over my knife's hilt. The emptiness of Mictlan filled me once more, the whole Fifth World turning into a hymn to death and decay. The smell of decomposition rose from the earth, saturating my nostrils, insinuating itself under the pores of my skin. Ichtaca's chanting faded into nothingness, replaced by the endless lament of the dead.

Shaking, I raised the blade, and struck. The thread linking the creature to the ghost tree snapped. It made that same cry of a baby dying, tearing at my heart for the children I would never have.

But the second creature was already reaching towards me, its claws not going for my arm or my hand, but towards my throat.

As if in a dream, I threw myself to the right and the claws raked my arm and side. Numbness filled me, collided with Mictlan's lament, becoming Father's empty gaze; becoming Mother's hands, still clenched in anger long after her death. I rolled over, gasping for breath. One creature had latched to Teomitl, feeding upon him with relish. The one that had struck my shoulder hovered over me, hesitant to approach.

I didn't give it a chance to reach a decision. I fell upon it with my knife, and sank the blade all the way in, until it plunged into muddy earth, the fragile obsidian snapping in two. The thread broke in two, and the creature screamed and started to fade.

Cursing, I withdrew my second knife from my belt, and ran towards Teomitl. Under my feet was not mud, but bones, breaking with every step I took – and the dead, whispering to me of my failures.

*Honour your parents and your clan…*

*Bring glory to your name…*

*Tell your children to enjoy the joys of the Fifth World…*

I had no honour; no glory; no children to come after me. But it didn't matter. It had never mattered. The dead could not touch me.

It was a lie: every whispered word hurt like a small wound; but still I managed to raise a shaking hand, and sink the knife into the creature latched into Teomitl.

As it started to fade away, Teomitl toppled into the mud, his eyes glazing over, his face locked into a desperate expression.

Cautiously, I slackened my grip on my knife, and knelt by his side, trying to shake him awake. "Come on," I whispered. "Come on."

Somehow, Neutemoc had woven his way between the creatures that opposed him, and left the altar and the dead child behind. Moving with a speed and ease I had not known he possessed, he was running towards one of the empty reed boats, his obsidian-studded sword weaving in and out of the creatures' embrace. It reminded me of two dancers I had seen a long time ago, in a deserted girls' calmecac; back when the whole affair had just been a missing priestess – and not this... monstrosity it had turned into.

No creatures remained to face me. They were all engaged in battle against my priests. Palli was standing in the water, his back wedged against one of the reed boats, keeping the creatures at bay with grim determination.

The battle between the priests of Tlaloc and Ixtli's men was still going on. Ixtli, with suicidal bravery, had leapt onto the barge of the leading priest, and was cutting his way towards the back. The priest, though, did not look afraid: he was watching Ixtli approach, his smile the same as the jaguar's before it leaps on its prey.

With Teomitl's loss of consciousness, the ahuizotls were no longer fighting: they stood, aimlessly wandering on the muddy earth. How long did we have before they started turning on us?

I shook Teomitl's slight frame. "Come on."

"Not... worthy of... her," he whispered. "I... should... have known."

The Duality preserve us. As if we needed more complications. "Come on."

"Choose... your... battlefield," Teomitl whispered. "Not... worthy..."

One more priest went down. Ichtaca had stopped chanting and was holding two creatures at bay, single-handedly. Over the water, Ixtli had only a handful of men left; but more priests of the Storm Lord remained, casting darts in a steady barrage. As I watched, a dart struck Ixtli across the chest. He wavered, his face set in a grimace, but went on, cutting down the last priest between him and the leader.

Neutemoc had reached the shore, four creatures lazily gliding after him. Palli rose from his crouch, and batted away at the creatures, while Neutemoc pushed a boat into the waters of the lake.

Without the ahuizotls, though, it was clear that we were doomed.

"We need you," I said to Teomitl, resisting the urge to shake some good sense into him. "Huitzilpochtli blind you, we need you, or everything is lost!"

"Mother..." Teomitl whispered. "I'm... sorry. Should... have... remained... true to Huitzilpochtli."

I flung his own words back at him. "There's no shame in having two allegiances," I said, urgently.

Ichtaca was down on one knee; and while Palli and Neutemoc had succeeded in getting their boat off the island, they had creatures chasing after them.

On the water, Ixtli and the leading priest were fighting sword against spear, rocking with the barge they were on. Only three Duality warriors remained; but one priest of Tlaloc floated facedown in the water, a magical sword embedded in his back.

"Teomitl," I whispered. "Ahuizotl. This is your testing ground. This is your battlefield. Will you run away?"

Teomitl's eyes fluttered open. He stared at me, without seeing me. "I'll... choose... my testing ground," he whispered. "Not this. I can't... The pain... too much..."

"Are you running away?" I screamed, shaking him like a rag doll. "Are you such a coward?"

For a long, long time, he did not answer. Palli's boat, with Neutemoc at the oars, was tracing a chaotic trajectory onto the waters of the lake, trying to elude the three creatures coming after it. It was going nowhere near the ghost tree.

"Teomitl," I said, slowly. "No one chooses their testing ground. Not even those of Imperial blood. And a true man stands by the consequences of his acts."

His eyes fluttered again, the emptiness replaced by anger. "You're a fine one to reproach me with that, aren't you?"

"I don't understand," I said, taken aback.

Teomitl tore himself from my grasp, every feature of his face becoming as harsh as polished jade. "So small, priest," he whispered, but it wasn't his voice. "So filled with useless regrets."

Chalchiutlicue. No!

"I don't understand," I whispered, even though I still remembered Her rifling through my thoughts like a peccary digging for roots, discarding what did not interest Her. "I–"

Teomitl knelt in the brackish water, gazing at the black clouds overhead, which showed no sign of dispersing. His fist clenched around algae, once, twice. When he spoke again, his voice was his own. "I was overwhelmed," he said, all the apology I would ever get. "Thank you."

His eyes narrowed, as the Jade Skirt's light streamed from every pore of his skin, and the ahuizotls were back into the fray. Several of them slid into the water, going after Neutemoc and Palli's boat, engaging the creatures chasing it. Neutemoc, after looking back, set the prow of the boat in the direction of the ghost tree – and rowed like a possessed man. Palli's face was grim.

Ichtaca resumed his chanting; by his rising voice, he was almost at the end of his hymn.

On the barge, Ixtli twisted and the spear spun out of the leading priest's outstretched hand, landing into the water. Ixtli raised his sword to strike.

I took hold of my knife, and plunged back into the battle, determined to dispatch as many creatures as I could. But something kept nagging at me, a sense that I was missing something. I avoided a claw-swipe that would have disembowelled me, and raised my knife to strike. But the creature had already shifted left. I sank the knife into the creature, under Ezamahual's shocked gaze. As it screamed and died, I stole a look at the ghost tree.

Mazatl still stood at its foot, kneeling with one hand on the roots. Magic streamed out of the tree, plunging into his whole body. Soon, he would be gorged with Tlaloc's magic, and dispatch us all with ease.

There was worse. The water, which had been up to my knees before, had now reached my waist. I retreated onto drier ground. The shores. I glanced at Teomitl, who had also retreated further inland. The waters of the lake were rising. The patch of earth we were standing on was shrinking.

Over by the boats, the leading priest of Tlaloc was facing Ixtli, both his hands empty. With a terrible smile, he lifted his hand as if to throw something into the air.

And something did leave his outstretched fingers, shining as it rose. A narrow beam of jade-coloured light formed, settled onto Ixtli. Ixtli's face contorted in pain; he went down on one knee, gasping in pain, the sword torn from his grasp. The leading priest was smiling. He lifted Ixtli's face to expose the throat, and raised a noose, whispering words I couldn't hear: a prayer to His god before the sacrifice, no doubt.

"No!" I howled, but I had no time to do anything. The leading priest looped the rope around Ixtli's throat in a practised gesture, and tightened it. Ixtli's eyes bulged.

Two creatures engaged me simultaneously; I ducked, but claws raked my back. Numbness filled me, transformed into images of Eleuia, alluringly dancing on the battlefield.

I had to help Ixtli... I rose, and one of the creatures leapt upon me. Ezamahual was fighting the other one, holding its full attention.

I ducked left and right as the creature attacked in a frenzy of claw-swipes, trying to keep an eye on the battlefield.

Teomitl was running, ahuizotls gathering around him in a gruesome escort. He reached the boats, and, arcing himself against the smallest one, pushed it into the water – and leapt into it.

On the barge, Ixtli was clawing at his throat, in a vain effort to throw off the noose. But it was futile; the priest of Tlaloc had won. Ixtli's death, as a sacrifice to his god, would only add to his power.

I feinted right and the creature followed, hissing as it opened itself for a fatal strike. I slid out of its embrace, and struck its midriff with the knife.

Two down.

There were no creatures in my immediate vicinity. I used the breathing space to take a look at the battlefield. Teomitl's boat was leaving the island, though he wasn't rowing. With a shock, I realised the ahuizotls, gathered under the keel, were dragging it forward, to where the leading priest was still strangling Ixtli.

As I watched, Ixtli flopped to the floor of the barge. There were now only two Duality warriors left; and a handful of priests of Tlaloc, gathering against them.

Over the lake, several of the creatures had succeeded in bypassing the ahuizotls. Neutemoc, frantically rowing, was already close enough to the ghost tree. But another creature had abandoned the fray on the island, and was gliding towards the boat, its hiss almost amused.

Palli, his face a mask of concentration, was already hard pressed to fend off both creatures. But the other creature was getting closer and closer, faster than the erratic trajectory of the boat.

On the shore, six creatures remained, three of them busy fighting ahuizotls, and the rest kept at bay by my priests. Ichtaca was opening the throat of a hummingbird, though the rain washed off the flow of blood on his hands.

Teomitl's craft crashed into the tangle of boats; the ahuizotls slid away. One by one, they started pulling the priests of Tlaloc into the water. Teomitl himself had leapt clear of his boat, and was running from vessel to vessel, intent on reaching the leading priest, who stood in his large barge, too far away from the water to be snatched by an ahuizotl.

It was clear where the urgency was: helping Neutemoc get to Mazatl. I sheathed my knife, ran to the shore, and pushed a boat into the water.

"You can't do it alone," Ezamahual said, behind me – climbing into the craft, taking the oars. "I'll row."

I nodded, and together we slowly got the boat out of the shallows, towards Neutemoc.

I turned, briefly. Teomitl had reached the same barge as the leading priest. The priest threw his hand up again; and the same light, expanding, covered Teomitl.

Teomitl grimaced. His face contorted in a painful struggle, and his grip on his sword slackened. He was going to die, like Ixtli – no...

But then a light as green as jade, as underwater depths, filled his eyes; and his features, softened by the inhuman light, became once again those of the goddess. The priest's spell fell around him harmlessly, shearing itself in two like a split obsidian mirror.

Teomitl shook his head, and walked forward, past the still body of Ixtli, smiling a smile even more terrible than the priest. His obsidian-studded sword was raised; and the leading priest had no weapon of his own, only magic that would have no effect on Teomitl.

Who are you?

*Ahuizotl. He who bears Chalchiutlicue's gift. He who bears Her protection.*

I turned away, keeping my gaze on Neutemoc. I did not see Teomitl's sword come down; but I heard the priest scream, a thin, reedy cry carried away by the wind; and then nothing, only the splashes made by the ahuizotls, and the soft raking noise of claws, tearing at flesh.

Ezamahual's quick rowing was bearing its fruit: we were slowly catching up with Neutemoc's and Palli's boat.

We were going to be too late, though.

Ahead of us, one of the creatures finally got past Palli's guard, and its claws raked the offering priest's arm. Palli fell to his knees in the boat, his face stretching into that familiar, terrible emptiness.

Now Neutemoc was defenceless. He did not give up. He went on rowing, intending to reach the ghost tree before the creatures could catch up on him.

It was never going to work... Never...

Ezamahual's oar-strokes quickened into a frenzy, but it wasn't going to be enough.

Ichtaca... Now or never.

And, for once, the Duality heard my prayer.

On the shore, Ichtaca laid both hands on the ground, and threw back his head with a triumphant scream. The circle blazed, spreading the Southern Hummingbird's light everywhere around the island, sinking into Ichtaca's flesh, outlining the bones of the priests in light.

The creatures, caught in the spell's hold, became paler and paler, vanishing altogether within the radiance.

It spread further, over the water – engulfing Ezamahual and me – reaching Neutemoc and Palli, and going on. For the briefest of moments, the ghost tree wavered and started to fade.

"No!" Mazatl screamed, in a voice that wasn't human any more. Magic poured out of him, going into the branches, sinking into the roots, and Huitzilpochtli's light finally faded into nothingness.

The ghost tree remained, but the creatures that had been clinging to its trunk were gone. And, on the island, not a single creature remained: just two stunned priests, taking care of the wounded, and Ichtaca, kneeling in his circle, breathing heavily.

"Do you think yourselves so clever?" Mazatl's voice was the hiss of a deadly snake.

From the tree's roots, a great cloud of magic spewed, roiling sickly as it merged with the water – higher and higher, until a huge wave travelled through the lake – aimed straight at us.

It reached Neutemoc's boat a fraction of a moment earlier than ours. I had time to see my brother pin Palli to the floor of the craft, and then the wave was upon us, an exhalation of water that sent us crashing into the warm lake.

## TWENTY-THREE
### *The Blessed Drowned*

I sank, my cloak filling with water, dragging me down like stone.

Under the water, everything was oddly quiet. Ahuizotls sang, far, far away, a gentle, soothing sound drawing me into Tlalocan. I hadn't had time to draw a good breath before sinking. My lungs burnt as I struggled to kick off my sandals, and undo the clasp of my cloak.

The fall into the lake had washed out the last remnants of the true sight: the water around me gradually became clearer – though I saw nothing but floating algae, and the light of the surface, far above me.

One of my sandals sank into the depths. A good start, but it wasn't enough.

For some incongruous reason, I thought of Huei, and of whether that was what she would feel when they drowned her. Would her gestures grow more and more sluggish as she sank to the bottom of the lake? Would she hear Chalchiutlicue's beasts summoning her to the bliss of the Land of the Drowned?

My hands slid over the clasp of my cloak, and finally prised it open. I kicked upwards, towards the light of the surface.

The rain was still falling when I emerged, gasping for breath. The lake was now scoured with angry waves. Nothing remained of the island save the stone altar, on which Ichtaca stood, directing the rescue of the priests who had fallen into the water. Teomitl was swimming on his back, surrounded by a ring of ahuizotls. He was holding onto Ixtli's still body, slowly, steadily pulling it towards the altar. Other ahuizotls dived into the depths, helping Ichtaca to get the priests out of the lake, though some of them were also feasting on the dead bodies.

An exhausted Ezamahual was clinging to the overturned boat; he blinked twice when he saw me, but didn't have the strength to do more.

And ahead...

Palli was still lying in the boat, unconscious. But there was no trace of Neutemoc.

Worry knifed my heart. I swam towards Palli's boat as fast as I could, took a deep breath – and dived into the depths of the lake.

The eerie underwater silence filled my ears once again. I swam downwards, with an ease akin to that of my childhood, keeping my eyes open in spite of the stinging touch of water.

Neutemoc...

Where in the Fifth World was he?

There should have been fish, or algae – even ahuizotls – but there was nothing. Just a spreading green light that gradually replaced the light of day – and, so close I could have touched them, the roots of the ghost tree, plunging towards the mud at the bottom: monstrous, shimmering things that seemed to beat with a life of their own. And, the deeper I swam, the larger they grew.

I had been swimming down for what seemed an eternity. Surely the lake was not that deep? It wasn't.

Surely, too – I should have run out of breath by now? I hadn't, either. But suddenly I knew why, and where the green light was coming from.

The time of the gods is not our own. And that was what I had strayed into by going so close to the ghost tree: to a different time, a distorted version of the Fifth World. The tree was a gate between Tlaloc's heartland and the Fifth World, pouring out the god's magic into the mortal world. Into the god-child Mazatl.

I tried not to worry about Mazatl. Neutemoc was the one I was worried about.

Neutemoc…

After what seemed an eternity, I saw a harsh glint, lost somewhere into the roots of the tree. It flashed on and off as I descended: the familiar, if toned-down, reflection of light on obsidian.

A macuahitl sword. It had to be a macuahitl sword. Please…

I found Neutemoc wedged into the ghost tree, one arm wrapped around a massive root, the other dangling, moved to and fro by the current. His face was pale, leached of all colour. His sword at his side was the only part of him that seemed to be alive: glinting coldly, malevolently in the green light.

With hands that seemed to have turned to tar, I disentangled him from the roots, pulling his body free from the tree with a wet, sucking sound, and passing his arm over my neck. Through all of it he didn't respond. Nor could I feel any heartbeat.

He wasn't dead. I hadn't died from falling in the water. He had to have survived. But he had fallen much closer to the ghost tree than I had, a treacherous thought whispered in my mind. I quelled it. I refused to listen to it, and focused on my leg-strokes – one, two, three – and on the light around me, pulsing as green as jade, as green as algae…

Neutemoc didn't stir, but grew heavier and heavier the higher I swam. Beside me, the ghost roots subtly changed, growing more and more solid, sending cold currents to wrap around my arms and legs.

Something tightened around us, sending chills through my bones. It wasn't anything material: more as if the water around me had suddenly contracted, growing colder and then warmer, like a heartbeat.

The light changed, became subtly dappled. Ahead of me, darker shapes broke the monotony of the water. Fish. I had reached the boundary of the Fifth World.

But, as I swam closer, I saw that they weren't fish at all – but bodies, their pale skin gleaming, their long hair streaming in the invisible currents. Their eyes were wide open, watching me impassively.

There were children: six, seven years old, their faces devoid of all expression, save for the tears running down their cheeks, inexplicably glistening in the water. There were women: young women with swollen skin, old women with a thin line of red circling their throats. And men, young and old, their skin as blue as unshed blood, their eyes bulging in their orbits.

The Blessed Drowned. The sacrifices to Tlaloc, to Chalchiutlicue, still weeping the tears that called down rain, still clutching their slit throats.

Neutemoc was heavier and heavier: not helping me, I thought, not without bitterness. If he became any heavier, I wouldn't be able to lift him and rise to the surface.

I kicked harder, knowing who I would see, at the end of this procession of the dead.

First was Eleuia, her empty eye-sockets still crying tears of blood; and etched on every feature of her face, the ruins of her beauty. Even pale and unmoving, even mutilated and reduced to this shadow of herself, her presence was still commanding – and she was still obscenely beautiful, she could still make me rigid with an alien desire.

She was singing, softly singing:

"*In Tlalocan,*
*No hunger, but maize always blooming, always putting forth flowers;*
*No pain, but the endless joy of the Blessed Drowned…*"

I turned my eyes away from her, unable to bear her empty gaze.

And after Eleuia–

Like Neutemoc, he was entangled in the tree's roots, his face pale and colourless in the green light, both arms pulled back and wrapped around separate roots, making him into a living quincunx. Unlike Neutemoc, his eyes were wide open, staring at me, not with anger or with rage, but with a quiet, sorrowful disappointment that made my heart twist.

"Acatl," he whispered, and his voice was the water surging through the roots of the tree. A few handspans above us, the roots broke the water's surface: the Fifth World, so close and yet so unattainable.

"Father, I'm sorry," I whispered, as I swam closer. The words came out of my mouth in a trail of bubbles.

Father's eyes held me, shining in the ghastly pallor of his face. He didn't look blessed, or happy. Just disappointed. Sad. The same look his body had had, even in death.

"Father…" I couldn't speak. I couldn't make myself heard. Father just shook his head, and didn't answer me.

Neutemoc was a dead weight in my arms. I dragged him closer, struggling to reach Father's body. If only I could be close enough, so that he could read my lips. If only I could apologise – for the vigil, for Neutemoc…

For myself.

"You still do everything as if he were alive, don't you?" a mocking voice asked.

Slowly, I shifted around, half-turned away from the tree.

The child-god Mazatl hung in the water, a few measures away from me. Green light flowed around him, outlining his body and the white tunic he wore. And in the light stood a monstrous figure with dark eyes, laying His hands on the child's shoulder, His fanged mouth resting close to Mazatl's ears, whispering words that the child flung back at me.

"Tlaloc," I whispered. The acrid taste of the lake's water filled my mouth, and only a thin thread of sound came out.

"Mazatl," the child said, a bare whisper that was almost human. But then he was speaking again with Tlaloc's voice, a thunder that made the water shake around us. "Or rather, not any more. Now I am called Popoxatl."

The Strength of Rain.

"Well named," I whispered.

I kicked, trying to rise to the surface. The end of the green light was so tantalisingly close. I could be out of the Storm Lord's territory, and into a place where the rules of the Fifth World applied. But Neutemoc's body, weighing me down, prevented me from rising any further.

An expression of animal cunning spread across Popoxatl's face: a sickening thing to see on a face so young. "You don't want to answer my question, do you, Acatl? Tell me."

"About what?" I asked, trying to keep my voice calm. I didn't know why I was seeking to gain time, but every instinct spoke against angering Tlaloc while I was still underwater.

"Your father, of course," Popoxatl said.

In the tree's roots, Father opened his mouth, revealing rows of yellowed teeth, struggling to speak, but unable to do so.

A game. Popoxatl was playing with me until I ceased to amuse. I tightened my grip on Neutemoc's body.

"Answer me," Popoxatl said. "Do you not do everything as if your parents had never died?"

"Mother died four years ago," I said, slowly. "Father, seven. I've made my own way. I don't see what You want." But I knew.

I wished Chalchiutlicue would do something, anything to rescue me. But despite the waters contracting around me, this wasn't Her dominion. The tree, and everything around it, belonged to the Storm Lord, Tlaloc.

Popoxatl laughed: a slow, rumbling sound that shook the roots of the tree. "Your own way? Oh, Acatl. You risk your own life to save your beloved brother—"

"What I think of Neutemoc has nothing to do with any of this," I snapped. "He's family – my own flesh and blood."

"Your parents' pride," Popoxatl whispered. "Among all the children, the brightest, the most successful."

"He chose his way," I said, unwilling to admit that the child's words hurt me more than they should have. "It led to glory. I don't begrudge—"

"Don't you?" Popoxatl asked. "Don't you, Acatl?"

Tlaloc's shadowy figure bent closer to his child-puppet. Between Popoxatl's outstretched hands, a dark shadow coalesced: a coiled mass of writhing threads.

In my hands, Neutemoc stirred. His eyes fluttered, but remained closed.

"Such a worthy man, is your brother. So much the pride of his children. Lusting after a priestess," Popoxatl whispered, and behind him came Eleuia's body, changing as it became closer to us, gaining flesh and colour and life – until she stood next to Popoxatl, her head cocked at a mischievous angle, her regenerated eyes sparkling with dark joy.

She started to dance: slowly weaving her way, with unbelievable grace, through the steps of some ritual. But in her eyes shone greed, and an unhealthy hunger.

The Duality curse her. Why did she have to tempt my brother?

Why did he have to be foolish enough to yield?

I backed nearer to the tree's roots, still clutching Neutemoc close to me.

Popoxatl laughed. "Such a whore, wasn't she?"

I said nothing. I could make no answer to this. I kept my gaze fixed upwards, towards the tree's trunk, which broke the surface just a few handspans away from me.

All I had to do was swim. But I couldn't. Neutemoc held me down there, as surely as I held him in my arms.

Come on, Neutemoc. Wake up.

"And still you cling to him," Popoxatl whispered, amused. "Still you make amends for him. Is he worth this, Acatl? Worth the wounds you suffered for him?"

I remembered battling the beast of shadows – the claws, sinking into my flesh. I remembered standing in the Imperial Court, withstanding Tizoc-tzin's amused stare. I remembered the Wind of Knives, lifting me high above Him, throwing me on the ground.

It was worth it. Neutemoc was my brother. My flesh and blood.

But I did not love him.

"He is—" I whispered. Everything I could not be. My parents' hope for the future. The perfect son.

Popoxatl opened his hands wide, and the dark shadows rushed towards me, wrapped themselves around me until they blotted out the world.

In my mind's eye I saw Neutemoc: not the bright, valiant warrior I'd always imagined, but a man mortally afraid – yearning for the bright simplicity of his warrior's life, never seeing that the past couldn't be called back.

I saw the hundred petty hurts Neutemoc delivered Huei – how he ran away from her in the birthing-room, as he had run away from Mother's death – how he sat away from her at banquets, his head turned towards his guests – how he heard but did not listen to what she said. I saw him turn away from his own children – too afraid of losing them to show them the least affection. I saw him walk into the darkness, willing himself to find the courage to end it all – never finding it.

He couldn't find it. He couldn't find anything.

Was this the man I had worshipped, the pride of my parents' eyes? This coward?

I saw him meet Eleuia, and how he made ready to betray his marriage without the slightest hint of regret – never thinking of what it would do to Huei, or to his children – never seeing how much Huei suffered from his pettiness.

In the end, he was the only one responsible for the failure of his marriage.

"Such a good man," Popoxatl whispered, his voice mocking. "Worth every wound, every injury, Acatl."

Worth… nothing.

It would be so easy, to open my hands. So easy to let him sink into the depths of the lake; and to rise myself, my knife in my hand, doing what had to be done to save the Fifth World.

What was a life, compared to what was at stake?

All I had to do was open my hands.

"The pride of your father's eyes." Popoxatl's voice was the thunder of the storm. "Such a strong man."

"Eleuia…" Neutemoc's eyes were open. He was staring at the corpse of Eleuia, his eyes mirroring the hunger in her gaze.

My hands tightened around him, as nausea welled up, harsh, uncontrollable. Could he see nothing but his lust?

He had grown heavier still, so heavy he was dragging me down. I arched my body, in a foolish attempt to resist his weight. But it was no use. I was sinking, going back to where I had come from, into the depths of Tlalocan.

"Eleuia is dead, Huitzilpochtli cut you down!" I screamed, shaking him like a rag doll. "Eaten by the ahuizotl. Dead and buried!"

"Eleuia…"

Everything shrank, in a mosaic of nightmare images: Popoxatl's smiling face, whispering of Huei's and Neutemoc's cankered marriage – Eleuia's uninterrupted, obscene dancing – Neutemoc's glazed eyes, still filled with that unquenchable, unreasonable hunger – images of him running away into the night, in unending cowardice – of Huei, standing straight and tall and unashamed of what she'd done.

The Duality curse him.

*Open your hands…*

All I had to do…

*Save yourself…*

He's deserved it…

The weight of the water was on my shoulders; and my hands burnt with the strain of Neutemoc's semiconscious burden. He was dragging me back into the depths, he and his accursed lust and inability to see that you couldn't call back the past.

*Open your hands...*

Sometimes, you had to make a choice. My fingers opened, almost of their own volition, and Neutemoc started slipping downwards, even as I rose.

For a moment – a split, endless moment as we hung suspended by the pulsing roots – our eyes met. In his was lust and hunger and an impossible desire for what he couldn't have, a desire that could only be ended by death...

And in my gaze, reflected in his...

The same.

The same hunger for the past, the same wish to turn back the flow of time, to have my parents' admiration; to be a warrior and the pride of my family.

*A true man stands by the consequences of his acts*, I had told Teomitl, and he had laughed at me, seeing what I had not been able to admit: that deep, deep down, I and Neutemoc were the same.

I hated him so much; but it wasn't him. It had never been him.

In less than a heartbeat, I dived, and our hands met, and clasped.

He was too heavy; he was still dragging me down. "You have to swim," I said.

His gaze was a mixture of hunger and confusion. "Eleuia?" he whispered, like a bewildered child.

"Swim!" I screamed.

He still wouldn't move.

So I did the only thing that would save us both: arching my body, I pushed him straight into the tree. He gasped as his body wedged itself in the hollow between two roots: nestling comfortably in the tangle of pulsing bark, sinking until his feet finally came to rest on a thicker root.

As best I could – not an easy thing given his unre-sponsiveness – I wrapped his hands around another buttress.

"Stay here," I whispered.

"Acatl?"

"Stay here." And, kicking upwards, I went back to Father and Eleuia – and Popoxatl. They would, I knew, be waiting for me.

As I rose, I drew the second-to-last of my obsidian knives, and the pulsing emptiness of Mictlan filled me; and the amused echo of the Jade Skirt's voice, boom-ing like underwater drums.

*A gift, priest.*

Father was still crucified among the roots, still watching me with that sad, disappointed gaze. But it wasn't real. Everything was Tlaloc's little game, as was Eleuia's slow dancing. Popoxatl was waiting for me, a smile stretched across his face. The Storm Lord, too, whispering words of poison in his puppet's ears.

"I see you've shed your burden," he said.

"What harm has he done you?" I asked, though I knew. Before Popoxatl had come into his power, Neutemoc's knowledge had been as dangerous as Commander Quiyahuayo's: what he knew about Eleuia might have stopped Tlaloc from achieving His aims. Now it was just endless malice.

"Don't you see, Acatl?" Popoxatl whispered, and his voice was that of a child. "He has no place in the new order. Warriors shouldn't rule the world. It's peasants who keep us going – and priests, shedding their blood to feed the sun."

I swam closer, knife at the ready, and Popoxatl watched me, dryly amused.

"Aren't you tired of the thoughtless arrogance of warriors? Of their endless staggering across our streets, conquering lands we have no use for?"

I thought of Mahuizoh's cavalier treatment of Ceyaxochitl and me – and of my parents' endless worship of war, slighting their own work to sing the praise of the battlefields. But it was not the way to change. It would never be the right way.

I was close now, almost close enough to strike, and still neither Tlaloc nor Popoxatl did anything. They just watched me. "What do you want?" I asked. "My collaboration? You don't need that."

Unhealthy hunger dilated Popoxatl's pupils, making me sick to the core. "Belief," he whispered. "I am the supreme god of the Mexica Empire. Everyone will abase themselves, and make their offerings of blood to keep me strong."

Belief. Commander Quiyahuayo had been right.

I swam closer; and when nothing happened, I sank my knife to the hilt into Popoxatl's chest.

Or tried to. The blade shattered, breaking on an invisible obstacle. And Popoxatl laughed, echoing the Storm Lord's amusement. "Did you think it would be so easy?"

It should have been. For all his powers, Popoxatl was only a god's agent, only a mortal. Surely a knife blessed by Mictlantecuhtli and Chalchiutlicue would kill a mere child?

Unless…

I pulled away, avoiding the child's outstretched arms. To my left, Eleuia had stopped dancing, and was coming for me with a sickening smile on her face.

I closed my eyes and extended my priest-senses.

And saw what I had missed.

Light streamed around Eleuia, limning the alluring curves of her body; but all of that wasn't just beauty, or charms – but the Quetzal Flower's grace, wrapped around her like a mantle. No wonder every man had been drawn to Eleuia: the

Goddess of Lust had rewarded her well for her services.

But that wasn't the worst.

Ichtaca's spell, which had dispelled the creatures, had done so by setting Huitzilpochtli's wards on everyone. Everyone human: the priests, Ichtaca himself, Neutemoc, me.

And Popoxatl.

The wards, anathema to Mictlan's magic – to Tlalocan's magic – spread around Popoxatl's body in a shimmering cover, leaving me no place to strike at.

I suppressed a curse; but it was hard, seeing Popoxatl's gloating face. Had I come this far for nothing?

Think.

The creatures had been able to whittle Mihmatini's wards away to nothing, and their magic had been of Tlalocan. And when Teomitl had rescued me in the Jaguar House, the rush of the Southern Hummingbird's magic had turned Mictlan's knives into obsidian dust. It worked both ways. Huitzilpochtli's magic would destroy Mictlan's; and Mictlan's magic would destroy those wards. I just had to summon it in the proper way.

Eleuia's outstretched arms closed around my chest. Without thinking, I slashed, and she fell back, screaming in agony. At least she didn't count as human, but she would be back. I couldn't kill her: she didn't belong to my dominion.

There was no time.

I thought of killing the beast of shadows, of the feeling of emptiness that had seized me as I lay on my back, that sense of *being* at work everywhere, in every living thing, coursing through my arm to strike – and drew another knife, my last.

But I couldn't summon that feeling again. Just the emptiness of Mictlan, waiting to blossom into something more, but not doing so. *Huitzilpochtli blind me!*

Popoxatl was drifting towards me, smiling in a decidedly unpleasant way. Beside him, Tlaloc was whispering something, dripping darkness into his ears.

There was no time.

I couldn't...

My hand tightened around the hilt of the knife. I was a priest of Mictlantecuhtli. Death was my lot, Mictlan the dominion of my god. I would never be a warrior, never bring glory to my calpulli – but I could make sure, now and tomorrow, that there would be other warriors to carry on, to fight the battles of the Fifth World and bring the sacrifices that would keep the sun in the sky.

I was a priest. And this, here, was where I stood. This was what I had chosen, what I had become.

Within me, Mictlan was rising: the keening lament of the dead, the grave voice of the Wind of Knives, the smell of rotting bodies and the dry touch of bones on my skin – my consciousness expanding, wrapping itself to encompass every living soul, the children huddled in the courtyards, playing games as the rain fell – their mothers, clutching their bellies and wishing for a quick birth – their fathers, resting with their macuahitl swords and their hoes by their side – the old men and women, chatting about the awful weather – the dead in Mictlan, making their slow journey towards Lord Death's throne and oblivion.

I was... everything I needed to be.

My arm descended; and the knife, scything through Huitzilpochtli's wards as if they were nothing, buried itself up to the hilt into Popoxatl's chest. He shrieked: a thin, pained sound like a dying dog, twisting at my heart. Tlaloc screamed, too, but He was already dissolving into nothingness, His voice receding further and further away as he was thrown away from the Fifth World.

The green light slowly faded, and a huge tremor shook the roots of the ghost tree, like a storm unleashing itself at last. The roots shook and shook, dislodging Father's body, which fell into the depths, still watching me with that unceasing disappointment.

But it didn't matter. Father was dead, and this mockery that the Storm Lord had called back into life didn't have any power to hurt. Not any more.

Around me, the Blessed Drowned were disappearing, one by one: turning into algae, into fish, into foam on the water. Popoxatl's body was sinking down as well, but not very far: ahuizotls were already gathering, tearing at it with their clawed tails.

My lungs were starting to burn. I welcomed the feeling, for it meant that the rules of the Fifth World applied once more. Now all I needed to do was rise back to the surface, and…

Neutemoc. He'd been in the tree's roots. But the tree had almost faded to nothing now, with only a few light reflections remaining. Where was he?

My lungs burnt too much. I kicked upwards, rose to the surface for a moment, under a rainy sky that had nothing of magic any more. Then I took a deep breath, and dived down again.

Far, far below, a dark shape lay horizontally in the water. I made my way straight for him, just a few handspans ahead of an ahuizotl; put both hands under his armpits, and pulled upwards. He was heavy, but not as heavy as he had once been in Tlalocan, and rising with him to the surface wasn't as hard as I had feared.

When I pulled him onto the shores of the small island and laid him down in the mud, though, he wasn't breathing any more.

## TWENTY-FOUR
## *Small Vigils*

I knelt in the mud, and pushed on Neutemoc's chest, struggling to get the water out of his lungs. Around me, the rain fell in a steady patter. But it was just rain, water falling from the darkened sky without Tlaloc's magic at the core of every drop.

The light was getting dimmer: the sun would soon set. It felt like too much had happened today. But then most of that day had been spent in Tlalocan, where the time was that of the gods.

The Fifth World would go on. But Neutemoc...

Surely... surely I hadn't gone all that way, done all I had, just to lose him.

Deep, deep down, I knew that the gods had their own rules, and the Duality even more so. I had made my own bargains; had saved Neutemoc from sinking into Tlalocan. But perhaps, in the end, it didn't matter. Perhaps, in the end, he would still be walking with Father in Tlalocan, basking in Father's admiration.

No. I couldn't accept that.

Neutemoc didn't move. My hands snagged on his ribs, and with every push I feared I was going to break bones. But still he didn't move. The tips of his fingers were wrinkled; and blood was starting to settle in the white oval of his face.

No.

"There's water in his lungs," Teomitl said, kneeling by my side.

He looked as if he had been through all the levels of Mictlan: his face as pale as the waning moon, his nobleman's clothes stained with mud and blood – and his eyes as deep as abysses, shimmering with the golden colour of the ahuizotls' irises.

I raised my gaze. Ichtaca leant against the stone altar, his eyes closed. Six or seven of the priests, mostly novice priests, were still unconscious. The others – Ezamahual and the two surviving warriors of the Duality among them – were tending to the wounded.

Ixtli's body lay on the stone altar, the priest's noose still tight around his neck. I closed my eyes, briefly. Had I not gone to him, he and his men would still be alive. Had I not asked a favour from him. He had been his own man. He had made his own choices; and they had taken him away from me. There was nothing I could do. Nothing but grieve.

"Ichtaca? Palli?" I asked.

Teomitl laid his hands on Neutemoc's chest, frowning. "Your Fire Priest is made of stone. He's full of scrapes and wounds, but I have no doubt he'll survive. The others–" he shrugged. "They're in the hands of the Duality."

Like Neutemoc.

Teomitl was probing at Neutemoc's bones, carefully. Magic oozed out of the pores of his skin, mingled with my brother's skin. "And your brother?" I asked.

He shrugged again. "Axayacatl? He probably survived. I don't think things would have held together otherwise."

I wondered how Ceyaxochitl was faring. Quite the gossip I was turning into. But I needed something, anything, to prevent me from thinking about Neutemoc.

Teomitl sat back on his heels, his face grave. "He's in bad shape, Acatl-tzin."

I knew. "Can you…" I'd done enough damage to my family: to Huei, to Neutemoc. Or, more accurately, we'd done enough damage to each other, but I'd still dealt Huitzilpochtli's share of it. "Can you do anything?"

Teomitl frowned. "I? No. The Jade Skirt, perhaps. But you know there will be a price."

"I'll pay it," I said.

Teomitl smiled, without joy. He seemed to have grown up immeasurably since taking on Chalchiutlicue's blessing, turning from a boy into a bitter adult in a matter of hours. "Always ask what the price is before accepting a bargain, Acatl-tzin. Have you learnt nothing?"

No, not much. Things about myself; about Father and Neutemoc; that was all. Teomitl was right. An adult, in all the ways that mattered. I didn't think he'd be needing any advice any more.

Teomitl laid his hands on Neutemoc's chest again, pushed down, hard. Light blazed from his fingers, wrapped itself around my brother's body: a green luminescence much like the reflections of light on jade, which uneasily called to mind the depths of Tlalocan, and the memory of the pulsing roots, and of Father, laid out among them like a living offering.

I heard Chalchiutlicue laugh, in my mind. *Priest*, She whispered, and suddenly She stood behind Teomitl, Her hands outstretched to cover his head, a mocking parody of the Storm Lord's position at Popoxatl's side.

You used Teomitl. But then we'd all used each other.

"He's in My land," the Jade Skirt whispered, and Her voice was the lament of the wind over the stormy lake. "But not so far gone. I can give him back to you."

"I'll pay the price," I whispered, again.

She laughed. "Such impatience. You owe Me a favour, priest. One day, I'll come and claim it from you."

And then She was gone, and Teomitl's magic had sunk down to nothing again. And Neutemoc was coughing up stale water, struggling to rise. I'd never thought I'd be so happy to see him moving.

"Acatl?" Neutemoc asked, his voice rasping in his throat.

I took his hand, pulled him to a sitting position. "Welcome back."

Neutemoc grimaced. "So is the Fifth World over?" He stared at the sky, and at the gathered priests. On the lake, a flotilla of boats was making its way towards us. In the prow of the first one was the familiar figure of Ceyaxochitl. "I guess not."

"No," I said.

Neutemoc closed his eyes. "I remember Father…"

I waited for him to remember the rest, how I'd almost let go of him in my selfish urge to judge him. But at length he said, "I guess I owe you."

I shrugged. "Nothing much." Chalchiutlicue would claim Her debt, but there was nothing I could do about that.

Neutemoc sat in the mud, watching the lake. I made my way towards the altar, and found Ezamahual tending to Palli. "How is he?" I asked.

"Nothing serious," Ezamahual said. "He hit his head when the boat capsized. He'll survive."

"And the others?" I asked, slowly, already knowing the answer.

Ezamahual's gaze was distant. "Two novice priests are dead. And some of them won't live out the night."

"I see."

"They gave their lives for the Fifth World," Ezamahual said, his voice toneless, as if reciting something learnt by rote. "It's our only destiny."

It was. But it didn't mean we wouldn't mourn them. Like Quechomitl, like Commander Quiyahuayo, they would ascend into the Heaven of the Sun, to find their afterlife far more pleasant than the toil of this world. But we would still miss them.

I, more than anyone: for I had used them, barely knowing them. I knelt, slowly, by the altar and Ixtli's body, and whispered the first words of a prayer for the Dead:

*"We leave this earth*
*This world of jade and flowers*
*The quetzal feathers, the silver…"*

When the flotilla of boats reached the island, Ceyaxochitl was the first on the ground. Accompanied by Yaotl, she made her way towards me with her usual energy, and a frown on her face which told me I would have a number of explanations to give her.

"I see you're alive," Ceyaxochitl said, with a snort. Her eyes took in my priests, slumped on the ground; Ichtaca, who still hadn't opened his eyes; Neutemoc, sitting cross-legged in the mud; and Teomitl, standing by my brother's side, oozing Chalchiutlicue's magic. "And I see you've had some interesting adventures."

"I'll–"

She raised an unsteady hand. Suddenly, I saw how tired she looked; how pale was her face, and how she'd wrapped her left hand tightly around her cane's pommel, to prevent it from shaking. Tending to the Emperor had taken a heavy toll on her.

"We'll get you back," Yaotl said. His face in the dim light was expressionless. "We can see about the rest later."

We had to leave most of the bodies in the water. The ahuizotls were feeding, and not even Teomitl's commands could make them abandon their grisly meals. Out of about thirty dead on our side, and the priests of Tlaloc on the other, we'd retrieved only four: two of my novice priests, one Duality warrior, and Ixtli.

On the way back, I found myself riding in the same boat as Neutemoc, watching the water part around the prow.

My brother was silent, as he had been on our journey to Amecameca. But this time the silence wasn't filled with pent-up aggressiveness, or things we'd failed to say to each other.

"You'll be fine?" I asked.

He said nothing. He watched the water, moodily. "I don't know."

"You can't go back," I said, finally.

"No," Neutemoc said. "You never can. But you can always dream of what could have been."

"And destroy your life?" I asked, more vehemently than I'd meant to. "Sorry."

Neutemoc shook his head. He dipped his hand in the water, watching the droplets part on his skin. "It doesn't matter," he said. He sighed. "Huei–"

"There's no need to talk about her," I said, more embarrassed than I'd thought.

Neutemoc didn't speak. "She told me to forget her," he said. "To find myself another wife, to raise the children."

"She told you that?" There would be no divorce, but nothing prevented him from taking on a second wife. He'd be more than able to support her.

"In the temple," Neutemoc said. "I don't know what I'll do."

My chest contracted. "You don't have to decide right now."

"No," Neutemoc said. "I guess not. What will you do?"

"I don't know," I said, truthfully. There would be accounts to make to Ceyaxochitl – vigils for Ixtli and the dead priests – and life would, I guessed, go on much as it had always done.

Neutemoc snorted. "A fine pair we make." His face closed again. "So you killed the child?"

"Yes," I said, curtly. And Eleuia, too; and perhaps Father. I wasn't sure.

"Going down alone into Tlalocan… You'd have made a good warrior, you know."

I shrugged. "Some things aren't made to be."

"Perhaps not," Neutemoc said at last. "But you'd still have made it, if you'd wished to."

"I didn't," I said, finally, and it was the truth, the only reason I'd chosen that path on exiting the calmecac.

We passed through the streets of the Moyotlan district, and saw everywhere the ravages of the flood: the canals which had overflowed, bringing water into the courtyards of the grand houses, knocking down the wattle-and-daub walls of the humbler ones. In the water were wicker chests, reed mats, codices – and the bodies of those caught by the flood, facedown in the canals, as unmoving and as unbreathing as Ixtli's warriors.

People were out in the streets, salvaging what they could from the retreating water. I saw a woman carrying a very young child around her shoulders, trying to recover a rag doll, and my heart tightened.

Ceyaxochitl's flotilla moored on the quays at the foot of the Sacred Precinct. Her warriors helped lift the dead and the wounded out of the boats.

"I guess I'll be going back to my household," Neutemoc said. He grimaced. "Mihmatini is going to flay me alive."

I could imagine what words Mihmatini would have for us. "Tell her you've almost died. That helps."

"It never does," Neutemoc said, with a quick, amused smile. He walked a few steps away from me. "You're not coming?"

I blinked, genuinely surprised. "No," I said. "My place is in my temple."

Neutemoc said nothing. His face had gone as brittle as clay. "Come to my house when you want, Acatl. I..." He struggled with the words. "It will be less lonely with you around."

My heart contracted to an impossible knot of pain; and the only words I could find seemed to come from a distant place. "Yes," I said. "When my affairs are in order. Thank you."

I watched Neutemoc walk away in silence. Next to the last of the boats, Teomitl was talking with Ceyaxochitl, punctuating his narrative with stabbing gestures. Giving a detailed account of what we'd done, I guessed.

They were both walking towards the palace. The palace, where Tizoc-tzin and Axayacatl-tzin would be waiting for their wayward brother: a brother who would one day, the Duality be willing, take his place as Revered Speaker for the Mexica Empire.

My work was done.

I turned away from them, leaving them to their conversation, and followed the warriors with the corpses, back into the safety of my temple.

• • •

As I'd foreseen, many things needed to be organised. Under my direction, the dead priests and Ixtli were laid in empty rooms, where the survivors could start the preparations for the vigils. The wounded were laid out in the infirmary, along with Ichtaca, though he seemed to suffer from nothing more than extreme exhaustion.

Once, I would have conducted the vigils. But instead, I made sure that everything was ready; then I retreated to the top of the pyramid shrine, where I browsed through the records of the temple, reading all I could about the dead novice priests.

Cualli of the Atempan calpulli, son of Coyotl and Necahual, born on the day Three Eagle of the year Five Rabbit... Ihuicatl of the Coatlan calpulli, son of Tezcacoatl and Malinalxochitl, born on the day Thirteen Crocodile of the year Six Reed... They had died for the continuation of the Fifth World; for what they'd always been pledged to. They were with the Sun.

But it wasn't enough. It would never be enough. I bore the responsibility for their deaths, and I would make sure that they had not died in vain. I would make sure Ixtli had not died in vain.

"I thought I'd find you here," a voice said.

Startled, I looked up, expecting Ichtaca. But it was Teomitl: still wearing his mud-stained clothes, still pale and exhausted.

"I thought you'd be at the palace," I said.

Teomitl shrugged. "Perhaps later. They'll be busy, in any case."

"They'll need you."

His eyebrows rose. "How about you?"

I made a short, stabbing gesture. "Me? I don't think so."

"You saved the Fifth World," Teomitl said.

"And I should expect some recognition?" I asked, more scathingly than I'd intended. "I don't think I'd accept it."

Teomitl laughed. "You haven't changed so much, have you? Still loathing politics."

I'd have to enter that arena, sooner or later. I'd have to second Ichtaca in the running of the temple, to take my true place as High Priest. But there were limits. "Why are you here?" I asked.

Teomitl said nothing. He walked towards the altar under the impassive gaze of Lord Death. "I have proved myself."

"You should be glad," I said.

He spread his hands, an unreadable expression on his face. "Perhaps. But it shouldn't end here. If I want to take my place."

His gestures were quiet, measured: the mark of an adult.

"Go," I said, gently. "Claim your place."

Teomitl shook his head. "Not without you."

"My place is here."

"I know," Teomitl snapped; and for a moment I saw again the impatient youth who had first come to me in my temple. "But I still need you."

"What for?"

He laughed, bitterly. "Do you think me wise, Acatl-tzin? Do you think me mature enough to handle the Jade Skirt's gift of Her magic?"

Startled, I said, "There will be plenty of priests willing to–"

"Flatter me for their own gain!" Teomitl snapped. "I came for you."

Unable to see where I stood, I flung his words back at him. "Do you think me wise? There's little I can teach you."

"You know about magic."

"A little," I admitted, cautiously.

"Enough for me, then."

I could probably teach him to control Chalchiut-licue's magic – and to have enough patience – but... "Is this what you want?"

"Don't be a fool," Teomitl said. "Do you think I came this way for nothing?"

In many ways, I realised, he hadn't changed: still impatient, abrasive, arrogant. But still quick to lend his heart, and to expect trust in return.

Since Payaxin, I had not taken on an apprentice, even less one of Imperial Blood. "I..." I started, and realised I had been running away from this possibility for so long I couldn't even envision it. "You'll have to show me some respect," I said, finally.

Teomitl's smile was like a sun rising. "I'll work on it. Besides, I have to get your consent for courting your sister, haven't I?"

I made a mock-frown, hiding the mixture of unease and pleasure his request gave me. "We'll see about that, young man. When this night is over."

I stood on the platform of the shrine, and watched the light finally fade behind the rain-clouds.

Below me, Teomitl was descending the stairs. "Come on, Acatl-tzin," he called. "The vigils have already started."

From behind him came the mournful sounds of the death-hymns, and the reedy music of conch-shells, signalling the first Hour of the night: that of Xiuhte-cuhtli, the Fire-God.

I sighed and gathered my grey cloak around me, before following Teomitl down the stairs in the growing darkness.

Above us, the clouds had broken a little, leaving just enough space for the light of one star to fall upon my temple. It was the most beautiful sight I had seen in a long time.

"Come on, Acatl-tzin!"

I was a priest of Mictlantecuhtli. I would neither have children, nor know the glory of warriors.

But this – the vigils and the conch-shells, and the setting sun that would rise again, and Teomitl, waiting for me on the steps with unbounded impatience–

This was my place, and my legacy.

# Cast of Characters

*Acamapichtli:* High Priest of Tlaloc.
*Acatl:* Narrator, High Priest of Mictlantecuhtli.
*Axayacatl-tzin:* The current Revered Speaker, Emperor of the Mexica.

*Ceyaxochitl:* Guardian of the Sacred Precinct, and agent of the Duality in the Mexica Empire.
*Chalchiutlicue (The Jade Skirt):* Goddess of Lakes and Streams; Tlaloc's wife.
*Cozamalotl:* Student at the calmecac.
*Cocochi:* Mahuizoh's mother.

*Duality:* The supreme deity, residing in the Highest Heaven, also known as Ometeotl.

*Eleuia:* The abducted priestess.
*Eliztac:* Priest of Chalchiutlicue.
*Ezamahual:* Novice priest in Acatl's temple.

*Huacqui:* Disgraced Jaguar Knight.
*Huei:* Neutemoc's wife.
*Huitzilpochtli (The Southern Hummingbird):* God of War and of the Sun, protector of the Mexica Empire.

*Ichtaca:* Fire Priest of Mictlantecuhtli's main temple, Acatl's second-in-command.

*Icnoyotl:* Poet.

*Ixtli:* Warrior of the Duality.

*Mahuizoh (of the Coatlan calpulli):* Jaguar Knight.

*Mazatl:* Toddler, Neutemoc's daughter; also the name of a child in the Floating Gardens.

*Mihmatini:* Acatl's and Neutemoc's younger sister.

*Mictlantecuhtli (Lord Death):* God of the underworld, Acatl's patron.

*Mictecacihuatl (Lady Death):* Mictlantecuhtli's wife.

*Mixcoatl (The Cloud Serpent):* God of the Hunt, Father of Quetzalcoatl.

*Neutemoc:* Acatl's older brother, of the Atempan calpulli; Jaguar Knight.

*Nezahual:* Priest of Tlaloc; Acamapichtli's envoy.

*Ocelocueitl:* High Priest of Huitzilpochtli.

*Ollin:* Neutemoc's infant son.

*Oyohuaca:* Slave girl in Neutemoc's house.

*Palli:* Offering priest at Acatl's temple, in charge of the storehouse.

*Papan:* Student at Zollin's calmecac.

*Patecatl:* God of Medicine.

*Pinahui-tzin:* Magistrate at the Imperial Palace.

*Popoxatl:* A child in the Floating Gardens.

*Quechomitl:* One of Neutemoc's slaves, usually on guard duty.

*Quetzalcoatl (The Feathered Serpent):* God of Creation and Knowledge, son of Mixcoatl, traditionally opposed to Tezcatlipoca.

*Quiyahuayo:* Jaguar Commander.

*Tezcatlipoca (The Smoking Mirror):* God of War and Fate, and of sorcerers.

*Teomitl (Arrow of the Gods):* A young warrior at the boys' calmecac.

*Tizoc-tzin:* Master of the House of Darts, heir-apparent to the Mexica Empire.

*Tlaloc (The Storm Lord):* God of Rain and Abundance.

*Tonatiuh (The Fifth Sun):* Incarnation of Huitzilpochtli as the Sun-God.

*Xochiquetzal (The Quetzal Flower):* Goddess of Beauty and Love.

*Xochipilli (The Flower Prince):* Xochiquetzal's consort, God of Youth and Games.

*Xoco:* Mahuizoh's wife (deceased).

*Yaotl:* Ceyaxochil's personal messenger.

*Yolyama:* Guard in the Jaguar House.

*Zollin:* Priestess in charge of the girls' calmecac.

# A BRIEF GLOSSARY OF
## Aztec Terms and Concepts

*Ahuizotl:* Beast living in Lake Texcoco, feasting on the
eyes and fingernails of the dead.

*Calmecac:* (lit. House of Tears) School where the children of the wealthy and those destined to the
priesthood were educated.

*Calpulli:* Clan. In reality, a clan had both a geographi-
cal extent (the calpullis owned their land, and
Tenochtitlan was split along the lines of calpulli
lands), and a political and religious one (the elders
of the calpulli were responsible for basic justice as
well as for worship).

*Chinamitl:* (also *chinampa*, Floating Garden) An artificial island used to grow crops.

*House of Youth:* The counterpart to the calmecac.
Trained warriors not of the nobility.

*Knights:* Elite corps of warriors, reserved for those with
strong prowess in battle. Includes the Jaguar

Knights, the Eagle Knights and the Arrow Knights.

*Macuahitl (sword):* A wooden club with embedded obsidian shards; the traditional Aztec weapon.

*Nahual:* Protector spirit, usually in the shape of a jaguar.

*Patolli:* Aztec board game, played with beans as dice.

*Peyotl:* Drug obtained from dried cacti (better known today as the basis for mescalin).

*Priests:* The priestly hierarchy had various ranks, the lowest ones being those of priestly aspirants, and of calmecac students. Then came the novice priests, who served a particular god in a particular temple. With time, they could be promoted to offering priests. Those cults which offered human sacrifices had a higher rank: the fire-priests, responsible for choosing the victims and for lighting a fire in their chests. Finally came the High Priests.

*Tzin:* Aztec honorific, equivalent to "Lord". I have taken the liberty of using it as a mark of reverence (much in the way of the Japanese "sama"), and not as an actual title.

# *About the Author*

French by birth, Aliette de Bodard chose to write in English – her second language – after a two-year stint in London. Though she has trained as a engineer (graduating from Ecole Polytechnique, one of France's most prestigious colleges), she has always been fascinated by history and mythology, especially those of non-Western cultures. Her love of mysteries gave her the idea to write a cross-genre novel which would feature Aztecs, blood magic and fiendish murders.

She is a Campbell Award finalist and a Writers of the Future winner. Her short fiction has appeared or is forthcoming in venues such as *Interzone*, *Realms of Fantasy*, and *Fantasy* magazine, and has been reprinted in *The Year's Best Science Fiction*. She recently finished her second novel, the sequel to this one, entitled *Harbinger of the Storm*.

She lives in Paris, where she has a job as a computer engineer.

**www.aliettedebodard.com**

## Author's Notes

### The Historical Setting

The bulk of this story is set in Tenochtitlan, capital of the Aztec/Mexica Empire, in the year 1480. Of course, the events in this novel aren't historical – but I have tried to keep the setting as historical as possible.

This has two drawbacks: the first is the scarcity of sources about life in the Aztec Empire. The second is that most of those sources were written after 1519: after the Spanish invasion, and forty years after the events of this book. Quite aside from questions of reliability, there is also the problem that the Aztec way of life had no doubt changed between 1480 and 1519. Also, inevitably, I will have mangled some of my sources; any glaring historical errors come from me, and not from the sources I consulted.

I did twist history in several respects. The post of Guardian, and its attendant worship of the Duality, is an invention of mine. The Aztecs did have a concept of the Duality as supreme gods, but they seemed to have been content to have that remain an abstraction, and worship mostly the expressions of the Duality (such as the Lord and Lady of the underworld). Similarly, I gave the clergy of Mictlantecuhtli the responsibility of funerals, whereas we have no evidence of a widely organised religious body in charge of that aspect of life (it's likely the clans would have taken care of their own). I also twisted their worship slightly by not having them offer human sacrifices; in reality, like most cults, they would have relied heavily on those.

Similarly, most of the characters in this book are fictitious, the exception being those of Imperial Blood. Axayacatl and Tizoc were both Revered Speakers of the Mexica Empire.

As for Teomitl... The successor of Tizoc was his brother, a young man named Ahuizotl. Not much is known of him, other than that Ahuizotl was not his real name, and he took it on ascending the throne – but no reason is given why. Ahuizotl is known for two things: his military conquests, which brought the Mexica Empire to its greatest extent yet; and his massive refurbishment of the Great Temple in Tenochtitlan. He died in a freak flood in the year 1502, said to be the anger of Tlaloc and Chalchiutlicue.

The "Obsidian Snake" to whom the Goddess Chalchiutlicue refers in chapter twenty is the literal translation of Ixcoatl, a previous Mexica Emperor who was the grandfather of Axayacatl, Tizoc and Ahuizotl.

As to the conflict between Tlaloc and Huitzilpochtli: an interpretation commonly put forward is that the Rain-God Tlaloc was the god of peasants and farmers, and that his was a very old worship. There is evidence that a rain-god with similar features to Tlaloc was worshipped in the time of Teotihuacan, about one thousand years before the beginning of the Aztec Empire.

Huitzilpochtli is a newer god, most probably the tribal god of the Aztecs – but the Aztecs elevated him to the highest rank in their divine hierarchy, twinning him with the Sun-God Tonatiuh and promoting his worship on a massive scale. Obviously, there was some room for divine discontent.

## Further Reading

Manuel Aguilar-Moreno, *Handbook to Life in the Aztec World*, Oxford University Press, 2006

Warwick Bray, *Everyday Life of the Aztecs*, Batsford, 1968

Roy Burrell, *Life in the Time of Moctezuma and the Aztecs*, Cherrytree Books, 1992

Inga Clendinnen, *Aztecs: an Interpretation (Canto)*, Cambridge University Press, 1991

Aurélie Couvreur, *La Description du Grand Temple de Mexico par Bernardino de Sahagún (Codex de Florence, annexe du livre II)*, Journal de la Société des Américanistes, 2002

Nigel Davies, The Aztecs: a History, University of Oklahoma Press, 1973

William Gates, *An Aztec Herbal: the Classic Codex of 1552*, Dover, 2000

David M. Jones & Brian L. Molyneaux, *Mythologies des Amériques*, EDDL, 2002

Roberta E. Markman & Peter T. Markman, *The Flayed God: the Mythology of Mesoamerica*, Harper SanFrancisco, 1992

Jacques Martin and Jean Torton, *Les Voyages d'Alix: Les Aztèques*, Casterman, 2005

Charles Phillips, *The Complete Illustrated History of the Aztecs and Maya*, Hermes House, 2006

Jacques Soustelle, *Daily Life of the Aztecs*, Phoenix Press, 2002

G.C. Vaillant, *Aztecs of Mexico*, Pelican, 1965


Aztec Calendar: *http://www.azteccalendar.com*

Sacred Texts: *http://www.sacred-texts.com* (most particularly the "Rig Veda Americanus" by Daniel G. Brinton)

## The Writing of *Servant*

I can trace the genesis of *Servant of the Underworld* a long way into the past. Like much of my fiction, it is irretrievably linked to books I read as a child and later as a teenager – before I was a science fiction reader, I was a mystery reader.

My repertoire was Sherlock Holmes (my copy of which was bent and creased from several re-readings); Agatha Christie (the French translations of her books being easily available, even in the bookshops of the small Spanish town where we spent our holidays); John Dickson Carr (a personal favourite because of his outlandish locked-room mysteries); and many more. Through them, I not only discovered the intricacies of a plot with many reversals, but also a sense of place. Indeed, all of those have a not-so-obvious common point: they portray a society of the past, one which might look familiar but is already no longer our own. Their characters – the retired army majors from India, the single girls taking positions as private tutors, the adventuresses in dalliances with the kings of small European countries – they were part of another universe, something delightfully quaint, which bore very little resemblance to the world I myself inhabited.

This sense of place persisted in another discovery I made in my childhood: Christian Jacq. He was a French author who found great success writing about Ancient Egypt, and I devoured his re-imagined court intrigues of the Rameses era – an utterly foreign land, filled with danger and magic. The books almost always had mystery elements, but the ones that stayed with me were the Judge of Egypt trilogy. Instead of having a prince or a nobleman as its main character, it focuses on Pazair, a magistrate slowly caught in the machinations of the Pharaoh's court, who uses his meagre resources to stay ahead of his adversaries, before becoming a masterly player of court games himself.

Another thing from my childhood that carried over *into Servant of the Underworld* was a fascination with mythology and fairytales. I was the proud owner of a full shelf of grey-jacketed books in the *Tales and Legends From...* series, ranging from the classics (Ancient Greece, Rome) to the more esoteric (Persia, China). They were windows into another world, and the weird creatures, places and deities filled me with a sense of unadulterated wonder and discovery I seldom found in classical French literature. That sense of both wonder and fear – for the ancient gods are fearsome creatures, and seldom benevolent – carried over into my first short stories, as I tentatively started to explore imagined and historical mythologies.

Aztec and Maya tales soon played a large part in my fiction. I'm not quite sure why, to this day. I think it's a combination of two things: the first is that Mesoamerica is one of the rare parts of the world I knew next to nothing about when I started writing (as opposed to Greek, Roman and Egyptian, of which I'd read so much they felt stale). The second is a purely contrarian spirit: the Aztecs frequently are the underdogs of fiction. Whenever someone needs a bloodthirsty, barbaric people to act as villains in the story, chances are they'll turn to some civilisation derived from either the Aztecs or the Maya. But, in reality, both civilisations had impressive scientific and political achievements: the Aztecs had one of the fairest systems of justice, which forbade torture and held noblemen to a harsher standard than peasants. I guess part of my motivation for starting to write in that setting was to prove that just because a civilisation seems bloodthirsty doesn't mean it's beyond the pale – thus adding my own meagre contribution to the ongoing war to rehabilitate the Mesoamerican civilisations.

The other thing I can see about the genesis of *Servant of the Underworld* is the way it grew out of my short fiction.

In 2007, I'd just come back from the Writers of the Future workshop, and I'd reached a crux in my own writing. I felt like I'd been writing the same short stories over and over, and it had become harder and harder to stay motivated. I toyed with the idea of writing a novel, but I was unsure of where to begin, or what the novel would be about. I'd always liked reading epic fantasies, but the idea of a multi-threaded, multi-character book scared me. I wanted to get my novel feet working on something smaller. Perhaps turning one of my short stories into a novel?

The one candidate that presented itself almost immediately was "Obsidian Shards", the story that had won me that Writers of the Future place. It was a magic mystery set in Aztec times, featuring Acatl, a priest well versed in magic and forensics. But I was still hesitant to commit: a novel was a big endeavour; I knew enough about Aztec culture to fake a short story, but nowhere near enough for a longer work; and a fantasy mystery set in a non-Western culture didn't seem like it would have enough appeal to be published at all.

And then I read two series of books that changed my outlook radically. The first was Liz Williams's Detective-Inspector Chen novels, a mix of police procedural, magic and science fiction in a non-Western culture; and the second, Elizabeth Bear's New Amsterdam mysteries, set in an alternative America where vampires and magicians were commonplace. And that set me thinking: perhaps, after all, this wasn't such a stupid idea...

In October 2007, I started the novel planning in earnest.

My writing process is very much an engineer's approach. I am an obsessive outliner, and tend to get as much of the research down beforehand as I can. The main reason is that I'm also fundamentally lazy: it's much less work to cut something at the outline stage than in the first draft.

In the case of *Servant of the Underworld*, I was comforted in that approach by the genres I had chosen to meld. Essentially, by choosing to make the novel a historical mystery with magic, I had to deal with two genres that required forethought. Historical settings can't be improvised, and I couldn't rely on vague ideas of daily life in Aztec times to start plotting – lest I end up discovering that I'd got everything wrong, and that the scenes had to be completely rewritten. As for mysteries... they're unforgiving in terms of plot. Everything has to hang together by the end. Of course, cutting and pasting and fixing works very well for some people, but I can't do that. I can't hold a whole novel plot in my mind, so I needed a relatively clear idea of where the novel was going and of the reasons behind the characters' actions. Better get the shape of the plot right, and then fill in only the little details.

Accordingly, I invested in research books. A lot of research books, that I read cover to cover in an attempt to get the bases of Aztec culture into my brain before starting to outline, let alone write. A lot of those books were on Aztec daily life, though I also had some on Aztec mythology, Aztec architecture, Aztec history…

Those last turned out to be crucial for the novel planning, because the act of turning a short story into a novel started with a very simple thing: I had to decide which era in history I wanted Acatl to have lived in. It wasn't that important for the setting itself. We barely have enough records of Aztec life in the time of the Spanish Conquest, so it was illusory to think that I'd have access to documents that predate it by decades. Though the setting had certainly evolved over history, I'd never be able to capture that. What it was important for was the context. After some discussions (in particular with fellow writer, Sara Genge), I'd decided that Acatl would no longer be a small priest in a small parish, but High Priest for the Dead, evolving within the political intrigues of the Imperial Court. That meant I had to know which Emperor I was dealing with.

Though the lifetime of the Aztec Empire was very short, it still covered about a century, and eleven emperors. The choice hinged on the setting I wanted: an Aztec Empire near the peak of its glory, stable enough to allow Acatl to investigate in an environment not riven by all-out warfare or invasions, but with enough political intrigues that I could drawn on later if necessary. For those reasons, I discarded the first few emperors, those of the humble beginnings; and the last one, Moctezuma II, during whose reign the Aztec Empire collapsed into oblivion. That didn't actually leave me much choice. It was a tie between Ixcoatl, who, like Napoleon in France, gave the Empire many of the structures that defined it up till the Spanish Conquest; and Axayacatl, an Emperor with few grand realisations, but one whose reign was relatively unmarred by war or famine.

One note caught my eye: Axayacatl's reign was succeeded by the short five-year reign of Tizoc, and then by the very young Ahuizotl, who extended Aztec domination into faraway places. Ahuizotl seemed a prickly character, prone to fits of anger, but fiercely loyal to his soldiers, seldom hesitating to share their lives on the march. His name was also that of a creepy water-beast I planned to use in the book, though no one knew why he chose it on ascending the throne.

I made some quick calculations: no one knew Ahuizotl's birth date, but assuming he became emperor at twenty-two – a very young age as emperors go – then he would have been seventeen in the last year of Axayacatl's reign. What if Acatl met him? That would give him one more reason to be embroiled in court politics; and Ahuizotl would be the perfect age to see Acatl as a father or older brother figure. Plus, that would allow me to work plot reasons why Ahuizotl chose his name, and there's nothing that titillates me more than the prospect of adding to a secret history (even though most people would miss it).

The last year of Axayacatl's reign would also be a time full of possibilities: the prolonged death of a long-lived emperor would give me a background rife with political intrigues and magical ones. And, as the emperor lay dying, the magical protection he'd extended over the empire would wane – leaving the gates wide open for the interference of other powers in mundane affairs.

Therefore, I chose to set *Servant of the Underworld* at the tail end of Axayacatl's reign.

Once I had done this, things fell into place: working out the history of all my characters, I realised that they'd all have been connected with the worst famine in Aztec history. That turned out to be a major motivation for Eleuia. The disastrous Chalca Wars that plagued Axayacatl's reign ended up as both an important part of Neutemoc's background, and the turning point for the divine conspiracy. Both Tizoc and the future Ahuizotl made appearances – and I was so interested in Tizoc that I have ended up making him a major character in the sequel, *Harbinger of the Storm*.

I wrote the synopsis, and tinkered with it over a week or so, trying to estimate how much plot would fit into 100,000 words. And then it was time to commit. I sat at the keyboard and started writing: a typical night for Acatl at his temple, though trouble was already afoot...

Of course, things never quite go as planned. The first I knew of that was when two characters stole the show. One was Teomitl, the young Ahuizotl. I had given him a role, but nothing like the mixture of arrogance and naiveté he soon exhibited. Originally planned to appear in a few scenes prior to the big showdown, he ended up having a much stronger role and more interactions with Acatl.

The other character had barely featured in the outline except as a placeholder, but Mihmatini, Acatl's sister, developed a strong personality, and turned from a shadow into a unique character. Every reader of my first draft loved her; and everyone also liked Teomitl: together with Mihmatini, they brought much-needed levity to a blood-soaked and grim storyline. From there it wasn't such a huge step to implement one of my fiancé's suggestions, and sketch in a nascent romance between the two of them.

Other difficulties included getting the setting across. I had deliberately twisted history and chosen short names for all the main characters (in reality, the longer Aztec names were the more prestigious), but I still had many difficulties visualising the locations of the scenes. Finally, I resorted to using a French book, *Les Aztèques* by Jacques Martin, which had reconstructions of the major sites, including temples, marketplaces and palaces. When nothing was quickly available, I left gaps in the manuscript, which I filled in later in dedicated sessions with the research books by my side. Several scenes ended up shifting slightly to accommodate the difference between my mental picture of a place and what it really looked like: chief among them were the Floating Gardens, which had been very vague maize fields in the beginning, and gained solidity as I researched Aztec peasant houses and the exact process of maize planting.

Localisation and timing also were a bigger problem than I'd thought: I finally got my hands on a scale map of the region in 1519 AD, accurate enough to allow me to determine what the distances were, but I kept having to refer to my maps of the Sacred Precinct and of the city to see where the characters were going. Halfway through the first rewrite, I also realised that Acatl had an impossibly exacting schedule, which saw him doing dozens of things per day, barely getting enough sleep, and never eating anything. I tweaked the storyline so that he was fairly busy, but over more days (though it's no wonder he ends up bone-weary at the end of the book, since he still snatches very little sleep overall).

The biggest rewrites took place near the beginning. I am not, by nature, a writer who plunges into the thick of the action, and the first version of Servant of the Underworld was hopelessly talkative. More importantly, it failed to set the tone: the time and place were unclear, and the first magic spell (the summoning to Mixcoatl) appeared only at the end of the second chapter. For a cross-genre novel, that was critical, and the agent rejections that I garnered complained either about the too-strong murder-mystery overtones, or the surprise shift into epic-ish fantasy at the end. Clearly, I had not managed to make it obvious that the book was both a mystery and a fantasy. I needed a better beginning.

My critique group suggested moving things around so that the magic spell opened the novel. It was a sound idea, except that no matter how hard I tried, I couldn't make it work. After much thought (and stupendous advice from Pat Esden), I wrote a brand-new opening scene, intended to replace the original first chapter. That one had a minor magic spell right off the bat; and the second scene that followed had Acatl trying to work out what had happened in the blood-soaked room by magical means, rather than have exposition handed to him on a platter by Ceyaxochitl. The first scene also ended with an aerial view of Tenochtitlan, which made it very clear where and when the story was taking place.

I kept, however, putting off submitting the new version for various reasons, the main one being that I was also embroiled in writing another novel at the time and couldn't find time to solicit feedback from readers. But, as fate would have it, that was around the time I headed to World Fantasy 2008 – and, though I had no intention of mentioning the novel to anyone, due to a plane cancellation, I found myself stuck in a hotel lobby with new agent John Berlyne and new publisher Marc Gascoigne, who both showed enthusiasm for my improvised pitch. On the way home, I finally got my act together, polished my new beginning, and sent it to them both.

And, wouldn't you know, you hold the result in your hands.

## Acknowledgments

First novels tend to have long acknowledgments; and I'm afraid this one isn't going to be an exception to the rule...

Acatl's adventures started with the novelette "Obsidian Shards", which was published in *Writers of the Future XXIII*.

The first readers and critiquers of those adventures were a great help in encouraging me to dig deeper into Acatl's past: Pat Esden and the gang at Hatrack, Chris Kastensmidt and the other critiquers at the Online Writing Workshop; my Writers of the Future class, and in particular Joseph Jordan, who first gave me the idea to turn "Obsidian Shards" into a novel. Pat Esden also read my revised first chapters and offered excellent advice on how to improve them.

The plot of this novel would not have been what it is now without those who attended the very first Villa Diodati workshop: John Olsen, Deanna Carlyle, Nancy Fulda, Ruth Nestvold, and Sara Genge brainstormed the novel with me, and offered me my very first batch of suspects. Sara, in particular, made the excellent suggestion I make Acatl a High Priest and embroil him in the court intrigues of the period.

Members of Codex offered to read my egregious first draft, and helped me fix the beginning: thanks to Michael Livingston, Ian Creasey and Meg Stout. Extra thanks to David W. Goldman, whose speed and encouragement were wonderful.

My most excellent critique group, Written in Blood, took on the task of correcting my revised version: Keyan Bowes, Dario Ciriello, Janice Hardy, Traci Morganfield, Doug Sharp, and Juliette Wade all offered me awesome feedback and line-edits. Traci, as always, helped me out with my Aztec research, and her enthusiasm for both "Obsidian Shards" and this project helped me out of a number of dark places.

Several people also helped me at the agent-search stage, by explaining the basics to me and offering me advice: Jeff Carlson, Stephanie Burgis, Patrick Samphire, Martin Owton, Gaie Sebold, and the rest of the T-Party workshop.

I never thought I'd write this one day, but I owe a debt to British Airways for cancelling my flight home from Canada after the 2008 World Fantasy.

It wasn't a pleasant experience to be stuck in a shabby hotel for one extra night – but it did allow me to meet agent John Berlyne and Angry Robot founder Marc Gascoigne, and to be cajoled into pitching the book to the pair of them. Amazingly, we found ourselves reunited again several months later, this time around a book deal for that very same novel.

Thanks to John and his agency partner, John Parker, for the lightning-fast communications, the negotiation, and the stupendous advice; and to Marc for the offer, his editorial work and helpfulness – and to all three of them for doing their best to dissipate my woeful ignorance of publishing matters. Thanks go as well to Angry Robot's Lee Harris for his tireless work on promotion, publicity, and the myriad other things I'm not always aware of.

To Linda Steele, Marshall Payne, Rochita Loenen-Ruiz, and Ken Scholes: you were around from the beginning. You offered me advice, comfort, and space to unwind. You guys are awesome.

My fiancé Matthieu not only read the first draft, but spent endless evenings with me brainstorming fixes, possible directions the plot could take, and sundry other things – not to mention bolstering my morale when it faltered. My deepest thanks for that.

I would not be where I am now without the endless support of both my parents and my sister. I'm grateful they bore with the bad quality of the very first stories and novels I foisted on them, and I'm overjoyed they get to brag about this one.

*Aliette de Bodard, Paris*

**ANGRY ROBOT**

*Psssst!*
Get advance
intelligence on
Angry Robot's
nefarious plans for
world domination.
Also, free stuff.
Sign up to our
Robot Legion at
angryrobotbooks.
com/legion
Because you're
worth it.